A Knight And A Spy 1411

Simon Fairfax

Published by Corinium Associates Ltd.

A CIP catalogue of this book is available from the British Library

Copyright Front cover images:

More Visual Ltd

ISBN: 978-1-9996551-7-4

Info@simonfairfax.com

www.simonfairfax.com

For my family for all their love and support as I continue to get lost without trace and travail through the 15th Century!

Other Books By Simon Fairfax

Medieval Series

A Knight and a Spy 1410
A Knight and a Spy 1411
A Knight and a Spy 1412

Deal series
A Deadly Deal
A Deal Too Far
A Deal With The Devil
A Deal On Ice

Acknowledgments

The moral right of Simon Fairfax to be identified as the author of this work has been asserted in accordance with the Copyright, Design and Patents Act 1988.

Published by Corinium Associates Ltd.

A CIP catalogue of this book is available from the British Library
Copyright Front cover images:
More Visual Ltd
Interior Layout: Corinium Associates Ltd
Copyright © 2019 Simon Fairfax. All rights reserved.
ISBN: 978-1-999 6551-7-4
simonfairfaxauthor@gmail.com
www.simonfairfax.com

Map of Journeys

Part One
The Midlands

Winter/Spring

Chapter One

Westminster Palace, London: January 1411

The man before the fire warmed his hands, stretching his arms forward towards the blazing logs, then as though seeking inspiration as well as heat from the flames he turned, his arms wide, plaintive and expansive, imploring the figures who stood before him. The flames reflected back upon the rich hues of the reds and golds of his silk sendall, the colours favoured by his countrymen despite the sobriety of his profession.

"I... My prince, I adjure you of all people, I implore you," he strained for the right words, as foreign to him as he was to England, "to hound these *bastardi pirati* to the ends of the earth. They thwart not just my trade and commerce, but seek to strangle the very soul of England's future. We have commitments, fiscal and irrevocable, that depend upon our trade with the Flemish. If these should fail, then..." He pulled hard at his neatly trimmed beard, then shrugged expansively in horror at the thought of the consequences. "Then too our banking system will fail. I need not tell you of the debts owed across Europe that must be honoured by my countrymen in *Firenze*.

These, my prince, must not fail. If they do it would imperil the treaty you have with the Flemish and the consequences for Calais and your father's holdings in France would be, how do you say, *un disastro*."

The prince, a tall and studious looking man, glanced across at his chief financier and advisor, Sir Richard Whittington, a serious figure dressed as became his stature in a deep hued doublet of padded silk and with a chain of office about his neck. Whittington oozed confidence and gravitas in equal measure; it seemed that nothing dismayed the elder statesman. The keen dark eyes saw all yet gave nothing away. He nodded in response to the silent request from Prince Henry without speaking, and the prince turned to the melodramatic figure before him.

"*Signor* Albertini...Filippo. Come, we understand your plight and have great concerns for you and indeed the security of your realm and mine. There is nothing more sacrosanct than the trade with the Flemish, and these Godforsaken pirates pillaging our ships and stealing our bounty must and will be stopped. Indeed matters are already in hand to capture them – or kill them, it matters not which. My Lord Courtney, Admiral of the western Fleet, is even now under command to sail forth and commence the scourging of our channel. And pray do not concern yourself as to the lawless actions of the pirates, for we will recompense you for any loss sustained or cargo taken."

The prince showed himself as a statesman in the making, his demeanour kind yet reassuring, treading the fine line between conciliation and regal arrogance. The Italian banker was mollified and appeared to retreat from the towering flame of indignation he had been but a moment ago.

"My lord prince, I am as ever most grateful to you. I had no knowledge that such measures were in hand. As for the debt, I shall bear my share for the sake of our close friendship and the security of the realm. I just ask that when these *pirati* are caught

I have my ship returned." The Italian smoothed his hand down the front of his doublet, lingered over the jewel-encrusted medallion at his chest and bowed deeply, his honour assuaged and his place secured at a time when foreigners were rarely granted security in England's realm. He nodded to Sir Richard and was further gratified by a gentle hand placed upon his shoulder by the long-limbed prince, who led him to the door of the chamber.

"Fear not, *Signor*, all will be well, we assure you."

Once the door had closed on the Italian, the prince and Sir Richard locked glances. A long sigh from the prince broke the silence before Whittington spoke "He has the right of it, despite his foreign manners, and by God's grace we must reconcile ourselves to capturing these pirates. Yet I ask in all candour, do we have the wherewithal to combat such a threat – and" he paused slightly before this last question, "is Lord Courtney up to the task?"

Prince Henry's brow darkened into a frown of irritation, and the puckered scar on his cheek showed white below the fashionably long hair that framed his face. At that moment he took on the mantle of the warlike prince of legend, showing his true worth and the steel within. He was aware of the comments his alliance with his close friend and advisor Richard Courtney would engender, as he was second cousin to Sir Edward Courtney, who would command the fleet. His voice when he responded had an icy tone that was unusual in his treatment of Whittington.

"We have every confidence in Sir Edward. He has promised fealty to our cause and we are satisfied with his word."

Whittington hesitated for just long enough to imply a question without actually asking it, offering nothing upon which the prince could pounce to further his cause. "For certes my prince, as you say," he replied.

Prince Henry continued in a warmer tone: "We shall give the orders to William Stokes and have the admirals – especially Worcester and Rempson – attend us in due course, with Thomas Beaufort. Needs must this be attended to as a matter of urgency, for everything depends upon our control of the Channel, and with it Calais's future."

"Amen to that, my prince. Now if your Royal Highness permits, I have orders to give and must press on with my work." Whittington bowed and made to take his leave, but not without a final comment from Prince Henry.

"Sir Richard, fear not, we all have the realm's best interest at heart. Be assured that we shall stop at nothing to secure Calais."

Whittington bowed again. "I too remain your most obedient servant, my prince, and England is my all."

Prince Henry gave a tight-lipped smile and bade him good day.

Chapter Two

The courtyard to the rear of Thomas de Grispere's house in St
Laurence Lane in the Jewry was blessed by a wintry sun sitting
low in a clear sky that shone down upon a deep frost on the
already hard packed earth of the yard, still glistening silver
despite the late-morning hour. Yet in this frosting an area had
been cleared, lying scuffed and bare to show the true colour of
the yellow clay beneath. On this cleared patch of ground two
figures pressed and retreated, dancing a deadly war pageant of
swordplay. Each man was clad in a padded gambeson, arming
gauntlets and a light helm over a coif. The strained cries of the
larger man reflected the sweat that covered his brow despite the
cold of the morning. His opponent was shorter, yet at six feet
he would be classed as passing tall in all the but the giant's
company.

Pressing on with his attack, using all the huge muscular
strength of his arms and shoulders, the giant forced his smaller
opponent to give ground. But in his overconfidence he forgot
his training and gripped too tightly as he committed himself to
a strong downward strike that had the full force of his immense

body behind it. It landed solidly – but not as he intended. It was blocked by the deft engagement of his blade half way along it, taking the force out of the blow. Then his opponent allowed both blades to close tip to tip, hilts joined, at which he grasped both weapons in his left hand, inserted the pommel of his own sword between the giant's grip and simply twisted the sword out of his large hand. He swept the pommel up to the larger man's face in a mock attack, stopping just short of his eyes before moving backwards.

The giant stood back, placed his hands upon his hips and gave a deep bellow, shaking his head in disgust at the ease with which he had been disarmed.

"By the rood, Jamie, how did you effect that? I thought I had you pressed to surrender at the wall."

His opponent smiled. "You used your strength and thus over-committed yourself to your course. The parry I have taught you, and the pommel is inserted thus..." he demon-strated the move "...which breaks your grip. Even you cannot withstand a twist with an angle such as this with your thumb awry. The thumb is the key. Break that clasp and you weaken a grip by over half, which is why we are better than the beasts that have no thumbs."

"Save monkeys." retorted a laconic figure who had been watching the swordplay from the side. A marled eye and single white scar falling vertically across his face bore mute testament to past battles and action, giving his expression a slightly lopsided countenance.

"Aye, John, our cousins from the animal world have our feature to use. Thanks be to God that they do not fight with swords," the younger man laughed.

"Now," John offered, moving forward, his posture still erect and strong. Despite the onset of middle years his physique was still hard and compact from constant training. "I remember teaching this young pup that very move, and it works well when your opponent is too confident and committed to the strike. Then, when he is off balance and has no chance of retreat, you deflect as Jamie did and reverse the grip. Here Mark, you try."

The former man-at-arms proffered a sword to the giant, who took it and readied himself to repeat Jamie's move. "That's it, slowly, build a rhythm 'til the mind thinks no more and just reacts. Again," he called, getting Mark to repeat the action until it became embedded in his muscle memory.

Jamie looked on thoughtfully. "The thought occurs that maybe it is the wrong weapon for you, Mark. What say you, John? He excels at the quarterstaff, yet we know that is no weapon for the field of battle. Yet mayhap the longsword would better serve? He has the build and strength to wield such a weapon at will and it may suit him better."

"Aye, forsooth it may, or the poleaxe. But enough for today – he has a good enough mastery of the arming sword, and with more practice will prove competent. Come, let us break now for food and drink afore this frost makes its home in my old bones." John grinned in a rare show of humour. Mark clapped him on the shoulder and the three men sheathed their practice swords, lifted off their helmets and made their way into the main house through the rear entrance.

"Come, Forest." Jamie called to a huge wolfhound, which rose and trotted silently at Jamie's heels, relieved from keeping guard to ensure her master did not sustain any harm. It had taken Jamie many hours of training to stop her from interceding in practice sword play to save him.

Drawing off their gauntlets, coifs and gambesons they proceeded to a bowl of steaming water a servant had fetched and washed away the sweat of exercise before a meal was brought from the kitchen below. As they sat down to eat, a figure shadowed the doorway, entering quietly and moving with an ethereal grace that gave the impression that his feet did not touch the ground. The dark, almost black hair and swarthy skin marked him as a foreigner to the English, and only the slate grey eyes prevented him from being taken for a Saracen. He was as ever flamboyantly dressed in bright silk doublet and coloured hose.

"Ho now, food arrives and the Italian appears as if by magic," Mark jested.

"There speaks the trencherman. If a man were to tarry, he would arrive at an empty table. I have been hard at work, slaving to work up an appetite." The newcomer moved his lithe arms expansively and gave a mocking courtly bow.

"I'll be bound that I should lief as not prefer your work to mine, Cristo. I pledge it would involve a certain Contessa?" Mark took his turn to bait the Italian.

"And how does my mistress Emma?" Cristoforo asked, scoring a direct hit as he alluded to the new romance between Mark and the daughter of a local mercer.

"Never you mind Cristo, for I have no idea of she of which 'ee speaks."

"Enough! Let us eat ere this food grows cold with your posturing like a pair of strutting cocks," John put an end to the banter. Jamie called grace and they set upon the bread trenchers before them with a gusto born of exercise.

Between mouthfuls Cristoforo asked: "Where does your father, Jamie, and Jeanette? I heard the midday bells toll on my journey here and tis unlike him to miss a meal."

"My father attends a meeting of his Guild. He is a senior member and needs must attend. As for Jeanette, why she travelled down to the wharf on an errand for my father and doubt-less tarried at shops along the way. You know more of women's whiles than I, Cristo," Jamie replied, now readily and affectionately using Mark's anglicized version of Cristoforo's name. "Were you at court this morning?" Jamie asked.

"Aye, that I was, and I'm reminded that I have a message from Sir Richard, who asks that you attend him before compline this evening." He paused, leaving the best for last. "The invitation also includes Mark of Cornwall and myself." The pause was well executed and all at the table looked at him in surprise.

"A summons for us all?" Jamie asked. "Do you have further intelligence as to the cause?"

Cristoforo enjoyed the consternation he had caused, shrugged in his Latin way and replied: "None."

"What can be afoot that demands all three of us to attend Sir Richard?" Jamie mused as his keen mind sought all sources of news that he had gleaned over the past few days. "Do you have no inkling at all, Cristo? No whiff of scandal that would demand a mission to include all three of us, for I suspect that to be the case. I hear that there are risings in the north, with Stanhope and his murderous band of cutthroats rebelling against the crown and its royal commands. He seems beyond reach of law and order and has friends vested in high places, apparently."

Cristoforo paused and gave thought to Jamie's question while John looked on, his own interest aroused. "Aye, mayhap we shall need to resolve his lack of understanding of the law. Yet events have occurred closer to home, although I have only heard a single instance from the Contessa. Her uncle Filippo had his latest cargo seized in the channel by pirates, and I understand he was furious and visited his case upon Sir Richard and the prince. But I know not the outcome of his plea. All I know is that he was in a rage according to Alessandria, and would vent his spleen with no care of rank or censure."

A frisson of excitement ran through Jamie's body. As a household knight he was bound most strongly to the prince, and that put him at the beck and call of Sir Richard Whittington – financier, advisor and spymaster to the crown.

Westminster Palace

As the sun began to set later that afternoon, the three young men walked off the still frosted street and into the antechamber to Sir Richard Whittington's private rooms. Each kept his own counsel, but they were united in one thought – the outcome of their talk with Sir Richard. Each suspected and half hoped for some intriguing adventure on behalf of the conspiratorial figure they were about to meet, aware of his power and his abilities to manipulate. Mark, alone of the three, had not been in this room before and looked about him, seeing a bright fire burning in the grate, fresh rushes on the floor and tapestries adorning the walls. Despite high set glazed windows, little natural light was thrown into the room, and sconces bore thick, bright candles to illuminate the work of Whittington's clerk Alfred. The clerk asked the three of them to await his master and left them for the inner sanctum, closing the door behind him.

"My lord," he began, addressing Whittington, "Sir James de Grispere, Mark of Cornwall and *signor* Cristoforo Corio are without, shall I bid them enter?"

"What? Oh of course Alfred, they are expected, send them in, do." He commanded.

Alfred moved to the outer room and beckoned the three men forward.

"If you please, messires, Sir Richard will see you now."

They nodded their thanks to Alfred and walked through to Sir Richard's sumptuous apartment. Two steps up from the outer office, this room had wooden floors and was very well appointed with silk hangings and a blazing fire glowing in an ornately carved fireplace. Up high a large and beautifully coloured stained glass window showing an image of St. Peter allowed a pale and baleful light into the room. A huge trestle table dominated the far wall, and Sir Richard stood up from behind it to greet his guests. "Gentlemen, I bid you welcome," he said. "Come, draw chairs near to the fire where we may talk in comfort on this freezing day."

The three shed their cloaks and fur-lined felt hats, hanging them on a rack and making for the fire where Sir Richard awaited them. The door re-opened and Alfred reappeared unbidden with a tray bearing goblets and a flagon of spiced red wine which he set at a side table near the fire. Sir Richard removed a poker from the fire and plunged it into the wine, causing it to froth and sizzle as it quenched the poker's heat.

"Come, seat yourselves, for there is much that I would impart – including the origins of this excellent Burgundian wine." Sir Richard looked to each man, seeking a reaction from the trio as he began his discourse. Only Mark showed any emotion, as he had been captured and tortured the year before upon the orders of the Burgundian leader, Duke John the Fearless.

"If it concerns that knave it will, I'm bound, be to no good," Mark muttered. Sir Richard gave a tight-lipped and mirthless smile. The three raised their goblets and saluted Sir Richard, Jamie eyeing him warily, suddenly aware of how this could turn out. Whittington continued in English, aware that Mark spoke little French and Cristoforo's grasp of the language over the past year had grown exponentially, allowing him to follow most of the alien tongue almost as well as a native of this strange land he now inhabited.

"Just so Mark, just so. This concerns affairs of state more here than abroad, yet as you will see they are as ever intertwined. I prithee that our discourse dost not travel abroad 'pon pain of death?" The three readily agreed and Whittington continued.

"Very well. The kingdom is riven with unrest and certain

causes are afoot that seek to destabilise it further, more particularly from the Stanhope faction to the north, which is causing his majesty much consternation. There is open revolt against taxes and the ruling of the country. Should this lawlessness spread it will doubtless inspire other minor revolts and rebellions organised by men who seek to gain through force what they cannot through fair trade and honour. As ever, money is at the root of it. Money and power.

"Let me go back to earlier years. You will recall the Pirate Wars and England's captains who were sent to avenge us and protect the safety of our waters?" Jamie and Mark nodded. Cristoforo had been in his native Italy at the time when the events took place. "Well, some of those self-same captains that served England so well are now freebooters. Disillusioned at their lack of reward and in want of destruction and easy trade, they rampage the channel stealing and looting almost with impunity.

"Latterly a carrick with valuable cargo was set upon by pirates in the channel and all was lost. I am sure *signor* Corio is well versed in this tale at least?" Whittington looked at Cristoforo.

"I will admit to learning of the event, my lord."

The deep, dark set eyes missed nothing and Whittington merely nodded, his suspicions confirmed. "Pain of death indeed. Court gossip shall be the death of us all," he muttered. "My prince has heard the pleas of those whose goods and ships have been raided, and will make orders for the hounding and arrest of the pirates at the next Council meeting. To this end he and William Stokes, along with certain captains and admirals, will put forward a plan to implement these measures."

Jamie had been following the discourse carefully, and had as yet heard nothing that would in any way cause him or his companions to be involved in the proceedings. "Sir Richard,

William Stokes is a renowned officer of the crown under whom a large number of men serve, and it is said that he commands a network of spies stretching the length and breadth of the land, in every port and town where revenues are paid. I wonder thus how we may be of assistance in this venture."

"Well put, young Sir James, cutting to the crux of the matter with the impatience of youth," Whittington grinned mirthlessly. "The prince intends to instruct..." here he paused, savouring the moment, "Sir Edward Courtney."

"The Earl of Devon?" Jamie exclaimed.

"Just so, James."

"This be the grandson of the tenth earl, Sir Hugh, who served the old king and who ruled Devon and Cornwall as his own fiefdom along with his cousin Sir Philip?" Mark exclaimed.

"One and the same. You know of him, I take it?"

"There bain't be no one in Cornwall that don't, beggin' your pardon, my lord. 'E were a holy terror, raiding and gettin' 'is own way. You crossed 'im at your peril, my father said. Now his grandson may or may not be cast from the same mould, but his brother Sir Hugh is the most infamous pirate on the waters," Mark explained, his obvious consternation making him talk more volubly than he would normally.

"Within this company alone I would say this: the prince may desire to set a thief to catch a thief, yet I doubt the strength of purpose lies within the earl or his son, also named Sir Edward, to carry out such a commission," Sir Richard explained. At this last remark, Jamie began to understand and became worried for his friend's sake as he could see where the discourse was leading.

"The importance of this trade is immense, and upon it England's future lies," Sir Richard continued.

"The Anglo-Flemish Treaty, to be signed this coming June.

Of course, my father has talked of little else these past days." Jamie interjected.

"For certes, and for his and so many of the guilds, their livelihood depends upon it. It must be signed on the appointed date of the fifteenth of June. Many on the Flemish side suspect us of trying to sabotage the treaty, and we need to reassure them. And Burgundian interests will intercede, I suspect, to turn the whole to their advantage. They would meddle in our affairs or more particularly ask us to meddle in theirs, for a civil war is coming to fan the flames of France's dissent. All lies in balance on the Treaty, and our trade with the Flemish holds the key to our fiscal wellbeing and upon that our ability to defend and hold Calais."

Jamie grasped the situation quickly. "Yet think on, for the Flemish lands and trade lie within the auspices of Burgundian holdings, and I fear undue influence here from Duke John."

"You have the right of it, and my deepest fear is that we shall be ambushed both abroad and at court. To which end I ask your help, each in his way. Mark, you as a Cornishman will fit very easily into the local people's confidence, and I ask that you return to your land and seek employment either ashore or at sea. The fleet will sail I believe from either Falmouth or Plymouth."

"You ask me to return home as a boon to you? Why I've not seen Cornwall in over a year. Christmas was all wrestlin' tourneys and such. I should like that, if it please you sir. Yet how will this square with his royal highness the prince, for he will want to know of my whereabouts?" Mark asked. "His wrestlers will be a man down and his countenance will be ill-set."

"Fear not. I shall make things right with the prince. All will be well as there is ample time, for the Council will not be set afore March." Whittington assured Mark. "There is no urgency in your regard, and late February will be the time to travel. I will avail you of names to contact and where they may be found. The servants of William Stokes will direct you and you should'st report to me as swiftly you are able. I wish to learn all that occurs, as even the simplest event may be of import. I trust not the earl, and more particularly the brother. Is that understood?"

"Yes my lord. T'will be good to return to Cornwall," Mark said.

"Now, *signor* Corio, I wish you to ride for Gloucester. The king sojourns there and will do so 'til called to Council. I wish him not to be ambushed and I trust none but one of you to deliver the missive I have for him."

Cristoforo in turn shrugged in his non-committal Italian way, bowed his head and answered: "I am as ever at your service, my lord. Suffice it to say that as long as my lord and master Sir Thomas agrees to this, as he is my benefactor."

"Indeed he does, and I am assured of his compliance. The circumstances are grave and I wish nothing to go untoward. Be wary on the road, for there are those who would thwart your venture, and I would have no one know of your intent."

"Yet I am puzzled, my lord," Jamie said. "For do we not in this go against the Prince?"

"We go against no one. We go for the Crown and the good of the kingdom. There are times when we must act in the best interests of those who know no better. This is such a circumstance," Sir Richard finished curtly, his tone broking no further discussion.

"As you wish, Sir Richard," Jamie replied.

"Now James," Whittington turned to the young knight. "We turn to matters within. I wish you to journey northwards and seek out the men under Sir Richard Stanhope, for they cause great mischief and I would lief as not know their aims and what their goals should be. They will not suspect you, an itin-

17

erant mercenary, perhaps late of the Borders and seeking pastures new mayhap?" At which the spymaster raised a querying eyebrow seeking assent as his gaze bore into Jamie.

"As you say, Sir Richard. I should be able to insert myself successfully, for as far as I'm aware I am not acquainted with Sir Richard Stanhope."

"Like as not, for although he is the former king's knight he has not been at court of late – and if he had he would not remember a lowly squire such as was your status."

"Sir Richard, I have cognisance of his deeds," Jamie stated. "I prithee would'st not it be more propitious to set a King's justiciar upon him, or the sheriff himself?" he asked.

"In faith it would," Whittington snorted in reply. "Thou should'st know that until recently he had a place upon the Bench himself."

"He was a magistrate?" Jamie said.

"A magistrate as was, and now a malapert rogue and worse. Yet no one will testify against him, and all fear his reach and his wrath should they do so. He has friends at court of some influence and was once a favourite of the prince, who fought with him at Shrewsbury. So, needs must we tread with care, and any evidence you bring against him must be watertight." Whittington finished.

"You would have me journey forth to Nottingham and return forthwith once I am replete with information of their cause?"

"Just so. Now, before you take your leave," Whittington stood and left the fireside for the array of papers upon his desk. He returned with a rolled parchment sealed with red wax and impressed with his signet ring. "*Signor* Corio, this is what I would have you deliver safely into the king's hands. His and no one else's, no servant or squire, do I make myself clear?" He asked severely. "It would please me greatly if you could journey on the morrow and await a response from the king as it pleases his majesty. Here is also a note for my family. They live in Gloucester and I would have you make yourself known to them, for they will treat you well upon my honour."

Cristoforo acknowledged the order and secured the parchment safely within his doublet, then re-fastened the buttons of the frogging.

"Now Messires, I should ask your forbearance, for there is much to do and I must press forward." The audience was clearly at an end and the three young men stood, acknowledged Sir Richard with a courtly bow and made to leave.

"I wish you good fortune in your ventures and adjure you to trust no one." Whittington's final words were ominous as they left his apartments.

Chapter Three

The oaken beams of the White Horse tavern were aged with the smoke of many a winter fire. A warm, snug atmosphere prevailed as three figures found a secure corner in which to confide their thoughts to each other. Each man sat his tankard of ale before him on the rough trestle table. Mark alone had his back to the room, while Cristoforo and Jamie sat opposite on a tall-sided settle. Although early evening, the tavern was already half full, offering shelter from the freezing cold night outside.

"My Lord Whittington is a sapient yet a cautelous fellow, for he stirs a pretty nest of vipers once he sees a cause and no mistake," Jamie remarked.

"That he does. Yet for me 'twill be good to see my home again. If there be no urgency I shall call upon my family to see how they fare." The wrestler rolled back his huge shoulders to relieve the tension as the warmth from the room seeped into his muscles.

"When will you leave, Cristo?" Jamie asked the Italian.

"On the morrow, as my lord intends. Tell me, is it the same road that we took for Worcester?"

"Aye, 'tis, yet go not that far north. At Oxford head due west through the hills – the Cod's Wolds as they call them there. 'Tis fine country and I can furnish you with places to stay through the trade of my father. It's grand sheep rearing country and I know it well from the wool trade. The market town of Chintenham lies a few leagues beyond Gloucester. There is a Royal manor there, yet the king resides in Gloucester castle. Chintenham is the sister town of Gloucester, where you needs must cross the Severn, for Gloucester sits right upon the river as Worcester does to the north," Jamie explained. Cristoforo had travelled all over Europe and had a keen memory for places and direction. Jamie doubted that he would struggle to find his way.

"'Tis kind, for an inn can be a difficult resting place when you are a foreigner in this land, king's messenger or no. And what of you? When do you journey to meet this errant knight? Where did he say? Nottingham?"

"That he did. It lies half way between here and the borders. I've passed through afore on my travels, though at this time of year with bad roads 'twill be five days ride if a day. It is rough, isolated country and Nottingham is the dominant town of the area. It is well placed for raiding, and Stanhope has gone rogue. He was one of the king's favourites, and as my Lord Whittington says he still has friends at court. He runs a secret covenant of men across the whole county and none can stop him since Sir Thomas Rempson died a year or two back. I know why Sir Richard is worried, for Stanhope's influence is great, running to piracy and smuggling I've heard, yet none will bear witness against him. He could drive a wedge across the land, for northern factions will often unite against a weak king. I shan't sleep easy 'til I have him for certes."

"Should you desire me to follow you northwards once I return from the mission to the king?" Cristoforo offered.

"That is kindly offered. Yet I would worry how you should

be received as a foreigner abroad in this land. More so to the north where their minds are closed."

Cristoforo shrugged and smiled in apparent acquiescence. "As you wish. But send for me should you have need."

Jamie nodded with a smile and clapped his friend upon his shoulder. "So you travel on the morrow, yet I fancy you will pay a call to Langburnestrate before the eve is done. All of Lombardy's financiers have homes from home in that street – as do their families, nieces in particular, so I am told."

"I know not of what you speak," Cristoforo answered, adopting an air of innocence. "Yet it now occurs to me that I do have business in that direction afore I return to your father's house."

The three men drained their tankards and rose as one. A figure dressed as a peddler, his cloak wrapped closely around him, studied them from under a brimmed hat as they left. He too moved off into the night heading back to the palace, bearing news that he knew would be rewarded with payment.

The three men separated just before the city walls, Mark heading north to his cottage in the new area of Smythefeld. Jamie and Cristoforo carried on into the city before parting, Jamie for home and the Italian for Langburnestrate.

Arriving in the wide street, Cristoforo made for the now familiar house of the Italian banker Filippo Albertini and his niece, Contessa Alessandria di Felicini. It was an impressive structure of brick and columns to the lower elevations, with only the upper stories infilled amongst the wooden framing with mortar and daub. The entrance to the building had a wooden portico and beneath it an impressive studded oak door that was already barred against the bitter cold of the night. Cristoforo banged solidly upon it with the hilt of his belt knife. The sound reverberated in the evening air and within a short time he heard the bar being withdrawn from inside the house.

The door was pulled back and a draught of warm air carrying aromas of spice and food wafted out towards him, reminding him of his homeland. A swarthy figure, not dissimilar in build or colouring to Cristoforo, stood in the half open doorway.

"*Buona sera Pietro, sono io. Come va?*" He announced himself.

The man before him smiled and rattled off a reply in rapid Italian, beckoning Cristoforo in out of the cold and bidding him wait within the large entrance hall where an open fire burned brightly in a large hearth. He heard the gentle sound of conversation in his own tongue emanating from the next room, accompanied by a tinkle of laughter. Shadows from the candlelight danced on the walls in grotesquely enlarged forms, like a puppet-show with unseen strings and malformed characters. The light was warm and rich and reminded him of home, for which he suddenly felt a great longing.

Then his world brightened, and the sight of the Contessa made him catch his breath, as she always seemed to do. She appeared in the doorway with a rustle of material from a deep blue gown of gathered silk that flowed out from a high waisted design, cinched by a wide doeskin belt tied at the front. She wore no wimple, and her hair was adorned with gossamer strands of pearls. Her beautiful dark almond-shaped eyes were touched with kohl and her lips glistened from the wine she had just drunk. Cristoforo held back a desire to kiss them. She moved forward to him, her feet light as a dancer's, and the subtle sweet perfume of spice and sandalwood, at once familiar to him, assailed his senses. She held her hands forward to clasp his.

"*Caro*, can you not keep away?" She mocked him gently.

"*Impossibile*, when I am faced with the prospect of such beauty." He replied.

"Fie on you, peacock. You flare your plumage so beautifully that you dazzle me with its brightness. Now before you burst, shall you take some wine with us? For we have supped and now recourse to conversation."

"I will indeed partake of wine. You are most courteous, *cara mia.*" Yet here he paused, a perfervid expression upon his face. "But you must forgive me, for on the morrow I have a fiat to attend on behalf of Sir Richard Whittington."

The words were not lost on the Contessa, and she feared the worst, knowing Cristoforo's proclivity for attracting trouble. "Not to France?" She whispered, dreading the answer.

"No, my love, merely to deliver a message to the king, A simple service easily rendered and I shall, God willing, return within a week. I merely wished to bid you adieu before my sudden departure."

"So where do you travel? You have not answered my question?" she asked suspiciously, narrowing her eyes in a feline manner.

"The place I believe is called Glow-star. Gloss-tar..." Cristoforo struggled with the pronunciation of the unfamiliar word.

"Gloucester," She corrected him, raising an eyebrow. "I have heard of it. What doth the king so far from his home?"

A heavier tread in the corridor behind them heralded the arrival of the contessa's uncle. "Ah Cristoforo, you are most welcome," he said. "Come, join us."

Chapter Four

Misty breath billowed from the mouths of the group in the courtyard as they spoke. Cristoforo made final preparations for his journey to Gloucester, while Jamie was setting out for Nottingham. Thomas had risen early after listening to Jamie's tale the previous evening, his sympathies lying with the fate of the merchant ships that were being attacked in the English Channel. Despite liking the man and knowing him well, Thomas and John both had a slightly jaundiced view of Sir Richard and the world in which he moved.

A man of middle years, Thomas de Grispere was prosperous. His doublet was well made and fitted tightly around his portly frame while his face showed a kindly disposition, soft now at the jowls but with deep set eyes that had seen much and missed little. The likeness between him and Jamie was noticeable in the early morning light, yet Thomas's darker hair was shot with grey, while Jamie's was dark red-gold, and his green hazel-flecked eyes were inherited from his deceased Scottish mother.

"You're takin' that vicious red goat with you, I suppose?"

John asked, nodding at the huge red-haired stallion that snorted and fretted as a groom led him carefully forward, avoiding his teeth.

Jamie laughed, ruffling the stallion's long ears, and upon his touch the horse calmed in a remarkable show of affection for his master. "I could not leave him here, he might eat you," he retorted. "I did consider Killarney, but Richard will be of more use. I believe I shall need his might and skill. I am lending Killarney to Cristo; she has speed and comfort that will better suit him."

Jamie embraced first his father then Jeanette. "Ho sister, come forward and say goodbye to your brother." He gently mocked any closeness the two might have, for since losing their mother at an early age Jeanette felt a strong bond with her brother and hated his departing.

"May God have you in his keeping, my brother," she adjured him, pushing back a braid of long blonde hair from her face. They hugged, Jamie crushing her slight frame to his, then he swung around and gracefully mounted Richard in one leap. The others moved back, knowing what to expect, for no sooner had he landed in the saddle than the animal jounced sideways, testing him as always. Forest jumped out of the way, barking at the errant stallion.

"Hey goky, listen!" He urged as he firmed his legs and sat more deeply into the saddle, quieting the horse's movement. The stallion was quite heavily loaded, yet he bore it well with a huge natural strength.

Once settled, Jamie pulled his new cloak about him: "I shall be glad of this, father, and thank you." The older man nodded at the gratitude, for he had made Jamie a Christmas present of the cloak. It was fashioned by a new process of his own devising: from wool boiled to shrink it, then covered with fine, tanned, supple leather, waxed to proof its wearer against all weathers. It was lined inside with silk and very warm.

"No mule?" John asked.

"I chose not, needs must that I may have to move fast and I'll not be encumbered, I shall perforce travel lightly," he explained. Clad in a thick gambeson, he had by way of armour but a maille coat and a bascinet helmet with a maille aventail strapped to the pommel. He also had his old shield that bore the distinctive arms of Sir Robert de Umfraville, bright red with a bold golden cinquefoyle slashed with a blue band, for he wished not to be recognised by his own device.

"Aye mayhap, and durst trust no one." John advised curtly. To which Jamie gave a nod and a one fingered salute.

"Ready Cristo?"

"*Si andiamo. Salute tutti,*" Cristoforo replied and the two men urged their horses forward, leaving the courtyard through the large double gates out onto St Laurence Lane, briefly heading south with Richard sidling all the while, continually testing Jamie until he was sure that he was capable of riding him while Forest kept a wary eye as she trotted beside her master.

Their way lay briefly together, and as they turned right onto Westchep Cristoforo asked him: "How does my Lady Alice? Was there time to see her ere you departed yester eve?"

Jamie snorted in response, "The earl, her oaf of a father, still considers me persona non grata. In his eyes only a duke would suffice to pay court to his daughter, and a royal duke at that. A household knight is not enough and he will never believe that the title of Lollard under which I had to shield was not merely an umbra despite the assoilment from a prince of the realm," he finished bitterly.

"*Si,* but how dost my lady view your cause? Is she willing, *amico mio?*"

27

Despite his sour visage Jamie had to smile at Cristoforo's native charm.

"You are a rogue, Cristo. A charming one, yet still a rogue." He pronounced with a smile. "Aye, as you suspect my suit there is well received and she pains no doubt at our parting. I have given Jeanette a missive to take on my behalf, and doubtless she will explain all. Yet with the passing of the hour there was little chance to meet, since she was not at court and we needs must steal moments when we can. I sought her at court for two days in vain. Mayhap they have travelled north to her father's estates."

"I suspected as much and instructed the Contessa to offer succour to your cause." He smiled at his friend. "For they are good friends, no?"

"Cristo, you are a prince among thieves!" And for the first time that day Jamie laughed aloud. Cristoforo, he knew, counted love as the most important thing in the world. At length they came to the end of the street passing on to Newgatestrete and at the corner of St. Martin's Lane they stopped as Jamie would head north to pass through Aldersgate and Cristoforo on to Newgate itself.

"So we part, Cristo. Please God we meet again soon."

"*Magari, speriamo*. Remember, if you need me send word, I am still indebted to your father and your life is my concern, *capsice*?"

"Fear not, I shall come through." Jamie assured his friend and they clasped in the Roman fashion, hand to elbow, saluted each other and turned their horses in different directions. Forest turned to follow her master as they parted.

They did not look back, but Cristoforo had the feeling that all was not well. Born of many trials and the life of an assassin, he had learned to trust his sixth sense. He looked around quickly, hoping to see something or someone. He saw nothing untoward, yet he could not shake the feeling of being watched. He pressed on through the early crowds, careful that his borrowed horse, Killarney, did not slip on the icy cobbles. She was a sure footed mare, that much he knew, brought over as foal on the boat from Ireland, and Jamie had chosen well. At this early hour the shops were being opened from behind shutters, and thankfully the new sewers meant that there was little effluence from the night's soil and the streets were relatively clear of rubbish and worse. Appetising aromas of fresh bread, cooked meats and pies wafted on the air, causing Cristoforo's mouth to water as he continued along Newgatestrete, fighting against the human tide that was pouring into the city with the early morning opening of the gates.

Heading north, Jamie had the same feeling as Cristoforo and many others who rode with danger and death at their heels. He would, he pledged to himself, ride with care. His first stop was St. Albans and then the market town of Northamptone, there to meet and stay with a wool merchant well known to his father. There was business to discuss and trade to agree. It would also give good reason for his trip northwards should anyone be following him, he reasoned.

The Palace of Westminster

Half an hour later, the courtier that had been following the two men reported back to his master. He still wore the scar upon his face following the beating given him by Jamie the previous year. He bore the livery of Sir Richard Tiptoft, yet reported directly to another: Sir Jacques de Berry.

"Ah you have returned. Now tell me where dost my lord de Grispere and that Italian jackanapes venture?"

"My lord, I know not. In truth they parted on Newgatestrete, de Grispere for the north and the Italian to the west."

"Indeed? No sign of the wrestler, for they were spied leaving the vicinity of Whittington's quarters yester eve. A company of three? I see Whittington's hand in this for he'd put a fox to shent ere his wiles are acted upon. Where dost thou journey and why westward, Italian?" he mused out loud, pacing in his room before turning to face the other man. "Did de Grispere have baggage or mule train?"

"No, just that red beast of his, lightly equipped and cloaked against the cold."

"And the Italian?"

"He too was of similar arraignment, my lord, with nothing to mark their intent." He stated calmly.

"Mmm, set to... That is all, I shall call in due course, now I must think on't." de Berry remarked, dismissing the squire.

— ✕ ✻ ✕ —

Unaware that their movements were causing such consternation, both men passed under the gates and out onto their chosen roads, each still wary. The feeling of being watched left them as both pressed on for their destinations: Cristoforo to Wicumun some thirty miles distant. He gazed upwards at a sky that was clouding with the promise of snow to come or he missed his guess. He pulled his cloak closer and now on the open road with less pedestrian traffic, pushed Killarney up into a smooth, mile eating canter.

It was three days later that Cristoforo came off the main London road to set above the town of Chintenham. He paused upon the escarpment of Leckhampton Hill, looking out over the valley and the natural basin below. Nestled there was the market town in the lee of the valley. It was approaching dusk and the red tongues of a setting sun were etched across the sky in many ribbons, heralding the promise of a good day on the morrow.

The snow that Cristoforo had predicted had not yet materialised, yet it was bitterly cold and a hoar frost glistened on the branches of the trees, which cracked in the freezing temperature. "Why does England have to be so cold? *Porca miseria,* I wish I was back home," he muttered to Killarney, who accepted the wish with her usual equanimity and tossed her head in impatience to be moving on.

Cristoforo pushed on down the steep road, heading for the town centre. He was too late to make Gloucester this day, and Jamie had made provision for him by letter and vouchsafed a warm bed and congenial company at the house of one of the merchants with whom they traded. The house was on the west side of the town lying on the river plain. It was dusk when he arrived in the village of Upper Hatherley, and amidst fields barely discernible in the lowering light he found, after asking direction, the home of Charles Boevey to be a grand walled and gated house, ominous in the gloom. A servant was in the process of shutting the gates when he arrived and demanded his business. Cristoforo proffered the letter, upon which the man bolted the gates in his face and left him waiting while he delivered the message to his master.

In short order he returned and with little grace, suspicious of the 'foreigner' before him, bade him enter into the grounds and thence the house. Dismounting Cristoforo asked that his horse be cared for.

"Be not afeared sir, oi be good with 'osses. She'll be well cared for, don't 'ee fret." He clearly cared more for the animal than himself, Cristoforo mused, stretching stiff muscles that had become unused to three days of long travel.

He hoisted his war bag and leather satchel from the saddle and was beckoned forth by a servant at the door to enter.

A mellow light from thick candles reflected back off the ochre walls, and a large fire burned in the hearth. A solid figure appeared of roughly Thomas de Grispere's age, well-padded against the night, with a flat velvet beret upon his head that accorded well with his disposition. His accent when he spoke was well bred, yet had a regional burr to it that Cristoforo had heard more and more as he travelled deeper into Gloucestershire.

"I bid you good evening sir, and welcome to my home. Forgive the stern welcome, these are trying times and to be caught abroad at dusk is to arouse suspicion. I am Charles Boevey, merchant and friend to Thomas de Grispere, whose bona fides you bear."

Cristoforo gave a small bow: "*Signor* Boevey, I am Cristoforo Corio, late of Firenze, and now in the service of my master Thomas de Grispere."

"Ah just so, just so. Come before the fire and have some wine. It is freezing without, and doubtless you will be chilled to your bones." Boevey bustled forth, motioning to the servant to pour some hot spiced wine. "Now, I believe that thou shall favour this, for I trade with Italians in silks and wool. And indeed with wine, for this is procured from them and I am assured that it is of good vintage. I prithee try it."

Cristoforo took the proffered goblet: "*Salute,*" he said, and swallowed a warm, rich mouthful of the crimson liquid. He was instantly transported a thousand leagues to a warm summer's day in his homeland.

"*Dio mio.* If I could bottle my country and bring it here, this would be it. *Sangiovese.*" He exclaimed.

"Verily so, and it would be a great wonder if you did not like it, for it originates from near Florence." Cristoforo took another mouthful, savouring the elixir, and from that moment the two men formed a deep accord.

Chapter Five

Nottinghamshire

Jamie's prediction of five days was holding true until the snow started to fall and he was forced to make for a village north of Nottingham. He had ridden past the town as he wished to enter from the northbound road to give credence to his story. The landscape was bleak in the cold, and the stiff breeze from the north east brought snow with it. The stark trees and bushes cut back from the road soon became etched in white, covered in thickening snow, falling faster now and blanketing the world in silence. Jamie was glad that he had no harness, for nothing robbed the body of heat like armour exposed to the wind. The maille hauberk was bad enough, but the new cloak performed its job better than he had hoped, sealing him in a blanket of warmth.

In the covering of snow, Jamie noticed tracks on the road lately made by a large party. By the way the snow had fallen he judged that the advance party was but a few minutes ahead of him. The road wound around the edge of thick forest, dipping and rising with the land. That and the thickly falling snow impeded any view of the group. Yet in the silence of the snow, sounds carried further than normal. Richard and Forest pricked up their ears: Richard quivered beneath Jamie as he recognised the sounds that came to him ahead of Jamie's cognisance – the unmistakeable sound of battle! Forest looked up at her master expectantly awaiting commands. As they rounded the next bend, metallic sounds and cries arrived on the air that were loud enough for human ears to hear.

Jamie flung back his hood, unpinned his cloak from the brooch clasp and laid it lengthways across the pommel in front of him. He did not want it to impede his movements should action be required. He retrieved his helmet from the saddle strap and pulled it on over the coif, laying the aventail flat over his neck and shoulders. Sliding his left arm through the arm straps of his shield, he was ready in a matter of moments and Richard moved smoothly into a canter, eager for the fray. Jamie eased his sword in the scabbard ensuring it had not frozen stuck, yet did not draw it forth.

"Ho Forest," he called to the now well-trained hound, whose back was covered in a thick saddle of snow, "listen by me 'til thou hears the command."

The dog gazed up at her master, seeming to comprehend every word, loping along by Richard's side. Though full grown in height, she would mature a little more with muscle, yet the wolfhound was a fearless hunter and war dog, trained to protect with a natural instinct. They sped onwards from bend, and before them lay a panoply of combat.

Descending to a small plain, the road narrowed between a rocky escarpment of sandstone. A horse-litter was stopped there, the front horse held by an ill-clad figure who stabbed upwards at the rider, who in turn slashed down with a heavy whip at his assailant. It was an ill matched fight, and as Jamie watched, the tip of the attacker's sword slid upward to pierce the rider's stomach. As the man doubled over in pain, he was summarily pulled from his saddle.

It was obvious that the attackers had war bows, as Jamie could see two arrow shafts quivering in the bodies of two servants lying to the side of the litter and a third buried into the shoulder of a further man who groaned, writhing in the snow that was turning red beneath him. A mounted knight was fighting two men, slashing with his sword, keeping them at bay while two men-at-arms engaged at unfavourable odds with the attacking vagabonds. A further figure armed with a bow stood back, frustrated at the lack of any distinct target in the mêlée before him.

Jamie instinctively knew that the archer was the immediate danger, and spurring Richard on to greater speed, he drew his sword and called: "An Umfraville! An Umfraville!" The old battle cry of his former lord was still firmly embedded in his psyche. He slammed down his visor in anticipation of the arrow strike. Forest, unbidden, ran by his side snarling, offering a second target to the archer.

Cushioned by snow and rapt in concentration, it was only then that the archer saw the new threat to the carefully placed ambush. He whirled with speed born of long practice, drawing the bow string back to his ear with Jamie less than a hundred yards away and charging down upon him. The string twanged with an evil snap and the whistle of the barbed missile sounded in the air. Face on, Jamie knew that the archer would choose the larger, sure target of the horse, aiming for Richard's chest to bring horse and rider down together. As soon as the string was drawn, Jamie swerved Richard to the right, creating a more generous target, yet one he was more able to protect. Hunching low, the action offset the archer's aim slightly, and Jamie dropped his shield to cover the horse from shoulder to chest as the thick leather saddle would give protection to the midsection. The arrow flew true, aimed at the point where the leg joins the torso, and struck the upper part of Jamie's shield. The mighty force of the concussion drove the shield back, shattering the arrow on impact and sending shards of metal and wood fragments outwards, some ricocheting off Jamie's helmet and visor, two lodging in Richard's neck enraging him further.

Jamie pressed on, finding himself laughing as the madness of battle took him, shouting the battle cry again at the top of his voice. The distance was now greatly closed and the archer fumbled at his arrow bag with cold hands. Normally he would have thrust spare arrows into the ground for easy access, but this had not been possible as the earth was frozen solid and the bowman thought he had no need of such expediency. He hesitated, for it takes a brave man to stand without cover when charged by a knight on horseback at full pace. He was experienced, probably from war or conflict, and it showed. Realizing his weakness he slid the war bow and held it two handed ready to smash the on-coming horse in the eyes or nose, unseating the rider.

Jamie saw the move and knew what to do. Leaving his sword in relief, pointing downwards on the near side, he curbed Richard. The horse fought the bit angrily, wanting to mow down the figure before him and destroy. He always thought he knew best, yet he heeded his master's unspoken command and slowed, regaining firmer footing in the soft snow. Locking up his haunches, he slid, paddling with his front legs and snorting angrily at the bit. Then, within feet of the archer, Jamie gave the final command and Richard reared upwards, lashing out with steel-shod hooves and slashing at the man in an evil fury. The archer, no longer able to swing at the head, tried for the body, but reeled back in fear as the bow met with an iron-shod hoof, snapping it. Landing on his forefeet, Richard lunged forward with his head, teeth bared, ripping at the bowman's left arm.

The man's scream of pain was cut short as Jamie's sword arm flew upwards, stabbing into his exposed throat and causing a spray of scarlet, bright against the white landscape. Richard kicked the figure as he fell, ploughing on towards more destruction as they turned towards the fighting near the litter.

One man at arms was down and bleeding badly, and the other was sorely pressed by two men. Jamie screamed his battle cry again, seeing only a red mist in front of his eyes as one of the men turned to face the new threat. The soldier, brave to the end, ran to meet the knight, swinging around aiming to catch the horse in the face with his sword. Richard half-passed deftly in a stride, Jamie deflected the lateral blow, pommel up, blade down. With the momentum he forced the blade around, slashing backwards as he passed into the helpless man's neck and killing him instantly.

He rode on to aid the man-at-arms, who was beset again by the attacker who was now keen to get past him. Jamie saw why; the outlaw who had attacked the horse litter was now astride the lead horse and urging it along the road with the occupants aboard, who were screaming from within. He looked down at his side. "Forest, set too!" He commanded.

The wolfhound needed no further bidding as she accelerated, bounding forward in long strides. When she was a yard from the horse Jamie saw her leap upwards with effortless grace, timing the strike perfectly as she crashed into the rider, jaws wide, ripping at the side of his face. The contest was ill matched as a hundred and twenty pounds of dog travelling at over thirty miles an hour rolled the vagrant out of the saddle and bit into his unprotected face as he fell to the ground. The man screamed a high, girlish scream as Forest's jaws closed.

Jamie saw that the man-at-arms had finally bested his man, who ran off into the woods. He spun Richard on his quarters and went to the aid of the knight, who had been wounded with a savage blow from a poleaxe that had penetrated his maille, leaving his leg bare and bleeding profusely. His horse had saved him so far. It jounced and pranced, kicking in vicious caprioles and keeping the two men at bay. The sound of Jamie approaching caused the man wielding the poleaxe to turn, snarling. He was large, confident and sure of his terrible weapon. He bore it two handed at half-guard ready to smash, stab or hook as he chose. The steel pointed tip of the staff was angled upwards and outwards like a driven stake. Jamie knew only too well how quickly the evil head of the hammer, spike and blade could be used to great effect.

He brought his sword over to the off side ready, letting it ride by his leg. It was difficult for the opponent to judge as the blade could be swung with full force in front of the body, free from encumbrance. Jamie placed himself side-on to the axe man and charged forward, ready with his shield. This time he forced the pace, making the defender rush his judgement. Sure enough, as Jamie came within the striking distance, shield ready to defend against the outward facing pole tip, the axe man spun the tip of the weapon through one hundred and eighty degrees, not seeking to cut with the axe head, but hook over the shield edge and pull, intent on dropping Jamie's guard and ramming home the evil spike into his unprotected torso, driven on by the impetus of the attacking horse.

Jamie understood how a poleaxe was used, having faced it many times on the battlefields of the Scottish borders, understanding its value as a hooking weapon, especially against armoured knights. He let the axe arc over and hook the shield, but instead of resisting, he allowed the shield to fall forwards. Bracing his left leg in the stirrup he stood up, swung over with his right arm and clove down hard with a diagonal stroke at the axe man. He ignored his helmeted head and the blade cut straight into the point where the neck joins the shoulder, smashing the collar bone deep into the chest below. Even if with his dying breath the man had wanted to thrust with his right hand, the arm no longer functioned with the shoulder muscle severed. The man sank like a pillar of salt, dropping to cast a crimson shade upon the white snow. Jamie twisted the sword free and sped onward towards the mounted knight, whose attacker turned just in time for Jamie's blade to sever his head. The man fell, his neck spraying blood in a long arc across the snow. The whole action had taken around a minute from start to finish, and the result was carnage. Already the snow was covering the evidence of the struggle, trying once more to return the ground to unsullied white.

Wheeling Richard around, Jamie pushed up his visor and trotted back to the knight, who was bent double, clasping at his wounds.

"Sir, how do you do?" Jamie asked in concern. In answer, clearly spent and weak from lack of blood, the knight fell down from his horse to lie supine in the snow.

Jamie was interrupted by snarling and barking as Forest savaged the body of the vagabond he had attacked. "Leave Forest! Here." He commanded, seeing the awful torn face and broken arm of the attacker hanging limply by his side. The man, now partially blinded, stumbled off, running more by luck than judgment into the woods after his luckless comrade. Jamie dismounted, ruffled Forest's ears as she trotted back to his side. He knelt by the fallen knight, seeking to aid him and wishing he had Cristoforo and his knowledge of healing with him. He gently eased the knight's head, and pulling up the visor, recognition struck him like a blow. "Sir Andrew Bloor!" he exclaimed. "Then that must be..." He looked back towards the waggon. His thoughts were interrupted as the man-at arms arrived, having tended to his comrade. Approaching his fallen master he addressed Jamie.

"Thank 'ee sir knight, for by God's holy legs you're most welcome and these bastard-born whoresons would've killed us all were it not for you," He said.

"'Tis my honour to oblige a man. See to your master while I retrieve the litter." Jamie ran the hundred yards towards the brightly coloured carriage, now stationary and whitening in the gathering storm. Jamie cursed as his boots slipped underfoot with the deepening coating of snow, which was now coming down in cyclical flurries driven by the wind.

He arrived, sliding to a halt, and reached forward to pull at the catch securing the velvet covered door, his heart beating against his chest for he guessed at what he may find inside. Pulling open the door he was cautious – and rightly so, as a dagger slashed outwards along with a cry of anger. "Villein! You may take me but you shall pay..."

"My lady, calm yourself. I mean you no harm and would secure your safety."

The lady within gasped: "Jamie, by the good Lord, Jamie! How come you here?" She cried.

"Providence, my Lady Alice, for I was on the road and heard a garboil ahead and sought to intervene. Praise God I did, for I was apt to be of service."

Another older voice from within the litter. "How does my husband, the earl?"

"At your service, Countess, yet for your husband I fear he has taken a wound which afflicts him badly and must be treated out of the cold ere it worsens."

"What? Is he dying?" She cried, aghast.

"No Countess, I believe not. Yet he is sorely injured." Jamie replied.

"Prithee aid me and I shall attend him." She commanded, attempting to dismount from the litter.

"My lady I adjure you, such action would be redless. Stay

within, for the snow is deepening and I will lead the litter back. The horses are unharmed." Reluctantly accepting his advice, the countess sat back down, shaking with concern and forcing her clenched fist between her teeth, deeply upset at what she would find. Jamie took the lead horse by the halter and led the litter back to the fallen earl. When he stopped the litter, the countess stepped down and knelt by her husband, her anxiety rendering her heedless of the wet snow.

She cradled the head of the unconscious earl in her lap, grasping his hand tightly. Lines of deep worry were etched into her face as tears rolled down her cheeks. "We needs must get him to shelter afore he worsens," she said, watching the blood from her husband's injury leaking into the snow beneath.

"My lady, permit me. I shall convey him hence." With that Jamie gently intervened, raising first the man's torso then shifting an arm beneath his knees. With a grunt of effort, he lifted the man and walked towards the litter. Alice went ahead to aid the laying of him within. There was only room for two and she left, allowing her mother to enter and comfort her husband.

"To where do you journey? Nearby I hope," Jamie enquired

"Indeed we do, for friends have a manor nearby and we are pledged to stay there this night. 'Tis but a short journey from here outside of Little Markham, yet my father suffers so." She murmured faintly, looking once again into the litter that bore the ailing earl, fussed over by his wife but still unconscious.

The man-at-arms came forward: "I know the way sir, yet I should be grateful if you wouldst attend upon us, for I'm afeared they may yet strike again."

"I doubt they shall, for their band is broken, yet I should be more easy to accompany you to the manor house." With that they laid the three dead servants under their cloaks and made fast the wounded man-at-arms astride a horse. It was only then that the problem of Lady Alice occurred to Jamie. Yet she was quick to assert herself, despite being visibly upset at her father's condition, her cheeks even paler than usual at the sight of the wounded earl.

"I am no mawmet to be easily broken," she responded. "Prithee fear not on my account. I shall ride with you and gladly, for I am not some shy maid of false modesty to melt in such conditions."

"As my lady wishes," Jamie acceded, admiring her spirit, "yet how would you achieve this aim for there is not a side saddle to be had."

She challenged him, her face in the shadow of her cloak hood, golden hair framed by the deep red velvet, her blue eyes deeper and darker in the failing light. Mocking, her voice took on a low husky quality. "Jamie, I am able to the task, my mother lies within," she nodded at the litter, "and needs must we press forward. If you do not tell then I shall not heed the cost. I shall ride astride, for as a girl I rode in such a fashion with my brother ere I could walk."

At that moment he loved her for her spirit and lack of false modesty. He laughed gently, looking a little down at her, for she was tall for a woman and lithe: "By the rood you show such spirit, I cannot deny you. Yet not a word, and wrap your cloak well about you."

With that he fetched a palfrey from one of the dead servants and gently set her astride the saddle.

As they rode together through the deepening snow and the day drew ever nearer to a close they talked at length, gaining a quality of intimacy that was not possible at court or under the eagle eye of her father.

"So once again you venture forth at Sir Richard Whittington's behest to face danger and chaos – much of which will perforce be of your own making," Alice chided him.

Jamie smiled in return. "Mayhap, yet I am a household knight and must go wherever I am bidden in the king's name."

"In the king's name or Whittington's?" she asked.

"Now you sound like John or my father, they are of the same mind. You have the right of it, yet I enjoy the cause and am loyal to the crown in whatever guise – despite what others may think." He answered, sending her a meaningful look.

"Oh sir, your barb strikes me a mortal wound and I am pierced." She mocked him.

"I was not aiming at you, fair lady, but at different sport. Your father cares not for me and rejects my suit for you."

"Yet I do not." And with that she turned to face him, deep concern and determination writ large upon her face.

"Thank you for that encomium, my Lady Alice. I shall persevere."

"Do, for my father will come about. He cares for me dearly as his only daughter, and perhaps..." she turned to look shyly at Jamie from under her hood. Jamie caught the look and laughed.

Chapter Six

Gloucester

The natural flood plain of the River Severn stretched out before Cristoforo, running amid a patchwork of fields as he made his way westward the following morning. The raw cold of the previous day had not abated, and if anything had worsened. He rode forward, approaching the bridge that led to the main eastern gate and Barton Street. Cristoforo noticed the life's blood of the area, the thick-coated sheep that were herded gently across fields silvered with frost, each nibbling at what scarce grass they could find. They looked fat, happy and warm, inured to the cold by their greasy coats.

Riding on, guided by the huge tower of Gloucester Abbey in front of him, he set Killarney to the bridge. He noticed that the whole town had been moated. By diverting the Severn they had created a virtually impregnable fortress, similar he thought to Calais. Looking down over the moat below, he saw that it had frozen solid and children were playing, slipping and sliding on the thick ice. He smiled to himself, remembering his own childhood in Firenze, where the river always remained in liquid form with the milder clime. *Water that ran as God intended*, he thought, shivering against the accursed English cold. He passed across under the guarded tower into Eastgate. He was to learn that the large town was divided into four sections, each with a gated tower guarding a bridge leading out over the moat. Once inside, the usual city smells assailed him, causing him to wrinkle his nose after the clean air of the countryside. The strong and pungent smells of animals, offal and dung came from the market to his left, and the streets were strewn with early morning soil as citizens clicked along in pattens that acted as overshoes, helping the well-to-do avoid the effects of the night's detritus on their soft poulaines.

There was a prosperous bustle among the crowds, exacerbated by the fact that it was market day. Carters, drovers and hawkers all vied for space, pushing and jostling, making Cristoforo glad to be on horseback as Killarney forced her way through the crowds. Finally reaching the crossroads of the four main streets he saw his goal, the huge square keep of Gloucester Castle to the southwest. Crossing into Westgate street he turned off left down Berkeley Lane, across Bear Land, then left down Barbican Hill. There the walls of the castle rose in front of him, the impressive central keep dominating the surroundings. Looking up he saw the royal standard hanging listlessly in the still air and knew that his journey had not been in vain. He crossed another internal moat to approach the main barbican, passing under the main gates into the outer bailey within the curtain walling. Inside, he was halted by the captain of the guard, who broke the seal of Cristoforo's letter of introduction and read the bona fides. He looked Cristoforo over suspiciously, as many did because of the hue of his skin, before telling him to leave his horse in the care of one of the ostlers. Cristoforo passed the man a coin, asking that he treat her well to oats and a good rub down.

Cristoforo followed the captain through to the inner bailey and then up into the vast keep. The castle was designed for war, with the first real windows set up high on the second floor letting light filter down into the main hall. Here was all urgency and noise, with courtiers, pages and fine ladies caught together in groups, excited at the royal presence, however briefly it might be bestowed upon them. An equerry approached him, and the captain wordlessly offered him the letter of introduction.

"The king will see no one. He rests in his private chambers. Present me with your missive and I will ensure that he receives it." The equerry held out his hand, refusing to meet Cristoforo's eye.

Cristoforo looked back at him, holding his ground: "That will not be possible. My orders are to deliver this into the hands of his majesty personally, and no other intermediary." He raised his head in a manner that brooked no argument.

The equerry snorted in disgust: "Await me here. I shall bring this to the attention of his grace Archbishop Arundel, for only he may intercede in such matters." The man walked off with Cristoforo's letter of introduction, leaving Cristoforo to look around and enjoy the comparative warmth of the hall. Under the eagle eye of the captain, he moved closer to one of the braziers that dispensed a modicum of warmth into the castle's huge interior. There he found a table bearing refreshment and helped himself to warm spiced wine. He sipped it carefully, finding it sadly wanting after the previous evening's vintage.

The equerry returned at length, perplexed and annoyed that this strange being before him should command an audience with the highest station. "Follow me," he said. "His Grace will see you."

Cristoforo hid a smile, shrugged and waved back to the surprised captain of the guard as he sauntered down the broad corridor after the equerry with a swagger in his step. Parading through the Great Hall he became the centre of attention, and conversation fell away as he left through a doorway that led him into one of the towers. He climbed two flights of stone stairs and the equerry beckoned him forward to a private chamber and thence into the presence of Thomas Arundel, Archbishop of York and Canterbury, adviser and close confidant to the king. The archbishop was a powerful force within the kingdom and a fierce opponent of Lollardy. Cristoforo recognised him instantly from his time at court and the burning of John Badby the previous year. He was not a tall man, yet his broad shoulders, stern countenance, cleft chin and wide-set eyes gave him an air of authority. Long brown hair flowed from underneath his episcopal hat of dark blue velvet.

He bowed before him: "Your Grace, I am Cristoforo Corio. I am at your service and the service of the king."

"Come hither, man. By your addresses, you are an Italian I perceive. They said you were a Saracen. Your countrymen have done our king great service in the past." The archbishop spoke in Latin. There was a power to him that Cristoforo decided was verging on the manic. The man was strong in his faith, yet zealous in his pursuit of his own definition of righteousness.

"As your grace sees," Cristoforo responded in kind. "May it please your grace, I have a missive that I was entrusted to deliver into his majesty's hands." He let the statement hang in the air, awaiting the rebuke that he was sure would come.

"Mayhap you come at the behest of Sir Richard Whittington. He is ever a good servant to my master. I pray thee present me with the parchment and I shall ensure that his majesty receives the contents forthwith. Come, be not afeared, for I assure you that it shall be so," he pledged, holding out his hand for the scroll.

"Ah, your grace, e'er it please you yet there was no ambage

in Sir Richard's direction. He made me pledge upon my life that I see the king in person and deliver this to his hand and his hand alone."

The archbishop's thick brows knitted and his shrewd eyes narrowed. "Then by the rood you will fail in your quest, for none shall pass by me and see the king."

Cristoforo shrugged. "As your grace pleases," He said in a kindly tone. He bowed and made to go.

"You are not dismissed," the archbishop exclaimed.

"Ah, mayhap I was not as fully cognisant of Latin as I had first bethought," Cristoforo offered lightly.

"You are a malapert rogue and I should have you clapped in irons."

"You may of course, as is your prerogative," Cristoforo continued, this time in French. "Yet it would be a great wonder that I would stay so imprisoned. Should Sir Richard hear of my treatment upon the king's errand as a messenger of his majesty, it would possible that our roles and our liberties be reversed."

A battle of wills ensued, which Cristoforo won. He had less to lose, and could afford to play for higher stakes. He had already formulated a plan to get past the defences and enter the king's chamber without the archbishop knowing.

"Very well, yet I shall remain in his presence the whole time."

"As your grace pleases." Cristoforo bowed again.

"Come hither," he ordered and with his robes swishing he made his way towards a rear door leading from the chamber. Cristoforo followed him into a large set of rooms that were fierce with heat after the Great Hall. The royal apartment was well appointed with rugs and tapestries and fed by two fires burning in large hearths to each side of the room. There in the centre sat the forlorn figure of King Henry – yet to Cristoforo's eyes he looked better than the last time he'd had sight of him.

There seemed more life in his face. It was still disfigured with boils, and his eyes were red-rimmed and rheumy, but there was a more spirited demeanour to the sovereign.

The royal figure sat in a grandly carved chair guarded by two men-at-arms. Three other noblemen were present: Sir John Prophet, Keeper of the Privy Seal and Sir Richard, Lord Grey of Codnor, Chamberlain of the King's Household. As Cristoforo entered the third man turned, revealing his face: Thomas, Duke of Clarence and Prince Henry's brother. His visage was dominated by his large, hooked nose, yet he was not unhandsome for all that. Lacking his brother's inches in height, he was stocky and powerful of frame as befitted a soldier renowned for his bravery on the battlefield it was said, seeking to prove his worth. He was also the king's favourite, above even his brother Henry.

The king, intrigued, beckoned Cristoforo to come before him. Cristoforo went forward, but was annoyed at the lack of care for the king's person. He had three weapons about him, any of which he could have used to kill the sovereign in an instant. The Italian moved as beckoned before the king, bowed three times and stood erect.

"May it please your majesty, I have here a parchment directly from Sir Richard Whittington who gave me a fiat to pledge this to your hand and your hand only," he said. He carefully undid the frogging at his jupon and removed the scroll of parchment from within. Two of the nobles tensed, the exception being Sir Richard, for he had met Cristoforo before in Shropshire, and there they had fought side by side. The archbishop took the scroll and passed it to the king, whose eyes were still able to see without ailment. He read through the words twice to take on board their full meaning.

"Sir Richard is as ever a good friend to us. With this document he warns us of an impending meeting of the royal council, where no doubt our son shall foment against us. He moves ever closer to the throne. Mayhap I shall outlast this latest of relapse and rally. 'Til then we see that he provides for Sir Edward Courtney to take to sea and thwart the pirates that are scouring the English Channel." He finished, his voice hoarse with emotion.

"Courtney, your majesty?" Archbishop Arundel enquired. "The Earl of Devon, cousin to Richard who even now causes dissention at your majesty's university at Oxford?"

"As you say, Arundel, and party to the royal council besides, no doubt. We perceive that the meeting shall be about revenue and the wool taxes."

"I see the hands of Uncle Henry in this," The Duke of Clarence spoke with ill-grace. "His estate is precarious, and mark my words should Courtney fail – and he will – my vision is that Henry will take up the gauntlet of his brother Thomas and gain the glory, thus entrenching his position within the realm."

The others, including the king, turned around to face him at the outburst, but it was the archbishop who offered him solace. "Fear not, my son, for we shall overcome both the Courtneys' position and the obstacle presented by Bishop Beaufort. I shall seek a papal bull in due course to ensure the alliance that you seek is successful."

Cristoforo did not understand the reference and wisely kept his own council, yet he marked the outburst and determined to seek Jamie's advice when they were reunited. The king turned back to Archbishop Arundel and continued in the vein of Whittington's message and the proposed council meeting. Yet before a discussion could begin, Arundel spoke to Cristoforo. "Italian, where do you stay? For needs must we give thought to his majesty's course of action."

"I am to lodge at the house of my Lord Whittington's

brother, on Northgate Street. Sir Richard has made provision for me there."

"Just so. I will send for you on the morrow."

Cristoforo was about to turn and leave when Lord Grey detached himself from the king's meiny and bowed to the sovereign. "Prithee, your majesty, I would have discourse with this man, for we were at arms together at Stokesay when we defeated the traitor Glyndower."

"As it pleases you, Sir Richard," the king muttered in response.

Sir Richard bowed again and turned to Cristoforo: "Come sir, do, for it has been months since we were engaged together and I would learn of all you have done since."

At the gesture Cristoforo realised that his standing would be raised by the knight's kindness, and he was grateful. The two men left the chamber with Sir Richard asking after the court and what prevailed there. In the corridor outside the king's chambers he spoke more plainly to Cristoforo. "The king rallies a little I feel, and may be well enough to attend and assert his will once more. Prithee tell Sir Richard that the winds of change are apt to blow afore the year is spent. But have a care on the road, for your presence here will have been marked and there are those who would know what message you carry from the king." He stared down at Cristoforo, a serious expression upon his face, then escorted him to the Great Hall once more.

Cristoforo sought the stables. He found his way to the main gate and made to pass through it when he was stopped by the captain of the guard, who appeared to Cristoforo to be much kindlier disposed. "Did you see the king?" he asked, seemingly impressed by this strange messenger.

"Aye, that I did, and I thank you for your help."

"I was glad to render service. Be you returning on the morrow? I ask so that I shall aid you in entrance to the castle."

"Ah, 'tis kind, yet I know not. I go as I am bidden for my duties," Cristoforo answered. He was not a trusting man and knew from experience that anyone who was kind to him either wanted something or was not to be trusted. With that he nodded at the guard and left, leading Killarney through the gate.

Mounting, he rode out and retraced his route to Northgate Street, where he sought the family home of Sir Richard Whittington's brother. Towards the end of the street he spotted a large house set back from the throughfare, impressive in its grandeur, reaching three stories from street level and dwarfing the adjacent properties. Dismounting, he walked up to the entrance and rapped on the studded oaken door. It was but mid-morning, he estimated, and the shutters were drawn back. Yet at length the door opened and an elderly servant appeared. He had a gravitas about him that bespoke character and intelligence. He gave Cristoforo a cursory glance that seemed to assess him in a single moment. The servant saw the well-cut expensive clothes, coloured in hues not native to England, yet he was not fooled into thinking him a Saracen as did many. The handsome face, olive skin and slate grey eyes bespoke a Mediterranean lineage, the servant knew, having travelled through Italy in his youth on a pilgrimage to the Holy Land.

"A good day to you sir. I am *signor* Cristoforo Corio, a messenger in the employ of Sir Richard Whittington, brother to the Lord Robert. I have here a letter from Sir Richard addressed to his brother. He asked that I deliver it and await a reply."

The servant noted the accent, which confirmed that the visitor was Italian. "Then you are to be disappointed, *signor*, for my Lord Robert has left for Pauntley Manor where he will reside for a sennight to settle affairs. I am his clerk and master of the house. How may I be of service?"

"I prithee take this and present it to my lord upon his return," he said, presenting the sealed message. "For I believe there is nothing of great urgency, and I cannot tarry nor journey forth to another town as I may be needed to attend the king and return to London forthwith." While heeding the words of Lord Grey, Cristoforo had his own senses to rely upon, and did not think Whittington's servant a traitor. He also knew that the mention of the king's name would gain him credence, and he was soon rewarded.

"You attend his majesty on Sir Richard's behalf? Please come inside and take some refreshment." The man responded. Cristoforo smiled, *I may yet spend a warm night in a comfortable bed*, he thought. And so it was that he stabled his horse to the rear and was summarily invited to stay the night. The following morning a page came from the castle to beckon him hence at his majesty's pleasure.

Chapter Seven

Nottingham

Jamie escorted the party to the manor of Alexander Meryng, an influential local land owner, and his son Sir William. The meeting had been propitious, for it had transpired that Meryng too was at odds with Sir Richard Stanhope, who had joined forces with one John Tuxford and was seeking to sequester lands owned by the Meryng family by force. Jamie now had the names of all the protagonists involved and was better able to understand the politics of the region. Sedition, he learned, was being sown by a handful of once loyal knights – Sir Thomas Chaworth, Sir John Zouche, Sir John Leche and Sir Roger Leek – who all now claimed that the king should abdicate and Prince Henry take the throne in his stead. It was treason by any other name, and once again Jamie marvelled at the perspicacity of Whittington in cutting out the canker before it became a more serious danger.

Yet worse to his mind were the blatant attacks on those within the county, attempting to seize their lands by force. Stanhope was using the might of knights and their followers to instil fear and take manors and holdings which did not belong to them. This was the beginning of lawlessness, and as Stanhope's power grew, so would his ambitions. Jamie had seen the actions of such men who relied upon their connexions at court to bolster their ambition and then use such influence to exonerate them of all crimes – all the while maintaining control over all they had seized. Such was the complacency that had festered under Henry's lax government in recent years. The king was unable to bring an iron fist to bear upon his realm and all were suffering the consequences – unless they were strong and ruthless and with little conscience.

"Stanhope is a clever and dangerous man, Richard." He muttered to his horse ruffling the stallion's huge ears. The snow had stopped falling by the following day, and Jamie bade adieu to Meryng and his son and rode off into the silent white world towards Nottingham, Forest ever alert to each new sound as it came upon the air. A strong easterly wind blew the snow into banks of drifts, the crests of which sparkled like a thousand diamonds, hurting his eyes as the pale sunlight reflected back. To keep his story about travelling from northern lands straight, he cautiously made his way to the north gate by a circuitous route. As ever he was impressed with the vast Sherwood Forest, and he smiled at the emerging legends of Robin Hood. Among the ballads and the manuscripts he had read William Langdon's *Piers Plowman* and his latest script *Dives and Pauper*, and the stories continued to grow. As Jamie's mind drifted towards the romance of the tales, he remembered his own ride in the snow with Alice at his side. He had not wished the journey to end, and they had seemed alone in a pure world of virgin snow and courtly love. It had been a perfect moment that had offered him solace from the evident disapproval of her father. *Yet mayhap that will change too, now I have rendered service to him.* Jamie thought. The knight was still in pain from his wounds, but

Meryng had found him a warm and comfortable bed and it was likely he would recover full use of his leg, although it would be some time yet before he could travel.

The road divided as the forest parted, and there above him, perched upon a sandstone rise looking out to the River Trent and the valley below, soared the mighty edifice of Nottingham Castle. He had seen the town before in passing, yet the castle never failed to impress him by its stature. He circumvented the outlying pastures, approaching through the vast level plains of Lingdale Field and Wood Field. The landscape was devoid of its normal grazing cows and pigs, leaving a few small herds of sheep watched over by shepherds and their dogs as they foraged for the brown winter grass beneath the snow. He called Forest to heel in case she was tempted to engage with the dogs or harass the sheep. He passed through the northern Cow Bar Gate and onto Backside. The covering of snow must have made the town appear more sanitary before it turned into the inevitable grey slush, and the effluent in the streets was now more apparent, cast as it was against the whiteness of the covering. Richard tossed his head in the crowds, snapping if anyone got too close. His size alone caused citizens to keep a wary distance, throwing Jamie the occasional curse and dark stare. Forest ignored them, gently padding along, taking in the smells of the new city.

With no knowledge of the town, Jamie followed the street southwards to the central Market Square, then feeling the appeal of a wider and less populous street he moved westwards into Timber Hill. Waggons loaded with lumber were on display, the sap of the newly cut wood smelling sweet in the air. The cries of the vendors were loud in the cold morning breeze. At the end of Timber Hill he turned left and found a side-street where the signs of two or three taverns swung in the breeze.

He chose the Running Horse in deference to Richard and bespoke a room and stabling. Then his stomach complained.

He had not eaten since breaking his fast at Meryng's manor, and his mouth watered as he smelled the aroma of frying bacon. He heard those at court boast of Nottinghamshire bacon from pigs that were allowed to roam free, gorging themselves on the acorns in the oak forests, fattening up for the winter kill. He ordered two trenchers stuffed with the meat and sat down with a tankard of ale to enjoy the food, throwing one of the trenchers and a slice or two of bacon down to the wolfhound. He was not disappointed with the food.

"Why landlord, 'tis surely the best bacon I have ever eaten," he said, and the landlord accepted the compliment.

"Aye, the pigs hereabouts feed right royally on the acorns in the forest. 'Tis good for the meat and no mistake. Another ale? For the salt will cure your mouth as much as the meat." They passed a few convivial moments discussing meats and the town, then Jamie said something that received a different reaction.

"I am lately returned from the borders, and a former comrade in arms said I might find him at the Wheatsheaf. Do you know where I might locate that inn?"

The landlord gave him a queer look: "I do, tho' I'd as lief not go there were I you – and if'n I did, I'd make sure my sword was 'andy."

"Well, he was rough fellow, so that sounds right." Jamie declared with a grin.

"Rough? Why he be keepin' comp'ny with a bad lot of malaperts and rogues." He dropped his voice and looked furtively around. "Them as drinks there are Stanhope's mercenaries, loyal to a fault so they say. Watch your mouth if you've soldiered for the king, and don't say as I didn't warn you."

Jamie pushed for more information, confirming everything he had heard from the Meryng family the previous evening. Stanhope's manors and estates were at Rampton, miles to the northeast, but he had a house near the town and spent much of his time there orchestrating his campaigns, Jamie learned.

"I bethought him a king's knight, or so my comrade said."

"Aye, that he was, and fought for the king at Shrewsbury, God bless 'im. But now 'tis as though he would build his own kingdom here, and right powerful he's become. None will gainsay 'im."

Finishing his ale, Jamie thanked the landlord and went out into the street, his immediate mission to buy a cloak of poorer quality, for an ordinary man-at-arms would never be dressed as he was. Walking through the town with Forest he found the Wheatsheaf and looked at exits in the nearby streets. His experience at Saint Omer with Cristoforo had taught him a valuable lesson.

He retraced his steps, bought a poor quality cloak, leggings and hat from a stall on the market. His sword and boots he could not disguise – yet he knew that many a man-at-arms had improved their lot in that regard through battle and corpse robbing. Now he needed to insinuate himself into the company of Stanhope's mercenaries and all would be well. A hint of a plan was forming in his mind as to how he might achieve this.

— × × —

Later that evening Jamie walked through the streets of Nottingham alone. He had bidden Forest stay in his room, knowing she would fight or rail against anyone who raised even a voice in anger toward him. He heard the church bells ring eight o'clock as he approached the Wheatsheaf.

Two ill-clad men stood outside arguing in a manner that implied too much ale and circumstances that were likely to erupt into violence at any moment. *I'm in the right place.* Jamie thought. He pushed open the door to the inn, walked in and stood just inside the door, allowing his eyes to grow accustomed to the dim light. Poor quality tallow candles served the taproom and men clustered round rough tables, the air a babble of talk. It was not a congenial atmosphere and Jamie would remember for a long time to come the hot and sweaty faces of coarse men who turned to stare at him. They were as rough a bunch of men as he had encountered anywhere in his young life, hardened as he was to war and bloody violence.

He stared back, curling his top lip in a mocking sneer that dared anyone to advance against him, taking on the persona that he knew he must inhabit to survive, for any kind of weakness would be his downfall. He pulled back the hood of his cloak, showing his dark red-gold hair that he had left unkempt and tangled by design. He looked sullen and dangerous. His hand lingered at the hilt of his dagger, ready to draw at any threat. With a purposeful stride he made his way to the rough-hewn bar, ordered ale and food and moved to a trestle already half filled with drinkers. He ignored the other occupants and sat down lightly, keeping a wary look about him yet pretending not to do so.

His ale and food arrived care of a serving girl who swayed her hips before him. Upon closer inspection he noticed that she was younger and less coarse of face than he had first imagined. A thin woollen coif did a poor job of keeping her dark hair in place and rosy cheeks glowed beneath her twinkling brown eyes. A once white apron was cinched at her waist, accentuating her curvaceous figure.

"Will that be all sir?" she asked, her eyes flirting.

"Aye lass, that it will for now." He answered with a smile of his own, deliberately accentuating the accent he'd heard for years on the borders, adding a lilt to his voice.

The words brought a scowl from a newcomer lingering at an adjacent table. He was young, broad and sullen of features.

Brawny arms showed beneath a leather jerkin and his huge, scarred hands were like hammers. Jamie sensed the change in mood and thought to himself, *ah, a chicken for plucking*. He ignored the look and broke open the meat pie, savouring the hard-crusted pastry and the rich gravy within.

The brawny man winked at his friends, put down his ale and swaggered over to Jamie's table, standing in front of him, huge arms swinging by his sides.

"Hey scullion, I saw 'ee looking at Beth, making sheep's eyes. Bog off, if'n you know what's good for 'ee."

Jamie ignored him completely and carried on eating, using the wooden spoon to collect the gravy before it soaked into the bread trencher beneath. He knew his lack of response would enrage the oaf before him, which was exactly his intention. This would be the kind of dirty fight he'd seen in alehouses all over the country. No rules, fighting tooth and claw to see who could be bested.

"Didn't you hear me, Red?"

Jamie looked up as though seeing the man for the first time and stressing his northern dialect answered: "Why don't ye go back tae your mammy. Ye'll maybe get back in time tae stop her sleeping wi' her next customer," he responded. He took another swig of ale, holding it in his mouth as if to savour it.

The man's eyes bulged with disbelief as the words registered in his thick head. No one dared speak to him in that way. He leaned forward, swiftly bringing both hands to grab Jamie's head and smash it into the table. Jamie merely looked up, and as the head and shoulders moved down he spat the ale into his attacker's eyes. The stinging liquid stopped the man, blinding him for an instant. In that instant Jamie stood, pushed the table over and grabbed the man by his greasy hair. He smashed his elbow into the man's nose, hearing the crackle of breaking cartilage and bone, and as his head reeled back he punched him in the throat. A keening sound left the man's lips as his blood-spattered mouth opened and closed in an effort to gain air, and he dropped to the floor gasping for breath.

The two men at the next table rose from their seats, daggers drawn, angry at the felling of their friend. Jamie knew he had to end it quickly or there would be others – friends who would attack and stab him in the back. He had no maille, and was wearing only a gambeson that would turn a blade but not to the neck or legs. His hand moved in a blur and before the two dagger men could react, they found themselves facing a sword. The point flicked out, left then right, cutting both of them, and the daggers clattered to the floor, followed by drips of blood as the men held their cut hands in pain.

Jamie slowly faced the room, circling, challenging. With a sword in his hand he would best any man there and they could see by the way he mastered the blade, perfectly balanced, ready, that lives would be forfeit if this attack continued.

From the other side of the inn a figure rose, dressed in gambeson and with shoulders muscled like Jamie's, lopsided from use of sword and shield. A kindred spirit if ever there was one.

"All right lads, you've had your fun. Now 'ere this gets serious I think yon mon here will have your lives next, not your hands. Put up your sword, man, give me your name and I'll buy you an ale. I admire a fighter." Advancing empty handed, palms raised, the newcomer came closer. The crowd relaxed. They clearly knew the man, who exuded leadership.

Jamie had seen such men before. A born leader and a seasoned man-at-arms by the look of him. He lowered the tip of the sword to the floor ready for treachery, but none came. The hard look around the newcomer's eyes crinkled into a smile.

"I would be as wary as you, mon, so I'll sit and show I mean no harm. Alf there," he nodded down at the recumbent figure who was still gasping for breath on the floor, "was ever a fool and loves to bait strangers. I'd say he's met his match. I'm Jack." He offered "You're new to the town, I take it?"

"Aye that I am, I've travelled down from Alnwick. My name is Jamie."

"Well then, Jamie of Alnwick, what do you seek so far from home?"

"A posting or position worthy of my abilities. I've fallen out of love with my master and seek new means to live."

"Then I may be able to help you. We can always use a good man in a fight."

"Who is 'we' and who do I have to fight?" Jamie asked, suspicion ringing in his voice.

"Well that depends upon what scruples you may have."

"If it puts coin in my purse and bread in my stomach, very few." Jamie answered.

"And if I had such a coin for every man I heard say that, I would never hunger," The man said, with suspicion. "Tell me how you came thus."

"You have seen my skills. My master saw them too, yet he set little value upon them. I seek a man who offers more."

Jack threw back his head and let out a roar of laughter. "A man for whom money calls louder than fealty. Plainly spoken, good fellow, and well met. Yet afore I say more, whom did you serve in Alnwick?"

"I was a little further north, near Berwick. I fought for Sir Robert de Umfraville..."

"What? You fought with de Umfraville, the Border warlord? Why man you must've seen some sport there, for the Scots are ever in revolt."

"Amen to that. They are, thus we raided and scourged them as we could to keep the Borders clear. 'Twas good sport as you say, and great were the spoils. But things have been quieter and more peaceful," Jamie spat the word out as if it brought a bad taste to his mouth, "since the Scots realised they had been bested. It won't last, but I crave action."

"Then what I have to offer should appeal, for we have similar work hereabouts. Do you know of Sir Richard Stanhope?"

"Aye I ken the name. Sir Robert spoke of him, he is a king's knight is he not?"

"Mmm, that's as maybe he was, but now he is for himself and who knows where, for he rules the district and seeks power and influence and land, as all knights seem to," Jack replied. "But come now, another ale and we'll talk more."

Chapter Eight

Gloucester

Cristoforo passed a congenial night at the Whittington home in the company of Sir Robert Whittington's servant Gareth, who knew many of the places and towns Cristoforo had visited in Italy. He even had a basic command of the Italian language and they talked until the early hours. Following his audience with the king the day before, he had spent an interesting hour or so roaming around the bustling town. He took a stroll down to the docks by the river port and then across to the silversmiths' shops for which Gloucester was famous, where he bought an ornate brooch for the contessa.

He found himself summoned to the castle the following morning at an early hour for an audience with Archbishop Arundel, who presented him with a message to return to London. There was no urgency attached as the meeting of the council was not set to take place until early March. As he made to leave, he bade the captain of the guard adieu.

"Where do ye travel now messenger, back to London?" he asked amiably.

"That I do. I shall travel back today. I thank you for your courtesy here, it will be noted when I make my report." He added. He would do nothing of the kind, but his suspicions were on high alert and he wished to set the Captain at his ease. Cristoforo mounted, and with a friendly wave urged Killarney out into the street. He would press on today while the light held, and hoped to make Barrington, some 20 miles to the south east, by nightfall. He passed by Chintenham and had started the long climb up the hill out of the town to Andoversford.

He looked out across the winter landscape and pushed Killarney into a brisk trot. She was a comfortable horse with a smooth action, and he was grateful to Jamie for lending her to him for this long journey. There were few travellers on the roads and all he passed were headed the other way, downhill to the town. The lifeless, leafless winter trees clawed upwards against a stark winter sky that promised snow as the grey clouds above him merged together.

As he climbed higher the first flakes started to fall, settling quickly, and he pulled his cloak closer about him. The road levelled out onto the main ridge above the rolling landscape and he gave Killarney her bit to catch her breath, walking her through the steady curtain of snow. All sound was deadened, yet another sense in him prevailed. He was, he knew, either being watched or followed by forces unknown. The straight Roman road dipped and rose, rarely transgressing from a straight line, offering him little opportunity to deviate and see who might be following him. "*Sempre dritto, cavalla, sempre dritto.*" He whispered to Killarney, urging her back up to a steady, ground eating canter. After a few miles, the road started to slope steeply downwards past a crossroads, where Cristoforo saw signs of other travellers who had come by foot, cart and horse. The snow was quickly covering the tracks so he pushed onwards before back-tracking to the left, seeking shelter in the trees that had been cut back to protect travellers from ambush.

Once in the copse he found a deep swale where locals had quarried the local stone for building. He dismounted, and leaving Killarney to munch on the brown winter grass that the trees had sheltered from the falling snow, he edged forwards to watch the road and wait. He did not have to endure the cold for long before three horses came into view, pushed too fast for the conditions by their riders as they slithered and fought for grip, the nails of their shoes saving them from falling. He let them pass undisturbed, smiling to himself. He had a further six miles to travel before reaching Little Barrington and a merchants' house where he would find respite from the weather and pursuers. It would be enough.

He remounted and pressed on carefully as the snow deepened and the frozen rutted road became more dangerous. Cresting a rise some two miles from Little Barrington he spotted the three riders in the distance, slowly retracing their steps towards him, looking down to the snow from time to time. Another grim smile crossed his lips.

He stopped Killarney, dismounted, unbuckled the leather satchel that was strapped to the cantle and produced a waxed drawstring bag. From within he fetched two parts of a crossbow. It was only a small weapon, about sixteen inches across the lath, which was laminated of wood, horn and sinew, riveted and glued. He slipped the waxed cord across the nocked ends, then clicked the lath into the short tiller. It was tiny weapon – an assassin's weapon – easily concealed and lethal at up to fifty yards. Three wicked looking quarrels were secured underneath the tiller in readiness.

Cristoforo turned away, keeping Killarney between him and the approaching riders who had spurred on, seeing his distant form. He unclasped his cloak, laying it over the horse's back to keep her warm as she waited patiently, ears pricked in curiosity as the three men drew nearer. He tensed his stomach muscles, lodging the stock of the tiller, pulled back with both hands until the bow string clicked behind the trigger that held it in place. As he did so, the pressure caused the trigger below to protrude, standing proud from the stock of the bow, protected by a thin steel guard to prevent premature release. Cristoforo placed a quarrel in the lock and bent forward as though to inspect the horse's hoof.

The three men arrived, their horses blowing plumes of hoary breath into the air. They formed a loose semi-circle in front of him. They were armed with swords and daggers, while one had a full-size crossbow strapped to his back and another a spear, the base of the haft resting in a fewter at his stirrup. They had cloaks, now open, showing no maille, just padded gambesons and one a leather jerkin.

"Trouble?" One of them asked gruffly.

"No, just snow driven into the foot." Cristoforo answered casually, remaining bent over, concealing most of his body from the three, "I thank 'ee for stopping, yet do not heed me, for I shall soon be on my way."

"We didn't stop to help," said the leader, lifting the spear.

Cristoforo straightened up, for he thought he recognised the voice. As the man's hood fell back he saw who it was.

"By the rood, captain, you're a long way from your home." He declared lightly.

"Not as far as you, Italian. Now let us have no badinage here, I'll have that message from the king e'er it please you," he held his hand out.

"*Dio mio*, but that will not serve, for I must deliver it to my master on a matter of a fiat."

"Fiat or no, I'll have that message, or by the Cross I'll have your life as forfeit."

"Ah now that is a pity…"

"Pity? Pity is it then, so be it." With that the captain raised his spear and his two henchmen began to draw their swords. As the haft of the spear came up, the captain flipped it and caught it underhand to throw. It was as far as he got. Cristoforo raised his hidden hand, holding the crossbow, aimed and the wicked weapon spat a quarrel that within an instant was protruding from the captain's neck. All thoughts of throwing the spear disappeared in a spurt of blood. Instead he dropped his weapon and clutched at his throat, vainly trying to stop the gush as he took his last breath.

His two companions looked at him in shock. Their victim had taken them all by surprise. In that moment Cristoforo came from behind Killarney, pulling his cloak with him as the two men spurred their horses forward, their swords drawn. Cristoforo's right hand dropped to his boot and flew upwards, launching a dagger that struck the throat of the second man, who fell backwards off his horse, gargling on his own blood. The third man was on him, but Cristoforo flung his cloak into the horse's face and the animal shied and reared, putting the rider off balance. The horseman sat it well, keeping his seat and his sword, yet as he tried to turn to face Cristoforo, he saw a flash of steel as the blade of a falchion sliced deep into his thigh. As he instinctively brought his hand down, the blade flew again in a back slash that neatly severed that hand at the wrist.

The injured man whimpered. "No, please…mercy," he cried.

Cristoforo heeded him not. He knew his life would have been forfeit even if he had handed over the missive, and with that knowledge he drove the point of the falchion hard into the man's ribs, twisting it and pulling backwards. Blood seeped out as the man fell from his horse, dying in the cold snow.

"You lay for me to kill and rob me, and now you cry

mercy?" he sneered. He spat at the dying man and used his cloak to clean the blade before replacing the falchion in the scabbard between his shoulder blades. Putting his foot on the dead captain's chest he tugged the spent crossbow quarrel from his throat and retrieved the dagger from the second man, returning it to its boot sheath. He then calmly disassembled the crossbow, returning it to the bag. Killarney was nervous and unsettled at the smell of blood. She was a palfrey, not a war horse, and it worried her. Cristoforo spoke soothingly, he did not wish to be afoot in this weather. He edged close enough to gently grasp her reins and mounted with care. He caught the reins of the three other horses and led them gently off into the snow, leaving the three dead men lying in the road.

A good day's work, he mused to himself. He feared no retribution, for he knew that to assault a king's messenger was a hanging offence. He had simply saved the executioner three jobs. Yet he would now walk Killarney quietly to the merchant's house without raising a hue and cry. *'Tis a shame*, he thought, *that there are no wolves in this country to clear up this mess.*

Chapter Nine

Westminster palace, London

Bishop Henry Beaufort's chambers were warm against the chill, yet the atmosphere within was frosty. His brother Thomas, Chancellor of England and Admiral of the northern fleet, stood in front of a large table, preoccupied and in ill humour, stroking his dark beard. With broad shoulders and a luxuriant head of brown hair he had the dark and striking looks of his father, John of Gaunt, and as such many features aligned with the king, his half-brother.

"So the Italian jackanapes returned, I hear, and in good fettle. The fiat upon which Whittington sent him was successful – and what I'd give to learn of the contents of that correspondence! How does the man survive? He has served two kings and now a prince, treading the line as assuredly as an acrobat." Thomas complained.

"Verily, so he does. He glides gracefully across troubled waters like a swan. All serenity on the surface, yet underneath, turbulence and force unerringly drive him onwards, unseen by others. Building a nest for the future, yet for whom? That is the question. A king, a prince or himself?" The archbishop's questions were rhetorical, and nobody moved to answer them.

"By the rood I know not, yet we shall see what is revealed at the March Council meeting, for now 'tis arranged, I hear. Our brother the king will be brought to brook I'll warrant, for he weakens as the prince grows e'er stronger. Yet still Prince Henry will make no move to take what should be his. The land needs a strong hand that no ill-made king can give. Uprisings abound and naught is done to stop them. Lollardy persists, yet only that old fool Arundel fights it and seeks to restrain the prince's favourite, Richard Courtney. Ha, it is a heady mess of potage and no mistake."

"Careful brother, for although we have power in title, we have no estates to bring to bear. Though the legitimacy of our being has been ratified, we are still vulnerable in all save name. That knave Arundel with the codicil holds us by the balls, yet mayhap we may relieve him of his power ere the prince accedes the throne. But we know that he conspires with prince Thomas to marry off our brother John's widow to his cause. And with such a marriage go all Margaret's estates into the hands of the king's favourite son, while we receive nothing. That is my pressing concern."

The warrior lord looked to his brother, worry writ large upon his face. "If Courtney should rise it would be a fine foil for Arundel and divide our enemies. To the north Stanhope causes unrest, and was ever favoured by the prince. With him and his men at our backs we could pressure our nevy to come to our cause and take the crown. Yet when last we spoke to him of the matter, he took it ill and dismissed such a route as mere janglery."

"Let us see what might prevail at the Council meeting, for that is but a short time hence. T'will depend on finances as ever, and the coffers of the realm are not deep. Money as much as power divides and rules this kingdom, so let us wait and see which way the wind blows."

Nottingham

It had been two days since Jamie had met Jack at the inn, and in that time he had used the Running Horse as his base, walking the town to familiarise himself with the streets and the layout of the city. He took Forest with him each time, for her keen ears and temperament would alert him to any revenge attack following the fight in the tavern.

He took Richard out for exercise and circumvented the town, visiting the busy docks and waterways of the Rivers Trent and Leen. The latter had been diverted to provide access to the bustling wharves at the foot of the great castle that towered above them. Looking up in admiration, Jamie was amazed that Richard's namesake, the Lionheart, managed to take the castle by siege in just three days. It looked formidable and indomitable, secure in its position on Castle Rock. Looking out he saw the Leen meander twixt meadows that were white with snow to rejoin the Trent further downstream. It was a picturesque setting, if one of frenetic activity as the steeves laboured hard to load and unload barges and sea going carracks bound for the Channel and Europe.

Sighing in the moment of respite, he turned Richard around and made his way back into the city followed by Forest. He was to meet with Jack at the Wheatsheaf early that evening, and from there he would be taken to Stanhope's manor outside the walls of the town. Arriving back at the inn, he went to the rear stable area, and in the deserted courtyard he practiced his swordplay for an hour. An old post was stuck into the ground and with the landlord's permission he used it as a pell, practicing strokes with his sword in the time-honoured way. Easing his cold muscles, he worked slowly at first, gradually speeding up the strokes. Cut, thrust, feint, the blows and moves flowed until his arms and shoulders burned with the effort.

After an hour he stopped, great clouds of white breath rising from him. He was sweating despite the cold and wearing just a linen shift. He made as though to turn away and stop, then span around at full speed his arms a blur of movement. Five quick, sharp moves landed on the pell, all of which would have been fatal. A grim smile broke across his face, for he loved the blade work and revelled in his skill and speed.

"A fine show, sir."

Man and hound span around as if by instinct, Jamie's blade raised and Forest with a curled lip, ready to attack. Surprised at the interruption, neither he nor Forest had sensed anyone arrive. Both man and beast looked to a window, where the landlord stood praising him. He recoiled slightly at the aggression, despite being safely inside.

"Ah 'tis kind of you to say so, and I prithee forgive me, for you startled me thus. I'm afraid I've notched your post a little in my efforts." He smiled, alleviating the tension.

"Ah, 'tis naught to worry. Come, you'll have worked up a thirst and a hunger." He gave Jamie a puzzled look before disappearing into his kitchen and Jamie wondered if he'd shown too much of himself.

Following his meal, Jamie found an armourer upon the landlord's recommendation to restore the sword's edge to its razor sharpness. The armourer had sinewy, corded arms protruding from the leather jerkin of his trade, and he held the sword with reverence.

"By the rood, 'tis a marvellous sword, and the blade be well forged. Where did 'ee come by it?" he asked.

"I retrieved it on the field of battle from a dead knight," Jamie dissembled, "I know not its origin."

"I'faith it's beautiful workmanship and the balance is perfect. Fortune smiled on you that day."

"Aye, that it did." He agreed. He did not like others handling his sword, and was keen to be gone from the garrulous armourer. Paying the man he left quickly, Forest tagging along beside him.

As dusk arrived, he made his way to the Wheatsheaf tavern, where he found Jack sitting quietly in a dark corner by the fire.

"Ah good, you've come. By the Lord Harry, that is a great hound." He exclaimed. Looking down, Jamie ruffled Forest's ears.

"Aye that she is, but friendly to those that know me." He warned gently, coarsening his voice.

"I'll mind that." Jack said, standing and lifting a thick travelling cloak from the settle. "Are you with horse, for we've a way to go?"

"I am. He awaits me at the rear of the inn."

"Then we'd best be quick, for thieves will steal a good animal and they're not too particular to whom it belongs."

"I pray they don't try, for 'tis hard ground for digging a grave," Jamie responded.

Jack raised an eyebrow and gave him a searching look. Arriving in the rear yard, he found Richard waiting patiently, Jamie's cloak upon him warming his back. Jack whistled, for even in the torchlight he could see that he was of quality and went to pat him. Jamie caught his arm in time as teeth snapped in the darkness

"I would not. He believes he is part wolf, and likes the taste of meat," he warned.

Jack shook his head in disbelief. "What a horse! By God I'm glad you stopped me. Now come, and bring your fierce flock with you. We make for Sir Richard's manor house." At which he mounted his own horse that was tethered in a vacant stable.

They set off into the evening and went to a small postern gate cunningly concealed behind two buttresses where the curtain wall changed direction, making the gate almost indiscernible from the wall. They dismounted to pass through and found that the gate moved on well-greased hinges and was barely large enough to accommodate Richard, who scuffed through under duress. Remounting, the two men moved off into the dark evening, heading west as fresh snowflakes started to fall. After a few miles of mostly walking the horses, they arrived at the village of Colwick and turned off on a side-track. They came to a dry moat and a gated curtain wall about fifteen feet in height. Jamie was surprised to see that it was castellated. *I doubt he has Royal consent for such works,* he thought as the torchlight brought the skyline into relief.

Jack called out to the guard on gate duty and the small portcullis was raised. *The place is like a small castle,* Jamie mused, and upon entering through the gateway he looked up to see narrow ramparts surmounting the whole wall. Before him there lay less than a manor house and more of a keep within a bailey, again with castellations running between four small turrets guarding each corner. It was, he decided, a fortress rather than a country manor.

The recessed door opened at a hail from Jack to the guard above, and they dismounted and moved inwards under the tall stone archway. The bailey was spacious, Jamie saw in the dim light, with wooden buildings and more substantial structures of barracks and stables to the left, where they were beckoned to leave their horses. Jamie gave a warning about Richard, bade Forest stay in the stables and followed Jack to the main door of the keep-like structure.

They passed through studded outer doors into a small entrance hall. *Those doors would stall an attack,* Jamie thought, looking left and right at the steps off on either side that led to a gallery or ramparts on the walls, Jamie surmised. They passed through a second door into to a main hall that was suffused with warmth. It smelled comfortingly of rich spices, dried rushes and lavender that gave it an opulent feel. Stanhope was not a man to eschew comfort, Jamie realised.

The two men blinked in the brighter light cast by the wall sconces. Standing in a loose semi-circle were five men. In the centre of that semi-circle stood a squat figure, seemingly as broad as he was tall. His heavy features rendered him almost ugly, plain at best. He had a heft to his shoulders that spoke of long hours with arms, and his exposed hands were criss-crossed with scars. Here was the man who had fought with the prince and the king at Shrewsbury. He was well dressed in clothes of quality that seemed somehow ill-suited to him. But the voice when he spoke was cultured, at odds with his appearance.

"I bid you welcome, sirs, to my hall on this snowy winter's eve. I am Sir Richard Stanhope," he said, his voice deep and authoritative.

Jamie gave a brief bow as befitted his role of commoner: "Thank you, Sir Richard. I am Jamie, late of Alnwick."

"Jack here," he nodded towards Jamie's companion, "has told me a little of your adventures further north, on the borders."

"Aye that's right," Jamie confirmed, stressing his brogue, "I served Sir Robert de Umfraville there for a time."

"So why did you leave his service? He is a good man and a grand fighter. Was the plunder not good enough for you?"

"Well my lord, it concerned a lady of good birth and a father who thought me not good enough," he lied. "In faith, there was a quality of intimacy between us not shared by her family. Men were sent to dissuade me of my amor and...well, here I am and here they are not."

Stanhope hid a smile: "So it can be with affairs of the heart.

Now Jack tells me that you accounted well for yourself against Alf in the tavern."

"I was a newcomer, he set me a trial of strength and will." Jamie shrugged as though that explained everything.

"Hmm. And you look for work that may make the best of your talents? If that be the case we may perforce have a use for you. But before I explain let me offer you a goblet of wine on this cold night."

A servant appeared bearing a tray. Jamie took the goblet of spiced wine offered and raised it to his lips, yet he sipped but little, for he knew that a test was coming and he would need all his wits about him. These were not stupid men and would not be easily fooled. Sir Richard continued without offering them a seat, moving so that his back was to the hearth where a fire burned.

"You should understand the circumstances abroad in these regions. There is *anarchia* here. The lands are ruled by might, not law, and different lords serve different rulers." He stressed the last word, the inference of which was not lost on Jamie. "To prosper, we must be strong to survive and cast our net widely, gathering all about us who would stay true to the crown. For the king ails, as we all know, and England needs a strong and youthful hand that can bring strength and order."

Here he paused, and Jamie caught a brief yet gravid look pass between him and one of the others. Jamie recognised him as Sir Thomas Chaworth, a member of parliament. He had seen the man but twice at court and then from a distance sitting in the House, and hoped that he would not himself be recognised. Jamie nodded and stayed silent, inviting him to continue.

"There are those who do not give a fig for law and order here, and would seize what they could in this time of unrest. We therefore," he gestured to his meiny who had drawn closer to him, "must strengthen our position for the day when we can support the king in his bid to restore law and order. Yet let there be no ambage – the king we wish to support is not yet crowned."

The shock of what he had just said hit Jamie hard: the words were treason! Fortunately, he had his goblet to his mouth and his features were masked. He gave a careless shrug, playing his part well.

"I care not for the like of kings and princes; for certes I have served causes afore to naught avail save more scars on my sword arm. If there is coin to be paid, that is my cause." He declared. "I'faith I ask why do you have need of me? You have Jack here, a goodly pack of malaperts from the tavern to do your bidding, and knights here too, I see," he nodded towards the gathered lords, "who themselves doubtless have men at arms to call."

Two of the knights frowned at the implied insult, particularly one of the younger men, yet he was stayed by a hand gesture from Sir Richard.

"Well said. Yet what we lack is men of middle rank. We have need of captains who have scourged and fought wars of raiding and attrition. In short, men with experience such as your own, who can organise men and weaken our enemies. What say you?"

"If'n you put coin in my purse and food in my belly, why I'll fight for your cause and gladly."

"Then I am pleased that you join us. Now, may I introduce these fellow knights? Sir Robert Strelley, Sir Thomas Chaworth, Sir John Zouche, Sir John Leek and Sir Roger Leche." Jamie made a brief bow to the assembled company including the still frowning young man, Sir Robert, who seemed less welcoming than the others. Jamie pushed his luck with his next comment.

"Sir Thomas, have we met afore? Mayhap you've travelled to the borders, for certes I'm sure our paths have crossed," he continued, planting a seed of doubt in case he had been noticed by him at court.

"I know not. I have travelled to the borders, yet I am likely to be seen at court or Parliament. Have you ventured there?"

"But once or twice on errands for Sir Robert. Mayhap that was the case," Jamie answered and let the comment fade. Satisfied, Jamie felt the attention of the company drifting to other matters.

"Where do you lodge, in the town?" Stanhope asked.

"I do, at the Running Horse."

"I know it well," he answered. "We can reach you there, and Jack will appraise you of your duties as they arise. I bid you goodnight and a safe return to Nottingham."

They were dismissed. Jamie made a light bow and turned to leave, his senses still on alert, and it was at that point when he heard the whisper of steel against wood, like the sound of two palms rubbing together and no more, followed by a gentle step towards him. He spun around, drawing his sword in a split second and bringing it to an upper guard in a sweeping movement, torchlight glinting on his blade, driven by instinct rather than thought. Jack too thought he was to be attacked, yet with his sword half drawn Jamie beat him to the move.

Flying down in the firelight came the blade of the young Sir Robert Strelley. Jamie intercepted the strike half way along it, allowing it to slide to the hilt. Stepping forward, he drew his dagger with his left hand and held it to the knight's throat, ready to slice it open.

"My lord?" He hissed in the man's face.

"Enough!" Sir Richard cried, a small smile on his face. "We merely sought to test you and you put us to shent. Sir Robert, you asked and were found wanting, Messires, put up your swords, there will be no bloodshed in my hall."

Jamie pushed Sir Robert Strelley backwards and retreated a

step quickly. Moving to the side, he bowed in mock humility, his face raised, eyeing the knight. "My lord," he said, a sneer in his voice. He took two further steps backwards, yet still did not sheath his weapons. Upon reaching the door he bowed again. "Thank you, Sir Richard, for your...hospitality."

Sir Richard uttered a coarse laugh. "By the rood you'll do lad, you'll do. I bid you goodnight."

Jamie disappeared through the doorway followed by Jack.

"Christ on the cross, I thought you meant to attack me." Jack exclaimed. "By God you're swift. How did you know?"

"A step towards me, the clink of a ring against a scabbard, a slight whisper of steel to wood and an instinct honed by living life at the edge of death. My time in the Borders taught me well. Now come, let us away afore they change their minds."

Inside the hall there was a sense of awe: "By the Lord Harry he's fast, and clearly trusts no one," Sir Thomas opined.

"A life on the Borders and service in Sir Robert de Umfraville's mieny will do that to a man. Yet I feel a little uneasy, I know not why. Too much hubris for a man-at-arms, mayhap? I shall send a messenger to seek proof of this warrior and his provenance," Sir Richard replied.

Chapter Ten

Laurence Lane, London: March

"When do you leave for Cornwall, Mark?" Cristoforo asked. They were sitting in front of the ovens in the kitchen of Thomas de Grispere's house. It was cosy and Cristoforo liked it there.

"Why on the morrow, for my Lord Whittington bade me wait until he was certain of how the council would vote, yet Lord knows how he would surmise such a thing."

"Mayhap it was what the king replied to his letter, for he is a cautelous and knowing man, as Jamie said."

"Amen to that. But I must bid farewell to Emma ere I depart, for the good Lord alone knows when I shall return. I'faith 'twill be good to see my family again."

"I am sure she will miss you dearly. Yet what of your cottage?"

As a result of their previous adventures, Mark and Cristoforo had received a bounty from the prince, and Mark for his part had bought a small cottage outside the city walls in the new area of Smythefeld on Chikenelane. It suited him well as it looked onto the market gardens fed by the river of Fakeswell and reminded him of the fields at home. New cottages were being built all along the lane, which although without the city walls lay just within the boundary of the City of London at West Smithfield Bars. It was not that far from the Dominican Friary, and Mark still called on Friar Vincent when he resided there and was not wandering and preaching.

"I shall lock it shut and my neighbour will look in to ensure all is well. I have naught to speak of and there ain't much of value to steal." He shrugged his huge shoulders and smiled down at his friend. "And what of you? Dost master Thomas bid you elsewhere, or Sir Richard for that matter?"

"Nay, apart from my usual duties to Master Thomas I have no bindings here and would accompany you to Cornwall, for I've not seen that part of England and you say it is warmer there and the weather fairer."

"Aye, that it is. Yet Cornishmen are strange folk and don't take too kindly to foreigners, begging your pardon Cristo. I'd lief as not be less noticeable by myself, not that I shouldn't like your comp'ny, for 'tis a long road. Mind, 'twill be better than when I travelled to Lunnon last, for Friar Vincent and I walked all the way! Now with my own 'oss, I shall travel in style." He proclaimed.

"As you say. I may take a journey north if master Thomas permits, for we have heard nothing from Jamie by letter and I have a feeling all is not well. My neck tingles, and I know not why."

"You and your feelings. They ain't never been wrong, mind. I miss his company as I shall miss yours ere we meet up again. Now I must be off for Emma and her mother expect me for supper and I do hate to miss my food."

Cristoforo laughed, clapping his huge friend on the shoulder: "Then I hope to God they have planned a feast, for you shall eat them out of house and hearth."

"Well I should be rude if I did not finish all as was set before me," Mark responded, managing to keep a straight face. "Now I shall see 'ee in the Spring when I return no doubt, and bid you well. If you see Jamie first then send him my regards."

"That I shall and fare thee well. God be with you."

"And you, Cristo, and you." With that the giant rose, moving lightly on his feet for such a big man, his body held perfectly in balance, shoulders swaying with his gait.

Riding through the city he made his way the short distance to the house and premises of madam Fitzwarren. She had married young, her beauty reflected in the bride price offered to her father. Her husband, Hugh Fitzwarren, had been much older than her and their marriage had been pleasant enough, though not a love match. He had been kind and she had absorbed all she could within his business, so when Hugh had been taken by the flux some five years earlier, Cicely had taken over all matters and made it a success. Her daughter Emma had been fourteen when her father died and was now blossoming into full womanhood. Jeanette had introduced them, playing matchmaker on the pretence of asking Mark to help her collect goods for her father. The introduction had, after some pushing on her part, been a success. Mark was essentially shy and it had been the lively young girl who, upon seeing the huge handsome Cornishman in his royal livery, had fallen in love with him at first sight.

He entered the front of workshop directly off the street. Like many of her calling, mistress Cecily lived above and behind her place of business. It was well appointed as befitted her status both in the community, and with a rare show of rank, within the Guild of the Worshipful Company of Mercers also. For they had permitted her entry to their ranks as she had proved her worth after taking over her husband's business and making it thrive.

One of the apprentice girls at the counter before him bobbed a curtsey and bade him good morning before leaving to fetch Emma from the workroom at the rear. The apprentice returned with a willowy girl of medium height, with the most striking head of hair the colour of Autumn. Her tawny and russet curls fought a losing battle against a plain wimple as they sprang forth to frame a pretty face. A sprinkling of freckles across her nose, along with her fair colouring, betrayed a Viking ancestry.

"Mistress Emma, good day to you." Mark said, becoming flustered as always when he met her in company.

"Why Mark, 'tis good to see you so early, come hither to the parlour where we can talk."

He followed her past the counter to a well-appointed room, comfortable and set with a fine woman's touch. Cushions bedecked deep settles either side of a fireplace in which a fire warmed the small snug room. A delicate window in one wall allowed rays of low sunshine into the parlour, yet candles burned giving a warm glow. Sandalwood and the smell of fresh, raw silks and fabrics pervaded the air. It was a comforting aroma. Mark relaxed as Emma took his hand and led him to a settle by the fire.

"My mother will be in shortly, so embrace me and tell me your news," she urged, a coy smile upon her face. Mark embraced her slight frame carefully, enveloping her within his huge arms as Emma melted in the strength she found there. He kissed her gently, savouring a slightly spiced sweet wine that lingered on her lips.

"By the Lord, 'tis good to see you, and I shall miss you all the more for it," he said and then cursed himself for his guileless tongue.

"Miss me? Why should you miss me? Do you travel abroad and tarry thus?"

"Alas, I spoke in haste without warning. Forgive me. Sir Richard has sent me upon a fiat at his command. I am to travel to Cornwall as a feudatory duty to the prince."

Emma was torn between the importance of the task and a man she had begun to care for dearly. She knew that the time apart would weigh heavily upon her heart. "By the rood, I suspect a mistress, yet I would know her form. Is she a lady of virtue or is it her jewel encrusted crown that steals you from me?" She said with a mocking smile.

"Ah Em, do not tease me so, for you run me ragged as it is. I should lief as not as take you with me, but the journey may be perilous and your mother would not permit it."

She pushed her index finger against his nose, delighting at the ease with which she could control this giant's strength. "Come then, tell me all that you may. Does it involve Jamie? For where he goes you do too, it seems."

"No, in fairness, it does not, I render service to the crown in Cornwall and Jamie is elsewhere." At which he explained what he could of why he was being sent to Cornwall and what he would do there.

"There has been much mischief abroad," she agreed. "We ourselves have lost numerous cargoes bound for our trade to pirates. Tis passing strange that you be indirectly to aid us in this duty of yours, and for that I forgive you your absence, yet will pine for you nonetheless," she said.

"The contessa's father says the same, and master Thomas fears for the Treaty. If it ain't signed there will be all hell to pay and the Devil take the hindmost. We all hope that whoever is chosen by the council will prevail and stop the pirates ere they strangle our cause. Or we shall all be lost, and Calais too most likely."

She placed her hands on his huge shoulders: "My Mark, your shoulders be broad yet they carry the world upon them, I fear. Come now, my Atlas, be not afeared on our account, for I am sure Sir Richard has a campaign planned to foil their schemes, and you a part to play in it. And with you on our side I am sure we will prevail." She answered pertly, confident in Mark's ability to succeed.

"I love that you have such faith in me, lass, and no doubt I shouldn't be so pebble-hearted. Yet I have seen the wickedness of the Courtneys in the past and I've no faith in them, truth be told. And I wish all three of us were together, for with Jamie and Cristoforo along we could go into Hell and steal the Devil's tail afore he'd notice."

At that point they heard Emma's mother's voice addressing a servant, and broke their tete-a-tete before she entered the room.

Lambeth Palace

The king had made the palace his residence since leaving the north some weeks earlier, and was now ensconced as the permanent guest of Thomas Arundel, the Archbishop of Canterbury. The king enjoyed the respite from the hurly burly of the Palace of Westminster across the river, a few hundred yards to the northwest. Here, with no direct bridge to connect the north bank nearby and only wherries providing a passage across the mighty Thames, he enjoyed walks around the magnificent gardens which even in the early Spring months seemed somehow lifegiving.

His health had improved with the weather. Although still troubled by his ailments, he nonetheless felt more invigorated and able to deal with matters of state and the swirl of rumours and treason that seemed to continually surround his court. A page and two men-at-arms provided a bodyguard for his safety, trailing some yards behind, leaving the king in peace to talk at leisure with the archbishop. Despite the softening of the Spring weather, both men were wrapped warmly in thick cloaks against the damp air, chilled by the wind that blew from the river as they sauntered through the paths of the palace gardens.

"The Great Council meets in three days' time on the fifteenth, and Parliament is suspended. It was well done by my Lord Whittington to warn you of the coming plot to wrest back control through finances. I wonder, my liege, if it was all the prince's doing or if there were forces at work pulling him hither and thither like a mawmet on strings?"

"To whom do you allude? Our half-brothers? You may have the right of it, for their ambition knows no bounds even when our realm is at stake. Yet if Whittington is right and Earl Courtney is to be tasked with leading a fleet, we needs must be ever aware of the peril both at home and abroad. My Lord Stokes informs us that it is William Longe who is the main culprit, and that he hides behind his badge of office at Rye. 'Tis distasteful to us, and with risings in the north all seem to have one aim, and everything seems to be conspiring to depose us from our throne. But praise God we are not done yet. There is still vigour in our old bones, and we shall come about and show them, my dear friend."

"Amen to that, my lord king. As God pleases, we shall thwart them and others in their plans. I trust not my nephew Arundel or Warwick, together with those in the Council."

"Their plans may as yet be upset, for Whittington tells us that France is rife with civil war, with Armagnacs fighting Burgundians and neither side prevailing, which is ever to our advantage. We shall look to the Channel and not be surprised ere a deputation arrives from France – though in whose name and in what regard we could not consider to venture."

"I am sure my Lord Whittington will provide answers, for he is as ever well informed on all matters pertaining to the French court."

"As you say, my lord archbishop, but now we must return. We are fatigued and shall require a rest ere more matters of the court place demands upon us."

— ⚔ —

The Great Council assembled three days later. The great lords and churchmen of England were present, yet factions were divided by an undrawn line between the king and his son. Ostensibly there were no divisions between the two that the factions were aware of. The Beauforts, as befitted their status of chancellor and archbishop, stood to the king's left, yet close to the prince who at this moment stood before the king. Their loyalties to both men appeared equal.

"I should always wonder how it is," Whittington fingered the chain of office about his neck and muttered under his breath to William Stokes, "that the Beauforts remain whole when they spend so many hours astride a noisome fence."

Stokes stifled a laugh at the observation: "Aye my lord, yet by the rood they perform most well. Their like is seldom seen without a circus."

Whittington turned to smile at his co-conspirator, a man who would be missed in a crowd. He had unremarkable features and dark brown hair and he was average of stature, yet he had a razor-sharp brain and planned his battles like a master general. With mathematical precision he saw the bigger picture where others did not, and was ideally suited to perform the role of financial spy. The assembled lords and clergy gave their agreement to various smaller items of protocol, then came the crux of the Council.

"Your majesty, if you will permit me," the prince said. "It has become apparent to us that certain fiscal dealings do not appear to benefit the realm. To wit I bow to the chancellor who will furnish us with the accounts."

Thomas Beaufort stepped forward and bowed to his brother, the king.

"Majesty, ere it please you, as your loyal chancellor I have here accounts prepared in your name and reconciled with the income for the kingdom. May I proceed?"

"As you wish." The king shrugged and waved him to continue.

"Thank you, majesty. We are all here most disturbed by the accounts that render a sorry story." He paused and saw the frown on the king's face deepen. Beaufort continued to address matters and finally summarized the position. "In short, majesty, the accounts show a wool subsidy of just £30,000, which is insufficient to meet the needs of the royal household at £22,811 and the defence of the realm at £42,115. The budget is adrift, and though it wounds me to draw this forward, a change must be made or we shall fall short in more than accounts."

The silence was palpable. The king, his face puce and his hands clenched upon his throne 'til his knuckles turned white with rage, said not a word, yet shot looks of scorn at Thomas Beaufort that were echoed by his son the Duke of Clarence at his side, who hated his uncles with a passion. The contestants gazed into the abyss waiting for a response, and it was the prince who finally broke the deadlock. He opened his arms in appeal. "Majesty, we feel we can reconcile the position, but only with your agreement and help," he said, seeking to draw the king away from a position from which he could not withdraw with his pride intact.

The king raised an eyebrow, his sole concession to having heard his son. "Your majesty," The prince continued, "it rests with income and is as ever tied to France and the Flemish lands. Our income is reliant upon our chief export – that of wool. The need for a treaty with the Flemish is pressing, and with it our ability to trade with the continent. Our trade is ebbing due to divers depredations, spoilation and robberies against Flemish mariners and indeed our own ships by John Prendergast and William Longe, two pirates who run the gauntlet of our ships to their own profit."

The king knew this was a trap of sorts, yet deliberately entered the jaws of the plot, knowing it would enable him to gain what he wanted, which was breathing space to seek his own path. He had been forewarned due to the timely arrival of Whittington's missive.

"How do we propose that this should be achieved?"

"Why majesty, we have in place a method whereby we release Sir Edward Courtney, the Earl of Devon and Admiral of the western fleet, and his son upon the pirates."

At this, two figures to the prince's left stood forward and bowed deeply to the king. Watching from the wings, Whittington saw a tight smile etch itself briefly onto Richard Courtney's face where he stood, as ever, by the prince's side. "They shall set sail and scourge the pirates in your name. We are sure master Chamberleyn and Sir Helmet Leget will accede to this order." At which he looked towards the two men who were making notes. They were the Clerk of the King's Ships and the Usher of the King's Chamber, both of whom were jointly responsible for the navy.

As the senior man, Leget offered a small bow. He was loyal to the king, having been in service with him since before his ascension to the throne and had fought with him at Shrewsbury. He had risen high in the ranks of seniority and now occupied a very influential position. "I should be honoured to serve in whatever way may render good service to his majesty," he offered.

He is prepared and forewarned, the prince thought. *Yet 'tis to our advantage*. He continued out loud. "Let it be so recorded," he commanded.

The king continued, outraged at the depredations of the pirates, and all were in accord. Both father and son realised that a difficult and embarrassing moment had passed, though cause and effect were still far from resolved. Guyenne, Calais and the Anglo-Burgundian Treaty were of top priority, for they represented both the physical and fiscal security of the Crown.

"And so it all moves, arsey versey," Stokes commented in hushed tones as an aside when the king had departed. "it would be a great wonder if anything other than finance were resolved over the next three days. Did you mark the quality of intimacy between my Lord Courtney and the prince? There is influence there – and not, I am persuaded, all to the good."

"Verily so." Whittington replied, "Courtney favours his cousin and keeps his Grace of Arundel busy away from any investigation into Oxford University. The Beauforts benefit too: Henry, for he finds Arundel disadvantaged and cannot fight on all fronts, leaving him clear to thwart the Duke of Clarence's suit upon his former sister-in-law and her estates. And as for Thomas, he too would reconcile such a cause. Perforce his ambition goes deeper, for he likes not the role of Chancellor in all but name and would rather be at war on sea or land, gaining glory and more funds I perceive. And so the wheel turns, whilst abroad forces muster to influence us further and uprisings in the north make the realm unstable, all to the cause of unseating a king."

"You have the right of it, Sir Richard. Too many pieces are moving on the board to untangle all the plots and plans or truly foresee the moves. I should be interested to see what mischief is cast abroad upon the ships of the Earl of Devon ere he set sail, especial in the cause of his son Hugh, a pirate in all but name."

"To that cause I am able to offer assistance of a most intimate kind," Whittington pronounced enigmatically.

Chapter Eleven

Bodmin

Mark set off for Cornwall after bidding a fond farewell to Emma, promising to return as soon as he was able. His journey was hampered by the freezing weather, and snow had fallen thickly across Bodmin Moor driven by an intense north easterly wind that found holes in every crack and seam of his clothing. He had purchased a thick lined cloak for the journey from one of the shops recommended by Thomas, and though it proved to be of excellent quality he was still chilled as he left the moor.

He twisted his shoulders back, pushing his bow bag into a more comfortable position. John had given him the idea of using a war bow bag to carry his great quarterstaff on horseback, where it would be protected from the weather and so much easier to carry raised, as mounted archers did with their weapons. Slung diagonally across his shoulder, he found the arrangement worked well and did not hamper him at all when riding.

Leaving the moor and entering Bodmin, he was driven forward by the wind and blinded by the swirling snow. He paused briefly, seeing the outline of the houses of his home town. Little seemed to have changed; perhaps a few more of the outlying cottages appeared to be lived in again after the ravages of the Black Death that had taken half the community in its terrible path. Smoke rose from the cottages and the slightly larger homes of merchants. A few passers-by looked up at him in suspicion, not recognizing the giant on horseback who was better dressed than the local villeins or townsfolk. With his fur-lined hood pulled forward no one would recognise him, he hoped, especially in the blizzard. He urged his tired horse forward through the main street of the town, passing the grand St Petroc's church and the lesser Chapel of the Holy Rood. Leaving Bodmin behind he pressed on, using roads that were once familiar to him, making the familiar journey to his parents' farm through the white and silent fields.

Coming to a ridge that looked out across a gently sloping valley he stopped, for below him were an assortment of buildings with dark tracks showing between them. The largest building had been constructed at right angles to the hill in the Cornish manner, a platform house that jutted out from the hill, safe from heavy rainfall. The natural fall of the land offered a perfect manger below for animals, while the other end of the ground floor was connected to the hillside by a small wooden bridge that crossed a narrow ditch that drained the hillside, stopping water running inwards. He noticed a new addition: a smaller cottage that ran parallel to the larger building. *That'll be Tom's new home*, he thought. He had heard that his younger brother had married a local girl. They had been sweethearts since youth. He had been sad to miss the wedding, yet could not leave the prince's service to make the long return journey home. *So much changes so quickly*, he mused. Friar Vincent had helped him to write two letters in a very poor hand in the year he had been absent. There would, he knew, be many questions to be answered. The light was starting to fail and the day was drawing to a close as he steered his tired horse towards the farm-house and buildings. Two dogs barked as he approached, yapping in the early evening gloom, straining against their leashes and bouncing on their back legs.

"Easy Lute, Tye," he called gently and at his voice the animals recognised their lost master and wagged their tails, whining. He slid from his horse, landing softly and went to stroke the dogs, who barked ecstatically at his return, for he had always had a way with them. They sniffed him, catching the strange smells. At that moment the door opened from the cottage, exposing a warm light from within.

"Now then, what be all this noise?" a figure growled.

"Father!" Mark called.

"What? by the good Lord, I don't believe it...Mark?" He cried and ran forward to be enveloped by the huge arms of his son. He was a strong man, but Mark's embrace took the wind out of him.

"By the rood you've grown stronger. You're like a bear." He exclaimed. "Come in lad, come in and see the family."

"I needs must tend to my 'oss." Mark replied, slipping back into the deep local accent of his earlier life. Father and son quickly stabled, stripped and fed the horse, and that done they went up to the house, Mark hoisting the large saddle bags he'd removed from the cantle. His father motioned for silence with an upraised finger and opened the door that his mother had shut harshly, berating her man to keep the heat in.

"Now, man," she began as he hove into sight, "what 'ee be doin' leavin' no wood in the 'ole?" she chastised him. "I told 'ee...Mark!" She broke off, seeing the hulking form of her son framed in the doorway and ran forward to embrace him.

"Now Mam, don't 'ee take on so. You'll smother me." he adjured her. His two sisters rushed forward to welcome him, along with Tom and his new bride. Mark looked around and smelled the familiar smells of earth, damp clothes drying and a savoury aroma coming from a pot that was supported by iron bars over the fire hearth.

"Sit down, son, sit down. Fetch some mead father, the lad will be chilled to the bone. Supper is cooking and'll be ready soon enough. Are you back for good? Tell us all." The questions battered him with no respite. Mark smiled at the warmth of his family; in truth he had missed them all, despite making good friends in London. When he was finally able to draw breath, his brother Tom started again.

"Now tell us, what is Lunnon like? And France? And you said you met the Welsh prince Glyndower?"

His mother called a temporary halt, telling them all that supper was ready. The meal was a hot, thick pottage of bacon, leeks and herbs with bread slices set on wooden trenchers. Mark set to with gusto, answering Tom's questions between mouthfuls. No sooner had he finished than he asked for more, so hungry was he. His mother ladled out another portion.

"I'd forgotten that you eat for two normal men," she laughed. "Now tell us, are you back for good?"

"No Mam, I'm afeared not. I'm on a mission of sorts for the prince in part and Sir Richard Whittington."

The family looked at each other in amazement.

"A mission for the prince?" asked his father in a tone of gravity. "Sir Richard Whittington? Be 'ee the same as was Mayor of Lunnon?" he asked in awe at the company his son was keeping.

"Aye, he were, and he's a good and noble lord who is my benefactor in many ways, along with Jamie and Cristo."

"Benefactor is it? Why lad, thou'll be far too grand for us soon." He chided. "And Cristo? 'Tis a strange name if ever oi heard one."

"He is Italian, from a place called...*Firrenzi*...that's 'ow he says it. We call it Florence. It's in the middle of Italy and one day I shall go there and visit with him."

"By the good Lord you've grown. Not just in stature, you've grown wings and flown," his father proclaimed.

"They'd 'ave be the wings of a dozen eagles to lift one such as you off'n the ground," Tom said, earning himself a playful cuff from his mother and a roar of laughter from his father.

"Now tell us all about what you must do for Sir Richard," Mark's father said, his eyes sparkling with pride.

For five days Mark stayed at his parents' farmhouse, relaxing more than he'd been able to do in a year at court, seeping into the old rhythm of the farm, waking with the dawn, tending stock and keeping the country hours of his home.

Once rested, he and Tom set off for Plymouth, where it was agreed that Tom would leave him on the outskirts of the town and return with both horses. Mark wished to appear more impoverished than he was, in need of work and without a home or a horse of his own. They parted company five miles from the town

"Now 'ee mind my mare Tom, for she's a good sort and well mannered," Mark told his brother. "I'll be back within a month to ride 'er again."

"Never mind your 'oss, 'tis you oi worry about. Take care Mark, for you go where I should be afeared to tread and no mistake."

"Don't 'ee worry, yet if naught is heard of me send word with Friar Vincent to fetch Jamie and Cristo, for with them at my back we'd face an army and no mistake."

They clasped arms, with a backward glance and a wave, Mark walked off along the road in the direction of Plymouth.

Chapter Twelve

Laurence Lane, London

"Master Thomas, I know that you travel soon, and I would render you service in any way that you ask and not shirk my devoir. Yet I prithee, may it please you, but I have a boon to ask."

"Why Cristoforo, 'tis unlike you to be so perfervid. Set to, man, set to, for the worst I can do is refuse you," Thomas joked, yet he sensed there was more coming than a common favour.

"It concerns Jamie. I have a feeling that all is not well, and I beg your leave to travel north to seek him out."

"Are you sure you do not have second sight? If you were a woman I should have thee burned, feckless Italian!" Thomas continued to ruffle Cristoforo's feathers, enjoying his unease. "For I was about to voyage abroad and cross the Channel. Knowing your aversion to the sea, I swear you foresaw my intent." He joked. "Why do you say this of Jamie? Have you had word?"

"*No lo so.*" He shrugged "I have the feeling like I have when

I am watched and followed, yet I see no one. This feeling, she is strong." Cristoforo finished, lapsing into silence.

"Very well. I've learned to trust you and your intuition. Travel with me north, for I venture first to Leicester then on to Lynn to journey across to Flanders. John will accompany me on the trip, with Will and others. I shall be well enough protected. I release you to seek out Jamie, and God be with you, for an Italian in Nottingham will not be well looked upon as a foreigner."

Nottingham

In the weeks since his initiation into the ranks of Stanhope's band, Jamie had proved himself on raids, directing war bands to weaken the local gentry into submission or fear. He had created havoc, seeking perfect opportunities to pillage in the manner of the Scots he had fought so effectively on the Borders.

Yet in all this, he had fought little directly, keeping as far away from the fray as best he could in his role as captain. On the odd occasion he was forced to fight he had bested his man easily, leaving him wounded in the melee. This was to change.

"Jamie, you fare well, Jack has told me," Stanhope addressed Jamie in his fortified country manor to the north of Nottingham. "The other lords abroad are in disarray thanks to your campaigns of harassment. Now with Spring upon us I seek new grounds to combine our campaign."

"As you wish, Sir Richard." Jamie nodded. "Where do we raid next?"

"We have been striking manors to the East, and we have secured new lands adding to my demesne and those of the other lords you serve. Those to the north of the county are ripe to sequestrate and we shall raid Alexander Meryng. We are building strong holdings here that will be held in the new reign, and you and Jack," he nodded to the other man at Jamie's side, "will be rewarded right well when the time is ripe."

Jamie feigned a deliberate ignorance with a frown. "My lord?"

"The crown lies balanced between father and son. A new king will be crowned soon and we shall prevail under the new ruler for we shall be an asset to him in the north and offer fealty with the strength of our income and support. For certes I'm not disloyal to the crown; the issue lies with the head upon which it rests. God knows I've served the king well, yet now a new era is to begin and we will make war in France again with glory, and land and riches shall be the reward. It would be a sapient man to choose the right side."

"Amen to that my lord. I am just a sely soldier, seeking naught but reward as my sword arm serves. Therefore, to where do we cast forth?"

"To the north, as I say, and the lands of another who has been growing stronger and would resist our cause. Alexander Meryng has banded with Sir John Zouche and forms a strong alliance to the northeast of Nottingham. Dost thou know them?"

Not by a line on his face did Jamie acknowledge his cognisance of the Meryngs. He merely shrugged as though it were another raid in his feudatory duties to Sir Richard: "No my lord, but I am at your command. Let us know how and where this is to be accomplished and we shall be ready."

"That accords well. I have in mind to raid them three days hence on Saturday, when I believe that my lord Meryng will be absent from his manor as he travels for London."

"My lord, with your permission. If Meryng is the weakest, should we not provide a diversion with a feint upon Sir John Zouche and yet strike hard upon the Meryng estate?"

"By the rood, I like your stratagem. So it shall be. Choose the men well and I will visit the inn beforehand. Have everything prepared for two raids. Now you must leave, for the time draws towards vespers and I have parties arriving on the hour."

Both men bowed and left the hall, passing through the shallow vestibule and out into the enceinte.

"I chose well with you, lad," Jack clapped Jamie on the shoulder. "And together we shall see some profit, I'm bound."

They strode towards the stables, and as they did so a party entered the main gates. It was clearly led by men of rank, evidenced even in the fading light by the quality of their clothes and horseflesh. The meiny that followed was well dressed in clothes of their class. The leading lords of the party wore cloaks and cowls trimmed with ermine fur, indicating that they were above the restrictions of dress code imposed by the Sumptuary laws. Those knights with them were again attired with very little restriction; gold and silver showed beneath their cloaks.

Jamie and Jack arrived at the stables before they were run down by the approaching party, and what Jamie saw shocked him to the core. Until that moment he had been unable to distinguish the livery of the arriving lords but now, as he hid behind Richard's neck, he saw it – the Earl of Arundel and Warwick, amongst others. The hoods dropped, showing faces familiar to him. *Christ on the cross, what have we here?* He thought. It became more intriguing as a new party arrived of just three men attended by no meiny. They had ridden hard, it appeared. Their cloaks were thrown back and upon their jupons was embroidered a coat of arms: the cross quartered shield in each opposite diagonal quarter showed three lions *passant* on argent and three *fleur de lys or* on azure – the House of Beaufort!

They were neither Thomas nor Henry Beaufort, Jamie saw, but esquires, emissaries who had come in their stead. He recognised one with whom he had trained at court and quickly pulled Richard away before he was recognised, for his horse was infamous, especially amongst the squires with whom he had trained. Luckily the light was poor as dusk settled and he moved into the shadows blending into the grey darkness. He was glad that he had left Forest behind on this occasion for she would have been a liability. He mounted quickly and coarsened his accent with a Scottish lilt, calling: "Come Jack, lets away afore we're overrun."

Turning Richard and keeping his hood up, they trotted off through the open gates. Jack followed quickly, unsure as to why Jamie was in such a hurry. They barely avoided a messenger cantering to the manor house on a tired horse. The messenger shot the two men a hard look as he closed with them and pushed on past without a word.

"'Tis passing strange, for I know that man. He is one of the Sir Richard's meiny for certes," Jack commented. Jamie said nothing, but brought Richard to an abrupt halt, causing the horse to rear its head.

"What ails you, man?" Jack asked.

"By the rood I'm a scullion," Jamie replied in mock distress. "I've left my gauntlets back at the stable. Ride on, Jack, I'll catch you soon enough for Richard wants to run and with the thaw he'll be safe enough."

"I'll daddle along 'til 'ee arrives, then. You'd shent an addle-brained fool with your memory," he chided, mocking Jamie.

Jamie returned to the gates, dismounting and leaving Richard outside the walls. He knew the horse would not stray and wanted no chance of him being recognised. He warned the guard against closing with the horse and went inside. He strode quickly to the main doors saying that he had left his gauntlets within and the guard, who knew him, readily gave him access. Once inside he silently climbed the spiral of stone steps that gave access to one of the towers and he hoped, the minstrel gallery above the Great Hall. Reaching the first level, he opened a small wooden door that gave off to the gallery. He dared not peer above the wainscotting to see below but made do with listening. The acoustics were not as beneficial, yet he heard much of what was said.

"What news from court, my lord?" Stanhope asked.

"The king ails," one answered. "His grasp on affairs grows weaker. More so, for his profligacy displays him not in good graces with the court or the council that have the ruling on all matters. The council is ruled by the prince and with it the crown in all but name. We grow stronger as the king grows weaker, and we seek to adjure the prince to persuade his father to relinquish the crown. It cannot be long afore too much goes awry. The Flemish Treaty flounders and the Burgundians need support against the Armagnacs who are destroying our trade and our wealth. Our land is at risk and we need a strong governance. The prince knows this, and God willing will move against his father soon to sue for the crown."

Jamie had heard enough, and dare not stay longer for fear of discovery. He had sufficient to sue for an affidavit indicting all below for treason to the crown. Any longer and his return to Jack would seem suspicious to him and to the guards below. He crept out of the gallery and slipped quietly down the steps below, remembering to retrieve the gauntlets from his doublet, waving them at the guard and shaking his head in self-deprecation. He strode out of the main gate to his waiting horse. He mounted quickly and rode off into the evening, his mind in turmoil.

Chapter Thirteen

Jamie arrived back at his room above the Running Horse, but it was not long before he descended to the tap room for food and a chance to think. Forest was restless, sulking because Jamie had left her behind, and with this in mind he made a decision. He would leave tonight and alert the Meryngs of the intended raid and warn them to be alert. He would find a suitable time to leave during the chaos of the raid. The melee would offer him plenty of opportunity to disappear before his absence was noticed. The chance would present itself, of that he was sure.

His time in the taproom and his meal gave Richard time to eat and rest, and an hour or so later he set out with Forest by his side for the hidden postern gate that he had now used with Jack on many occasions. Richard had become used to pushing through it, yet he still protested at the indignity.

"Easy boy, easy." Jamie calmed the horse before remounting and setting off into the night. The snow had ceased to fall, revealing a bright moonlit night, radiant with stars across the sky and casting a sheen upon the white landscape, as dark trees loomed upwards, etching their spectral fingers against the canvas of the night sky. The winter had been long and hard. Jamie remembered the snow that had fallen earlier in the year when he had rescued Alice and her father from the ambush. The cold had not let up since then, and although it was now March the snow still held the landscape in its icy grip. It was but three quarters of an hour's ride to the Meryngs' manor house, and in the clear moonlight he easily retraced his journey of a few weeks before as his thoughts turned to Alice and wondered how her father fared. He hoped that the earl had been well enough to travel and that they had moved on from the manor to their own estates further north and away from the danger that this area represented.

The manor house was set at the end of a private track off the main highway, and when he arrived all was barred shut for the night and a solitary torch burned above the gate. There was no sign of any guard or gatekeeper and Jamie knew that he would be treated with suspicion for arriving at this hour. He led Richard to the door and hammered upon it with his fist, the sound echoing through the stillness of the night. He heard no sound and hammered again, and this time a door scraped and banged shut within the gatehouse of the surrounding curtain wall. Boots sounded against stone as someone ascended the steps within, and a wary face appeared on a platform above the gatehouse, shrouded in a heavy cloak.

"Who goes there? Show yourself!" a hoarse voice commanded.

"'Tis Sir James de Grispere, friend to my lord the Earl of Macclesfield and his daughter Alice. I attended with their party some weeks past. I have urgent business with your master Alexander Meryng and his son Sir William. Open the gate man," he ordered imperiously, "I have no time to tarry and must return forthwith ere I'm missed."

The guard was not to be bullied and ordered him to await

without whilst he attended his master. Jamie fumed, knowing that time spent away could be his downfall if he was discovered out of his lodgings and without the town. Muttering to himself, he finally heard the bar being withdrawn on the inside and the large double doors opened showing two men-at-arms eyeing him suspiciously in the torchlight.

"Let me pass, man," he ordered again and rode past the two guards, who could perhaps have been forgiven for thinking that anyone this arrogant had to be there as of right. Forest trotted by his side into a small courtyard. He unhooked his cloak, draped it over Richard's back, warned the guards not to approach his horse and then man and dog strode into the open doorway of the manor house. Entering the great hall, he saw both Alexander and Sir William, who appeared to have been woken from their beds. The family likeness was evident between them, more lines and grey hair on the father whilst the son showed Jamie how the older man must have looked in his youth.

"Master Meryng, Sir William, I bid you good evening and crave your pardon for calling unannounced and so late. 'Tis I, Sir James de Grispere, late of the Earl's company you may recall."

"Aye, we do," the older man replied. "What brings you to my manor so late at night that it be so urgent to raise us from our beds?"

"Messires, I apologise for the late hour but not my errand. For I bring you warning of a raid to be led against your lands forthwith. I believe you travel for London these two days hence."

"I do, yet how could you have cognisance of this?" Sir William asked askance.

"Someone within your household betrays you, and passes your confidences abroad for others to benefit. I say once more, a raid is planned by Sir Richard Stanhope with a feint upon Sir John Zouche to weaken your cause and then raid your manor. You must be prepared and warn Sir John."

Father and son looked to each other aghast.

"How can you know of this if you are not one of them?" Sir William asked suspiciously.

"In truth I have infiltrated their ranks with subterfuge and guile, the better to betray them. You must trust me on this, for I have a fiat directly from the court to bring about their downfall. On the day of the raid you will see me in their ranks bearing the shield of Sir Robert de Umfraville, an argent shield with blue cross and cantered cinquefoil. Prithee, ask your archers to have regard and spare me, for I support your cause."

"Thank you for these timely tidings, Sir James."

"I serve the crown and Sir Richard Whittington, and seek to despoil any treason within this realm," Jamie replied. "But tell me, how fares the Earl of Macclesfield and his meiny?"

"He recovered well, and departed ten days since for his northern estate, along with his daughter and remaining servants. They became restive, waiting for a spring that appears not to be coming," Sir William replied.

Jamie breathed a sigh of relief. "Now I must away, for every moment here causes me more chance of being undone. I bid you good night, and to beware on the Saturday hence, for chance will bring a raid to your doors." With this he bowed and swept back, Forest at his heels.

"Wait, Sir James, what form will this raid take? We know so little." Alexander called after him.

"As do I, yet forewarned is forearmed. I cannot tarry thus." He left in a flurry of activity, brushing through the manor door, striding to Richard and retrieving his cloak. He mounted in a swift movement, beckoning the doors to be opened for his withdrawal, and man and animals disappeared into the night,

Forest barking in excitement at the unexpected nocturnal activity.

Jamie found his way back with ease, and slid through the postern gate and then through the centre of the town, avoiding the Watch and finally finding his rest at the Running Horse. He had a strange feeling of being followed within the walls, but could detect no one, yet he was on his guard – his sixth sense never failed him. However, he did not see the shadow that slipped by the tavern's doorway as he passed to the stables to settle Richard for the night.

The dawn revealed a crisp crust on a white frozen world as the temperature dropped still more. In Sir Richard Stanhope's manor, the messenger who had returned the previous evening bided his time. His master had a foul temper in the mornings and he wished not to suffer his ill humours. Finally Stanhope appeared, looking creased and scowling with a sour visage. The night had been a celebration of sorts, and the lords had stayed the night as guests after consuming a large quantity of wine as plans were laid.

Seeing the messenger and his Steward waiting for him he growled: "Well?"

"My lord, I bring news from the Borders," the messenger answered, keeping his distance from the foul tempered lord as he drained a pitcher of bitterly cold water in an attempt to stop his head from pounding. "I have made inquiries as you requested upon the identity of Jamie of Alnwick."

Stanhope exploded. "Well dolt, tell me! Christ on the Cross, my head pounds, my blood courses and I have little patience."

"Continue, Ralf." The Steward urged him.

"My lord, no one knows of such a man-at-arms that has

recently left the retinue of my Lord de Umfraville." Stanhope raised an eyebrow. "I gave a description, a goodly one, and I was told that there was a man who favours his bearing but who left Sir Robert one year previously." Stanhope jerked his head upwards at the words and instantly regretted it as the pounding returned and the room span. "This man was an esquire in training, by name James de Grispere, oft called Jamie. He left for London and parted on good terms with my Lord de Umfraville. So much so that he presented him with a destrier for saving his life. The stallion was called Richard, and is a bright chestnut."

"What?" Stanhope roared, "And you waited 'til now to tell me? Scullion, dost though have turnip for a brain? Begone now, I needs must think." Sir Richard slumped to a chair his mind reeling. *By the rood I knew it, he was too confident and well trained.* Stanhope wondered what de Grispere was doing here in Nottingham, and who had sent him. *Could they know of our plans?* he thought. He decided to question his allies, knowing that if de Grispere had served the king's court they would know him as knight or esquire now that he had his name.

His head pounding, Stanhope paced the hall, his mind awhirl as he awaited the awakening and arrival of those who had been present the previous evening. When the company was finally assembled in the same numbers as before, he imparted the news received from his messenger and spy. The esquire with whom Jamie had trained spoke forth.

"This man-at-arms, my lord, you say he rides a chestnut stallion, large and handsome, with whom he is asotted?

"Aye, do you know of him?" Stanhope demanded.

"Mayhap. Stands he uncommonly tall," here he motioned with his hand, "with red gold hair, sure of himself and a connexion with de Umfraville?"

"That he does. Tell me his name and rank for I believe he is false." Stanhope demanded.

The esquire snorted. "My lord, I would adjure you to give him a wide berth for he is a swordsman of renown. His name is Sir James de Grispere, and he was knighted by the prince himself for deeds of valour – to wit the breaking of Glyndower after beating his champion, Black Rhys."

Two of the others cursed, for they now knew who the mysterious soldier was.

"Edward is right, the man is lethal with a blade and rumours swirl about him," Arundel commented. "'Tis said he thwarted the proposed siege of Calais ere it started. He is well connected at court and flies well in the prince's favour."

Stanhope had heard of the raid at Stokesey castle that had been routed after Glyndower was ambushed. Meanwhile the fire at Saint Omer had become the stuff of legend, with none knowing the cause and how it came about that a cathedral should set afire from within, destroying a huge siege engine bound for the re-conquest of Calais by the French. He cursed savagely, at which the earl of Warwick counselled him: "My lord, think on. What harm can he do? I'faith he has seen us not, nor does he know of our plans. We visit here in a sely cause, and do not aid you in your ventures – for God's truth you do not need us. Everything is rumour, and within the course when the prince shall come to power all will be forgiven. This de Grispere is but one man, who will gain little but witness raids." The earl shrugged. "I say let him be, until such time as he stops an arrow or fails to turn a blade in a melee. It has happened, and will do so again."

Stanhope made to tell them that he had imparted something of their plans to Jamie, yet halted himself in time. Warwick made sense, there would be a time for retribution and naught would go awry until the opportunity arose to settle the account with Jamie. "As you say my lord, all is well. Yet I wonder who can have instructed him to venture here and to what end?"

"There are many forces at work in the court and all is aswirl with fog and rumour. I shall seek the truth of this upon my return, it will out for certes," asserted Richard de Beauchamp, the earl of Warwick. He too had fought in the wars with Glyndower and at Shrewsbury, yet was aware that England needed a new and stronger king, and thus supported the prince.

Chapter Fourteen

Jamie awoke that morning in the tavern none the worse for his adventures of the previous evening. No one had challenged him and he found all was well when he returned to his lodgings at the Running Horse. He bespoke a breakfast of local bacon and was then met by Jack in the alehouse.

"Come, we must talk," Jack said. "Let us walk the town." With that he went outside into the cold and frosty air, where his breath billowed in front of him as he spoke. "This Saturday is the time for our raid on Meryng's manor. We will strike at midnight, set fire to what we can, steal what cattle we find and burn his hayricks. We will bring him to his knees as we have the others."

"Aye, 'tis a time-worn method, and no man can stand with no stock and an empty belly. How far be it to the manor, and what is it like? Fortified or no?" Jamie asked.

Jack smiled at the thoroughness of the man he had come to know well over the past weeks of planning and raiding. They walked in a wide circle through the streets of Nottingham and came upon a friar pleading for alms.

Jamie was puzzled. "'Tis passing strange, for look, he is garbed in brown, not grey," he said, commenting upon the friar's habit, which was circled with a string of rosary beads and a belt of corded rope. The hood was pulled forward, covering his head and shadowing his face that was bent forward in contrition and humility.

"Aye, he'll be of the Order of Assisi, from Italy," Jack replied. "They are mendicants, travelling to and fro, and they meet with the Grey Friars here," he pointed to the huge friary newly finished on Broadmarsh.

"Ah, I once had a comrade in arms from Italy. I shall give freely in his memory." With that Jamie fetched a coin from the purse at his belt and dropped it into the wooden cup.

"*Prego, signor, grazie mille.*" Came the heavily accented response from the cowled figure. Forest, normally diffident at best towards strangers, sidled up to the friar, whining. The man patted her with his free hand, stroking the coarse grey fur over her ears.

"Why 'tis odd, she normally eats strangers, not befriends them. Forest, come." Jamie called.

Jack smiled: "No, 'tis but natural, for Saint Francis was the patron saint of animals."

Jamie laughed and Forest loped obediently to Jamie's side and the friar moved on, praying as he went.

That evening both men went to the Wheatsheaf to meet with the other men-at-arms who were to lead various sections of the raid. The tavern was noisy and covered their conversation, which was carried out in hushed terms although all in the taproom were sympathetic to their cause and strangers were not easily tolerated.

"You, Alf," Jack instructed Jamie's one-time opponent, "will lead ten men on a raid against Sir John. Do not press it home. Fire his barns, make a noise and then leave, no more. He is well provisioned with men-at-arms and they will put up a fight. Your attack will be a feint, so pull back quickly ere you are chased and they attack from his manor house."

The others nodded in agreement, and as they did so Alf turned slightly, catching Jamie's eye, a knowing sneer on his face. Jamie shrugged, yet Alf's expression worried him. Why would he now have the confidence to display such an open sign of dislike when Jamie was one of the trusted captains? Time to be off, he thought. He would slip away in the middle of the raid. At that point the door to the tavern opened, admitting a cold draft of air and disturbing his concentration as he and many others glanced to see who the newcomer was. It was the friar from Assisi. He rubbed his hands together as he entered the warm tavern, making for the bar taps, the cowled hood still forward, making it impossible to see his face clearly. With his back to the company he asked for hot spiced wine at the bar, yet was not understood.

"Vino. *Vino Caldo.* Wine hot, please?" he said in a heavy accent.

Beth caught on. "You sit down over there, father, by the hearth," she motioned "I'll bring you a beaker of hot wine to warm your body as well as your soul."

The friar muttered his thanks in his foreign tongue and shuffled over to the fireplace and the smoky fire. A single seat was vacant, and even the rough crowd made room for a man of God.

"Do we need worry about him?" Alf asked, jerking his thumb at the friar.

"No, mon. Why he barely speaks a word of English. Do you think a mere monk will spoil our plans single-handed?" Jack scoffed. The others laughed at Alf, who offered another surly expression and buried his face in his beer mug.

More matters were discussed, the company broke up and

Jamie got up to leave, casting one more glance at the friar before leaving the inn with Forest at his side.

— ✕ ✤ ✕ —

The next day was Saturday, and as was their custom they met at the inn in the early evening then left to assemble at a set of ruined barns a few miles beyond the town. Most of the thatch was still in place on one, and here they joined before a smoky blaze that sent tongues of fire upwards to exit through a hole in the roof. Many of the men lived outside the town, either working the land or employed directly by Sir Richard and others as their villeins or men-at-arms. In all some twenty-five men were assembled and it was a rough, harsh company dressed for war. Most had mail shirts or hauberks, some leather breast plates and many wore helmets of various vintages. The horses stamped in an adjacent barn in an effort to keep warm. They heard a distant church bell chime the eleventh hour of the night, at which Jack called them to leave.

"'Tis the hour to depart. Mount up, and let us go forth to cause mischief this night. Alf, Jamie, come hither." The two men turned, Jamie a little puzzled. "Jamie, I want you to attend Alf and his company. Don't take this wrong, Alf. You're a good man but 'ee do get carried away and I want a short raid and nothing more. They will be too many and strong, so come away quickly and heed Jamie's command. Understood?" Jack urged.

"Aye Jack, be not afeared, I know my duty." Alf replied. Jamie shrugged and agreed with a nod, the back of his neck tingling as it had on the Borders when all was not well.

The men all mounted and then divided into their respective groups, riding off in two different directions, with Jamie and Alf at the van of the group that was to attack Sir John Zouche's estates.

They rode over unfamiliar territory for around half an hour, heading northwest. Cresting a small hill, they saw below the distant outline of a deeper black against a canvas of dark grey, indicating the walls of the manor. All seemed quiet and still. Brands burned at the side of the gatehouse, yet nothing else stirred.

Alf, who had assumed command for now, spoke in a hoarse whisper: "We go slow, down the 'ill, then light our brands and throw them at the ricks. You two," he nodded at men who had dismounted and were nocking their warbows, "Make for the gates, get within range and shoot fire arrows over the walls."

"Remember," Jamie added, "a single run. We hit hard, harry them and run back. No staying to fight or we'll be surrounded and killed as soon as they get organised. We use this ridge as our rallying point and meet back here after. You two archers keep a wary eye once you've shot your fire arrows. Look to our backs and cover our retreat."

The two men nodded in agreement, pulling the yard-long shafts from their arrow bags carefully so as not to damage the fletchings. The main party separated, leaving the archers behind, and at the last moment they moved into a canter over the remaining few yards. The firebrands – lit at the last moment to prevent them from being spotted from within the manor – whooshed through the air as they were thrown, and still no hue and cry came from within the manor. Jamie had taken his shield from his back, and with his arm through the straps he stayed back to repel any foray from the manor while Alf, the lust of battle upon him, whooped and cried in excitement as they fired the ricks, moving on to the outlying buildings.

Yet as soon as the fire arrows flashed through the sky and flames cast eerie shadows across the land, figures appeared upon the walls hunched over crossbows, and quarrels hissed into the night air, carrying death towards the company.

"Retreat now, retreat," Jamie called, and with visibility poor in the light of the flames, his voice marked his position. Just in time he raised his shield bearing the crest of de Umfraville as a crossbow bolt thudded against it, the head protruding on Jamie's side of the shield as the force of the strike bent Jamie's arm inwards. A flurry of arrows flew upwards from the raiding party as the archers returned the fire that was coming from the manor walls.

The gates, which had been pulled partly open, had caught fire, flames licking hungrily at the seasoned wood. One mounted soldier on a brave horse managed to jump the fire, and he ran forth shouting his battle cry. Jamie span Richard around on a hind leg to face the oncoming threat, all thoughts of restraint banished as the urge for battle seized him. He knew that he must protect the retreat before it became a rout.

In the half-light he saw that the mounted soldier had a spear raised, carried underhand ready for a throw or to drive forward and down, using the advantage of height and distance. As always when in battle, actions and time seemed to slow to a crawl, such was Jamie's focus and awareness as muscles trained from youth in the pageant of war took over unbidden. He moved his shield below Richard's neck to the left, hidden from sight, and allowed his sword arm to drop by his right leg, then released Richard straight into a fast canter to meet the oncoming threat.

Jamie watched intently for any backward motion indicating that the man would throw the spear, but none came. Richard accelerated unbidden, relishing the fight as much as his master as the two men raced towards impact, neither giving ground. Then Jamie watched as the oncoming rider raised his arm and stood up in his stirrups, gripping his horse at the knees in a solid lock, ready to drive the spear down into his seemingly hapless opponent.

Waiting until last second, Jamie brought his right leg back behind the girth, nudging Richard slightly to the left at his quarters, pointing his head at the opponent to change the angle of his own strike. He saw the spear arm draw back slightly and brought his shield to bear, deflecting the blow while whipping back his sword arm in a wicked arc that slashed the blade across his opponent from shoulder to hip. He did not wish to use the point as he knew not what armour or maille he faced, nor lose the sword in the strike. The shield drove the point of the spear up and over, exposing the opponent's body. Jamie added a twist of his torso to increase the force of the cut, the full impact taking the opponent's shoulder. From experience he knew it had pierced the maille hauberk as a howling scream came to him in the night air.

Yet he had no wish to finish the man, and wheeling Richard around in a sharp one hundred and eighty degree turn Jamie raced off into the night as his wounded opponent slumped forward in the saddle. The others, he saw as he galloped to the ridge, had already assembled, with two of their number missing.

"Come, let us not tarry. Away now ere we are trapped." He urged, galloping on as the rest of company followed suit. They rode off in the moonlight. Slowing to a canter when they were well clear of the Zouche manor they pulled up their blown mounts, and Alf sidled up beside Jamie.

"They was waiting for us, if I ain't mistook," he snarled.

"I know not. They recovered quickly and launched a counter attack with crossbows." Jamie raised his shield to show the wicked bolt that was still protruding from it. Alf snorted in disgust.

"We lost two good men to them bolts. 'Ow'd they know, eh? I reckon someone told 'em, that's how."

Jamie turned to face him, his lip curling: "What is it that you say, man? Out with it. If it concerns me, say so and I'll make it three men lost tonight. For by the rood I'll kill you with no compunction this time, like I should have done last, mayhap." Jamie pulled his sword free, half drawn. Alf sneered under hooded eyes and pulled back from the threat. With men behind him, Jamie knew he had no chance of slipping away in the darkness unnoticed. Within half an hour they were in front of the postern gate at Nottingham, forming a single file to enter. As Jamie slid from Richard's back he heard a vague whisper of air and then there was nothing but blackness as the club smashed into his helmet. He collapsed to the floor, stunned despite the protection of the steel and coif. A second blow landed between his shoulders and he lay concussed. Richard shied and sidled, preparing to protect his fallen master, but his bridle was seized and he could not fight the curb as a staff forced his teeth to a safe distance.

"Tie him and drag 'im in. Sling 'im over his horse and we'll take 'im to the Wheatsheaf. Sir Richard warned Jack and me all might not be well and what to do if'n it weren't." The men obliged curious at the strange turn of events, yet unwilling to go against Sir Richard Stanhope's direct orders.

Minutes later after manhandling an unwilling Richard through the streets to the inn, cursing at the horse's attempts to bite them, they lifted Jamie from his horse's back and dumped him unceremoniously on the floor in a corner of the inn, where he slumped, half conscious. No customers remained save the friar, who was curled up asleep by the fire and remained undisturbed by the commotion. The landlord appeared with Beth, both rumpled and with sleep-drugged eyes.

"What happened to Jamie?" Beth cried in concern.

"Ain't no need to worry yourself none at him," Alf snapped. "He's a traitor. Sir Richard knew it and bade us take care. Good job we did for he led us wrong and no mistake."

"What? You jest, for Jamie is a good man and has led you well in the past," she protested.

"Hush, girl," her father admonished. "'Tis naught of our affair and Sir Richard's word is law. Now, back to bed with you," He ordered her. She cast one more look at the Jamie's semi-conscious form and left the taproom. What's 'e doin' here?" Alf asked pointing, at the figure of the friar curled up by the fire.

"Oh, he ain't doing no harm," the innkeeper replied. "He was shut out of the friary from what I can tell, for he speaks little English, and returned just afore closing time. So I let him sleep ere the night and he'll chop wood in the morning for me as payment."

"We'll get this one in the store behind and await Sir Richard in the morning then his fate will be decided. I 'ope he's for the sword. He's a wrong' un, an' I'll enjoy killing him, so I will," Alf said. The landlord shrugged, used to the rough ways and lawlessness of the land. With two of the other raiders, they carried Jamie to a store and barred him within.

"Is that red beast of his secured?" Alf asked of one of his party, a man named Joe who was limping badly.

"Aye, we've locked the bastard in a stall, let him cool off. He kicked me and I was lucky, Blackie has a broken leg from him. Wanted to take his sword to him but I said no as you'd want 'im for yourself."

"I do. 'E's a grand horse and I'll tame him no mistake," Alf said. "Stay with me the night to guard *master* Jamie." He mocked, "You others go home and we'll meet in the morning."

He and Joe stayed behind, getting a beaker of ale from the landlord before he retired. They made for the fire and the sleeping form of the friar, who snored gently, stretched on a settle wrapped in his voluminous cowl. The landlord retired and left them alone with their prisoner.

After an hour, as the fire died down to glowing embers, the recumbent figure of the friar gently stirred, listening to the sounds in the room. Satisfied and with a seemingly effortless movement that belied his earlier demeanour, he sat upright on the settle in perfect balance, pushing back his cowl to better hear any movement. The exposed head showed curly dark hair, an olive complexion and slate grey eyes. The nose was long and aquiline.

His movements were careful and silent as he straightened his legs and began to move gently and quietly around the pair of sleeping guards, all his senses alert for any movement. On the balls of his feet, he made his way delicately towards the store room door. It was a simple wooden latch to ensure that the door remained closed, with a wooden peg that prevented the bar moving upwards, making it impossible to move from the inside. He glanced back again at Alf and Joe. Satisfied, he gently pulled the peg outwards. It was a simple dowel and withdrew easily from the hole, worn from long use. The friar eased the locking bar upwards from its slot and then realised the danger. The door swung outwards. If Jamie had recovered within and was waiting to surprise his captors, he would strike hard and fast before he realised his rescuer was friend, not foe, yet he dared not speak to warn him in case it woke the guards.

The decision was made for him. The stairs creaked as someone made their way down appearing at the dog-leg. It was Beth, carrying a bowl of steaming water and some towels over her arm. She gasped when she saw the friar opening the store-room door, and the two consecutive sounds woke Alf, who spluttered back to full consciousness quickly followed by Joe.

"What? By the rood, a viper in our nest. Friar or no, I'll stop 'ee!" Alf cried rising and rushing at the figure in front of the store room, dagger in hand. It was a mistake for he knew not the quality of the man he faced. The friar stepped to the left

121

away from the doorway and brought up his right leg, clearing the cumbersome habit as his hand met the top of the boot. As the friar stepped forward, his arm whipped up as he threw the dagger underhand straight into the unsuspecting Alf's throat. Alf stopped as though he had run into an oak door, gasping and dropping to the floor, his opened throat spurting blood in fountains across the inn's floor. Joe was already advancing, with his sword drawn looking down at his fallen comrade with incredulity, yet remaining poised. Alf had been a tavern brawler, a tough man but ill-trained. Joe had learned with a sword, as evidenced by his manner. Seeing the dagger protruding from his dead friend's neck, he grabbed a stool to use in the manner of a buckler and advanced on the friar.

"Come then father, lets send thee to meet thy maker," he grunted. The friar was not perturbed as he reached up over his shoulder, but he suddenly needed to cover his back as he heard the storeroom door move behind him.

"Jamie, have a care, *sono io...*" he cried, and then Joe rushed him. A falchion appeared in the friar's right hand and another dagger in his left. Joe came within range and jabbed with the stool, raising the sword above his shoulder to slash downwards. The friar stepped to the left on the outside gate of the sword, hindering further use of the stool as he met the downward slash of the blade with a crossed sword and dagger, thrusting upwards to meet energy with energy. Joe could not believe that his sword had failed to connect, locked as it was against the hilt of the falchion by the dagger. The friar immediately pulled back the dagger then drove it straight between Joe's lower ribs, level with the lungs, once then twice, and a woosh of air escaped from the wounds, bubbling the blood that came with it. The man dropped his swords and collapsed in agony.

Beth stood in shock, aghast at what she saw. The bowl of water she had brought with the intention of bathing Jamie's wounds fell from her hands and clattered across the stone floor, its contents mingling with Alf's blood. It happened so quickly that she could not reconcile what she was seeing. Then Jamie staggered into view, wielding a small flour sack ready as a makeshift cudgel.

"*Ho, amico mio*, you are *troppo tarde*," the friar joked.

Jamie blinked, not believing what he was seeing. "Cristo! By the Lord Harry. Hell's teeth, I was never more glad to see you." He cried, staggering towards him and clasping his arm. Cristoforo supported his friend.

"Nor I you. How do you do?" Then he turned quickly to comfort Beth who stood shaking in fear. She had witnessed tavern brawls before but nothing like Cristoforo's brutal and efficient killing of the two guards. It was made worse by the fact that he appeared so calm and clinical as he killed.

"*Signora*, please be not afeared," he adjured her, flashing his teeth in his most winning smile, "I mean you no harm. I just wished to secure my friend's release."

There was not a woman born who would not succumb to that smile and charm as well he knew. Beth was no exception and the spell of fear was broken.

"'Ee be a friend of Jamie's then?" she asked

"Aye, for my sins, and they be many. Could I trouble you for a cup of wine and a fresh bowl of water and cloth? He appears to have a lump upon his head the size of an apple, and needs must it should be attended to."

Beth turned as though pleased of a distraction that gave her the chance to drag herself away from the dead men, the pool of sticky blood and the invasive metallic smell of it that pervaded the air. She moved towards the bar, returning with all that was asked, the water cold this time, as Cristoforo eased Jamie onto a settle so that he could look at his bruised scalp. Beth skirted the two bodies, averting her eyes and holding an apron to her mouth to mask the smell of death. She skittered away after Cristoforo had thanked her for the water and cloth, running to the stairs.

"How goes it, Jamie?" Cristoforo asked. "'Tis good to see you, *amico*."

"Aye, and you," Jamie replied. "Is there something you can do with your herbs to send forth the man in my head with a hammer? For he seems intent upon thumping a hole in my skull. By the rood my shoulders are sore where that whoreson beat me a second time to the floor." He nodded at Alf's body and gripped the settle arm tightly as Cristoforo bathed his head, then inspected his shoulder where it met the neck. "*Mama Mia*, a huge haematoma. I have some salve for it, yet we should not tarry here, for this man Stanhope returns, and maybe some others. Can you fight?"

"Aye, so long as there's blood in my body, why?"

"I shall go to fetch Killarney and Forest. The landlord showed me a side door and told me how to open the latch. You stay here and we shall depart upon my return through your postern gate."

"So, it was you I saw the other night, watching as I returned?"

"'Twas me, yet I knew not who else might hear us and your dog came close to betraying me, foolish beast that she is, so I kept my distance to better the ruse. I was good no? Only Forest knew me." He boasted at his skill. "Now I go, for no one will trouble a friar even at night."

Jamie shook his head then regretted it. Cristoforo fetched Jamie's sword and dagger from the table where Alf had sat. "Do not try to put your helmet on, it will hurt," he adjured nodding to the helm on the table that showed a slight dent.

"It must have been an almighty blow to stun me so through

my helm. Yet I was not prepared, and such attacks are the worst when they come from behind unbidden."

"Stay here, I will return anon."

Jamie nodded gently, drawing his sword and feeling comforted at the feel of the weapon in his hand. Cristoforo seemed to float out of the room and through the inn door, lost to the night, departing as silently as a wraith.

Chapter Fifteen

Cristoforo returned after what seemed like an eternity, tapping gently on the inn door, which Jamie unbarred.

"I had to avoid the Watch, but the snow muffled the horse's steps. Come, we must fetch Richard and leave, *subito*."

Jamie retrieved his cloak, strapped his sword belt around his waist and picked up his dented helmet. There was no sign of his shield, which must have been taken by one of the others in the company and not valuable enough for Alf to commandeer. Forest brushed against him for reassurance then moved on, excited to be out in the night again. Jamie's head still span and he had moments of dizziness that blurred his vision. He moved to close the door and saw Beth on the stairs.

"Thank you, my lady," he whispered.

"God speed Jamie, whoever you are."

He nodded, smiling gently at her, then shut the door softly. He managed to get around to the stables at the back, and for once Richard sensed his master's unsteadiness and permitted him to mount easily, without any of his usual tricks. They moved quietly out into the snow-covered streets, making for the postern gate, which they slipped through unnoticed, out into the white countryside. Keeping to the shadows where they could, they aimed for the darkness of the forest and took the main road south. For ten miles they rode into the freezing night, and heard five bells ring out across a harsh landscape from the village church at Kegworth. The wind had started to drive in from the east again, bringing with it the promise of more snow. Cristoforo looked across at his friend in the silver light. Jamie did not look well and needed rest.

"Come, we will stop awhile here. Let us get into the forest and we can light a fire. I do not want to be in the open if they catch up with us." He led Jamie off the road and into the forest.

"Here, this swale will do well." Cristoforo said, and looked across to see his friend shivering. It was unlike Jamie, who usually bore the cold well.

Leading the horses into the dip, Cristoforo moved them away from two yew trees that had sprouted there and were poisonous to horses. Tethering them to a beech tree a few paces away he quickly formed a windbreak of woven branches. Returning, he bent over three small pine trees and stripping the yew of its supple branches wove them together and pulled the young evergreens down to form a crude but effective shelter. These he wedged into the boughs of the nearby beech and they soon had a living cave made up on three sides with a lean-to roof. He threw ferns and bracken onto the floor of the shelter and bade Jamie sit, with Forest watching his every move. More woven branches narrowed and lowered the entrance to a tunnel at waist height. Lastly, Cristoforo wrought a shield-like windbreak that he pushed against the opening, blocking most of the driving storm from the low, narrow entrance to their shelter.

This attended to, he left Jamie well wrapped in his cloak seated on a bed of ferns and went in search of firewood as Forest lay down by her master to guard him in his weakness and provide him with extra warmth. Cristoforo broke off old tree branches and scraped bark from the underside of a log. Thus equipped, he returned to the windbreak with some bark, dry leaves and tiny twigs. A few stones were visible from previous excavations, and he fashioned these into a crude hearth.

Pulling a small pad of old wool from within his gambeson, he then set about the kindling with a flint, until he produced a strong spark that smouldered and smoked, finally offering a small flame upon which he blew gently. The dry wool flamed and he carefully added the leaves and dry bark until at last it supported the twigs which caught well in the flames.

The process took less than an hour. How many times, Cristoforo wondered, had they done this together on the road? Even a crude camp such as this offered a form of comfort against the storm, and they had both survived worse. Yet looking at Jamie, who still shivered under his cloak, they needed more. It was not a good sign and Cristoforo knew that a fire and some hot food would aid his friend's condition. The flames began to lick hungrily at the twigs that crackled and spat, gorging on the kindling. Adding larger bits of wood, the fire began to produce meaningful heat that was reflected back into their small hovel by the stones that Cristoforo had built up behind. He set up his metal pan and using thick, green sticks, he raised it above the fire on two tiny chains before filling it with snow to melt and boil. He crawled out again, reluctantly leaving the warmth of their den, to attend to the horse's shelter and fetch more firewood.

The horses began to snuffle and forage, kicking in the snow in search of rough grass. But they were well fed with stable grain and would, he knew, last without any meaningful food for some time. Retuning again he was surprised at how comparatively warm the shelter had become. A thick layer of snow had settled, sealing it snugly against the wind. Jamie had his hood down and was holding his hands out in front of the blaze. Cristoforo pulled a small, waxed bag from his satchel and dropped some dried herbs into the melted snow, waiting for it to boil. He then moved to examine Jaime's head where a huge purple bruise throbbed, swelling tight against the skin.

"Jamie, the blow to your head was severe and the evil humours within must be released. Your skin is stretched and hot to touch where the blow landed and I must release the pressure and let the humours fly away, *va bene*?"

"As you wish, Cristo, you have more knowledge than me in these matters as you have proved before. If you can rid me of these evils that invade my body and take away the devil banging in my head, do whatever you wish," Jamie replied, knowing that Cristoforo possessed medical skills above most surgeons. The Italian nodded, slipping a wickedly sharp dagger from his boot and holding its tip in the bluest part of the flames, twisting it in the orange light.

"What, you try to burn me now?" Jamie said grimly.

"No, the old man who trained my family said it was important to use flames to cure the blade of ill humours. I know not why, yet I have never seen a wound rot after so doing. I will allow it to cool ere I cut you."

After a few minutes he asked Jamie to bend towards the flames as he was not able to stand within the small shelter.

"Ready?"

"By God I am, just kill me and be done," Jamie growled.

Carefully Cristoforo cut the hair away near the purple lump and then using a spotless cloth, dipped in a strong-smelling spirit, he smoothed the area clean. "Now here she comes, *il coltello*."

Gently, with steady hands that many a surgeon would have envied, he sliced carefully into the throbbing lump and was rewarded with a squirt of blood and milky liquid. Jamie hissed, sucking his breath in and swore harshly at his friend, cursing his ancestors and all foreigners as necromancers and charlatans.

"Christ on the Cross but that hurt!" He finished.

"The evil has gone and with it the bad humours of heat. Now she will heal. Await now, for I pour some spirt on the wound, you record how you did for me in France?"

Jamie did remember. He'd seen how it stung his friend's wound, so he knew what to expect. Yet he had been assured that this would stop the green rot setting in.

"Hell's teeth, that stings. By God man, you should be a torturer, not a healer. Yet even now it throbs less, or is it just the pain of that spirit that succeeds to battle for my head?"

"Cease your constant moaning, you are worse than a woman! I will now bind it against the elements of ill humour and we will see how it heals."

With a light poultice soaked in the herb water from the pot, he bandaged Jamie's head and tied it gently but securely.

"Now food," Cristoforo adjured, at which he produced a haunch of bacon and brown bread bought from the innkeeper of the Running Horse. The bacon he sliced and cooked over the amber coals at the side of the fire on green branches and the bread he cut roughly to accept the meat. The two men ate in companionable silence, glad to be out of the storm and to have full bellies. Jamie threw a lump of fatty bread to Forest, who caught it in her waiting jaws. She had caught a rabbit in the night –prized delicacies for a wolfhound, it would seem, as all that was left were the ears and paws.

Jamie took a mouthful of water from his canteen. "I believe we should wait for full light then move on as quickly as possible," he said. "There will be pursuit as soon as Sir Richard learns of my escape."

"They will come to the inn to break their fast, and finding you flown they will sally forth on the London road with all due speed. They will be on good horses and will mayhap catch us afore nightfall."

"Yet we have little choice. If we tarry and seek shelter, word will out and we will have to ferret around in the cold, moving at night. The horses need fodder. I say we press forth and move as far south as we can and find a large town to hide in. Leicester is but a good day's ride even in these conditions, and my father has friends there with whom we can beg shelter."

"Then we go as soon as the storm abates or the light is upon us," Cristoforo said. "You sleep now and I will stay awake and watchful."

Jamie made to protest but Cristoforo waved him away, crouching and moving to the entrance to their lair. Peering out he saw that the wind still whirled the snow in flurries and pirouettes, and once away from the fire and the warmth it was bitterly cold, robbing all heat from a man's body. Cristoforo cursed. *In my country it will be Spring now,* he thought. In the fields outside *Firenze* the farmers would be sowing their seeds and moving the cattle and sheep up onto the higher pastures. The city would be luxuriating under the warm sunlight. *Damn this Godforsaken England.* The horses, he saw, were still there and stood nose to tail seeking heat from each other's bodies. They were protected from the worst of the weather by the windbreak he had fashioned.

Cristoforo watched the dawn rise, dressing the world in a blue tinged glow. The storm had mercifully blown itself out during the early morning, having filled every hollow and covered every bank in diamond crystals of ice. None of their tracks from the road were visible and all was quiet. Yet they knew speed was of the essence and they must move quickly, for pursuit would be hot on their heels.

Jamie had slept fitfully, nodding in and out of a deep sleep, and Cristoforo checked on him regularly, not wishing him to lapse into a sleep from which he would never wake. His great great grandfather had been taught healing and medicine by a healer whose life he had saved in the east, and the learning had been far in advance of western surgeons and physicks. The lore had been passed down through his family as it was so important in their chosen profession. Now he shook Jamie gently awake. "Jamie, Jamie, *amico*. We go, *andiamo.*" He urged. Jamie woke from a stuttering sleep, his eyes groggy and somehow shrunken as he mumbled into wakefulness.

"Now let me see your eyes." The Italian looked at the pupils, making sure they were the same size and focused. "Good, you recover. Now we go, *subito.*" Jamie crawled forward into a white world, standing and moving towards Richard. Speaking to the horse in a calming voice, he threw his cloak upon his back to warm it, and fetched the saddle from their hide. In moments they were saddled and the two men mounted. As they passed the trees, Cristoforo saw what he had failed to spot in the dark – the red and yellow bark of a willow. He halted Killarney and broke off a thin branch. He took out his belt knife and slit the stem revealing a white pith within. "Here, this will aid thy head," he told Jamie. "Suck out *il midollo*. She will taste bitter, for I have no time to make a tincture, yet by God's grace, it shall cure your thumping head."

Jamie took the proffered stick and duly sucked on the bitter tasting pith within, pulling a sour face as he did so, yet trusting his friend's remedies. "Thank you, Cristo, for your ministrations and care," he said. "I am again in your dept. But now to Leicester, and the hope of real shelter."

Chapter Sixteen

The horses were glad to be moving as their cold muscles relished the work, restoring heat to their bodies. They found the great south road which led to Leicester easily enough and made steady progress despite the banks and drifts of snow. The best pace was a trot as they dared not risk cantering on the uncertain surface and it would tire the horses to walk them on the verges by the road.

For three hours they rode through a wintry landscape of virgin white. The old Roman road edged towards Loughburga and they stopped briefly to water the horses at an inn outside the town and to buy a bag of feed before pressing on. The going was hard on the horses, with deep drifts blocking the road through which they were forced to paddle like huge swans, each horse taking a turn to break a path through the snow that the other followed.

"We shall be easy to follow now." Jamie remarked, looking back at the trampled snow of the last bank they had forced their way through. "'Tis but ten miles now to Leicester, and the merchant's house of which I spoke lies to the east of the town.

He serves on the local judiciary bench and will have law and order to aid our cause and safety."

They skirted the city moving east to meet the main road to Stamford, Peterborough and Lynn. They joined that road and saw a caravan of travellers with pack mules in the distance making steady progress towards them. Then Forest's ears pricked, and some instinct made both men turn – that sixth sense that always served them well. There in the distance behind them they saw what Forest had heard: a party of horsemen making fast going in the snow that they had stamped down.

"If we press on we'll never make our destination afore they catch us," Jamie said. "These malapert curs are pressing their horses enough to make them falter badly. Please God one falls and breaks his scullion neck. How many, Cristo?"

"I count six. Good odds," Cristo replied, pulling up his satchel to fetch out his crossbow. "This will level the odds further and we'll toss a coin for the odd man out." He continued in a fine frame of mind.

"What I wouldn't give for my old shield now, for I'll wager that they have spears." Jamie opined, and suddenly he felt good. The throb in his head had subsided with the aid of the willow pith and it accorded well with his disposition. The thought of a good fight brought a panacea to his ills. "We will divide and narrow their target. Force them if you can to throw early with your bow. They'll not expect it." Against mail he knew it was good for fifty yards to pierce and kill. It was extremely accurate and Cristoforo practiced weekly on the butts in Laurence Lane.

Jamie dismounted and fastened Forest's war collar around her neck. It was of thick yet supple leather and bore studded spikes facing outwards to protect her neck and act as a deterrent to grab her there. She faced forward, aware of what it meant and stood ready, watching the approaching enemy. Re-mounting, Jamie felt Richard fret as he nodded his great head up and down. The small vibrations transmitted from Jamie down the reins and through his seat called to the receptive stallion as his excitement rose. He knew what this was: war and battle.

With his crossbow now assembled and cocked ready, a quarrel in the tiller groove, Cristoforo kept it from sight behind Killarney's neck. The two men moved apart, putting fifteen yards between them, and watched carefully as the six men drew ever closer. Jamie cast one more glance over his shoulder to see that the caravan of travellers had split, three men breaking away and making good time on the snowy road, pressing down on them hard. Was this a trap? Were they to be pincered between them? No, the direction was all wrong. Maybe the party from the east would aid them – yet why? He then turned forwards again, time slowing as it did before battle, the quiet peace before the mayhem and rage that always took him. He undid his cloak, laying it across his pommel to free his movements, his dagger and sword drawn.

There would be no *paroli* here, he knew, just death. All the men he saw had spears resting in their fewters, and now as they closed, they raised them, changing grip for a throw. The leader led the van in a small vee. He was mailed and carried a shield bearing the livery of Sir Richard Stanhope. So be it, Jamie thought, to the death with no quarter given. He knew that twenty yards was the maximum range at which they could throw, and with confidence and no defence on their behalf they would maybe come closer. Nearer they came, and Jamie heard the panting of horses from his right as the other three men closed from the eastward road, yet he dared not look, concentrating as he was on the oncoming riders.

At thirty-five yards Cristoforo's arm rose, he took careful aim and the quarrel buzzed forward. The leader saw the action and took too long to realise his fate, so intent was he on spearing his seemingly defenceless prey. He began to raise his shield, but it was too late. The quarrel thudded home smashing through his breast bone, the impact sending him backwards off his horse. The other five men were startled, reeling in and halting their gallop. Cristoforo quickly pulled back upon his bow placing the butt of the tiller in his stomach, yet even as he did so he realised it was futile. He would not have sufficient time to draw, cock and release a bolt before the spears would be thrown. He flung the weapon aside and prepared to fight the two men bearing down upon him, their spear arms raised for a throw. He focused, drew falchion and dagger then nudged Killarney sideways. She was nowhere near as quick as Richard but responded well, as if she knew that a moving target was harder to hit. Then a strange thing happened; one of the men sprouted a crossbow bolt to his shoulder, causing him to drop his shield and instinctively raise his right hand to the wound. He cried out in pain and his companion looked across in dismay and launched his spear. The missile whistled through the air, but with just one spear to contend with Cristoforo timed the strike well and batted it away with his falchion. Now it was one on one. The oncoming soldier drew his sword, shouting his war cry. Cristoforo halted Killarney and waited. At five yards his arm flew back and the wicked dagger span in the air, lodging in the man's exposed cheek, all thoughts of attack forgotten. He spurred Killarney and slashed the falchion across his opponent's face, blinding him as he passed by. Curbing his horse he halted, turning to witness a strange sight.

Jamie spun Richard, who caprioled suddenly, taking a soldier by surprise, kicking him broken from the saddle. Yet beside him fought another man, with a shield whose device he could not see. He was angry, shouting a battle cry of King Harry, and as his face turned, he saw a marled eye and a long scar running down his face: John! His opponent had kept his spear, jabbing overarm, standing in his stirrups, trying to best the shield John was using to such good effect to fend off the longer weapon.

As the soldier stood again to strike down, John slid the deadly point of his sword into his straightened leg, pulled back quickly and as the spear hand dropped, he slashed at the exposed shoulder, cutting the maille and driving the blade home. He sawed backwards, releasing the blade and was rewarded with a howl of agony from the man. At this he rotated his wrist, bringing the blade slicing down into his neck in a killing stroke, piercing the metal and leather of his habergeon. The man dropped from his saddle to fall lifelessly to the trampled snow. Cristoforo wheeled around, looking for the sixth man, and saw instead a supine body impaled on a second crossbow bolt lying in the snow.

Jamie looked on in surprise and delight written across his face: "John, by all that's holy, you are well met! How come you here in such timely fashion?"

"Ha," John snarled irascibly, "have I not taught you better than to face a spearman without a shield?"

"Would that I had one – but it seemed a fair fight, Richard and no shield against a spearman." He quipped lightly.

John snorted, then smiled: "Lucky then that we were on the road, for it seems that you have not lost the knack of making enemies wherever you go. Was it the father of some wench you swived?" he mocked.

Still tense from the fight, Jamie laughed back at his former mentor. "Aye, but she was worth it," he said. Then he looked along the road and saw that the rest of the party had caught up with John, Will and Edward, the latter who had fired the crossbow bolts with such success. "Father!" Jamie called, recognising the portlier figure, well-padded against the cold. "'Tis good to see you, yet why do you not journey to Flanders as you planned?"

"Jamie, my son, I am by God's grace glad to see you hale and well." He puffed, dismounting and walking towards his son, who held Richard back as he stamped and pawed the snow. "We planned the journey yet the foul weather and storms at sea prevented it, with no man prepared to sail – wisely as it happens. By the Lord I'm right glad we did not, for fortune smiles upon us to be here at such an opportune moment. Who are these men and why do they seek your demise?"

"They serve Sir Richard Stanhope. They seek me because I escaped with the help of Cristo, and have news most pertinent to Sir Richard Whittington and the crown. For Stanhope controls a nest of vipers who foment treason and unrest. Yet the stain of such a cause does not lie with him alone. It seeps deeper into the court than one could imagine." He looked at his father, a perfervid expression upon his face.

"Come," his father adjured, "let us not tarry here, for we must make de Lacy's house by evensong. There we will find a better reception and respite from this Godforsaken cold that chills my old bones." Thomas de Grispere clasped his son about the muscled shoulders and went to remount his horse. "Now tell us all that has occurred. Praise God that he brought us together when he did, Cristoforo, for it is now I that am in your debt, it would seem."

Cristoforo just shrugged and bared his slow smile. He liked his new found friends and family, enjoying the action and drama that constantly surrounded Jamie in his present role as a knight and a spy.

Chapter Seventeen

The short journey to the merchant de Lacey's home proved uneventful – at least compared to the astounding news Jamie imparted to his father and John on the road there. No word was spoken of the events in Nottingham once in de Lacey's company, for they wanted the information to remain a secret between them at least until they returned to London and could inform Whittington. Yet the enormity of what Jamie had discovered shook his father to the core.

On the road home the following day he spoke with his son.

"You will only be safe once we are returned to London and you sign an affidavit swearing all that you have seen and discovered. Yet still you must be on your mettle for these lords make powerful enemies and their reach rises to the prince himself."

"For certes, yet I am in an unenviable position of treading the line between king and prince."

"Mayhap, for we do not know if the prince is but a sely pawn in a noble's game. It has occurred before and will again, God knows. Tread carefully, my son, trust only Whittington, for it was he that set you on this errand and he alone that can free you of the shackles that bind you to his cause."

The wise words stayed with Jamie on the days south. The weather became more clement as they came closer to London and offered a better reflection of early Spring. Any evidence of snow disappeared and the brown grass was starting to turn green again as they passed through the meadows surrounding the capital. The wind changed direction, and as they entered the gates of London the gentle breeze blew salted air upon them from the south, flavoured with the tang of the sea and the river.

The salty air reminded Jamie of Mark and his mission to Cornwall. "Has aught been heard of Mark since he left for Plymouth?"

"Nary a word," his father replied. "Jeanette called upon mistress Emma, but she had received no missive of his condition or whereabouts."

"That does not fill me with surprise, for Mark is ever faithless with a quill," Cristoforo commented.

"Now we rest, but once we have eaten I would adjure you to get yourself to the palace and Whittington as soon as you may. For only then will you be safe. The lords of Warwick, Arundel and Beaufort have a long reach and dangerous power." His father advised.

An hour later, with the stain of travel washed from them and full bellies, Jamie and Cristoforo set out for the palace and Whittington's chambers. Once within, they found themselves ushered without delay through to the private chambers of Sir Richard, who was pleased and relieved to see Jamie, having heard no word since receiving a note from the Earl of Macclesfield a few days past.

"The earl mentioned of your intervention and within was a separate missive from his daughter, the Lady Alice, who was..." here he paused, "...a little more forthcoming, perhaps."

Jamie interpreted the meaning correctly: "Ha, so the old goat still disapproves of me, despite saving him and his family from a terrible fate. He is a cantankerous old devil, for certes!"

Whittington made no comment but smiled benevolently, commanding him to give an account of all that had occurred. When Jamie came to the meeting of the lords at Stanhope's manor Sir Richard held up a hand and interrupted. "James, make no mistake here, for more than a man's honour is staked upon your words. Are you certain sure that it was these very lords and the livery of Beaufort's men that you saw?"

"I am, and I would stake my honour and life upon that which my eyes witnessed. Of Beaufort's esquire, why I have shared a sword and a cup of wine with him at court."

"They saw you not, yet still you were undone?"

"Verily, for they were suspicious and placed me within a party where I could be set upon. Mayhap I was seen or recognised. Maybe word reached Stanhope that I was not of the same station that I pretended to be, maybe word came from the borders. I know not."

Sir Richard stood and paced the room. He looked down at the carpets upon which he strode, seeing their patterns and hoping perhaps that their intricacies would unravel the puzzles in his mind. He turned and placed the figures upon the metaphorical chessboard in his head, searching each move that the pieces could make and the outcome. Almost absentmindedly he asked Jamie to continue with his narrative. Then he had Cristoforo relate the story of his movements and intervention in Jamie's fate.

"By the rood you were fortunate, James." He declared, concern in his voice.

"Aye, that I was. If not for Cristoforo and the ministrations of loyal subjects at the Running Horse inn I would doubtless now be gracing my Lord Stanhope's dungeon – or very probably worse."

"'Twas timely to meet John and your father on the road. This cursed weather has been of use to some, I'm right glad to hear."

Sir Richard hurried on in his habitually precise manner, skipping forward as he made plans to thwart enemies, always one step ahead of where he should be. "Needs must we shall have you and *Signor* Corio sign affidavits of all that has occurred. These will be kept safely away from prying eyes, yet I will let it be known through Lord Grey as the king's chamberlain and Bishop Arundel that information has been gleaned and vouchsafed concerning treason and insurrection in the north. The parties concerned will be put on their guard and worry about what has been discerned. Stanhope will quieten for a while and Meryng should be safe for now."

"Sir Richard, may I ask how will this be felt by the prince? For he is indicted in his absence by association, and he would be held in poor estate by his majesty should this be put abroad."

Flint came into Whittington's voice again and his tone changed. "Do not concern yourself with such matters, James. I shall tread that fine line between a king and a prince, keeping both at ease for the sake of peace and the kingdom. I am ever the diplomat and can sense which way the wind blows. Say naught of this matter to anyone. It will out in time, I'm sure. There are other things keeping the crown and Council occupied in the meantime. I am informed that trouble flares again in France, where neither Armagnac nor Burgundian factions can gain the upper hand. This, allied to the imminent signing of the Anglo Flemish treaty, will bring us once more into France's affairs. Those lords whom you have indicted with your words will soon find themselves embroiled in the affairs of state both here and abroad. I shall make certain of it."

Whittington offered Jamie and Cristoforo a mirthless grin. "The prince will find himself for once a pawn that is pulled this way and that as the balance of power tips back and forth. Any adverse weight that may be placed upon these scales would be disastrous to us and to the future of England. So we will be judicious with the information that you have provided, and use it carefully and most importantly at an opportune moment. 'Til that time arrives, I will continue to gather evidence and strike against those who seek to steal the crown and undo them in their cause – and in so doing I shall assoil the prince of any wrong doing."

"As you wish, Sir Richard." Jamie answered.

"Good. Now to you both I adjure caution. Watch carefully the shadows in which you may linger. The court is as dark and unstable as it ever was, if not worse. Should these hornets whose nest you have disturbed be aware of your hand in this – and for certes I believe they already are – then you must be extra vigilant."

"Indeed, Sir Richard." Jamie answered curtly.

"Come now, young James, let there be no churlishness here. We are friends who fight secretly for England's cause and whomever may offer her good fortune," he said, clasping Jamie's shoulder.

"Aye, that we are," James expressed a breath he hadn't realised he'd been holding. "And as we talk of friends, I would ask has any news been heard of Mark since he left London?

"I have received word that he has taken work at the port of Plymouth and has reported back all of import. The fleet sails soon – with most interestingly Sir Hugh Courtney as one of its captains." Sir Richard paused to let the words sink in.

"The pirate? Is this not putting a fox in the hen house?" Jamie questioned.

"There is naught that I can offer in that regard. William

Stokes has men about in the ports, especially Plymouth, yet no word has been received on his account. I will keep you abreast of any information that I should receive of your friend, rest assured. The devoir of this fleet and those who command it is to capture and produce the pirates. If they fail, I suspect that the task will fall to the lord admiral."

"Sir Thomas Beaufort," Jamie whispered.

"Just so, and consider further. The prince has strong connections with the Courtneys through Richard, their cousin and closest friend. If they should fail, it makes the Beauforts' suit stronger and offers Sir Thomas the chance to engage in action, gaining both favour and power. He likes less the role of Lord Chancellor and would rather a sword in his hand to further seek his future power.

"'Tis indeed a heady brew from which he would drink. And with the prince divided in loyalty, they may influence him the more to press for the crown and with it their standing. They may be half-brothers to the king, but since when has blood been any impediment to power?" Whittington finished, looking hard at Jamie and Cristoforo, ensuring that the full import of his words had struck home. "Now I must beg your forbearance, for I need a lawyer and witness to swear your affidavits. After that they will be lodged with the Lord Chief Justice, Sir William Gascoigne and their contents sent thence to the king's ear."

At which he called for Alfred to fetch a lawyer to begin the laborious process of scribing the document that could well prove the downfall of Sir Richard Stanhope and his comrades in conspiracy and arms.

Part Two
The English Channel

Spring/Summer

Chapter Eighteen

Plymouth

The cold weather that had brought snow to the northern half of the country had not reached the southern ports, and Plymouth was no exception. The bustling fishing port boasted a wide and well-appointed harbour suited to launching a major fleet of ships. When Mark broached the ridge above the town, he looked down in surprise. The port had changed since he was a boy. The old king had ordered a castle built on the promenade of Sutton Pool, the harbour to the south of the river Plym. Here Mark saw the new building was being topped off with the castellation of its walls and its Barbican strengthened to incorporate a mechanism for raising and lowering the gigantic chain that guarded the harbour.

The huge guns of which his father had spoken faced across the entrance, and Mark had been told that they had seen off a French attack earlier, at the turn of the century. Plymouth was a fortress town that held the key to the southwest and the ports of England. The town itself too had grown since he last visited it as a boy so many years before. If he had not lived in London this past year he would have been impressed and awed at the criss-cross of streets and the bustle of the shopkeepers, fishermen and traders all vying for position. The smell of fish and the tang of the sea was strong, blown in on a south westerly breeze.

Mark moved easily down the road into the town, drawing no attention as he had changed into some old clothes from the farm. A borel sack was slung easily over one shoulder atop his cloak and whilst he still had his father's old sword at his waist, this was not such an unusual sight. Most men carried a weapon for protection, although many were little versed in its use. The quarterstaff in his right hand was still where Mark would place his faith if he was set upon.

He went down into the town, passing under the town walls, just another traveller seeking work in the port town. Keeping the castle on his right as a reference point, he walked on towards the docks. There was no brick here, he saw. The buildings were of local stone infilling as nogging, and the mighty beams of oak supported houses that seemed to lean in as they reached skywards. Some of the wealthier merchants' houses had latticed windows to protect their occupants against the storms that prevailed here, storms he knew only too well. Just before entering New Street, he set eyes on the friary on Rag Lane of which Friar Vincent had spoken during their time on the road together when he first left Cornwall. He carried a letter from his friend for the head of the friary and had promised to deliver it for him.

Mark carried on down the steeply sloping road of bright cobbles after delivering his letter, and rounding a bend he caught sight of the docks and the sea beyond. The narrow frontages of the shops and houses bore tribute to the value placed upon them by their closeness to the sea and each, he knew, would stretch back in long strips of garden or workshops.

The cobbles led him downwards towards the quays, where gulls soared above, cawing and fighting in flight or swooping neatly to sift through the fresh rubbish discarded by the fishing boats in their wake. The activity was frenetic, with each of the berths occupied by an eclectic mix of seagoing craft, from small wherries to large cogs. He heard the resounding hammer of mallets and the rasp of saws, and realised that the ships were being fitted with high castles fore and aft. They were being turned into warships! They threw a wide draught, being flat bottomed, and he knew that they could carry greater tonnage than their Mediterranean counterparts. Yet they would be similar, if not identical to those used by the English pirates and any battle would be from an equal platform.

Steeves scurried about in lines narrowly missing each other as they jumped from plank to ship and back again. A senior man with a rough creased visage was giving orders. He had a woollen hat upon his head, and wore a shiny leather breast coat over a filthy linen shirt. His fingers played with a piece of cord which he knotted at intervals to mark the number of planks going aboard as the men fed the labouring carpenters. Before him was a tally stick which he marked at intervals with a sharp knife.

"Good morrow sir, be 'ee the master 'ere?" Mark enquired politely.

The man turned a seamed face the colour of walnut to look at Mark through bloodshot eyes, taking in the giant before him noting the huge breadth to the shoulders and thews of his legs.

"I am, but busy here as you can see."

"Ah, busy is good, for I seek work hereabouts and wondered if 'ee be the man to speak with," Mark answered. He had slipped back into his Cornish accent since being back on the farm, and all manner of London bronze had now been hidden behind that of a yokel villein straight from the fields.

"I may be, what can 'ee do? Are you trained to an apprenticeship?" he asked, looking back to check the steeves carrying lumber and supplies to the waiting cogs.

"Well, I'm good with my hands and helped with framework on the farm and such like. I'm strong too, and happy to toil for my keep."

"When the church clock strikes the hour of sext, come to the yard there," the man pointed at a rough wooden building by the docks attached to a warehouse. "I may have work for you."

With that he turned away, leaving a smiling Mark to wander about the quays and wharfs admiring the ships and frenetic activity. The hour arrived and he was taken on by Carac, the master of the steeves. He settled well into the work, and was found a bunk above the warehouse where many of the men slept.

— ✕ ✦✕ —

Mark had a generous disposition towards his fellow man, and soon ingratiated himself well into their company – not least because his immense strength made it possible for him to carry almost twice as much as the other workers. As the weeks went by he became accepted as one of the team and often sat with them in the evenings at the Minerva tavern in Looe street, just up from the docks. Most of the fleet had been finished and refitted for war, with just two more carracks and barges to be brought up for fitting out. They would later follow the fleet, which was to sail on the morning's tide under the command of the earl Edward and his son Sir Edward as joint admirals, along with the earl's brother Sir Hugh Courtney.

The steeves settled down in the tap room to celebrate. Mark had learned a good deal in his time there. Messages had been passed to Josef, one of the local revenue officials responsible for the receipt of kaiage, who regularly attended the wharf to oversee the landing of goods and ensure all duty was paid. He was an innocuous, scholarly man who was ideal for his work and sent messages back from Mark to William Stokes.

They were a good-natured crowd, tough and hard of hand, used to manual work. They worked hard during the days and drank hard in the evenings. Some of the crew from the war cogs were also there that evening, including the captains. Most were genial and enjoyed the camaraderie of like-minded men, but not all were of this stamp when the ale started flowing.

"Come on then, I'll take on all comers. Who'll wrestle me?" Mark heard the cry as everyone turned to see the muscled figure of one of the steeves, an overseer called Merek. He was a brute of a man, with a slab of a face, piggy eyes and big scarred hands, which he flexed by his sides as he rolled his shoulders.

"Come on 'en, who'll rough 'n' tumble?" He challenged again, smiling through stained and broken teeth. Conversation quietened, groups of men sat with their ale cups and most avoided his eye. Others smiled, shaking their heads.

"Old Merek's bin drinkin' again," one lad seated at Mark's table muttered. He was a young boy of sixteen and just maturing, easy of nature and gentle among the rough company.

Merek caught the words and moved over, a nasty look in his eyes. "What? What's that'ee say boy?" he called, his blood up. "Come on, spit it out. Does 'ee want to wrassle?"

"No Merek, not I," the boy answered gently.

"I can't 'ear 'ee, boy." Merek answered, seizing the boy's ear and twisting it, making him howl in pain. "That's it, cry to your mammy. She'll be 'ere as soon as the last sailor's paid 'er," Merek sneered. He slapped him hard across his face, spilling his ale.

The lad was game and span around with an ill-timed round-house punch that was aimed at Merek's hard, paunched stomach. The blow landed, hitting the slab of fat and muscle and Merek just laughed, driving down a huge fist onto the boy's head just behind his ear, dropping the lad cold. As he went down, Merek swung again to smash him. The blow never landed; Mark caught his hand in mid-air.

"He's 'ad enough. You've knocked him senseless, what more do 'ee want? Leave him be." Mark said gently. He did not like bullies.

"Who are you, his sister? Why you're pretty enough," he jeered, shaking his hand free. "Come on pretty boy, will you wrassle with me? Or are you too frightened of hurting that pretty face of you'rn?"

"Go on Mark, take him." One of the men at the table urged. Others followed. Mark liked a fight as much as the next man, and he was torn between fighting and keeping a lower profile. But it was too late, the die was cast.

He stood, weighing up the man before him who swayed slightly, a sweaty, ale induced sheen upon his face. He'd had a few too many ales, but Mark did not underestimate him. He was a tavern brawler with a good deal of experience and beneath the slab of fat at his stomach lay a hard and powerful layer of muscle.

Mark unbuckled the belt around his waist, giving Merek nothing to grab onto. Others stood, pushing chairs and stools into a rough ring, and men began exchanging odds on the outcome.

Carac sidled near, "'Ee be careful, it'll not be like the wrestling to rules 'ee may have done before. This be vicious and he loves to cripple a man. If 'ee go down 'e'll stick his boots in and stamp you," he warned.

Mark nodded in acknowledgement of the words and realised this was more than a rough and tumble wrestling match. But he'd been in tavern brawls before, both here and

London, and knew the score however this might be dressed up as a 'match'.

The two men faced each other within the loose circle of cheering onlookers. Merek rolled his shoulders and moved his huge hands back and forth, feinting for a hold or grip that would give him the chance to throw Mark. There was no stickler to shout 'wrestle', and the two men just set to.

Mark stood relaxed, bent at the knees and waist, one leg forward for balance. Merek lunged and the two men clashed to shouts from the circled crews. Mark took his favourite grip of the shorter man: right hand behind the neck, left to his right wrist and sleeve, but he wasn't expecting what happened next. Instead of a wrestling grip, Merek drove his hand to grip Mark's upper arm, driving the thumb deep into nerves that lay between triceps and biceps, causing mind-numbing pain. Even Mark's huge, iron hard muscles could not protect from this attack. There was a natural join there that could be exploited, yet the move was illegal in a true match.

At the same time Merek's right hand rotated, breaking the grip, and he slapped across hard, aiming for Mark's ear to burst the ear drum. Had he succeeded, Mark would lose all balance and pivot to the floor. Mark saw the move and reacted fast, tilting his head, but in doing so exposed the hinge of his jaw and neck. Merek seized the opportunity driving the hard thick little finger of his hand into the point just behind the ear. The result was agony, sending pain through the nerves of Mark's neck. His body tensed against it, pushing himself off balance as he drove his left hand up to force Merek's elbow up and away to break the grip. But as he did so the other fingers gripped his ear and pulled, and at the same time Merek drove his hip in and up, pulling on the numbed arm.

There is a point when a wrestler knows, even in a clean match, that he will be thrown, and it is sometimes better to go with the movement, relax and control how and when this happens. Not all Mark's fighting had taken place within the clean rules of Cornish wrestling, and he had engaged in his fair share of tavern brawls. He expected to be dragged to the floor with an elbow to his throat or fingers in his eyes and kicked between the legs. So he did the unexpected: he sprang forward with the movement, going with the pull of his opponent's strength. In doing so he surprised the man, who relieved of the full load came forward as Mark flew over his hip in a perfect roll to land shoulder first. Yet instead of letting go with his right-hand Mark continued with the movement pulling Merek's head, aware that where the head goes, the body follows. His opponent's nerve grips were only good in one place and were weakened and broken in his spin through in the air, while Mark kept his hold on the rough leather collar of his opponent's jerkin and strands of his lank, greasy hair.

Landing lightly and rolling, he pulled Merek on, and for good measure he kicked him hard between the legs. He was rewarded with an *ooof* of expelled air as his opponent sailed over his head and crashed to the hard tavern floor. Mark stood quickly, rubbing his sore right arm, which was still slightly numb from the nerve hold. *Someone had taught Merek well the art of dirty fighting*, he thought. Mark waited, not wishing to re-engage until his arm was fully recovered.

Merek swore in rage and pain as he rose unsteadily to his feet. "You bastard, I'll 'ave 'ee," he spat. He jumped up and down, gently rubbing between his legs to alleviate the pain. An angry man was a disadvantaged man, Mark knew and sought to make it worse. "You're naught but a scullion, pissynghole. My sister could wrassle you to the floor on her worst day." He taunted, wanting to make the man as mad and reckless as he could be.

This was no wrestling match now, this was maim or kill for

Merek. He roared like an angry bull and charged at Mark, hands forward to grapple and smash his head into Mark's body. It was a foolish move brought on by anger and taunting, but it was exactly what Mark had wished for. His arm was still slightly numb and he needed to end this quickly.

He timed it perfectly. Pivoting on his left leg, he moved out of line of the full force of Merek's charge and drove his right knee upwards with all his might, pulping Merek's nose. Merek looked for a split second as though he was travelling in two directions at once as his legs went forward and his head flew back. Mark grabbed his greasy hair in the charge and released with his left hand smashing his elbow to same point behind the ear and jaw that Merek had used on him. It was a wicked blow, driven by immense force, and it struck the sweet spot where all fighters seek to land a punch. It knocked Merek cold and he dropped to the floor. The tavern erupted in cheers, yet for a moment Mark thought he had killed his opponent and knelt quickly to ascertain if he was still alive. Seeing the gentle rise and fall of his chest he smiled and rose, welcoming the applause from the tavern.

A captain of the fleet came up, offering a jug of ale. "You're a grand wrestler lad, I like that in the man. Would you like to join my crew?" He offered, half joking.

"No, 'oi be for land, tho' I do like the sea." Mark replied, gulping down the ale as the post-fight reaction set in, allowing the adrenalin, so quick to be released, to seep slowly from his system. He sat down to cheers of his mates feeling drowsy, and within half an hour he had fallen asleep at his table with his head upon his arms.

Chapter Nineteen

Mark awoke with a groan, his head throbbing. He blinked against the light of the sun that probed around the canvas sheeting as it billowed above him and struck into his eyes like sharp knife points. He raised a hand to protect his blurred and clouded vision, praying for shadow or better still darkness. The ground was moving beneath his body as he lay supine, the world seeming to heave and haw.

"By God am I mad? Have I slipped into an abyss and gone to hell?" He moaned, but then his other senses took over and the strong smell of the sea, ripe fish, tar and hemp all fought for his cognisance with the shrieking of gulls. A merciful shadow fell across his face as a figure stood above him, blocking out the sun.

"Not hell lad. You're aboard ship – a good ship an' all – on a glorious spring day with a fine nor' wester blowin' across our bows." Blinking up, Mark recognised the captain who had given him a tankard of ale the previous evening.

"A ship? Was I bedevilled with ale that I fell asleep on this ship? Or did Merek hit me harder than I thought?" he moaned.

The captain laughed gently: "neither lad, 'twas the dwale I slipped in your drink. Leaves a man uncommon ill and deep in slumber. Now you serve me and his majesty, for I've need of strong souls aboard who can fight, and ye be of the right stuff to serve. I fetched your garb, your staff and sword from Carac, and it be stowed in your war bag aft. Be glad, for the king pays better than a steeve's coin and we go to catch pirates and fight those who would ruin our land. We make for So'ton, then to the English Channel to follow our search for the rabble."

Mark looked at him uncomprehending and made to stand, then swayed as the huge cog moved beneath him. He made a grab for the spar of the deck and steadied himself.

"'Tis but the dwale. Drink water and rub vinegar upon your cheeks, it'll pass soon enough. Then get your sea legs, for you'll need 'em ere long," the captain ordered, swaying easily with the movement of the deck as he walked off. Mark shook his head and made for the huge central mast and the large barrel roped to it. Lifting the lid, he used the wooden cup that was chained there to drink the fresh water from the barrel. It tasted a little brackish, but it was a blessed relief to his parched throat and sore head. He squinted again against the low-lying April sun. *What now?* he thought. Part of him was angry to have been hoodwinked into serving aboard the ship, and part of him was pleased to realise that he had managed to get where he wanted to be with no suspicion attached to the process. He would now see exactly what action was to be taken. Yet how was he to impart whatever information he should gain back to Sir Richard?

Puzzling this, he staggered aft to the bulkhead and through to where the cook was preparing food. He asked for some vinegar and the cook pointed with his ladle at a flask on a barred shelf. Removing the stopper, Mark rubbed the vinegar into his skin and despite his scepticism felt almost instant relief.

"Dwale, was it?" The cook asked in a coarse voice that bespoke too much brandy and salt air.

"So the cap'n tells me, and my head can't help but agree."

"It be a bastard brew, that. Devil's work. Henbane, opium and suchlike. Still, you're aboard now so make the best of it. You'll want your gear. 'Tis aft through that door." He swung a floury thumb behind him as he made pastry for pies. "Don't forget to duck. Big'uns like you allus forget."

Mark thanked him and went to find his borel sack, sword belt and dagger. There on the floor was his beloved quarterstaff. He left off the sword as it was too cumbersome for everyday duties and strapped on his belt with its sheathed dagger and went forward, remembering to duck his head. The light seemed easier now, thanks to the water and vinegar.

With the strong breeze behind them and the sail stretched wide, the ship made for the open sea before turning to the northeast on a course for Southampton, the crew pulling hard on the ropes that held the sails as the cog creaked and groaned under the wind that now came at from the port-wise direction, tipping the ship a little as the sails caught the breeze and drove it forward. Mark looked up and there, perched high and swaying with the movement of the ship, a man stood in the crow's nest, eyes alert. Looking from one side to the other he saw two more ships on a parallel course a hundred yards apart, with more behind and one in front in the van.

Mark began to sway with the ship, steady on his feet. Like many of his Cornish countrymen he was a natural sailor. He went to the forecastle that had so recently been constructed of linden wood, now brightly painted in red and gold. The smell of paint and freshly cut wood came to him over that salt tang of the sea. He knew a little of ship's lore, and as he mounted the steps he called out, "Permission to enter the fo'c'sle, cap'n?"

"Aye, come ahead lad," came the response. "You're better then?"

"By the rood, my head's still thumping, but I'm on the mend and no mistake."

The captain, whose name he discovered was Ralph, questioned him more on his origins and observed that he had clearly been to sea before. Mark just managed to bite his tongue before he mentioned his trip to France the previous year, and just added that like all good Cornishmen he had been to sea many times. Satisfied, the captain turned to look at the sail and watch the flagship in front. Like the shields hooked to the sides of the castle, the flagship bore the Courtney crest: a bezant background with three bright roundels in gules, the red in stark contrast to the gold behind. Above was the bright azure bar of the label with three points.

So we're off to fight pirates, he thought. Somewhere, somehow, he needed to let Sir Richard know of his whereabouts.

His thoughts were interrupted by another figure who ascended the wooden steps to the fighting platform. He needed no permission to enter, and Mark had seen him before. He was not especially tall, yet bore the musculature of someone trained in arms. His face showed breeding and he wore a thick moustache in a rakish manner that gave his features a piratical air. His sandy hair was swept back and fell long at his neck. He was well dressed in a fine deep blue padded jupon with elaborate frogging on the closings. His boots were polished leather and gleamed in the sunlight.

"Sir Hugh, good morrow to you," Captain Ralph addressed him.

"And to you, captain. We have a good wind I see. If it keeps up we'll reach Southampton in less than two days, I perceive," He said.

"Aye sir, you have the right of it if the wind holds, and I believe it will."

Sir Hugh looked up at Mark's giant form and was impressed. "A new man?"

"Aye sir, Mark of Cornwall, the man who defeated Merek yester eve. Mark, this is Sir Hugh de Courtney, vice admiral of the fleet."

Mark tugged at his forelock and offered a bow. "An honour to meet you sir," he said, feigning an obsequious demeanour. He had after all been honoured by the prince himself, but he knew he had to play the game.

"Ah, so you're the man that bested him. Why you're the talk of the town this day. He is a beast when in his cups, and no mistake. He's broken many a man," Sir Hugh continued. "Can you fight as well with a sword? For if so, you're my man."

"Aye, Sir Hugh, I get along and my father taught me well."

"Well by God we'll see fighting I'm bound, and I'll mark you well." With that he turned to the captain. Mark felt himself dismissed, and turned to find duties to which he could attend.

Chapter Twenty

London: April

"What ails Father, Jeanette? He looks sickly and pale of disposition. Does the physician cast any opinion upon his case?" Jamie whispered by the door to his bedchamber.

His sister herself looked pale, he thought, tired with nursing their father. When she spoke it was in a timorous voice that belied her usual fortitude. "He says father has a flux. He has bled him to release the cold within and sought his charts for an explanation. Yet he does not rail to recovery."

"Bled him? I am no physic, God knows, but I'd rather trust Cristo and his healing than any other. I shall fetch him and see if aught else can be done. By God's Grace he must recover, for he is dear to us."

"Amen to that, and I pray that he will. Go and fetch Cristo, for with his magic he knows more than any in England, it seems."

"Sssh! Speak not of magic, for though he might appear a necromancer at times I would not have it put abroad that he was such lest his fate as a foreigner be sealed by a burning."

Jamie and Cristoforo returned, the latter carrying his satchel which he had replenished after their journey to the north. He looked at Thomas de Grispere and examined him before looking up at the two expectant siblings. "His lungs are congested with bile, he ... *come si dice*? *Sibili*?" with which he made a rasping, laboured sound in explanation.

"Wheezes?" Jeanette suggested, mimicking the sound.

"*Si*, wheezes. I need to see the apothecary and purchase oils of mustard, camphor, *rosemarino* and mint. When I return, have a bowl of boiling water ready and a clean cloth, this big." He mimed with his hands.

"As you wish, Cristo," Jeanette agreed. "Shall I go in your stead?" She offered.

"No I need to see the quality of these herbs and ensure that the apothecary mixes them *perfettamente*." He assured her. With that he rose and left the room in that silent way of his with which they had become so familiar.

Jamie's father, who had been conscious all this time, smiled wanly. "By God it was a good day's work when I spared that boy and took him to my meiny. Now James, come hither, for I cannot shout and needs must have your ear. I weaken, I know, and afore Cristoforo's healing will out I must ask you to render me service."

Jamie was puzzled, but came to sit on his father's bedside as bidden, concern writ large upon his face.

"Now my boy, the Guild met this week and all was concern at the chance of the treaty, for the date marches towards us with alacrity. I was to travel to Flanders this week, and I am glad I did not, for two more ships were lost to the pirates and the Flemish merchants are in uproar. They blame our navy and declare the Channel unsafe. To wit..." Here he paused, coughing and slumping back on the bolsters. Jamie offered him a beaker of water as the fit subsided.

"Father I adjure you, this is of no import. Your health–"

"Shh, boy, listen. I failed to journey there in March and now all our cloth and goods lie in Flanders, taken in without payment and ready to ship. Yet none will transport it and I blame them not. If the treaty fails, as I suspect it will, those goods will be impounded and seized in lieu. We will lose our profit for the year. You must go, James, in my stead. Pay the kaiage and transport the goods to Calais where they will be safe on English soil. Do not seek to ship the goods until all is safe across the Channel. Swear to me now?" Here he gripped his son's hand with surprising strength.

"I so swear, father. Now rest."

"Good. For even with Cristoforo's aid you and John cannot best a fleet of pirates. A final boon. I have written a letter to Sir Richard asking for your release from duties and that he acquiesce to my favour. Leave and do not tarry, for time is our enemy. Eighteen ships have been lost to these scullion whoresons, Jamie. Eighteen!"

"I will father, I swear. Now rest, I prithee." He patted his father gently with his large, calloused hand and took the sealed letter from the small table at his bedside.

Westminster Palace

Sir Richard was, as ever, pleased to see Jamie, yet he seemed preoccupied and his brow was creased with worry more than usual. He pulled at his ear in thought and distraction, a habit that Jamie had begun to look for and understand. The idiosyncrasy manifested itself when Whittington felt excessively pressured by his duties for the realm. Yet now Jamie surmised that he too felt the bite of the treaty's effects, for as a major mercer and trader in wool and cloth, his exposure could be greater than their own. Jamie knew that he was not paid by the Crown for his endeavours but was instead compensated through exemption, paying no tax or kaiage on his goods. It was a cautelous move on Whittington's behalf, Jamie knew, yet to make profit it relied on being able to transport goods and trade across the Channel. If this was impeded, he would lose a good deal of money.

Breaking the seal, Sir Richard frowned as he read the letter from Jamie's father. Taking in the words, he looked up, startled. "'Tis not the Black Death? Pray God no, for it has risen its ugly head again in parts and your father travels hither and thither and it spreads like a wildfire, unseen and unchecked."

Jamie crossed himself: "We think not, God be praised, for his skin has no discolouration and he has ailed for three days now. All testament declares that those who contract the plague die within that time. We believe it to be a congestion of the lungs with bile and ill humours that lie within."

"Please God he recovers, and as to his favour of course James you must away. I have naught for you to do at present on the Crown's behalf. The prince is sorely tried, as embassies are to be broached upon us by the Armagnacs, so my spies tell me. Neither faction can prevail, and armies battle to and fro within a hundred leagues of Paris. They will seek a force from England to tip the balance of power in their favour."

"How does the prince fall? Is he for or against their suit? And what of King Henry? Does he still prevail against ill health as was the case at the Great Council? May God be with him."

"The prince will support the Armagnacs, I feel, yet I will not foretell the future, for Burgundy is a fox and will upon hearing of their embassies send forth his own to further enhance his cause and muddy the waters of diplomacy. Of his majesty, I regret that he is again unhale. He called for the arch-bishops to pray for his eternal soul but two days past. He is unsettled by the feud arising between his two eldest children."

"May God have him in his keeping," Jamie prayed, crossing himself before continuing: "By the rood 'tis a strange irony that our enemies should come to us to settle their case when we should make such bloody war on them so often." Jamie shook his head in disbelief.

Whittington smiled a secret smile and as though instructing a child. "The twists and turns of men's minds would shent a viper on both sides of the Channel. They seek but one thing: power and the ability to rule a king, for both Louis and his majesty suffer so. Those that would steal a crown care not whose forces they would use to achieve their end. It is our duty to ensure they do not succeed."

"Amen to that, Sir Richard."

"Now go James, and may God be with you. Report back to me on all you find in Flanders and the mood in Calais. I have great use for such intelligence as the talk within Calais holds our future in the balance. If you can seek out David, Bishop of Chichele and Nicholas Ryssheton t'would do well, for they negotiate on our behalf and will give thee a most timely report. It would render us all great service – yet I would adjure you to slip in and out of that town without any save them knowing of your presence. For there are those that would seek to prevent news arriving safe to this side of the Channel."

Jamie nodded in assent, left and made his way back to Laurence Lane. Cristoforo accompanied him to the London docks, to return with his horse.

"Cristo, I thank you for all your healing of my father, and I pray that he recovers."

"By God's grace he will. Fear not, I shall do all in my power to revive him. Do nothing redless whilst in Flanders," Cristoforo warned.

"I go to transport cloth from one town to another, what chance is there for me to stray into trouble?"

Cristoforo merely raised an eyebrow in mockery.

"Yet for all that, if I am not returned by a sennight look for me at the English ports and seek word of any ships that may have been captured or distressed. Oh, and I would ask a favour that you deliver this to Lady Alice, for I have not been able to see her since our meeting on the road." He passed a sealed note to Cristoforo.

"For certes, that I will. God speed, Jamie." Cristoforo said as they clasped arms and Jamie stepped down into the low-lying caravel that would outrun any pirate cog. It was of a Mediterranean design, built upon the Genoese pattern with two masts and sails instead of one and two banks of oars. It had less cargo room but plied its trade as a fast and safe way to cross the Channel.

The port of London disappeared around a bend in the river as Jamie gave a final wave to Cristoforo. Taking to the open sea upon leaving the estuary, the caravel leapt to life, carving a perfect wake through the choppy Channel waters. Under the guidance of the experienced captain the craft made the crossing three quarters of an hour faster than any cog Jamie had previously travelled in. They saw sails upon the horizon from time to time, and once it seemed that two ships began to bear down upon a course that intercepted their own in unison. To no avail, as the nimble craft easily avoided any contact, finally finding the harbour of Dunkerque and safety.

Chapter Twenty-One

Harfleur

As Jamie was landing at Dunkerque, further south down the French coast a flotilla of three warships and two lesser Genoese barges, manned with crossbow mercenaries in French employ were sailing steadily down from Harfleur. The small fleet moved with grace along the Lézarde River towards le Havre and the open sea of the English Channel beyond.

Knowing the scale of pirate activity in the channel, the French took no chances and enhanced the number of protective ships escorting the convoy, as the vessels held the cream of French aristocracy from the Armagnac dynasty. The single sails were stashed against the prevailing wind and the banks of rowers heaved on the oars, powering the mighty ships towards the estuary and the open sea of the English Channel. The ships were a pretty sight made up of gaudy flags, brightly painted shields and banners hung abreast, heralding the might of the French party. Once into the Channel the large vessels tacked to make progress against the wind, driving them westward towards the Thames estuary and the shores of England.

The young Duke of Orleans stood on the fighting platform at the front of the war cog, the wind blowing back his long dark hair that bespoke his Italian heritage. The older man at his side addressed him.

"What are your thoughts, your grace?"

"I know not what to think, nor of the reception that awaits us upon our arrival at the English court. I hear rumours, as do we all, that the king is unwell and we shall only receive an audience from the prince. This would be a great loss, for I feel any sympathy the English court has towards us lies at the king's behest, not the prince's. What say you, John?"

The older man, the Duke of Berry, smiled in admiration at the sixteen-year-old boy in front of him. After the loss of his father at the hands of assassins four years ago, the duke marvelled at how he had grown in stature and matured beyond his years. "As you please, Charles, but it would accord well with us if we could unite both the king and prince, for we will need the whole court to agree to our proposals for the future of France and the good of our kingdom."

"The king is already in accord with me. Recall the quality of intimacy between him and the Duke of Milan. It was the duke who fashioned for him the famous armour that King Henry was to wear in the tourney with his enemy the Duke of Norfolk. It was, I am told, the most beautiful workmanship any has ever seen, of the finest Milanese plate."

"It would be a great wonder if there were not a deal of *sympatico* between our cause and his. The restoration of Aquitaine will allow us the advantage, I feel."

"We shall seek his mind and fathom what may best be done. A mutual collaboration of enemies is the key. That and the sealing of the Treaty."

"Amen to that," The Duke of Berry rejoined.

The Palace of Westminster

A day later they made the port of London, where they were met by heralds and horses to escort them to the Palace of Westminster. The majority of men-at-arms were bidden to stay within calling distance of the ships. The main duty of the knights and soldiers had been to guard the Channel crossing, and an emissary to the king of England required no special protection. The streets of London were thronged with people as the procession of French nobles made its way along the banks of the Thames to the Palace.

Once dismounted and their horses stabled, a reduced party of some twenty men entered the palace through the east entrance to the accompaniment of heralds and trumpets. They were dressed in the latest fashions from the Parisian court – richly coloured silk sendalls, multi-hued hose and boots of supple doe skin – and they were led into the main hall, a vast beamed structure, magnificent in size and designed to impress all who entered. Carpets of red, blue and gold had been laid for them and they moved forward in procession towards the throne at the western end of the vast hall.

As the cortège moved steadily to the front of the court and his majesty, the duke caught the eye of his nephew, Jacques de Berry, who acknowledged the royal duke with an almost imperceptible bow of his head. A contact made and a message passed. To lesser men, the passage before the English court all under scrutiny would have been intimidating, but to the royal dukes of the French court it was a seemly affair.

As they entered and came to within a few yards from the dais they saw King Henry. If the French dukes had been unmoved by the pomp of their welcome they were certainly shocked at the sight of King Henry before them. His pallor was grey and sickly, the boils about his face were rank and red with the excretion of suppurating sores. The hair, streaked now with grey, was lank and unkempt. His breath came in rasps and his voice when he spoke was hoarse.

The cortege halted and the leading members of the party, the dukes of Orleans, Berry and Brittany, bowed deeply three times, while those of lesser rank behind kept the heads bowed a little longer.

"Your majesty, it is gracious of you to honour our humble souls with an audience. Your cousin, his royal majesty King Charles of France bids us wish you well and we submit his most gracious felicitations upon you in his name," offered the Duke of Orleans, who despite his youth was the highest ranking of those present.

"We thank you for our cousin's kind words and would ask that you reciprocate our blessings upon him in our name."

"Majesty, if you will permit," the Duke of Orleans beckoned with a wave of his hand, his eyes never leaving the king's face, "a token of his esteemed majesty's regard."

Two caskets were brought forward by esquires, both of which were opened to display gifts. One stood out, as it contained a luxurious velvet pillow, upon which was laid an elaborate ornament. The Duke of Orleans bent and lifted the pillow so that all could see it held a masterful rendering on two gold shields bearing the coats of arms of both Henry and Charles, wrought in intricate enamels and inlaid with gold filigree and jewels. It was fashioned in the most exquisite workmanship and would have been worth a king's ransom.

As the chamberlain of the household, Lord Grey moved forward to receive the gift on behalf of his majesty, duly presenting the pillow closer so that the ailing king might have a better view.

"It is a most wonderous gift. We thank our cousin for his generosity and thoughtfulness," King Henry said.

"As your majesty pleases," the duke bowed.

A silent communication passed between the king and Prince Henry, who stood at his father's right-hand side. "You will no doubt be fatigued from your journey," the prince said. "And we pray that you will accept food from our table within the hour, before which time you will be escorted to your quarters, which we hope will be sufficient unto your needs during your visit to our court."

"Your royal highness is most kind and we would indeed be pleased to join with you at *déjeuner*," the duke responded.

With the courtly pleasantries at an end, the French visitors and their meiny retired, escorted by royal pages to the lavish quarters that they had been allocated. The rooms were located in a secure part of the palace of Westminster in the newly constructed west wing. They were on an upper floor, offering greater defence against intruders. The walls were of stone and wainscoted to half height, with wooden floors and glazed windows. The chambers had been fitted to the highest standard, boasting to their guests of England's advancement in culture and comfort.

Once the doors had been closed and the pages had departed, the three dukes and Bernard, the Count of Armagnac, gathered in front of the fire that burned brightly in the generous hearth before them.

"Hells teeth it is damp and cold in this Godforsaken country," Berry grimaced. "If ever we should rule here, as is our right, I would lief as not be assigned to govern for I'd die of ague within a month." The others agreed and then became serious.

"It seems propitious that the king and prince are united in their will to meet with us. This bodes well, does it not, Duke Charles?" the count asked. At fifty one years old, the count was an elder statesman of the house of Armagnac and carried a certain gravitas that was respected by the younger members.

"Verily it does, and is more than we could have prayed for in that regard. But now comes the test to see if the terms we require will be met. I expect your nephew to come hither, John, for we must learn all we can before our next meeting with the king. When shall he arrive?"

"I expect him as soon as he has executed his feudatory duties and is able to come alone." John de Berry answered.

They had little time to wait and discuss other matters, for within ten minutes there was a knock at the chamber door announcing the arrival of Jacques de Berry.

"Why nephew, you are well met and timely so." His uncle greeted him. With his usual arrogance, Jacques de Berry greeted all those present as equals, save in address.

"Now, what news have you on the courts stance to our suit?" asked the young duke.

"It is as you saw. The king and prince appear united in their support of your cause. In line with this will lie the future of Aquitaine and the security of English lands in France, together with the recovery of Guyenne." Then even Jacques' cockiness faltered. "There is another matter of great import, however, and one that could tip the balance against us. It concerns the Welsh prince Glyndower, for as I understand you seek his recognition for past alliances."

"We do," confirmed the duke.

"My lord duke, this condition may unsettle their majesties enough to reject the codicil. We and the English both know the importance of allies, yet the English see Glyndower as an outlaw and a traitor to the crown. I doubt they will recognise his alliance and we may have to abandon him ourselves."

"We will address this issue as it becomes necessary, for if England should land in favour of the Burgundians our cause will be lost."

Chapter Twenty-Two

The English Channel

The *Shield of the Cross,* in which Mark sailed, made the port of Southampton within two days along with the rest of the fleet. They passed into the Isle of Wight channel, then pushed northwards up the Solent estuary to Southampton Water.

Mark had settled down, learning the nautical names and the ropes and lines that aided the sails and rigging. He was, he found, a natural sailor and did not suffer the dreaded sickness so many landsmen did when shipbound. He remembered how his friend Cristo, so brave, light-footed and expert with his assassin's weapons, was laid low when at sea. It was the only thing he feared. Standing now on the forecastle looking out with interest, he spied the imposing Arundel and God's House Towers, and he saw how the construction of Catchcold Tower was progressing as it came into view off the headland to the west of the town. The mighty city walls were imposing as befitted the Royal Docks, and newly installed cannon and guns bristled through the purpose-built portals that housed them. The ships made for the South Gate. It was an impressive structure of ramparts and machicolations, from which defenders could pour boiling oil and scalding sand down upon any attackers.

By God the French will have their work cut out if they ever dare attack here, Mark thought. Any attacker would be caught in a crossfire if they tried to enter through the main gates. The rowers pulled slowly back on the oars as they docked at the main quays alongside the fleet and slipped in gently to bump against wooden rails that were set into the stone. Steeves threw cables from the shore and tied off the great warship against the quay. A boarding plank was thrown down from the deck and the crew began to disembark.

"Mark," called the captain as the Cornishman made to slide down the steps from the forecastle to the deck below and freedom. "You've taken the king's coin and you are one of us. To run now is be tried for treason, so don't ye give cause for me to indict you."

"Aye, Cap'n. I have no wish to leave. Running is the coward's way, and this is a grand adventure. My indenture to you is sealed, fear not," Mark replied.

Captain Ralph just nodded and turned away. As Mark left the ship to explore the town and docks, the captain spoke quietly to two men aboard: "Keep a wary eye on that one. He's new and not yet to be trusted, despite his fine words. If he makes to leave, stop him or kill him."

The two sailors were seasoned and experienced men who had witnessed such behaviour often. They nodded and made to follow Mark ashore.

The captain need not have worried, for Mark had plans of his own. He had been forewarned by Whittington that the quays and ports were full of William Stokes' spies and needs must they would be working close to the revenue inspectors and port officials. His problem was how to find the right man and ensure that a message was returned to Stokes and Whittington. He wandered along the quays, a newcomer gawking at the new sights far from home. As he wandered, he noticed certain officials taking a little more interest in him, perhaps wondering if he were a French spy.

Mark sidled up to an official marking off cargo from an unloading merchant cog and began a conversation with him, during the course of which he managed to ascertain the location of the chief customs officer's rooms. The official pointed to an imposing stone building next to one of the many towers that had been built into the city wall near the God's House Tower. Mark ambled along as if to no true purpose, noting the office of the inspector without entering. Opportunity would no doubt arise at another time to meet the official and he was, he realised, still within sight of the ship and possibly the captain. Instead he passed under one of the many gates and made for a tavern, where he settled down to enjoy a beaker of ale. Others from his ship were there in the tap room, yet apart from a perfunctory nod he ignored them and they left him alone. He supped his ale, but soon afterwards his ears pricked up when he heard the language of his dear friend Cristo.

He looked up to see the source of the words and saw a group of five men speaking to each other in Italian. The group was loud in the way of Cristoforo's countrymen, and knowing that they were not understood they cared not a fig for what they said. The group were not sailors, steeves or soldiers. Their flamboyant dress marked them as wealthy merchants or bankers.

"By the rood," Mark muttered to himself, "They'll be Cristo's countrymen as sure as like." He wondered if they might be connected to *Signor* Filippo. He drained his ale he moved in a circuitous route to the bar, gently bumping into one of the men as if by accident. He turned to offer an apology, hands up and palms out, as the man span around on his stool.

"*Scusi, Signor.*" He began with the words he had heard Cristoforo speak many times.

The Italian was so surprised at hearing his own language spoken that any possibility of an aggressive response to Mark's apparent carelessness left him.

"*Parli italiano?*" he asked

Mark guessed at the meaning and answered in English. "No oi don't, but 'appen a good friend of mine does. He comes from Italy too, a place called Frenzy or some such."

The Italian beamed in response after a moment of puzzlement. "*Firenze! Bello.*" He proceeded to rattle off a sentence in his own tongue of which Mark understood nothing.

"Steady now, I speak very little only what oi've 'eard my friend speak in Lunnon," he protested with a smile, thinking how like these men Cristoforo was in manner and speech. "*Parlare lento,*" he improvised.

The men laughed, and in the welcoming manner of their race they bade him sit and join them. It transpired that they knew *Signor* Albertini, and one of their number was in his employ. They insisted that he dine with them at another tavern and the group moved on. The two sailors from the cog shrugged and followed them out, completely at ease and not in the least suspicious: it was to them a normal night out in a port. Mark was enjoying himself and making new friends who appeared perfectly innocent, even if they were foreign.

— ✕ ❋ ✕ —

The following day back on board the *Shield of the Cross*, Mark had a sore head ¬– yet not as bad as when he had been drugged with dwale, he ruminated. The captain took the two men aside before Mark arose.

"Did aught occur abroad with Mark yester eve that was suspicious?"

"No cap'n. He wandered along the quays like, then went to the tavern and bumped into some foreigners, Italians maybe. I know they weren't French because they didn't speak that perfidious tongue, and pirates wouldn't dare come openly to So'ton. They just got talking and he went drinking with 'em and came back on board. Naught suspicious and no attempt at escape."

"Italians, you say?"

"Yea, the town's full of 'em. Merchants and bankers, sorting cargo and warrants for coin. There be plenty here for official work and the like. They're a friendly lot for the most part, strange mind, but amiable enough, especially when a big oaf like him bangs into them." The sailor laughed.

The captain pulled at his chin, yet seemed happy with the account.

The fleet set sail that day to patrol the Channel, proceeding in an eastwardly direction from Southampton along the coast. They passed the headland at Eastbourne, with Mark gazing up at the pure white cliffs of chalk in wonder, before turning slightly north east and sailing to Hastings. No convoy of ships was spotted, and nothing that resembled a pirate fleet. They turned back and docked in the safe harbour at Eastbourne, yet only a few were allowed ashore. Mark was ordered to stay aboard. He chose the opportunity to speak with the captain, who was pacing the deck, clearly pensive and awaiting orders from Sir Hugh upon his return.

"Are we to put out again, captain?" he asked.

"Aye, that we are. We must scour each port for news and see if any of the pirate cogs have been spotted abroad. Yet we cannot move against them in port. We need to catch them in the act of piracy. If rumour be true, the pirate leaders are knights and connected with the court. One be the mayor of Rye and Sir John Prendergast so they say – and good men they were too."

"How so?" Mark asked curious as to their change in allegiance.

"They were pirates or privateers all along, and were gifted an unofficial warrant by the king to raid all enemy shipping from France to Spain. Yes, you may raise an eyebrow, but they served a useful purpose and gave one fifth of what they took to the crown. It kept the enemy ships at bay and brought coin to the realm, so they served their purpose and prospered to boot. But now, as we sue for peace, they have become bored and dissolute, seeking plunder and action at any cost, caring not whom they harm."

"You sound as though you admire them, cap'n."

"Aye, lad, mebbe I do in a way. 'Tis like a wolf being suddenly told not to take any more sheep and to tend them instead. It won't serve and it never will." The captain said. "Just you take Sir Hugh. Why he's done his share and may again, who knows? For 'tis a fine line between piracy and fighting for the crown and no mistake." The captain pulled himself up, gave Mark a knowing look, then moved off as though he had said too much.

Within the hour they shipped out again, with Sir Hugh on the forecastle with the captain. Now as the fleet passed out on to the Channel it sailed north-eastwards, hugging the coast. Within five hours the ship made Rye. Signals were sent from the flagship to the *Shield of the Cross*, and she made to port heading into the harbour at Rye with her sister ship, the *Swan*. Mark was puzzled, yet kept his own counsel as he watched the rest of the fleet sail away up the coast.

Chapter Twenty-Three

The two ships made for port at Rye. The harbour was impressive – and so it should be, for as Mark knew it was the main contributor to the Federation of Cinque Ports of which Prince Henry was now Warden. It also housed the largest and most impressive Royal Dockyard on the South Coast.

"She be a fine port," A sailor called Jim commented, standing at Mark's side. "If you've not been here afore, feast your eyes. She'll take up to three hundred ships 'tween here and Winchelsea," Jim nodded at the nearby town on the shale bank. Numerous inlets and islets showed themselves as the ship passed. *A smuggler's paradise*, Mark thought. The water looked deep to his eyes, easily capable of floating any ship even at low tide.

Ships of all shapes and sizes were moored here, from fishing boats to full size cogs with fighting platforms and battle-hardened crews. The town was set on a raised island that rose up from the port, set inside city walls that were commanded by a castle of four semi-circular towers. The Land Gate stood to the fore, a forbidding portal of two strong towers and a large arch with its portcullis raised. The two ships found suitable berths in the immense port, and once everything was stowed away all seamen, soldiers and knights were given shore leave. The seaside tang of rotting fish was once again prevalent, mixing with old tar, mouldering hemp and the usual smells of a lively and busy town.

Market Street stretched up before him and he had a mental note in his head of his intended destination from *signor* Vittorio Loggio, the banker who worked for the Felicinis. In the evening he had spent in the Italians' company, Loggio had given Mark two connections – one here and one at Dover – hoping that one or the other would suffice. The two addresses were written on a scrap of parchment which Mark had concealed about his person. Now Mark wandered the streets, looking for the address. He found what he was looking for in a prosperous street with houses of quality. Half way along he found the right address and knocked upon the door, turning with a final glance to make sure no one was following him.

The door was opened by a well-dressed figure who was obviously Italian from his oiled hair, olive skin and well-tailored clothes down to the doeskin boots on his feet.

"Good morrow," Mark said. "I come bearing the compliments of *signor* Vittorio Loggio and would ask that you allow me an audience with your master concerning the affairs of *Signor* Felicini and others." The court had served him well in smoothing his manners, Mark thought.

The Italian waited a moment then beckoned him in: "*Prego,*" he offered sweeping his arm in a dramatic gesture and standing aside.

Mark entered, removing his woollen seaman's hat and standing expectantly, aware of how unkempt he must look in the fine surroundings of the house. A magnificent carved oak staircase swept upwards leading to apartments on the first and second floors. The door off the entrance hall opened and he was summoned by the same servant to enter another room. This room was a snug chamber containing dark furniture with deep red drapes framing the windows. Sunlight peeked through the expensive glass that filled the window frame, and the room bespoke wealth and opulence.

As befitting such a setting, a well-groomed individual stood in front of a hearth laid with a good fire that brought the room to an almost unbearable temperature for Mark, who had become accustomed to the open sea and all the depredations of its weather. The man standing before the fire was clad in a magnificent silk sendall that would not disgrace the court, girded at the waist with a jewelled belt supporting an inlaid dagger. His hair too was dark and swept back in a sleek manner, the eyes dark brown and questioning. He ran his glance over Mark, noting the coarse dress and rough manner of his speech.

"*Signor* Collazzo, may I present Mark of..." The servant hesitated, looking at Mark.

"Of Cornwall, *signor*," Mark finished. "*Buongiorno,*" he offered, using one of the few words he had learned from Cristoforo.

A thin smile creased *signor* Collazo's lips. "You are most welcome sir. May I offer you some wine?" Mark accepted and with the drink poured, *Signor* Collazzo continued after sipping the spiced wine.

"Now sir, you have mentioned two men whose names command that I listen to you. Prithee, how may I be of assistance?" he asked in heavily accented English.

Mark explained who he was and his connection to Cristoforo, *signor* Felicini and Sir Richard Whittington. At the mention of the latter's name, Collazzo's eyebrows shot upwards.

"And what, pray, would you have me do to forward your obligations to Sir Richard?" Collazzo asked.

"Why *signor* I would ask that you write a letter to both *signor* Felicini and Sir Richard informing them of my condition and where I am bound. For by God the last they would know is that which was passed to him by the kaiage master at Plymouth who served master Stokes and with him Sir Richard. Since this time past there would have been silence."

"*Va bene,*" Collazzo declared. "This I can do with ease. It serves me well, as *signor* Felicini and I are partners in many ventures and we stand to gain much by the destruction of these *bastardi pirati.*"

Collazzo marched to his large desk with a purposeful swagger. He seated himself, and picking up his quill and drawing forward a new sheet of parchment he proceeded to scratch away, dipping his quill at regular intervals as the ink flowed. Satisfied with the result, he read it back to Mark who asked that he make a small addition on his behalf.

In a similar vein, he repeated the process with a letter to Filippo Felicini, asking that he contact Cristoforo Corio at his best speed. This done, he spread blotting sand upon the scripts, blew this off and sealed both documents with wax and the imprint of his signet ring.

He moved around the desk and summoned his steward. Pausing, he asked Mark: "I have but one question. *Madonna,* how do you, a man of the sea, survive in this Godforsaken country when it is always so cold!"

The two men laughed, breaking the tension, and Mark thanked Collazzo and left the security of his house to wander further around the quaint town that harboured such potential for strife. Coming to a break in the city walls, he looked out over a low parapet to see the River Rother meandering lazily out towards the estuary mouth. He threw a stone, skimming it as he had done as a boy, and was delighted to see it hit and jump eight times before it disappeared beneath the surface of the river. Anyone seeing him would think he was just an aimless visitor from aboard ship with not a care in the world.

Chapter Twenty-Four

Dunkerque

Jamie found it strange to be back in Dunkerque, the town from which he had made such a dramatic escape the year before. It seemed unreal to him that the town had not changed at all, and it was comforting in some small measure to hear the accents of his father spoken again so readily. He adopted it easily, slipping back into the less formal manner of speech.

He made for the Customs and Revenue office that oversaw all goods that came in or went out of Dunkerque. The building was guarded by two men-at-arms, who nodded as Jamie went through the outer gates into a huge courtyard stacked high with goods upon which excise duty had yet to be paid. Much of it was raw wool that had been imported from England and not yet collected. Open bayed warehouses stood behind the offices protecting the cloth stored within against the elements. The floors were dry, but the bales of cloth and other goods had been raised onto wooden slats to keep them off the earthen floor.

Two officials with boards and keys to the open slatted gates stood guarding the stock. Jamie spoke with one, who pointed him in the direction of a stone building at the rear of the courtyard. Presenting his warrant of payment raised under *Signor* Felicini's banking system, he paid the kaiage and left with an itemised certificate which he presented to the officials. They checked the sealed stamp and began to unlock the large gates, beckoning Jamie to follow them into the cavernous warehouse. Looking at the bundles of cloth that were stacked high, he realised that it would take four or five waggons to transport the goods to Calais.

Two hours later he returned with carters and five waggons that he'd hired for the forty-five-mile journey. Once across the border into English territory he knew the goods would be safe from French *routiers*. The journey would take two days with an overnight stop at Bourborg. The carters and mules entered the compound of the customs office, and the men began loading the bales of cloth and goods. While this was in progress, Jamie sought more information from the officers in charge.

"Has there been much sailing across the Channel?" he asked. "For it seems impossible to get passage for my goods."

"Nay, no one will take the risk with the pirates abroad. All are afeared of losing cargo – and their lives, more like."

"Yet we sailed across without hide nor hair of them seen."

"And well you might. 'Tis my belief they have spies in the docks here informing upon those foolish enough to sail from the ports on this side of the water."

"That would cause mischief abroad and no mistake. We durst not trust anyone, for these are dark times. What of the treaty? Do you think it'll be signed?"

"The treaty?" The man spat at the floor. "A pox on the Treaty! While the English cannot control the sea nor vouchsafe for any poor traveller venturing abroad there'll be no treaty.

And you mark my words," the man continued, "my lord of Burgundy will have a lever to force open the gates and link us closer to France, and with such a course war with England or gain Calais, whichever he desires."

"Then by the rood I'm right glad I fetched our stock, for you paint a terrible picture of dissent, and one to which I'd lief as not be party."

"Amen to that, for I see naught but strife ahead," The official concluded.

Jamie thanked the warehousemen for their help, and seeing the waggons all loaded he moved to lead them forward on a hired horse that was saddled and waiting. The company edged forward slowly as the mules pushed into their harnesses, egged on by the cracking of the whips above their heads.

— ✕ ✤ ✕ —

Two days later, leading the procession of waggons moving southwest, Jamie saw Calais come into sight as he led them down for the last part of their journey. The company entered through the north gate into the outer bailey of the fortress town. Looking up, Jamie saw new building works in progress, strengthening the town walls and gatehouse. There was a siege mentality in the air and Jamie wondered if the duplicitous Sir Geoffrey de Haven was still in the position of castellan for the castle.

The town was bustling, and as always he was surprised to hear English spoken on this side of the Channel. The houses were different, with an eclectic mix of architecture betraying the broad nature of those within its walls. This was, he knew, England on French soil. Upon the walls it was not just crossbowmen he saw, but groups of archers with their fierce looking longbows, feared by the French since Crecy, when the scion of

French chivalry had been decimated by the common English archer.

The streets were laid out in regular shapes, much less erratic than those of London or England's much older towns. The distances between the buildings too were greater, offering less chance for the spread of fire in a time of war. It was a living, breathing fortress town that had been much improved since it had fallen into English hands nearly seventy years before, when King Edward drove most of the French citizens out and filled it with Englishmen to better defend and secure the town.

The procession of waggons made its way through the wide streets heading towards the western gate and the port. They passed through under the watchful eyes of the guards and went out to the port and storage area. The sea had been let in and redirected to form a natural harbour and moat around the town on all sides, and next to it secure warehouses had been built on one of the man-made islands that were kept under heavy guard at all times. Stone bastions housed huge cannons pointing seawards, threatening any attack on the port and the town from that direction, and the mouth of the harbour itself was guarded by an ominous looking tower and castellated battlements that housed more cannon and a huge sea chain that could blockade the harbour. The waggons moved across the land bridge that led onto the island and the warehouses and customs office.

The officer knew Jamie of old, and his father regularly held goods here pending transport to England. Here Jamie heard the same story; the warehouses were nearly full as no one wanted to risk passage with the pirates at large unless they sailed as part of a huge convoy, and no one was prepared to risk organising such a thing.

"Is there anyone that will give me passage to England, Elias?" He asked the older customs officer as both men saw a swift-looking caravel cast off and bounce into the Channel with the wind in its favour, leaving in a hurry towards England.

"They could've," he answered, nodding at the vessel. "Mind, I'd soon as not travel with those scullions, for if they be not pirates or excise runners I know not who is."

Jamie looked with interest at the racing caravel scudding across the sea.

"What about that cog there?" he pointed at a vast and well put together vessel that looked brand new or recently painted.

"The *Juliane*? Well, she leaves on the morning tide if'n you can get passage. She be Prince Henry's ship and will only take his personal retainers and household."

Jamie smiled, *so there was some benefit to being a household knight after all,* he thought.

"By the Lord Harry that will do me well, Elias! Now I will give you payment in lieu by warrant on the Italian's bank and see the men off, for I have to sail on the morrow's tide and have matters to which I must attend."

Elias was clearly bemused and thought Jamie would try in vain. He was unaware that Jamie was now Sir James de Grispere, knight of the royal household, with a personal connexion to the prince. Jamie walked from the office and thanked the carters, who had all performed well and had transported the goods in record time. After paying them off he moved across to the wharf, where he saw that the final preparations for setting sail were taking place aboard the *Juliane*.

"Ahoy aboard!" He called out, and was met by a reply from a lean man bearing the mark of authority in his captaincy. He had a strong, capable face, showing intelligence above that of the common sailor beneath wiry steel grey hair. He eyed Jamie suspiciously at first.

"What be your business sir?" he responded gruffly.

"Prithee, you are the captain; and this is a ship of the prince royal?"

"Aye that I am, and she is of the prince's fleet. Now time is tight, we sail on the morning tide and there is much to do." At which he nodded to the open harbour where the waves were breaking upon the rocks and walls of the breakwater.

"Then I'll not waste it. Mayhap you can aid me, for I am on a fiat of Sir Richard Whittington and through him the Prince, as behoves one of his household knights. I need passage to England on important matters of state."

The captain looked Jamie up and down as though seeing him for the first time, fighting back a look of disbelief.

"How are you called, sir?" he asked with a little more respect in his voice.

"I am Sir James de Grispere and I am commanded by the prince."

"May I see your bona fides? For these are strange times and I'll not take just anyone aboard. Yet step up to the deck and mind, for the plank sways a bit as she saws." He advised.

Jamie stepped on to the wooden platform and felt it move beneath his feet as he adjusted to the swing. Three swift steps and he was up onto the deck, leaping as the cog swayed on the tide. Opening the frogging of his doublet he removed a letter sealed by Whittington and the prince asking all and any to provide aid and passage to him as demanded. The captain read it twice, then looked up, raising an eyebrow. He nodded then declared: "Well sir James, 'tis to England we travel – and so now do you. Welcome aboard. I'm captain Ernald of Dover, which is where we be bound."

"Well met captain, and I thank you, for you have aided me and your help will be mentioned to those who matter."

"That can do no harm. Now fetch any baggage that you may wish safely stowed."

"Aye cap'n." Jamie called, making the perilous journey to retrieve his warbag.

"Stow your gear aft, it'll keep dry there," the captain nodded to the rear of the ship then moved away to continue supervising the final stowing away in readiness for the voyage. Jamie took the opportunity to look around. The ship was new, as he'd suspected, with bright paintwork and clean rigging. Everything looked tidy and efficient.

Jamie made to leave and seek food in the town with a final word of warning from the captain.

"We sail at Lauds, so be sharp after sunrise or I'll sail without 'ee and no mistake."

"Aye cap'n, I'll be here for certes." Jamie assured him and risked the perils of the plank once more. He made for a tavern that he and his father frequented on such occasions, where he sought to learn as much as he could of conditions and feelings on this side of the Channel. Once he had bespoke a bed for the night, he walked through the town to the inner enceinte that housed the castle and was reminded of the last time he'd been here with Cristoforo on their mission to Paris.

He was allowed through the gateway after showing his papers that identified him as a royal messenger, and one of the sentries directed him to the quarters of the English delegation comprising four household knights together with the eminent lawyer and diplomat Nicholas Ryssheton, who Jamie sought. He found the keep guarded, and sent a message via one of the pages asking that Lord Ryssheton attend him without mentioning his name. Jamie had learned through his dealings over the last year that secrecy was everything and that no one could be entirely trusted. A few minutes passed, and Jamie was beginning to wonder if the message had been delivered when a thin figure appeared, wrapped up well in a cloak against the evening chill. He seemed in poor temper and of sour visage.

As he approached the gate, he demanded of the page: "Well, where is this messenger?"

The page pointed towards Jamie, who stepped out from the shadows. "My Lord Ryssheton, a good evening to you. I trust I find you well." As the page disappeared, he continued. "I am Sir James de Grispere of his royal Highness's household knights at your service."

"De Grispere? Why of course I have seen you at court, sir. Yet why do you tarry thither? Come in man, out of the cold evening air."

"Sir, I would rather not, for mayhap my welcome within may be warmer than I would like." Jamie answered enigmatically. The lawyer was no fool, and caught his meaning immediately.

"Just so, just so. Now tell me what news you have, or is it I that must update you with the state of the negotiations?" he finished with a gravid look in his rheumy eyes.

"As you say sir, I come at the behest of Sir Richard Whittington and from him the prince whom we serve. He would know what has been agreed and what matters of import have yet to be discussed. In short, will the treaty be upheld and signed or will it fail?"

"In that accord I have news that will alarm both the prince and Sir Richard, for I fear that as matters stand the treaty is doomed to failure. The heart of the account lies with the safety of the seas. The Flemish contingent are convinced that we cannot guarantee safe passage across the Channel, and in this accord I am at a loss to offer such an undertaking. They also veer towards a feeling of accusation that the loss of shipping and trade is sanctioned unofficially by the realm of England." He almost whispered the last words, afraid of the reaction that it would invoke.

"By God's grace that is a lie!" Jamie replied. "The king and the prince are at one accord in their desire to ensure that the seas are made safe again and the pirates taken in chains or killed. Their majesties would be araged to hear such rumours spoken abroad or even considered."

"Of that I am in no doubt. Yet consider this: who controls the Flemish lands? 'Tis Burgundy. And who would benefit from a delayed treaty? 'Tis also Burgundy. Then think on't – should he sue for peace with England in return for arms to thwart his nemesis, the house of Armagnac, and sway the Flemish to the table of diplomacy?"

"By the rood you have the right of it." Jamie considered "And by so doing he would divide the realm. For the king favours the Armagnacs, yet I hear rumours of the prince siding with Burgundy, who wouldst promise the return of lands in Aquitaine and elsewhere. Such a return to arms would please many as a chance for glory and ambition as I've heard abroad across the realm."

"Now make this known to his highness the prince, and with that accord he'll not take to being made the dupe of Burgundy and you will render great service to the crown. Now tell me, how does the king, for rumours spread abroad of his return to ill health?"

"He was unhale when I left the court and calling to be shriven, yet rallies at length from week to week. I know not any more than that."

"Sir James, 'tis best that you depart now and may God have you in his keeping, for much depends upon your presenting the facts to Whittington and the crown."

"I bid you adieu my lord, and thank you for the intelligence. Good night, and not a word I prithee of my presence here, for my journey will be perilous enough without adding to the strain."

"You have my word of honour, now go."

With that Jamie strode off into the night, pleased to be leaving the castle.

The following morning, he arose at dawn feeling refreshed and hurried down to the quay, being one of the first to pass through the newly opened west gate and down to the harbour side. The *Juliane* bobbed with the change of tide as though eager to be off and seemingly frustrated with cables that tied her to the shore. He marched up the gangplank, bade captain Ernald a good morrow and took a position amidships.

Jamie saw that two fighting platforms had been built fore and aft and were occupied by a few men-at-arms. There appeared to be no archers, just a few crossbows hooked ready for action later.

If we are attacked will there be enough men? he wondered. Looking at the sail he knew she would be faster than cogs of war, but if the pirates had sleek caravels they would be over-hauled, new ship or no. The soldiers looked competent and tough, with good mail and swords, and their shields hung outside on the rail in the usual manner. Jamie's observations were disturbed as the captain gave the order to cast off, his voice carrying strongly in the breeze. Looking over the side, Jamie saw a large rowing barge heave to at the prow, attaching a huge cable. Once it was secure two banks of oarsmen heaved at the bosun's command, pulling the cog away from the quay and out into the shipping channel. The wind was a south-easterly that blew in their favour. As soon as it was safe, the captain gave the command and the huge mainsail was unravelled. It slapped and cracked as it came down, to be arrested by the bowlines holding the weather edge, and finally it billowed as it caught the breeze. The cog seemed to almost lurch forward as the wind caught the sail, and the ship seemed to become a living, breathing entity in its own right.

With shouted commands, the cable was slung off the barge

and the rowers pulled to escape the path of the cog that was steadily gathering knots.

Jamie rejoiced at the feel of the sea air as the wind blew his hair from his face. It was good sailing weather, and a pale dawn sun made its way into an azure sky as sparse banks of white cloud fluffed along northwards in time with the ship.

Chapter Twenty-Five

Rye, England

Mark wandered through the pretty port town, admiring the cottages and simple cobbled streets. It reminded him a lot of the towns of his Cornish homeland, yet nothing compared to the vastness of the harbour that stretched from Rye to Winchelsea across the Puddle, as it was known. Even now he saw three huge and well-appointed cogs enter the harbour in trim order, followed by two smaller sleek, twin-masted caravels. Yet these were not merchantmen, he noticed upon closer inspection. They were cogs of war, unless he was mistaken.

He walked quickly to the quayside to gain a better vantage point and see what was happening. Something was amiss, he was sure, yet he knew not what. The ships moored against the outer quay and he saw a group of men make for the *Shield of the Cross*, where they were welcomed aboard by the captain and Sir Hugh, among others. Mark heard the bells ring out for sext and his stomach protested at the lack of food. He made his way to The Olde Bell, an inn that had been pointed out to him by his shipmates as a good place to meet. It was located close to the shore on the high street, and he saw that it was already half full of sailors and men-at-arms.

He bought a beaker of ale and sat with his companions. He had settled well into the ship's company as always, and was making friends easily.

"Dost know of the new ships that have called into port?" He asked of Jim as he finished his first pull of the rich dark ale.

"I caution 'ee not to look too closely, lad, for if I don't miss my mark that be those whom we seeks." At which he winked surreptitiously at Mark, who caught the faint smiles of those around him at the table.

"But I..." he began.

"Give us no buts lad," another continued in quieter tones, "for you'll see soon enough what's to 'appen. The masters will tell us in time and we'll go with what they say, you just mark me."

Mark knew when to keep quiet. His thoughts began to race inwardly and he did not like the conclusions that he came to.

As the day drew on, bosuns and sergeants-at-arms came to the Bell and called for all men to return to their ships by the hour of Nones. At this, some started to drink up and wander slowly from the tavern towards the quay. All were curious to see what developments were to be made known.

When they returned to their ships, the men were given orders to restock for setting to sea and told that all shore leave was cancelled. The activity became frenetic as time wore on and crews in the fading light to have all five ships re-stocked and ready to sail. In the middle of the night, all five ships quietly slipped their lines and sailed out on the River Rother estuary into the starlit night on the full tide, the mysterious new ships in the lead, as they clearly knew the river channels well on the half mile journey to the sea.

Westminster Palace, Prince Henry's private chamber

The two young men could not have been more unlike each other, sharing only the long dark hair that was so characteristic of their father. As blood royal princes of the realm their status, like their height, was not quite equal. Prince Henry was the heir apparent and Thomas second in line to the throne. It was acknowledged that the younger Prince Thomas, Duke of Clarence, was the king's favourite. Both men knew, yet neither would ever utter the truth of it. Thomas was more devoted to his father and had not formed a Council in direct challenge to the king's sovereign power or his absolute right to rule.

"Brother, we are private here and no audience listens to our discourse. So hear us well, for we were promised by your own lips to favour my suit for Margaret. You gave your approval if recollection serves. Why then do you tarry now and hesitate to give full consent?" Thomas cried, anger in his voice, aware that they had quarrelled so in their boyhood, and were oft at each other's throats. Thomas was broad and strong, while Henry had a whipcord strength born even then of greater height, and had as often as not managed to win such childhood conflicts.

Prince Henry turned away to better husband his strength of purpose and prevent his anger erupting upon his younger brother, whom he knew had the right of it. Yet Thomas was the king's man, and the Beaufort brothers – their own uncles at least by half-blood – had brought pressure to bear. He pinched the bridge of his nose twixt finger and thumb, rubbing gently as if to ease a headache, while the old scar on his cheek throbbed. At length he turned back to Prince Thomas: "Brother, the promise you bring to us is just, yet the suit be wrong, for with it you divide us against France, our common enemy. The kingdom is already riven with discord, with rebellion and risings in all corners. And now you would bring it home and lay it upon our doorsteps.

"Shrive me if you will, and by God's witness I admit that I

favoured your suit with Margaret. But by the rood I cannot now give my blessing; so beshrew your heart, for the pressure brought upon me is ineluctable. I need unity of the kingdom and this will cause a schism within the Council, and with that a weakening. You are cognisant of how ill is our father? Think ye he will go to war if called? Does he grip the kingdom thus," he raised a clenched fist "as he once gripped his sword, with a steel fist? No. His grip is now soft as a maiden's on a knight's pizzle. So we must be sword and shield to this realm, both within and without."

"For sure the true meaning of your words stands clear, my brother." Thomas spat. "You find yourself in a cleft stick. Support me and you lose those of the Council who would support you, more specifically the Beauforts. Those bastard halflings would seize the crown themselves if the opportunity arose. Instead they machinate and posture, awaiting every opportunity they can, gradually clawing their way upwards as accords so well with their disposition.

"Fie on you brother, for I see your mark well. So be it. You mention our father, his majesty, in terms so light, yet he will rally, for see how he met with the Armagnacs and stood firm on matters of the realm. There is a steel there that none would suppose existed, and he may well outlive us all, God be pleased. If this be your final word then I am done and I will not beg. I shall instead call upon the Holy Father for a Papal see to which even my lord Archbishop Beaufort cannot deny, and marry Margaret I will." With which he bowed to his brother and stormed away.

"Thomas, brother, be not hasty..." The Prince called to the back of the Duke of Clarence. He stood then alone in his chamber as the door crashed shut, wringing his hands and raising his head upwards: "God give me strength, for I have not even gained the crown and yet still it weighs heavy upon me."

Chapter Twenty-Six

The English Channel, May 1st

The *Shield of the Cross* sailed slightly abreast of the flotilla to avoid foundering in the wake of the other ships. They made a good speed at about four knots and travelled steadily north east, passing by the headland of Dungeness before hugging the coastline up to Dover.

The wind was from the southeast and not fully in their favour, yet they made Dover by the time the yellow slits of a morning sun ribboned out across the dusky sky to illuminate their way. The sea had a gentle swell, pushing the huge cog in a gentle rocking motion that lulled the senses. Mark stood on the forecastle, at ease with the sea despite his sense of foreboding as to how events were unfolding.

By God he thought, *I wish I was with Jamie and Cristo now, for I am sore afraid and no mistake.* He looked around unbidden across the forecastle decking to see the captain and Sir Hugh in conference, watching carefully as the morning light brought all four ships into view and the aft beacons were extinguished. It would be a matter of half an hour or so, he had been told, before they spotted the distinctive cliffs heralding the port of Dover. He assumed they would bear a new course eastward from there to intercept whatever was travelling from France.

He walked forward along the deck heading for the forecastle ladder which he scaled.

"Permission to enter the fo'c'sle, cap'n."

"Aye Mark. Now listen, for our mission has changed. Sir Hugh and *The Swan* have switched allegiance. We now strive for ourselves as privateers. The Treaty with Flanders will fail and with it our chance of any more booty and coin. What say you?" Mark just looked at him, saying nothing, for there before him was the change of loyalty that he had feared – he was now a pirate. There was nothing that he could do about it short of jumping overboard. If he made his feeling known he would be caught up in any brawl that ensued and he would have to fight for his life, he knew.

"Well, cap'n, oi reckon I'm for it as oi could do with some coin. Yet what of the others, the ships of the earl and such? Won't they scupper our plans?"

The captain smiled a thin-lipped smile. It was not a pleasant expression. "Don't be afeared, for they will be gone up the coast towards the Thames estuary when we reach Dover, whether by design or with no agreement I know not, and nor do I care. For with the Treaty gone, war will come and the king will need all the men and ships he can get and devil take the hindmost. We'll be heroes paid to pirate, you'll see." He declared confidently. "These other ships, as well you know I'm sure, are captained by Sir John Prendergast and William Longe, mayor of Rye. They'll lead us this day and with direction from one of the caravels on the Channel we'll catch our prize."

Mark allowed himself to be swayed in order not to arouse suspicion. He shrugged, agreeing to the captain's explanation.

"Good lad, now go and practice with that staff and sword, for my guess is that we'll need both afore the day be out."

Mark nodded and left the forecastle, sliding down the wooden steps to deck. There was a feeling of expectation aboard the vessel as others sharpened swords or made to clean helmets and what little armour they had. Mark fetched his quarterstaff and removed it from the waxed bow bag where he kept it to protect it from the moist and salty sea air. He began a series of moves to stretch and rehearse long practiced forms, practicing strikes and blocks that he had known since childhood. He had also kept up with the swordplay that Jamie and John had taught him back in London.

He found to his surprise that he was one of the best swordsmen among the crew, and only one or two men-at-arms or knights could best him. They enjoyed the fencing and often asked to practice with him. Now he belted on his sword and felt the unfamiliar weight at his side. He had a helmet and padded leather arming coif to ease rubbing and cushion the blows. He produced a pair of padded gauntlets and a gambeson he could wear when ready. The nervous tension spread and men joked coarsely as they often do before battle or conflict to ease their nerves.

They had turned east just before the port of Dover and made a course for France. Two of the cogs had split away from the main flotilla, heading slightly northwards in good order. They had been met by an agile caravel that had scudded in from the east and moved smartly about to run alongside them within easy hailing distance. Mark had not heard the discourse but assumed they were passing information about incoming shipping that would be their prey. He was correct, for within twenty minutes they saw a large broad sail above a cog heading on a north-westerly course. The flotilla changed course slightly to intercept it. The vessel would, he knew, be caught in a pincer movement from the unseen cogs that had headed north and their own ships. The wind was with them and the lone cog had to tack slightly to make the best of the wind. She was doomed in her attempts to evade them as they started to gain steadily upon her, swooping inwards in a vector.

Mark watched from the deck as they closed the distance and saw now the frenetic activity aboard the approaching vessel. Pale grey smoke plumed from the braziers fore and aft on the fighting platforms as the crossbowmen made ready their fire quarrels to launch at the coming armada. Men were strapping on armour and readying their swords while others climbed the rigging to best secure themselves to throw down spears and rocks onto the pirate ships. They were not going to surrender, and the battle would be fierce.

For his own part Mark pulled on a simple bascinet helmet over the padded coif and made sure that the strap could easily be released in case he fell overboard. He heeded Jamie's warning of old and wore no armour or maille, knowing if he ended up in the sea it would pull him to the bottom before he could release the steel bonds.

They were now some hundred yards away, and the first of the fire bolts flared across, aimed at the mighty sails of the cogs or the platforms fore and aft. It was a thankless task in the rolling sea to get the accuracy needed to land a good shot. Yet some he saw, hit their targets. One slammed into the sail and mast of the smaller carrack, spluttered then caught, as the pitch-soaked tow ignited the sail, the flames that licked at the canvas were fanned by the breeze. Crossbowmen from the pirate ships shot back yet did not use fire arrows. They wanted the prize of the ship, not a burned-out hulk.

The gap shortened to twenty yards as the pirate cogs eased closer, judging the angle of attack carefully to collide yet not be run down by the impetus of the large cog. Mark looked out across the closing gap and saw the name of the ship they were attacking.

It was the *Juliane.*

"Ready now!" shouted the captain, "we board and fight for our lives for they give no quarter."

Mark looked up to see him and Sir Hugh deeply focused on the timing and angle of their interception, the fighting platform of the *Shield of the Cross* now obviously higher than that of the *Juliane*, giving a huge advantage to the attacking ships. They could bear down and rake the decks with spears and quarrels, aided by the extra height. It made boarding easier too, with a downwards swing on a rope as the gap closed. Already men had fallen on both sides as red gore slicked the decks along with the voided bowels of the dead and dying, the stench of battle driving all else from men's nostrils. Shouts and war cries went up from both sides as each man called the cry of battle, egging their comrades on in a fever of battle lust. As the grey hulking pirate cogs closed but yards away, it was as if a clutch of beggars scampered, harrying a lord, brightly coloured in his splendour, who tried unsuccessfully to shoo them away.

The ships were close now and the air was punctured with a new sound: the whistle of rope and steel as the grappling hooks were spun, gaining momentum ready to be thrown, tying in the ships. *The Shield of the Cross* made contact slightly ahead of the northern ships and there was a moment when it seemed as though the *Juliane* would escape, pushing away and through a gap to run for Dover. Then the hooks bit hard into the timber and rigging of the *Juliane* as the leading southbound pirate ship's prow thudded home with a screech of rasping timber and a force that rattled Mark's teeth as the ship absorbed the blow.

Faces drawn in a rictus of hatred looked out at them from the bows and deck of the *Juliane*, shouting insults, blood lust raised to fever pitch. The men could be seen and distinguished as human, yet they seemed like animals, ready to kill to preserve their own lives. Looking aboard Mark readied his quarterstaff, taking his turn behind to grab a boarding rope. Then to his horror he saw a familiar figure amidships – Jamie!

By the good Lord no! he thought, and as if to confirm his worst fears, Sir Hugh shouted from the forecastle as loud as he could above the din of pending battle.

"Surrender your ship, and as God is my witness we shall spare your lives. You have my word of honour." He cried. A stilling of noise ensued as those aboard all vessels sought to hear the reply.

"Never! This is the prince's ship and we'll die rather than surrender to you traitors!" Captain Ernald shouted back, at which there were cheers from his crew, who bravely turned to face their fate.

"Board them!" Sir Hugh raged in response, and the slaughter began.

Men flew in from both sides and the defending crew of the *Juliane* were forced to divide and fight to both port and starboard. The first few to swing across were cut down like a field of ripe wheat, for the defenders were trained men and used to the call of battle, prepared and ready to die for their prince they served.

Inevitably, the tide of numbers told its grim story. First a group swung together and secured a tight beachhead on the forecastle, sweeping down from above to the clash of swords and the cries of frightened men. With this distraction, men swarmed amidships onto the open deck, and here the fighting became fiercest. Mark swung across in the second tranche of men to board as the ropes were pulled or swung back for more of the pirates. He landed well, catching his balance and thumping his staff for extra purchase onto the red slicked deck. A shipmate fell before him to a man-at arms; at which he instinctively raised his quarter staff, parrying the next blow in a strong cross, following the movement with his right hand jabbing the shorter end into his assailant's stomach and as he doubled over in pain slamming the left end over to send him stunned to the deck. He hesitated, not wishing to kill a good and loyal Englishman. He kicked him hard instead, and stepping over the prostrate form he looked for his next victim. The din of battle was set to an awful cacophony of wounded men, screams of rage and the mewling sounds of the dying calling for their mothers.

Then he heard a different voice: *"An Umfraville! An Umfraville!"* The mighty war cry pierced the air and he looked across to see a sight that would strike fear into any enemy – Jamie in full battle lust, all reason gone, a red mist before his eyes and at his feet six men already dead or dying. His battle axe whirled to smash another through his helm and face, dropping him in a spray of crimson. A sword point jabbed through the seemingly open guard at Jamie's torso, exposed at the end of the axe swing. Jamie's left arm flew up, holding a shield borrowed from a dead man-at-arms. As he drove the blade up, tilting the shield, Jamie drove its point down into his attacker's sternum, snapping one of the leather straps with the force of the blow, before back slashing with the axe, laying open his stomach to release a writhing rope of intestines that fell to the deck. He kicked the man backwards flat footed to keep an open area for his feet.

Two men came up and the axe again performed a butterfly arc, slicing through the arm of one and the helm of the other, dropping them to the deck.

Jamie stood to face the next attacker, his chest heaving with exertion and his eyes wild with rage. But they held back, fear in their eyes at the ten men lying at his feet. Watching with awe, Mark heard a curse at his side: "I'll take the bastard." He watched in horror as a man-at-arms pulled back on the cord of a crossbow, his foot in the stirrup, straining against the force for the click of the catch. Mark knew he could not let this happen, for a quarrel at this distance would pierce all but the best plate and maille combined. Jamie wore only a padded gambeson and the crossbowman was hidden from view.

"Leave him, 'es mine," Mark snarled, knowing that he may be going to his death with Jamie in such a rage. He knew that he could not see his friend cut down by a cowardly quarrel. As Mark strode forward, he saw a huge man approach and swing with an axe. He watched as Jamie stepped back to avoid the blow but slipped on the gore splattered deck and fell backwards, raising the ruined shield as a defence. Mark heard the axe head thud home, nearly rending Jamie's shield in two, and he saw a grimace of pain flicker across Jamie's face as the blow landed. Rolling to his left as the axeman was exposed. Jamie whipped his own axe across, using only his wrist. It was enough, as the target was soft and sea boots were no match for a battle axe. The axeman screamed, unable to comprehend the fact that his foot had been cut in half. Unbalanced, he fell back howling, rolling across the deck to get away from Jamie as he rose swiftly to finish him.

Mark pushed men out of his way with his staff calling out "he's mine" as he went. The men parted gladly, letting him through. There were now only small groups fighting as inevitably the numbers told the tale of advantage. Then Mark dropped the staff and drew his own sword.

"Come on then man," he yelled. "You think you can take me, sword to sword?"

Mark watched as Jamie looked at him through the red mist of battle. He saw Jamie's mouth twist in a sneer, then he spat, and for one terrible moment Mark thought he was going to charge in an insane suicidal rush to the midst of the pirates, killing as many as he could before certain death. Those watching thought Mark mad. They had seen his swordplay, yet none were certain that he could defeat the killing devil in front of them.

Almost imperceptibly Jamie appeared to relax, throwing off the broken shield and dropping the battle axe, releasing the leather thong hooked over his thumb, and drawing his own sword, that whispered against the wood and greased wool as he released it from the scabbard. "Whoreson traitor, by Christ I'll have your eyes ere I meet my maker," he shouted.

"He's mine no one else's," Mark warned, taking a fighting stance, the sword familiar to him in a half guard position, covering his torso, point outmost. A perfect stance. Jamie watched, taking a high guard, feeling good to have a blade in his hand once more, and then he attacked. Driving right with the force of his shoulder then left with a flick of his wrist. Mark shuddered at the power of the second strike, not believing such force could come just from the wrist. If it had not been for his huge strength he would have lost the grip on his own sword.

He recovered well, as Jamie seemed to hesitate for a split second, allowing Mark's muscle memory to take over. He drove his bent elbow upwards, crossing the guard and rendering the line of attack impossible. Jamie slipped the guard, rotating through a hundred and eighty degrees allowing his elbow to go with the pressure, freeing it for a horizontal strike across his body to Mark's right. The giant sensed the move and knew it was what they had practised. He pivoted on his left foot to meet the attack squarely. Mark knew he had to press home his attack and not be on the defence or he would lose the fight. He began a series of fast, cutting strikes aimed at the head and upper body. Jamie had an answer to each, yet was seemingly hard pressed, not given an opportunity to respond with an attack of his own. Mark saw him retreating.

Then Mark drew an immense strike overhand that was barely met by Jamie as swords clashed hilt to hilt. Expecting the parry, the giant gripped the blades high up with a gauntleted hand, clasping them tightly. He slipped the pommel of his sword under Jamie's and rotated sharply, breaking the grip and pulling both swords away. Jamie cried in alarm and went for his dagger – too late. For Mark thumped him between the eyes, and as he fell he pressed a sword tip to his throat.

"Do 'ee yield, on your word of honour?" Mark growled.

Jamie, half-conscious, nodded assent in seemingly bad grace, as he saw stars before his eyes from the mighty blow.

There was stunned silence from all around at the vanquished figure on the deck. "Kill him," someone shouted.

"Spare him," came a command from the forecastle. "He fought well and we have use for such men. More than this pebble hearted whelp." He sneered at the dying figure of Captain Ernald and with one blessedly clean strike killed him with his dagger. Jamie, even in his stunned state, stared up at the ruthless figure and swore vengeance, for he had liked and admired the brave captain.

Chapter Twenty-Seven

"Bring him hence to the fo'c'sle," the figure on the fighting platform commanded.

Taking his dagger and sword Mark stepped back, allowing Jamie to rise as all fighting had now desisted and groups of wounded men begged mercy in the strange silence that always pervades after a battle. Jamie staggered up across the deck, rubbing his forehead where Mark had struck him. He looked down at the bodies of the crew whom he had watched and spoken with over the last few hours now lying dead or wounded on the deck. He made his way to the wooden ladder and up to the forecastle, joining a small company of men there, including the man that had killed captain Ernald, who stood with his feet braced apart and a raffish look upon his face. His broad shoulders and raiment bespoke a man of wealth, and his face had intelligent features but a cruel mouth. He was a man not to be trusted, who would take your life as soon as you looked the other way, Jamie decided. His hands were clasped behind his back, sea legs easily weathering the swell and fall of the deck beneath him.

"My compliments. You are a worthy fighter and passing quick with the axe. 'Tis fortunate that you are not so skilled with a sword or our giant friend down there would not've been so fortunate." The man nodded at Mark who was on the deck below with maybe a hint of suspicion in his devious eyes. Jamie wisely said nothing and merely stood with a truculent expression upon his face.

"Well, what say you? Do you have a tongue, scullion?" he sneered. Jamie bit back a comment at the insult.

"What would you have me say, I prithee?" He replied. "Beg for my life? For if so the world will end ere you hear those words pass my lips."

"By the rood you've spirit, yet I would expect nothing less from the way in which you fought. Tell me, how are you called?"

There was nothing to lose by dissembling, so he answered truthfully. "I am called Jamie."

"From whence do you hail? And on what duty did you attend aboard the *Juliane*?"

"I live in Shopereslane, near Westchep in London," Jamie offered, giving the name of a street where many of his father's merchant friends lived and providing one of their names as his employer. "I was overseeing the transport of goods on my master's behalf to ensure they arrived safely." He finished.

"You gave good account of yourself for an overseer," the man next to Sir John commented. He looked almost as a merchant but for the well-used sword at his waist and the sly countenance of his face. He was not as well built as Prendergast, but had the look of office about him and carried himself with an arrogance born of rank. His clothes fitted well and were not common threads, and his gambeson, though torn, was well made.

"I was once a man-at-arms for one of the prince's knights," Jamie replied, giving some credence to his obvious martial skills.

"Ha, so that explains your skill at arms," the man said, "Well, would you join us? For we've need of men such as your-self and it would be a wonder if our rewards were not much greater than that of your current employer." He laughed and the others murmured agreement.

"Do I have a choice? If I do not oblige, I fear I'll be in for a long swim or probably worse. For this was Prince Henry's ship by all accounts, and for certes you will let no man tell the tale abroad to bring down his wrath upon you."

"Aye, 'twas the prince's ship and he'll take it ill. Yet he'll have no use for it save to escort his missives back to France and return with a tattered treaty to bear witness to a land that calls for war. And, when that war comes, he'll ask not only for his ship, but for strong men to command it, and we'll oblige his call to harry the French and make war upon them in the king's name."

Jamie shrugged as if considering for the first time both the information provided and his situation. "Well, if that be so, my choice appears for made for me as I'm just a sely soldier with little to commend save a strong right arm, and I was expecting little more than death from your giant, so I'll take a chance and your coin."

The man laughed again, and the laugh sounded as false as the man himself appeared. "Well said, young Jamie, and welcome to our ranks." Jamie nodded and left the forecastle as the man rounded on the crew, calling to them to make ready for port and their destination: Rye. He called down to Mark. "Attend me on the fo'c'sle, giant, for I know you not. Yet by God's grace you gave a good account of yourself today and I'll reward you in kind when we return to port."

Mark scrambled up the wooden steps. "Thank 'ee sir, I'm

Mark of Cornwall and I sail with *The Shield of the Cross* under Captain Ralph."

"Mayhap you can do a favour for me. The new man there, Jamie, whom you bested in the fighting," He tipped his head at the departing figure who was now out of earshot. Mark looked back and nodded. "Keep a wary eye on him, for we know not his loyalty yet, and I'll trust no one 'til they're tested."

"Aye, cap'n. He is in my debt and will trust me for my mercy," Mark assured him. He was happy at such an outcome as it would give him the chance to talk to Jamie without arousing suspicion.

"Captain? No lad, I'm no captain. My name is William Longe, and I am mayor of Rye," he laughed, clapping Mark on his huge shoulder.

Mark turned, smiling to himself as he went in search of Jamie, whom he found aft picking up his battle axe. Jamie welcomed him with a careful nod of recognition. "'Twas not 'til you punched the light of battle from my eyes that I recognised you, Mark," Jamie said quietly. "And that of course is why I let you win. We are well met in this terrible place."

"Treat me as a stranger to whom you owe a debt of clemency," Mark whispered. "They be a distrustful lot up there," he nodded to the forecastle. "They saw us fight, and fight well. We shall forge a new friendship in their eyes from our contest. And by all that's holy I beat you fair and square."

Jamie stifled a laugh and nodded. The deck was being cleared of the dead and swabbed with buckets of water to wash away the detritus of battle. He began to lend a hand to the crew, who gave him a wide berth.

"Mark. 'Tis Mark, is it not?" Jamie called loudly. "Prove your strength once more and aid me here if you can, for this one's a lump and no mistake." Mark grinned at Jamie as the two men took each end of the large pirate Jamie had killed. They stripped him of his sword and axe and anything else of value and threw his body overboard. With space apart from the others the two men winked at each other. "By the rood, you've a punch like a mule's kick," Jamie remarked, speaking loudly once more and rubbing the lump that was rising on his forehead.

"Aye, 'twill no doubt be the colour of a thundercloud by the morrow," Mark joked. "And I'll not chance a turn with you again. Your face bespoke your thoughts and I thought I'd lost to your battle madness."

"'Twas a close run thing. I was lost in Ares' creed and no mistake, but by God's grace you not only saved my life but gained me a more worthy pursuit with your crew."

"I foresee great sport to be had fighting at your side," Mark said. "And now look lively. You have provided us with many bodies to cast into the sea." He moved off beckoning Jamie to follow, and the two men laughed.

Up on the forecastle Sir John turned to Longe. "Many an unlikely friendship is forged in battle," he commented.

Longe looked at the retreating figures of Jamie and Mark and kept his counsel.

A few minutes later, the ships were turned and the *Juliane* sailed alongside them with a new crew now in control, heading for the port of Rye. They made the harbour before sunset and heaved to against the quays to unload the looted goods from the *Juliane*.

Then looking towards the quay, Mark ducked behind the rail. For there in the fading light was the portly figure of the Bishop of Chichester, standing before his horse-drawn waggon in all his papal splendour. They had met at court after a wrestling match and the bishop would recognise Jamie immediately as a household knight. Mark moved carefully away from the rail to find Jamie and warn him.

"Why the hypocritical cur." Jamie muttered when Mark explained. "Rumours were struck abroad of his taking goods from privateers in return for turning a blind eye to their deadly trade."

"Now keep out of sight on the port side. He'll be gone once his waggon is loaded with goods and we'll make for the Olde Bell and maybe a friend," Mark said.

Jamie was puzzled, but Mark raised a warning finger and shook his head.

An hour later they left the *Juliane* and wandered ashore, making for the inn. They managed to get a corner seat where they could watch the tap room from a vantage point. It was filled mostly with seagoing men back from the day's raid and a sprinkling of merchants and local fishermen. Their conversation was hidden beneath the noise of the tavern as the pirates celebrated their victory. "Now you must tell me all that has occurred since you left London, for I believe our paths have crossed again at a most propitious moment," Jamie said.

Mark began to carefully narrate all that had happened since he'd travelled to Cornwall at the winter's end. Jamie listened intently, interrupting occasionally to clarify a point or two.

"Thank God I met you on the boat today or it would have gone ill for me, I fear," Jamie said when Mark had finished.

"Aye and thank John for teaching me the move that broke your grip. I knew not if you'd remember and skewer me afore I had chance to defend myself."

"The wink and the stance told all, I then knew what you wanted and hesitated an instant to allow you to come around and defeat the riposte."

"Praise be that John taught me the move in the yard, for I needed that time. Hell's teeth, you're fast when your blood be up."

They laughed and ordered fresh ale. "Now tell me of this

merchant here, *Signor* Collazzo?" Jamie said.

"He sent word by messenger to *Signor* Felicini and to Cristo at your father's house. The latter bidding him come at all haste to Rye. So, he should be here on the morrow at the earliest."

"That may be too late for we need the means to send a message to Sir Richard ere the *Juliane* is hidden and her crew silenced." Jamie pondered. "We are watched, I must assume, and never to be let off a leash."

"Well you at least. and if either of us manages to escape, the other's life will be forfeit."

"Then there is naught we can do but await news from London. Sir John Prendergast I like not, he has the looks of an eyasmusket, while William Longe is honey smooth but would slip a knife twixt your ribs as soon as you turned away. For Sir John I have promised vengeance on captain Ernald's life and one day shall take his in return." Jamie swore.

"Amen to that and I'm right glad that I killed not a man who was aboard your ship, though some'll 'ave sore heads and broken bones like as not," Mark joked.

The two men supped their ale and watched the night progress and then two newcomers arrived who were not of the ships or the sea. One was the steward of *Signor* Logazzo and the other, Mark and Jamie saw to their eternal joy, was Cristoforo Corio. The two men made for the bar, but not before Cristoforo, as was his habit stalled just inside the doorway as he scouted the room looking for danger and assessing everything in a sweeping glance. He spotted his two friends but not by a flicker of an eye did he register or acknowledge their presence.

Apparently satisfied, he moved with feline grace across the floor of the tavern poised and alert, floating as though on air. The two men arrived at the bar having twisted and turned to avoid the crowded tables. Jamie and Mark looked on and could barely suppress a grin at each other. Almost as one they drained their ale and Jamie picked up the beakers and sauntered to the bar looking for all the world like a man with nothing on his mind save more ale. He found a space aside of Cristoforo and nodded as would a stranger. He spoke very quietly to him in Latin, knowing that few if any in this company would speak the scholarly language.

"You know me not." Cristoforo barely acknowledged the comment and did not make eye contact, he just gave a minimal nod of his head "Pissynghole in a few moments," Jamie finished.

With the ale served, Jamie made his way back to the table and joined Mark, where he explained what he was about to do. Within ten minutes he saw Cristoforo head for the rear of the tavern. Jamie stood, patted his stomach gently, made a show of nodding at Mark and then made his way in the same direction, taking off his cloak and leaving it on the settle as sign that he would be returning for those who may be watching him.

Outside the door he could barely see anything as the yard was illuminated by a single brand. Then a grey ghost materialised from the darkness in a completely different place to where Jamie had expected.

"Cristo?" he called gently.

"*Si, amico mio,*" came the soft reply. "Don't worry," he adjured as Jamie went to check the wooden stalls. "No one is there, I have checked."

"By all the saints it is good to see you." Jamie continued in Latin. "How came you here so quickly?"

"The countryman of mine whom Mark met in Southampton passed word to *Signor* Felicini on the day they met, saying they were sailing up the coast. I spoke with the contessa and her father and they mentioned a man of business, *Signor* Collazzo who resided here, and *eco mi,*" he finished as though it were perfectly natural for him to arrive where and when he should.

"By all that's holy 'tis good. Now we must be brief for there is much to tell and little time. I am under suspicion still and if I tarry and do not return forthwith men will be sent for. I prithee before aught else, how does my father?"

"He rails against the fever and mends right well, be not concerned. Now, *dimi tutti*."

Jamie explained everything that had occurred to date until the taking of the *Juliane*.

"You must ask *Signor* Collazzo to send a message back to Whittington or the prince telling him of the *Juliane's* capture and the treachery of Sir Hugh, Longe and Prendergast. The royal fleet will not know of it and will be sailing into danger or looking the wrong way. They'll not take the ship back out to sea, but will hide it here somewhere until they can disguise or use it again under different colours."

"I understand, and it will be done. Just one more question. How did you come by your black eye?"

"'Twas Mark. He claimed he needed to thump some sense into me," Jamie laughed.

Cristoforo's teeth gleamed white in the darkness as he recalled his immensely strong friend. "*Dio mio*, then I am surprised that you are alive, for his fist is more dangerous than a mace!"

"Amen to that. Now we must away back to the tap room." The two men sauntered back in at slightly different times ignoring each other as they returned to their respective companions.

"'Tis done," Jamie said to Mark. "Cristo will send a messenger to London this evening via *Signor* Collazzo. He will then stay here to watch our movements and report back to London."

Chapter Twenty-Eight

Westminster Palace, London: 4th May

The messenger arrived on a blown horse lathered in white foam from the neck along its flanks which heaved with exertion. It was the third horse the man had ridden and he was exhausted from his efforts. He had been paid well by the Italian merchant, but had earned his coin.

Entering the palace stables, he flipped a coin to the waiting groom, bidding him to walk the horse gently until its breathing returned to normal and only then to permit him small sips of water at a time. Assured of the horse's welfare, the messenger mounted the steps to the southern entrance of the palace, where a man-at-arms stopped him and demanded his business. Minutes later he was admitted to Whittington's quarters and Alfred took his sealed missive into Sir Richard while he warmed his aching legs and back before a fire until he was called before Sir Richard.

"How long since you left Rye?" was Whittington's first question.

"I know not, sir. I was on the road for some two hours, yet I was the second in the relay. From his words, I'd say he left early this morning as soon as the light permitted."

"And now it is sext," Whittington mused. "My thanks to you and your master. Avail yourself of some refreshment. Alfred will see to your needs, for God knows you have done your country a service this day." Whittington moved off, concentrating his mind on the problems ahead and planning his next move.

"Thank 'ee sir. Yet I durst not daddle, for I've another message to relay ere my day is done."

Whittington turned on his heel to face the messenger. "To whom is this message to be delivered?" he demanded.

"An Italian sir, *Signor* Felicini."

"Ah, just so. Again, my gratitude."

The man bowed and left the room. Whittington paced the floor, thinking hard about what he had just learned. His mind made up, he left his quarters and walked hurriedly along the corridor to the council chambers, where the final day of talks with the Armagnacs was taking place.

The courtier at the door was at pains to persuade him that none were permitted to enter or disturb the proceedings with their majesties.

"I would adjure you most strongly to interrupt them. All fault will lie with me and me alone, and you shall not be made accountable."

The courtier sighed and braced himself against the course of action that he was about to take. "Await me here, Sir Richard, and I will avail their majesties of your need." With that he nodded to the guards, knocked and entered the chamber. As he entered, the discussion stopped and the prince turned in his seat scowling at the impertinence of the courtier.

"What is it? We demanded that we were not to be disturbed," he said.

"My lord prince, I do heartily beg your pardon, yet Sir Richard Whittington is without, and he most urgently begs a private audience with your presence."

"Can Whittington not wait?" the prince demanded.

"It would appear not, your royal highness, he was most insistent and declared that it was of the utmost import."

"Very well." The prince turned back to assembled parties around the table. "My lords, your majesty. I would beg a brief reprieve ere we continue. I shall be but a moment." Then as an afterthought and in need of evidence that nothing untoward was in play he summoned Sir Richard, Lord Grey, Chamberlain of the household, to accompany him without. The two men stepped outside the chamber to be met by Whittington, who gave a brief bow to acknowledge the prince.

"Your royal highness, Lord Grey. Thank you for agreeing to meet with me, for the news I have is pressing and has a direct bearing upon your discourse with the Armagnacs."

"Brevity is the order of the day, Sir Richard. We are sorely pressed in all matters and cannot reach agreement at this juncture with the emissaries. Therefore, any intelligence that may aid us is important, so pray continue."

"My prince, I have news direct from Calais and more that will disturb you greatly, for it affects both your royal highness and the realm in equal measure." At which the prince raised an eyebrow and gestured impatiently for him to continue.

"First of Calais. I have news directly from my Lord Ryssheton. He informs that the talks falter and rumours are put abroad – by the Burgundians, he suspects – that England wishes the pirates to continue their plunder of the Channel and bring the treaty into disrepute." At which both Lord Grey and the prince shook their heads in dismay and anger.

"Beshrew your heart, Whittington, for I fear the rest is yet worse. What do you conceal?"

"My lord prince, it concerns the *Juliane*, she is taken by the pirates – to wit Sir John Prendergast, William Longe...and mayhap Sir Hugh Courtney."

"What?" he roared. "When did this occur, and how came you by this intelligence? Is it verified?"

"I fear it is, my lord prince, directly from the pirate fleet from Sir James de Grispere..."

"De Grispere? Then it will be true, for we owe him much and he is ever loyal. Now tell us all that you know."

Whittington passed over the letter that he had received from *Signor* Collazzo. It was informative and passed on all the salient details from Mark's embarkation on the *Shield of the Cross* and his apparent change of allegiance to the fight at sea and the taking of the *Juliane*. The prince's frown grew deeper as he read through the letter, and as he finished he involuntarily clenched his fist in anger, crumpling the parchment.

"Have Lord Beaufort attend us here immediately." The prince snapped at Lord Grey. He looked into the middle distance and fumed, pacing the ante-chamber as Whittington wisely stayed silent, awaiting questions that he knew would come. He had rarely seen the prince so vexed before and he let him play out his anger. The door to the council chamber opened and through it came Lord Grey and the Lord Chancellor, Thomas Beaufort.

"My prince?"

"Thomas, from this moment onwards we relieve you of your role as Lord Chancellor and beg that you attend us by finding the pirates who hound our seas. Secure them and bring them back in chains. Do you hear? They have taken the *Juliane*, my ship! By all that's holy I will have them in chains at my feet and dispense my justice in person. For if we cannot save our own ships how can we promise to protect the ships of other nations? What use is the treaty while such business continues?"

Then without waiting for a response he turned to the courtier who was at the desk writing as the prince spoke, and continued. "Have this entered in the royal warrants: Sir John Prendergast and William Longe, mayor of Rye, are indicted as traitors to the realm. Hold any action against Sir Hugh until we have further proof of his involvement. But all rights, properties and status of both of the other men are revoked with immediate effect." The scribe nodded and scribbled faster.

"My Lord Beaufort," he continued, "you are to continue to aid us in your capacity as Admiral of the Fleet forthwith. Have it noted that we will assign the sum of one thousand pounds to be put at the admiral's disposal, and all means and circumstances are to be made available to aid him in this matter."

Whittington's eyebrows shot upwards. A thousand pounds was a vast sum of money and would represent a goodly percentage of the court's annual budget.

Thomas Beaufort's eyes glittered at the prospect being offered to him: "Your royal highness, I shall not disappoint you. I will have them back in chains within a sennight. With your permission, my prince, I will take my leave and begin preparations at once, for there is much to be done and I shall not tarry."

"As you wish," the prince replied. "The funds will be made available this day, together with royal warrants of office and authority. Attend us later on the hour of nones in our private solar."

"As you command, my prince," Beaufort answered, bowing to his nephew and sweeping out of the room, energy and anticipation of the task ahead emanating from him.

"My Lord Whittington, thank you as ever for your propitious intervention. We are indebted to you."

"It is my pleasure to serve your royal highness. I would ask a further favour perhaps to better aid the endeavours?"

"Pray speak, my lord." The prince offered.

"My prince, 'tis a delicate matter, and one concerning which I would beg a private audience – with your presence, my Lord Grey, and that of the Lord Chief Justice Sir William Gascoigne."

"Have Sir William join us from the Council..." the prince began, then he halted. "No, for this brings an entanglement upon all matters pertaining to the Armagnacs, who will learn soon enough what has occurred this day. Let us return to the chamber, for I believe this will terminate all discussions once we have broken the news of the pirates' tyranny. Sir Richard, attend us in my private quarters within the hour." The prince and Lord Grey returned to the chamber.

An hour later, Whittington attended the prince and his lords in his private chamber. They were arrayed before the large table, each man betraying the tension he felt. "My prince, my lords," he began. "I have information that I would pass to your royal highness that I would not have known abroad in the palace. Sir William is already aware of what I am about to impart." The prince frowned, but let Whittington continue telling the assembled nobles of the plots being fomented in the north and the involvement of those – including by implication the Beauforts – at which his face slightly reddened, whether with anger or embarrassment Whittington could not tell. The blue eyes turned to ice as he heard more.

"You say that the Beauforts were not there in person?" he asked at length

"No my prince, only their servants."

"Why was I not informed?" The steel was back in his voice again.

"It was but a recent event, and truthfully there is insufficient evidence to fully complete a prosecution of all those that were present. I did not wish to cast aspersions upon your uncles, the Beauforts, until such time as I knew the full story. And you were exceeding busy with the treaty and concern for your father's health."

The prince looked askance at Whittington, believing not a word of his excuse. A thin-lipped smile came to his face, for he knew that he owed the man much and gave forbearance accordingly. "De Grispere again, and he has signed an affidavit to this effect?"

"Indeed, my prince, with my Lord Chief Justice as witness," he gestured at Sir William. "I have others less well placed than Sir James who are reporting back to me in this matter, and the news is not as we would wish. A rivalry grows apace with accusation and unrest as Stanhope's power rises."

The prince thought for a moment, considering all that he had been told, and his mind jumped to the conclusion Whittington suspected it would.

"We suspect that this is not the whole story, as you asked for that permit for Sir James and others to travel abroad?"

"As you perceive, my prince. I have been aiding my Lord Stokes in matters pertaining to the royal fleet, and as such I have now two men aboard the *Juilane* who are favourable to our cause." Here he paused for effect and was not disappointed.

"My dear Sir Richard, you are verily a wonder to us and a valued friend in many ways, rendering us great service. How by the Lord Harry did you achieve such a feat?"

Whittington nodded graciously, acknowledging both the compliment and the extended olive branch. "My prince I thank you for the encomium, though it was but my devoir to the realm."

At which he proceeded to explain Mark and Jamie's actions and how they came to be aboard the *Juliane*, and of Cristoforo's involvement on land. "I would therefore ask that you advise my Lord Beaufort accordingly, as these two men are owed much and remain faithful to the crown."

"Mark of Cornwall. I remember him well. A giant of a man and an able wrestler. Side by side with de Grispere they will be a formidable combination – especially if the Italian works with them. Never have I seen such stealth and cunning in a man. I would rather he work with us than against us, by God's grace. It seems that we are again in their debt," the prince said. "Just so, we will make it clear to my Lord Beaufort that these two are to be watched for and treated accordingly, and mayhap a warrant can be prepared exonerating them of any and all misdeeds in case of their mistaken capture."

"Just so, my prince."

"You kept this close, my lord Gascoigne," the prince snapped.

"At Sir Richard's behest, your royal highness. For if you were informed, then needs must his majesty would have had to have been informed too, which would have done ill to his disposition." The Lord Chief Justice answered suavely. The prince then turned to Lord Grey.

"My lord, once we are secure against the pirates and the treaty is signed, we must turn our mind to these malaperts in the north and put paid to their efforts once and for all."

"Indeed, my prince. Mayhap we can press William, Lord Roos, into service? He is well placed in that quarter and would serve well as a steady yet firm arbitrator."

"Quite so. A good choice and one of which we approve. Make it so," the prince concluded.

Chapter Twenty-Nine

Rye

Returning to Rye, the messenger found *Signor* Collazzo's house with ease, where he passed the two documents from London to *Signor* Collazzo, his steward and Cristoforo. Once he had left the room, Collazzo broke open the first document and read it carefully, his face taking on a surprised expression as he did so.

"By the good Lord, the prince moves swiftly. He has ordered Lord Thomas Beaufort to command a fleet and make all haste to apprehend the pirates, inditing them as traitors to the realm. The fleet sails as we speak and makes to blockade the harbour. There is a second warrant here," he raised it in his hand, "providing safe passage and certifying the innocence of your two comrades, Cristoforo, in the event that they be captured. This should be taken to them without loss of time, for they will be in great peril of being imprisoned or worse should the *Juliane* be taken with them aboard."

"I will take it to the tavern this evening. The cogs are still harboured and none has sailed," Cristoforo replied.

Mark and Jamie had agreed that if Cristoforo should appear on the quays, one of them should come ashore and seek to make contact either near the house of *Signor* Collazzo or in the Olde Bell. Both men spotted him ambling on the quayside aimlessly, and Mark – who was the more trusted of the two – asked permission to go ashore. Once at liberty he made his way along the sea front, then up to Church Square upon which *Signor* Collazzo's house was situated.

He leant against the wall there, looking across to the harbour and waiting for Cristoforo to come into view. As he did so, Mark moved innocently into St Mary's church and took a pew near the back, looking over as the mighty door squeaked again to admit his friend. Cristoforo wandered near the pew and admired hangings on the wall. Having ascertained that they were alone he spoke quietly, informing Mark of the imminent arrival of Beaufort and the fleet, and left the warrant of their offices to the crown near the steady flames of the candles. Cristoforo lit one, genuflected towards the altar and then left. Mark waited a little while before copying his actions and lighting a candle of his own. Placing it with the others, he retrieved the document, hid it within his doublet and made his way back to the ship.

The captain watched Mark's movements as he returned sometime later with wares purchased from shops in the town, including two eel pies to which he was partial. He moved to stand beside Jamie and handed one of the pies to him, aware that they were being watched from the forecastle.

"You were followed. Did all go well?" Jamie spoke quietly between bites.

"Aye, I saw Cristo and we went into the church separately and then left just so. No more than a sely sailor offering prayers for deliverance," he declared with a grin between huge mouthfuls of pie.

"Please God that it be so, for we are still not trusted and must have care."

The next day a messenger arrived in great haste as the church bell struck noon. He slipped from his horse at the quayside and scanned the large ships moored there, reading the names painted on their bows.

"What do you seek, sir?" Mark hailed across, intrigued by the messenger's arrival and hoping to learn whatever he may.

"*The Shield of the Cross* and Sir Hugh de Courtney."

"If you pass it thither I will ensure he receives it, for *the Shield* is moored to our port side," Mark offered.

"Nay, I durst deliver it only into his own hand as I am bidden."

"As you wish. Follow the plank up and I'll show 'ee the way."

The messenger came unsteadily up the plank and was shown across to the ship tethered to the *Juliane*. Jamie and Mark watched with interest as Sir Hugh was summoned from his cabin aft and presented with the missive. His gambeson was adrift and he looked unkempt from lack of sleep as he squinted into the bright spring sunshine.

"Sir Hugh de Courtney?"

"'Tis I."

"A message sir, for your person alone, I was bidden to say."

Sir Hugh took the rolled message and broke the seal and read the words before him:

5th May, year of our Lord, 1411

Sir,
Forgive my brevity in haste. Beaufort is instructed and sailed on the tide with a fleet. The Juliane *is to be retaken and all those caught be chained as traitors – flee!*

For ever yours,
R

The knight looked upwards as though to seek inspiration from God. He read the brief note a second time, then turned to his captain who stood by: "Make haste to have the ship ready for sea within the hour. We must be away ere the tide turns."

Men set to immediately at his remark, and which Jamie and Mark shared a meaningful look.

"I hope Cristo is keeping watch, for my heart tells me we too shall soon be sailing. Yet where and what has caused my Lord Courtney such concern I know not. What I wouldn't give to see that letter!"

Within the hour the *Shield of the Cross* and the *Swan* set sail, pulling out into the estuary on the turn of the tide that eased them gently out into the Channel.

In the early hours of the following dawn, once the tide was fully out and had begun to turn, captain Ralph accompanied by William Longe and Sir John Prendergast all came aboard and the *Juliane* was made ready to sail, yet not in the manner Jamie and Mark had imagined. In the twelve hours between tides the crew had been busy, and they thought it strange to be fighting against an incoming tide and were puzzled as to why they had not shipped out earlier.

"Cast off!" came the cry as the plank was raised.

Cables were slipped as the bargemen heaved at their oars, pulling the *Juliane* out, moving sluggishly at first. Then the incoming current became stronger as the run of the sea turned the ship, aided by an incoming breeze that lifted the slack from the mainsail as it was unfurled. The cog glided gracefully into the centre of the estuary – and then the tiller arm connected to the huge rudder aft was pulled to port, pointing the *Juliane* up the river Rother.

"By the rood, we travel inland. Is the river navigable thus far?" Jamie asked.

"I know not, yet she draws only a shallow draft and is flat bottomed save for a central keel," Mark replied. "Why by all that's holy she'll barely draw more than a barge, and as lightly loaded as she is she'll likely carry us to Scotland." The rowers pulled hard, bringing the ship into line as the tide and wind pushed her gently upstream into the quiet waters of the river Rother. The course of the river initially ran northeast, almost parallel to the coast. The pilot barge stayed with them, running along under its own small sail saving the might of the twin banks of oars for when they might need them to help the *Juliane*, which sported only a few oars on each side. Mark asked Jim where they were bound.

"Why Smallhythe of course, hast no one told 'ee? Master Longe has a smallholding there and a manor nearby. We'll likely lay low 'til the fleet has come and gone," He chuckled.

When he had moved off Mark muttered, "That's some nine miles by road, I've heard. I hope that Cristoforo has seen us leave the port."

"Fear not. It's a port, and as full of janglery as a court full of women. If he did not see us with his own eyes it will be fully abroad by sext." Jamie predicted.

After about two miles the river took a sharp turn to the northwest, and after another mile it forked, with one tributary heading eastwards up towards the hamlet. It was this tributary that the *Juliane* floated along, now aided by the rowing barge helping the ship to greater speed as the breeze and current were against them. It was hard work and the oarsmen sweated and cursed as they pulled the cog up the final mile of river. The watercourse narrowed again, yet it was still some twenty yards wide and deep enough for the shallow-drafted craft. The banks gently sloped onto flat, verdant floodplains, shrouded with lines of whispering willows that swayed gently in the breeze. Sheep grazed on the new shoots of grass, the tranquil scene at odds with the nature of the newcomers.

The final mile of the tributary wended its way towards Smallhythe, taking them to a small manmade basin that allowed the *Juliane* to come about, ready to face downstream. They were still a half mile from the hamlet, and concealed within the trees of a copse. A narrow landing stage edged from the bank, barely discernible from the water course.

"Heave to and tie off the lines, yet be ready to sail again as soon as the order be given." Prendergast ordered. He was now clearly in command, knowing all the secrets of the backwaters that were so close to his holdings.

Two stone barns stood nearby, and it was to these that the crew gravitated, making fires and preparing a meal. Two sheep were killed and quickly butchered, jointed and roasted over the firepits. Jamie and Mark were wary, helping as they did to appear part of the adventure but constantly alert for any sign of trouble.

— ✕ ✳✕ —

They did not know it, but the moving of the *Juliane* was only just in time. The royal fleet under Beaufort's command made good speed on their journey down from the Thames, covering the ninety nautical miles in less than a day's sailing. The fleet consisted of three war cogs, two carracks and a barge. Only the flagship sailed into the harbour, the others waited, battle ready to block any who sought to escape. They entered the river estuary arrayed for war, weapons ready, shields and helmets fixed and bows strung. The scene before them was bustling yet peaceful, a typical maritime town with an eclectic mix of craft moored in the vast harbour. They scoured each inlet on their way through, yet saw no sign of the elusive *Juliane*.

Thomas Beaufort stood on the fighting platform of the forecastle, clad in a bright blue gambeson with a beautiful Milanese plate bascinet helmet upon his head with the visor up, exposing his strong features. The captain was at his side and a few of the household knights including Sir Christopher Urquhart, who had trained as an esquire with Jamie and had been elevated to the knighthood earlier that year.

"All looks to be without the pirate's presence," Beaufort said. "There be no sign of the *Swan*, *Shield* or the *Juliane*. The birds appear to have flown, but 'tis no surprise, given the court is rank with spies and a fast horse would have journeyed thus far in less time than we could sail."

"Aye, your grace. I wonder who could have informed upon our mission, given that we saw no sign of the Courtney fleet on our voyage here," A knight asked with a cynical edge to his voice.

The duke snorted. "I would adjure you to look no further than the name you just mentioned, for the Courtneys have a long reach and their cousin Richard is ever at the prince's side when not fomenting heresy at Oxford."

This drew grim smiles from the assembled company. They all knew of the influence Richard Courtney appeared to have over the prince as friend and confidant. It was for this reason alone, it was supposed, that as Chancellor of Oxford University and one who promoted and protected liberal doctrines including Lollardy, no action had been taken against him or the university's teachings.

"Why Sir Thomas, I don't believe my eyes, is that not our Italian friend from court, Cristoforo Corio, who hails us from the quayside?"

The duke squinted ahead to see Cristoforo waving at the incoming ship.

"I believe that you have the right of it, Sir Christopher," he grunted, seemingly annoyed at the presence of Cristoforo. He had been informed by the prince of Jamie and Mark's presence, yet had not thought to pass this on to any of his crew or knights. He was aware that Jamie had been in Nottingham and had certainly been spying for either the king or Whittington. If he were to be killed in the action of taking the *Juliane*, he reasoned, that would be one less witness against him and his brother.

As they closed, Sir Christopher returned the salute and hailed him loudly with the excitement of youth in his first action. "Cristoforo, why 'tis well met and most surprising for I did not think to meet with you here."

"'Tis a long story to be told another time, for I needs must have speech with your commander my Lord Beaufort. Is he aboard?"

Those on board could not but fail to hear the discourse and came to the rail as the mighty cog heaved against the wooden rail of the quayside, bumping with the swell. The tall muscular figure came to the rail and called down to Cristoforo as the plank was dropped to the quayside, seeming to take it ill that Cristoforo should be present.

"I am Lord Beaufort, commander of this fleet. If you have news for me, pray come aboard," Thomas said haughtily, knowing full well the identity of Cristoforo, yet pretending lack of recognition for one whom he despised.

Cristoforo came aboard carefully, his hatred and fear of the water all too apparent to those who watched him navigate the gangplank. Once safely aboard he bowed, glad to feel a firm deck beneath his feet.

"My Lord Beaufort, I am Cristoforo Corio, and I serve the

household of Thomas de Grispere. In that cause I must inform you that Sir James de Grispere and Mark of Cornwall, who both serve the prince in his household, are aboard the *Juliane* as agents for the crown serving his Royal Highness's interests in an act of subterfuge. They beg me to inform you that the ship has sailed inland up the river Rother but an hour past."

"Thank you for the intelligence, but I have already been made aware of the presence of Sir James and his companion." The comment drew a frown of puzzlement from Sir Christopher, who turned to the admiral yet said nothing. "Dost thou know of the destination?"

"The rumour is Smallhythe, my lord, some nine miles by road to the north east, yet much longer by river. I was awaiting your arrival to render service and intended to follow by land the better to direct you once I have discovered their place of concealment. With your permission, my lord, I would depart in all haste better to get abreast of them?"

Beaufort waved him away in a dismissive gesture. "As you wish, we shall look for you on the road." With that he turned away to give orders to the crew and make arrangements for the other ships in the fleet to enter the harbour.

Chapter Thirty

Cristoforo had his horse saddled and waiting for him, held by one of *Signor* Collazzo's servants. He had the chance for brief word with Sir Christopher before he departed, and hoped that this would be enough to keep his two friends safe from harm's way when the *Juliane* was captured, for he trusted not Lord Beaufort and was only too aware of everything Jamie had discovered during his mission to Nottingham.

Once mounted, Cristoforo left Rye, making for the country lane he had been directed to that led to Smallhythe. As he rode away, it seemed that he was journeying in the wrong direction as the lane took him away from the river's course. But once past the village of Iden he crossed the Rother and bore left towards Wittersham. From there he had a clear view of the river as he moved west through a narrow lane cutting across the flat landscape. At the fork of the river, where the tributary wended its way north-eastwards, he saw the tall mast of the *Juliane* edging its way up river. He had found them!

Cristoforo retraced his steps back to the Wittersham road and headed north again, through Peening Quarter, where he had a clearer view of the river shaded in the distance less than half a mile south of Smallhythe. In this more secure position, he slipped off the horse and crept closer for a better look at the ship and its crew. It was not difficult to spot Mark as he was a head taller than his shipmates, and where he was, there would be Jamie. Both seemed well and able bodied, which is all that Cristoforo cared about. He marked the men on the forecastle, having seen them when the boat was in port.

For another ten minutes he watched as the large craft was led into the basin and turned about. Satisfied that this was the ship's final harbour he remounted and set out to find the royal company. It didn't take him long. They had made good time, eschewing the cogs and coming instead in sequestered nimble caravels and two barges full of oarsmen and men-at-arms. He caught them before the tributary and explained how the *Juliane* had peeled off to the smaller watercourse. The river was narrow enough here that he could shout from the bank, so the party of craft continued on their way unhindered.

With the information given Cristoforo shadowed the fleet, keeping slightly ahead to alert them. Just before the harbouring point and the basin he bade them stop, walking the horse into the shallows so that he could be heard without raising his voice.

"They are three or four hundred yards around the next bend in the river." He informed.

"We have them." The duke smiled, thumping his fist into his palm. "Now hark all, we want them in chains taken alive to suffer a traitor's death. Go to and take the ship. A party of men under my captain-of-arms will land here and go by foot to prevent any escape. Set to, oarsmen, for they are within our grasp at last."

The three caravels were easily pulled the final distance against the wind and current as they steadily closed on the bend that would reveal them to the pirates.

Although well aided by Cristoforo, the attack did not go as planned. Sir John Prendergast and William Longe were wily and had posted guards to alert them of any attack. One was in the crow's nest of the *Juliane* and two more were on the perimeter of the camp in the trees. The flat land which had aided Cristoforo now came to the rescue of the pirates. As soon as the sentries spotted the masts of the caravels, they alerted the camp.

Only half the crew had been allowed ashore at any one time, with Jamie and Mark opting to stay aboard as much as they could. The camp turned into a nest of angry bees; fires were ignored as they all rushed for the safety of the *Juliane*. At Longe's command, the men salvaged what they could and rushed back to the ship. Jamie and Mark had hoped to cut free the cables and let the ship drift, but at no point had there been the requisite small numbers of men to ensure that the plan would work and allow them to escape with their lives. Now, with the deck swarming as the crew returned together with men-at arms, the *Juliane* once more became a living breathing entity.

"Slice those cables," Prendergast called as the last man slipped aboard and the plank was withdrawn. "they're in caravels you say?"

"Aye sir," called the man from the crow's nest.

"By the rood we'll sail over them. Unfurl the sail, boatswain." With that the men lowered the huge mainsail, which caught in the southerly breeze and snapped open, pushing the ship sluggishly forward, moving gently towards the current in the middle of the river. Jamie and Mark saw what would happen as they stood above the deck on the aft castle platform. The *Juliane* would ram and sink the oncoming caravels and all aboard, being substantially bigger and heavier, with a correspondingly large hull and a huge forecastle that would dwarf the low-slung caravels and barges. It would be an unequal fight, and the royal fleet would lose. Once out on the water the *Juliane* would sail for the open sea to be lost to all retribution.

"Why they'll turn the caravels to kindling, leaving them smashed in their wake. We have but one chance." Jamie whispered. "Think you can steer the helm alone on the rudder if I dissuade these scullions of their desire to fight?"

Mark looked at the huge rudder bar that normally took two men to lever and manoeuvre the ship. As the wind fetched out the sail, the long bar was at this moment being pulled to navigate out into the main stream by two men who hauled at the rounded branch of oak that was bolted to the rudder below. "Aye. I think I could manage that," he said.

"Go then, and God be with you. Look not to me, for the stakes be high and I shall prevail, fear not." Jamie encouraged.

Mark nodded, grasping his staff and moving across to the rudder men. "Ho lads, let me help you heave to." He called as their struggles to pull the ship about increased. Mark strode across to the tiller as though to aid them. As he approached, he raised his staff looking for all the world as if he would wedge it between the deck and the steering arm. The staff flew with incredible speed, dropping first one and then the second man unconscious to the deck. They had no time to defend themselves as the staff connected with their heads. Mark dragged the men away from the tiller and seized it in his huge hands, bracing his shoulders and thews of his legs, taking the strain as he flexed against the current that was starting to pull the immense arm away from its natural course, fighting the natural line of the current. His feet sought the wedges of wood set into the deck in a semi-circle to better aid the tillermen and prevent their feet slipping in wet conditions. The ship creaked and snapped with his efforts to move it away from the course of the stream.

There were nine men on the aft fighting platform, of which two were crossbowmen and four men-at-arms who stood looking over the rail at the deck below and forward as the royal fleet hove into view. Another sailor was hauling ropes, and the last two men were Prendergast's captain of arms and Sir John Prendergast himself. All were focused upon the impending collision between the Juliane and the low-slung approaching caravels.

Jamie waited, wanting to give Mark as much time as possible to alter the course of the ship before anyone noticed. In doing so he put himself at risk, for the longer he left it to retaliate the more opportunity there was to be attacked en masse by those on the aft platform.

"Ho men, look alive!" called Prendergast, who was the first to realise they were diverting off course as the bow started to veer away towards the opposite bank and across the current.

"Aye sir." Mark called to allay his fears. Sir John still did not take his eyes off the approaching craft as missiles began to fly between the two factions. Jamie gave one final look over his shoulder to see Mark bent with effort as his muscles cracked and popped fighting with the strain of steering, holding the tiller to his will. Beads of sweat arose on his brow as he brought all his immense strength to bear on the rudder. The ship was fighting a losing battle with the current and Mark's determination.

As the *Juliane* inexorably changed course, Sir John Prendergast finally looked back to see Mark slaving over the rudder. "By God's holy balls, leave go of that tiller," he roared.

As soon as Jamie saw him begin to turn, he flew at the four men-at arms on the rail, his arms wide, catching three of the four above their centre of gravity and toppling them head first over the rail to the hard deck below. The fourth man, whom he had missed in his assault, had been grabbed by the three falling men, and in an effort to save himself dangled by his arms from the fighting platform. Jamie came behind and heaved as the men tumbled to the deck below. Their cries of alarm were soon quelled as they slammed into the deck, dead or unconscious. The two crossbowmen were bent over their weapons re-cocking them, and were caught unawares as Jamie flew forward, slicing with his battle axe, killing them both in two strokes.

The sailor, seeing the fierce knight before him, gripped the rope he was holding and swung down to the deck below and safety. Jamie, seeing Mark's plight, ran to position himself between the two remaining men as Mark continued to pull on the tiller, taking the ship out of the path of the caravels.

The captain at arms had a shield and sword and was mailed in a short hauberk. He came at Jamie warily, relying on his shield as protection against the axe. He was experienced and did not fly in but tested Jamie, his sword flicking out to find a weak spot and exploit the gap. Jamie could not afford a long-drawn-out fight as Sir John sought to round the fighting pair and kill Mark before the ship was run aground. Jamie danced, leaping away from the captain, slashing obliquely with his axe and forcing Sir John to pull back. Yet with the move he exposed himself to the soldier, who flew in with his shield raised and sword point lunging at Jamie's legs to bring him down.

Jamie circled with the axe, sweeping the blade aside and continued the arcing movement, bringing the lethal weapon over to slice his opponent. The man was not fooled, and brought the shield to bear, protecting himself from the axe that split the willow board and lodged there. The man pulled. Experience in the battles with Scots in the shield wall had been a hard school and had taught Jamie many tricks. He went with the pull, seemingly off balance, and fell to the deck releasing the thong of the axe from his thumb. Free of any resistance, the man stepped back heavily. Jamie went with the fall, pulling his dagger with his left hand and driving it hard into the exposed foot of his opponent, pinning him to the deck. The man howled in agony, unable to move as blood sprayed from the wound.

The cry halted Sir John, who turned from his rush at Mark, seeking to slash Jamie as he lay on the deck. But Jamie was already moving. *Never stay still,* had been John's mantra, *keep moving whether you're armed or unarmed.* Jamie rolled away once, twice, three times, as fast as he could, finishing in a backward roll that brought him to his feet. Sir John came at him fast.

"You've lost your axe, whelp. Now you're mine," he sneered, relying on Jamie's demonstration against Mark when he had lost the sword fight. Jamie ignored the barbed comment and drew his sword, remembering the look of wretchedness on Captain Ernald's face as Prendergast killed him in cold blood. He cast one last look at Mark, who now had the tiller at full arc and looped the rope stay over the bar as the *Juliane* headed for the opposite bank where it would wedge solidly.

Both men had arming swords of similar length, and there was little advantage to be gained. Jamie twirled his blade at the wrist in a flourish, but instead of finishing in a guard position he stamped forward, bringing the blade point first at Sir John's chest. Prendergast parried hilt to tip, forcing Jamie's blade away to his right, and his counter move came in fast, driving his sword point forwards with his arms raised high, held two handed with a clasped thrust pushing for Jamie's sternum. The driving point nearly struck home as both men had their arms up, crossing in the upper guard. Jamie was now at a disadvantage, forced to cross the centre line with no vantage to be gained from the point. He took a gamble and span, turning his back on Sir John in a fast turn. There was no time to bring his blade to bear, nor was there a need, for in the turn he brought his elbow around, driving it hard into Sir John's ribs, bringing a gasp of air from his opponent, who bent at the waist, losing his continuity of movement.

With space gained, Jamie continued the turn, stepping out and away and giving himself room to bring his blade to bear, although without full force. Sir John's gambeson had been well made, with crushed woollen layers double stitched in three lines of hemp cord, stud buttoned for extra strength. But Jamie's wicked blade was sharp enough to slash at the padding of Sir John's gambeson, damaging the skin and muscle beneath that covered his bruised ribs, which Jamie hoped he had fractured.

Jamie's blade continued, not allowing Sir John respite as Jamie repeated with a forward slash across his torso that Sir John barely had time to defend. The move caused him pain from his damaged intercostals and he sought to drive the point of his sword inwards to effect a counter attack. Jamie parried the stroke easily, driving Sir John's blade down, and Prendergast moved again to an upper guard, retreating in fear at the savage onslaught that had been unleashed upon him. They caught again hilt to hilt. But this time Jamie's sword sliced across the guard, cutting John's right forearm. Dropping his sword, Prendergast pivoted and leapt over the rail of the platform, flying cleanly in an arcing dive into the river below.

He disappeared from sight and Jamie had no time to seek him further as Mark cried for help. He had been holding the wooden steps giving access to the fighting platform and was now being hard pressed by the crew who were retreating in front of the invading royal force that had fought its way aboard the *Juliane*. His quarterstaff whirled again, smashing a pirate on the side of the head, yet as he did so a quarrel whistled past by his ear from above as another man swung in on a rope from the rigging, axe in hand.

Jamie ran, plucking his dagger from the mewling captain-at-arms, who sat propped against the rail in a pool of blood from his skewered foot. Now well armed, Jamie faced the axe man, who swung wildly at head height. Jamie ducked, lunged and brought the dagger up into his stomach, driving through the jerkin to gut him. He pulled the dagger from the wound that sucked against the blade, twisting it to aid release. Ignoring the dying soldier, he ran to help Mark, crying *"an Umfraville!"* as he ran, slashing one pirate across the back as started to turn, catching another with the thrust of his dagger. A mace came crashing down, and he blocked it between his dagger and sword, not daring to allow it to slide off and hit Mark as he kicked the man, who fell backwards down the steep ladder crashing head first into the deck. Two more remained, Mark drove his quarterstaff into one while Jamie speared the other through the side.

Then, as quickly as it had all begun, resistance ended. Longe was captured and men had seen Prendergast leave the ship to its fate when he dived overboard. The pirate crew threw down their weapons, surrendering as a familiar mocking voice hailed Jamie.

"By the rood, Sir James de Grispere, you acquit yourself well. Durst thou leave any action for us!"

"Kit! By all that's holy, what do you do here?" Jamie exclaimed to his friend and former squire in arms with whom he had trained at the palace.

"I came with the company of the crown and my Lord Beaufort who you see here before you. May we enter the fo'c'sle, captain?" he enquired mockingly, excited beyond measure at having won his first real engagement.

The two men climbed the ladder to the aft platform, where Jamie and Mark offered a bow to Sir Thomas Beaufort, Admiral of the Fleet.

"Well met, Sir James. Christopher has the right of it, for you have acquitted yourself well," Beaufort said, looking around at the carnage on the deck. "And our thanks are to you for foiling their plans. We should have been tinder wood if the *Juliane* had sailed over us." Yet he continued reprovingly, "I see you let that malapert rogue Sir John Prendergast escape."

"I had little choice, my lord. The coward leapt the ship and I could hardly follow with the battle in full array. It would be a great wonder if he gets far, for he is wounded and I did not see him rise from the dive. He was not in maille, yet he wore a heavy gambeson. There appears to be no sign of him."

"Well, we must look to what we have gained. I will send out scouts to root him out if his body is not found." The knight turned and addressed Mark. "You are the wrestler in his highness' employ, Mark of Cornwall?"

"Yes, my lord."

"How came you to be embroiled in this web of deceit?"

"It is a long tale my lord, yet to shorten it, I am loyal to the crown and go where I am bidden to aid the prince as is my duty." Mark answered, showing his newly acquired courtly manners

"'Twas bravely done. For certes there are few I know who can force a tiller so, to turn a ship single handed against a current as you did. You saved our craft, God be praised."

Mark blushed at the compliment from the eminent knight and nodded his thanks at the praise. Beaufort cast a final glance around the platform and moved off to organise the return to Rye.

Chapter Thirty-One

Launceston Lane, London

"Father, you look much better than when last I laid eyes upon you," Jamie said, smiling and taking his father's hand in his.

Sitting at his side, Jeanette was warmed by the intimacy between Jamie and their father. As their mother had died in her childbirth, she had been the only real female influence and source of intimacy within the family; at times being a surrogate mother to Jamie despite being younger. Now she was delighted to witness a moment of affection between her two men. Looking across, she thought not for the first time how long and tapered were Jamie's fingers; more like the fingers of an artist than a soldier. While the hands were thick with sinew and tendons, the joints had not yet thickened as so many did with exercise or use of arms. Maybe that was why he was so fast, she mused, not being weighed down with heavy muscle in the lower arms.

The colour had returned to his father's cheeks and he could

now sit up in bed, his breathing all but normal, with no signs of the wheezing that had characterised it when Jamie had last been here.

"'Tis true, I feel much more hale, yet nothing is a better tonic to me and a panacea to my ills than to have you safely back home." Thomas said. "To wit, prithee tell of all that occurred for I have not been about and I am starved of news both here and abroad."

"To ease your burden, father, all is safe and well with the goods, which we placed in safe storage in Calais. By God's grace I am glad that we followed your advice and did not ship with the *Juliane*, or our cloth would be gracing the Lord Bishop of Chichester's rotund form by now."

"So 'tis true, the wily old churchman is as iniquitous as ever?"

"Aye, that he is, the old goat. We saw him posturing on the quayside taking goods aboard his waggons – bound for the church, I'm sure," Jamie answered scornfully. The two men chuckled at the thought of the hypocritical clergyman, then Thomas became more serious asking for more details about what had occurred in the Channel and afterwards at Rye.

"Cristoforo gave me scant details upon his return, saying only that there had been an affray, devil take him. An affray indeed!" he raised his voice as much as he could. "The man is insufferable. The whole world appears one huge jest to him, and the only one topic he takes seriously is that of love. He departed ere I could question him further in search of his beloved contessa," Thomas complained. Cristoforo had left Smallhythe ahead of the fleet and ridden back to London with the search party and men-at-arms, seeking the whereabouts of Prendergast as he went from town to town. Nothing had been reported of his presence since his dive from the ship. "Yet by God he did rightly create a miracle with his potions, curing me with a hood of linen that he fashioned, making me breathe the steaming unguent that he prepared. I thought it like to kill me at first, yet by the rood it was my salvation."

Jamie found his friend entertaining. Nothing seemed to trouble Cristoforo much and he made light of every danger, taking the view that life was to be lived to the full and for the moment. He proceeded to explain to his father all that happened.

"So 'twas by God's grace that Mark was aboard the *Shield of the Cross?*"

"'Twas ever thus. Fate casts her bony hands and we must grasp all chances that are offered and pray God it keeps us alive," Jamie shrugged.

"Amen to that, my son. Now, what of Sir John Prendergast? Has aught been heard of him since he dived to the water?"

"No. A thorough search was made on all the land holdings thereabouts, yet there was no sign. He may have drowned, but his body has not been discovered so far. My Lord Beaufort was araged at his escape, and for certes the local populace love him and would like as not harbour him in secret. I know little more, but would dearly like to engage with him again, for I have an unfinished pledge that I must honour." The words came out with such menace, so at odds with the atmosphere of his father's bedchamber that Jeanette recoiled slightly at his venom.

"We shall disturb you no longer father, and allow you to rest," Jeanette proclaimed. "Come brother, let us away and leave father be."

Westminster Palace

The royal audience were debating the events of the past few days when news came to the chamber from a courtier, who begged a conference with the prince. The others present watched the transformation of the young Henry.

"He has done what?" he roared. It was the second time in

days that Sir Richard Whittington had seen the prince lose his temper so violently. Prince Henry turned from the courtier to tell the others what he had just heard in disbelief: "That whoreson Prendergast has taken sanctuary – in Westminster Abbey! He is in Westminster Abbey bold as brass! How came he there, my Lord Beaufort, for we bethought he drowned or was at large to be captured?"

Thomas Beaufort's eyes widened in rage at the news and his fists clenched at his side in anger. "My lord prince, I know not. Yet as an indicted traitor he does not deserve sanctuary. I will go hence myself and remove the cur at swordpoint, church or no."

"No, for we should have another martyr like Archbishop Scrope on our hands, and for that naught would be served." The king spoke across the chamber, his voice strong and hard, and all present turned in his direction. The court were aware of how much damage the execution of Scrope, who had raised a rebellion in arms against the king, had done to the king's reputation. Many saw him as a martyr, and his death had caused great damage to the king's reputation. None wanted to see this repeated. "The traitor Longe, when is he to be arrayed?"

"We have no date as yet, majesty," Sir William Gascoigne replied. "He awaits our pleasure, chained in the Tower."

"Good. Let him rot, for we are in no hurry to deal with his case. As to Prendergast, he has forty days remaining, then he can be fetched out when his sanctuary is expired. Yet, hear us well, we want him alive and taken to custody unharmed."

"As your majesty pleases." Sir William agreed, passing a knowing look with Beaufort, both thinking the same thought, that the food due to Prendergast as of right by law might well be in short supply over the forthcoming weeks.

"We are most concerned as to how this delay will affect the treaty. We wanted Prendergast and Longe's heads in a timely manner to help the treaty. Do we prevail in that regard? For I would still aid the suit of the Armagnac faction if we could agree on the subject of the traitor Glyndower. We believe they will make war upon Burgundy with or without our aid. All efforts must be made to align the terms of the Treaty of Brétigny with those of the Flemish Treaty. Without such unison we would lose the power to rule Aquitaine, and with it our concession to the French realm," The king said, showing the steel that he was regaining as his health once again improved against all the odds.

The lords surrounding him were amazed at his strength of purpose, not believing the rumours of his miraculous recovery. The king had been told years before in a prophecy made by a seer in whom he believed deeply that he would not die anywhere other than in Jerusalem. With this driving him, the court believed that he would not give up his iron hold on the crown until he returned to the Holy Land and his fate.

"Amen to that, my lord king." His son exclaimed, showing to one and all that king and prince were in accord on this matter if not others. The prince continued in this vein, seeking to consolidate his father with a single purpose. "Think ye, majesty, that the Burgundians will also attempt to sway us to their cause with emissaries begging for help?"

The king turned his rheumy eyes directly at his son, from whom he had encountered so much resistance and suspicion.

"We know not for certes, yet we suspect that nothing will occur until the ink is dry upon the Flemish Treaty. For Burgundy is a wily foe and will pledge allegiance as he sees fit to further his cause. The Burgundians would have France and with it the Armagnacs under their yolk, ceding lands as their due. Be it a fair trade or a temporary dam to stem the tide, we ask you?"

Silence fell upon the company, for in one fell swoop the king had outlined the strategy of France as many saw it more succinctly and clearly than any treaty could. His summary begged the question that was in the mind of all those present: which faction would gain England the most power and land?

Part Three
The English Court

Summer/Autumn

Chapter Thirty-Two

Westminster Palace: late June

The council chamber was presided over by the Bishop Chichele, Thomas Earl of Arundel, Sir Hugh Mortimer, Sir Henry Beaufort and John Catterick – all eminent members of the Council and close confidants of the prince. Neither the king nor the prince were present, neither were any of the king's coterie, who had also been excluded from the talks that were at this moment being held in secret. Seated around the table were royal emissaries from the French court and ducal envoys. An eminent member was Sir Gaillard de Durfort, who represented the French court.

"Messiers, we are empowered to offer substantial benefit to your prince and the realm of England," Sir Gaillard pledged. "The treaty has been signed by his grace the Duke of Burgundy, and now that the seas of the Channel are calm we are in unity." The Frenchman shrugged as though there were no reasonable impediments to any accord between the two countries. The men opposite sat stony faced, waiting for Sir Gaillard's effusive monologue to finish. They were masters of the negotiating table and very experienced. "We are prepared to concede the region of Aquitaine for certes, and mayhap there are ways to encourage parts of Normandy to be added to the lands of England. What say you, Messiers?"

Mortimer spoke quickly and in English, knowing how hard the French found it to understand the language. "I trust them not. Remember how they pillaged the bags of the Armagnacs and found the agreement to treat with King Henry as sovereign king of England, thereby recognising his disputed position of absolute power. Why do they now agree to all that we could wish for?"

The speech had been delivered in his northern accent, making it virtually impossible for the French to keep up with. Sir Gaillard frowned, trying to comprehend what had been said.

"Yet they can offer more than their royal cousins – with no holding out for a recognition of Glyndower. There is more here," Carrick, who was the lawyer for the English side, offered. "I can smell it. Wait on't, for I believe we are about to be delivered of the full offer."

Archbishop Chichele smiled benevolently and responded in French: "My lords, pray continue."

Sir Gailliard looked around at the other members of his embassy and as if by some unseen signal continued. "My lord the Duke of Burgundy has authorised us to propose a marriage of allegiance to seal the fate of our great countries, and will offer the Lady Anne, his daughter, in marriage to be betrothed to his royal highness Prince Henry."

The English contingent had to school themselves quickly to give nothing away, and merely glanced at each other at the magnitude of the offer.

The Earl of Arundel spoke up as the head of the English contingent: "We thank his grace the Duke of Burgundy for his generous and very attractive offer of the bride price for the Lady Anne. As I am sure you understand, we needs must communicate all matters to his royal highness before we can comment further. As the hour is late, I propose that we break for supper and reconvene on the morrow. There is after all much to consider from your generous proposal." The earl's expression brokered no argument. His suggestion was accepted and all rose and bowed before leaving the chamber.

— ✕ ⚜ ✕ —

"Well," Whittington demanded. "What occurred?"

"It was as you suspected, my lord. De Berry was summoned to their chamber and was there long enough to reveal all that had been discussed," Jamie answered.

"We shall learn soon enough if it be true, for if my informants at the French court are in the right of it, they are to offer the Lady Anne as bride to sway the prince. The marriage promises not just a bride for the prince but the unison of the two royal houses. Yet 'tis a poor foundation upon which to build a kingdom," Whittington opined.

"Rumours already abound, for upon leaving the chamber of the Burgundians, de Berry roamed the court whispering hither and thither, to wit the intelligence is as you say my lord."

"By the rood I know not why we let that jackal off the leash, for there are times when he does more harm than good – yet mayhap the devil you know," he mused. "Go to, now, James and seek Bishop Arundel or Richard, Lord Grey, with whom you are well acquainted. Ensure that the king hears of this from our lips before the rumours reach him from other sources."

"As you wish, Sir Richard."

"Before you go, I have another deed for you. Once you have informed the king, I would have you travel to France and seek out the Duke of Armagnac or a loyal follower and ensure that they know of all that has occurred here this day. Needs must they be aware of what has been offered. I suspect the bait laid by the Burgundians will pit king against prince and that as a result there will be arms and aid given to the Duke of Burgundy. It will put us all in an invidious position – and if the Armagnacs fall, France will be united and the stronger for it. I shall have a letter ready upon your return, now go with all haste, for much is at stake," Whittington finished.

Jamie left Sir Richard's quarters and made for the river, where a wherry transported him to Lambeth palace. The short journey across the Thames was a pleasant one in the bright sunshine, yet the summer brought with it the strong smell of humanity that used the Thames as a sewer. He would not wish to fall overboard, he reflected, and welcomed dry land on the opposite bank after avoiding collision with the many craft that navigated the busy waterway.

The landing stage was guarded by two men-at-arms who demanded his rank and his reason for entering. They summoned a courtier who accompanied him through to the inner sanctum and thence to the royal chambers. He was made to wait upon the king as a member of the royal household entered to see if he could be admitted. After some minutes Lord Grey emerged from the chambers led by the courtier.

"Sir James," the knight greeted him genially, "what brings you to this side of the river?"

"Lord Grey, I bid you good morrow. I come at Sir Richard's bidding with news for the king."

The Chamberlain frowned, knowing Whittington rarely sent anyone on a fool's errand, and that if Jamie had been so tasked it would be of some importance.

"I prithee tell me all," he encouraged.

"There was a secret meeting twixt the prince's proctors and

the Burgundians this day. It has but recently finished and rumours already abound. Evidently negotiations were made, and seems that the Duke of Burgundy has offered his daughter, Anne, as a marriage sop for Prince Henry's alliance and favour. This along with other incentives were given for the country to side with the Burgundian cause against the Armagnacs."

Lord Grey's face spoke of his anger: "A secret meeting? By God's grace, did the prince know aught of this?"

"I know not, my lord, but he was not present at the discussions." Jamie answered tactfully.

"You have done well, de Grispere. I will ensure that his majesty hears of this and is forewarned. It will surely go ill with him, for the king is I believe more favoured towards the Armagnacs and seeks to plan a campaign to that effect."

"Is there any message that you wish returned to Sir Richard?"

"Prithee offer him my thanks for his consideration. Kindly inform him that I shall visit him later."

Jamie left and returned to the palace across the river and Whittington's quarters.

"Thank you for advising the king," Whittington said. "His majesty will be furious and may resolve to take a stronger course of action as his health improves. Now James, to France. Travel at your best haste to the Armagnac court and let it be known what has occurred here today with the Burgundian embassy. I will commit nothing to writing, so you must inform them of today's events. Their greed for power and hatred of Burgundy will do the rest."

"I am confused. Why would you side with the Armagnacs? I bethought them out of favour as they demanded that Glyndower be taken back into the fold and pardoned? Alas, if the king favours one side and the prince the other, do we not divide the realm by our own actions by providing intelligence to the Armagnacs?"

Whittington sighed as though explaining something to a child. "If nothing else, James, it shows your heart be true. As a loyal subject, you should not go forth afore you know all the facts. In faith I do not seek to aid one side above the other, nor to give either a distinct vantage. No, what I seek to achieve is disarray, for if one faction should gain the upper hand and take command of France they will unite the country and England will be in greater peril.

"I predict that the prince will sue for aid to the Burgundians and the king will not be drawn. The king seeks only to retain full rule over Aquitaine as was provisioned in the Treaty of 1360 and to retain Guyenne, securing the lands around Calais that must never fall. I seek to set one side against the other, to ensure that neither gains vantage. A divided France is a weak France and one that we will easily defeat and keep at bay. For by God's grace if the king continues to rally as he is now doing and regains his health, he will travel in person to Calais and there commence a campaign to retake the lands that are rightly his. France riven by civil war is what I seek. It offers an open gateway for the king and a path to unity between monarch and prince." Whittington's voice had gained power as he spoke in the distinctive and incisive way he had when he was impassioned.

Jamie stood before him seeing the right of Whittington's actions. Sir Richard was a man who was clearly driven by his love for England and the king he had so loyally helped to protect. "I understand, Sir Richard. I will make plans accordingly and leave this very day," he replied.

"You are best placed of all my *insidiores*, for reasons known to us both. I am sapient of the dangers and would adjure you to have great care: an Englishman in France at this time will not be popular."

"You are aware that I speak French like the Flemish merchants of my father's race, and as ever I will go abroad as such. I shall leave for Le Havre, the less time to spend on French soil. My father has connexions there and I will use these to my vantage. My route will take me from there to Rouen and the Armagnacs."

"May God have you in his keeping, James, and I shall look for your safe return." Whittington dismissed him with a smile.

"Amen to that, Sir Richard," Jamie smiled back, then in a flurry of excitement he was gone.

Chapter Thirty-Three

London

The court, as ever, was a place where a man could earn a coin for the right sort of information, and Jacques de Berry, straddling the fence betwixt the Armagnac and Burgundian camps, had many about him who would watch, follow and inform. One such was Crispin de Lourds, who following his master Sir John Tiptoft's fall from grace now supplied de Berry with information and was handsomely rewarded with illicit coin from de Berry's pockets.

De Lourds still carried the legacy of the beating Jamie had given him the year before, and bore great ill will towards the prince's knight, vowing to bring him down if he could. De Lourds had followed Jamie from Whittington's quarters, watched him cross the river to Lambeth Palace and return, and reported his movements to de Berry.

"So, he moves hither and thither passing messages in the way only a trusted lieutenant would do. Causing mischief and no doubt relating all that is rumoured about the court to his majesty. Well it is too late, de Grispere, for the meeting has occurred and an accord is all but reached, please God, for the good of France."

"Shall I follow him further, Jacques?"

"No, for he made to leave and rode eastwards, probably to his home in the Jewry. It will serve and you shall be paid well, for this is interesting news. Whittington plots and turns the court around his finger as ever, yet he is too late. Send Isaac to me, for the Jewry is his land and he will not be easily spotted."

Isaac followed Jamie back to Launceston lane and waited patiently through the day. He was rewarded after sext as Jamie appeared to the ringing of the church bells, trotting out with a mounted servant by his side. His huge wolfhound whined at the gates, held back with some difficulty by Jeanette, who waved him farewell. He rode Killarney, making it easier on the groom to ride back leading the spare horse home from the river port. Isaac followed them carefully, keeping well-hidden as a mark of respect to the calibre of the man he was following.

At the river wharves, he watched as Jamie handed over the horse to the groom and boarded a sleek caravel, well prepared and ready to follow the tide that was on the turn, beginning to flow seaward once again. Even on the faster caravel Jamie knew it would take a day and a night to arrive at le Havre, but it was safer to make the time at sea to save time exposed on French soil despite the supposed truce between the two countries. The signing of the treaty and the capture of the pirates made it less likely that they would be set upon in open waters, yet still he carried his battle axe and a small buckler in his war bag. There were two men-at-arms aboard, both armed with crossbows, but with a fleet ship and supposed peace, there seemed little likelihood of attack. Jamie had been granted rough quarters for the crossing, but it was a berth and a roof over his head, and he had known worse privations.

For the time being the sun shone and the salt spray blew all the cobwebs away. As there were no other passengers, Jamie whiled away the time asking the men-at-arms if they would humour him with some exercise at sword practice. There was just room on deck and it was good to practice in a confined area because it meant that footwork was the key. To prevent slashing the ropes or rigging they used weighted wooden swords for their work and set to, parrying, cutting and thrusting. He took each man in turn, then asked if they would attack simultaneously: two on one. They grinned, agreeing readily to the request.

It was excellent practice for Jamie, and as the two men-at-arms soon discovered it was hard to attack completely simultaneously. If one struck with slashing edge, the other had to either wait or lunge with a thrust, being careful to avoid the downward slash of his friend's blade. It required coordination by the attackers, and in the restricted area Jamie had the advantage. The two started a rhythm but this too had a disadvantage, for as one held back until his friend attacked, it left him open if the single man were fast and understood the tactic.

Twice they tangled each other in their enthusiasm and each time Jamie exploited it, dancing away to the outside gate, putting the attacker in the position of blocking his waiting friend. After an hour, all three were blowing hard, and Jamie called a halt to the relief of the other two men.

One of them, a man called Alan, wiped his brow and asked: "Where did you learn such skills, for we've never been tasked to fight one to two, except unlooked for in a melee. Mind, it is right good practice and sharpens the eye no end."

"That it does," Jamie replied. "My father's retainer was a man-at-arms in the wars in the Holy Land and insisted I learn the use of the sword since I was a boy." Although it had been Sir Robert de Umfraville who had honed those skills. As his squires practiced he would roar: "You can't choose your enemy in a battle. He chooses you, and like as not you'll be outnumbered, so you'd better learn to fight more than one man."

The words came back to him, forcing a smile, along with the memory of bruises and sore heads and hands from the early days until he had learned to anticipate and turn the advantage of superior numbers against the attackers. It had been a hard school, but a valuable one.

Alan broke Jamie's brief reverie: "Well I've learned a new skill today and no mistake. When we've recovered, I'll be the odd one out and you and Walter can attack me, and we'll see how I fare."

— × ✱× —

Isaac returned to Jacques de Berry in his private rooms, bearing news of what he had seen.

"A caravel? Did you find out for where it was bound?" de Berry asked.

"I did my lord, and she was bound for le Havre."

"Le Havre, and from there to the Armagnac court at Rouen, I'm bound, to pass on the Burgundian terms and stir a nest of vipers to Whittington's vantage." He growled. "Thank you Isaac, you have done well." He passed him six pence. The boy was delighted with the amount and departed, assuring de Berry he was forever at his service. Almost as soon as the door had closed there was a knock upon it. A page stood at the door: "My lord, you are bidden to attend the Burgundian envoys who would wish you to sup with them."

De Berry left immediately for the private chamber of the French emissaries. Food was brought to the chamber and they were not disturbed.

"You have served us well, for rumours abound of the proposals to the prince," Sir Gaillard said. "When we meet with the king it will be embarrassing for him, as the prince will strive even harder to break the bonds of his father's yoke and push to aid our cause."

"I have just learned of an element that may upset you and hurry the timing of your negotiations." De Berry paused as de Durfort and the others frowned in puzzlement. "I believe that a messenger has been sent to France, more specifically to the Armagnac court to advise them of what has been offered. They will be infuriated and concerned at the threat of aid to the duke. You must beware of them striking early towards Paris. If they gain control, they will pressure the king and the duke's power will wane."

"When did this messenger leave?" de Durfort asked so quietly as his voice was steeped in menace and anger.

"By today's tide. He travels for Le Havre and will arrive at Rouen within four days. With a Calais crossing and fast horses, a message can be delivered to Paris in five or six days. It will be too late to stop him yet will offer the Duke of Burgundy advance warning of a possible Armagnac attack, and as such he will be all the better prepared to meet it."

The French nobleman swore harshly: "By God's legs, who orchestrated this relay of information? Nothing remains secret for ever, yet I believed that we should embarrass the king and drive a wedge between him and the prince. I did not think we would alert the cursed Armagnacs to war at this early stage." He thumped his fist into palm and strode the chamber as the others looked on in consternation.

"What would you have me do my lord? I am at your command," De Berry said.

"Do? Why, if you are able, I wish you to travel to Paris and warn my lord of Burgundy that he is to expect an escalation of war."

"As you wish, my lord. I shall board an evening ship bound

for Calais and be within Paris in five days." With that he ignored all offer of food and excused himself to make ready for France.

The talks progressed for two more days amid swirls of rumour until the French deputation was brought before King Henry at a full meeting of the Council. The terms were laid out clearly and concisely: treasure, the promised reparation of land – and the ultimate jewel, the offer of marriage between the prince and the Lady Anne, daughter of Duke John. It was an attractive proposition to the prince.

As always, two distinct factions were lined up, drawn almost imperceptibly by loyalty: the king on one side with his loyal followers of Lancastrian knights such as Sir Robert Waterton, Sir Thomas Erpingham and Sir John Norbury; the prince and his proctors on the other. To this was added the Burgundian embassy that was all charm and manners, appearing to favour neither one side nor the other, supposedly offering the most innocuous of solutions to a potential escalation of hostilities relating to the English ownership in France.

The king himself was not present, and Sir Richard Grey, as his Chamberlain, spoke out, asking the question that was on everyone's lips.

"My lords, we thank you in the king's name for the gestures and tokens that you have kindly offered to bestow upon his majesty and his royal highness. But there is one position that requires clarification and as yet remains unspoken in this regard." There was a collective silence and the court was electric with a frisson of excitement. All within the English contingent knew what would be asked. "It therefore behoves me to ask it. Do you acknowledge and accept in all matters and rights due, recognising his majesty King Henry Fourth of England as the rightful ruler of this realm?"

Everyone held their breath as they all looked to Sir Gaillard de Durfort and the ducal embassy. The knight's face turned red with anger or embarrassment, it was hard to tell which. He had been wrong footed, never expecting to be called out in so direct a manner. Finally, after a pause he replied: "I have no authority on behalf of my lord the Duke of Burgundy, either implied or explicit, to confirm such an indictment. We have an ineluctable desire to see harmony between our nations to foster the good-will of his grace, and Duke John will respond in kind, of that I am certain."

Sir Richard Whittington was distanced from the company to the side of the chamber, yet he heard what was said along with everyone else present. As the babble of voices grew, he murmured to William Stokes at his side: "They twist and turn as eels in a barrel, and I would trust them no more to policy as a fox in a hen house."

"Amen to that. The king will never accept such an answer, and I perceive that the Burgundian cause will obtain no offer of aid from his majesty. As to his royal highness, that may be another matter."

Lord Grey, ever the diplomat, responded in kind.

"If my lords would be gracious enough to take instructions in this matter, we should be thankful."

Prince Henry stood perplexed, feeling once again thwarted by his father, even though he was not present. His scar throbbed and he gently massaged the old wound. He felt the need to intercede somehow, but the matter was taken out of his hands by Henry Beaufort, Bishop of Winchester and the king's half-brother.

"My lords," he began, quieting the hubbub of noise that surrounded the chamber. "May I say with the permission of the prince that we look favourably upon your suit, and that we are sure that some amicable position can be met that is suitable to all parties."

The bishop studiously avoided the eyes of Lord Grey as he spoke, knowing he was crossing the Rubicon in terms of relations between prince and king and with it discarding his position of impartiality. It was a dangerous game to play, he knew, and represented a huge gamble in his political career. Upon making eye contact with the prince, he was gratified to receive an almost imperceptible nod of gratitude and a faint smile. Invisible lines had been etched still deeper into the English court as everyone there saw and understood the significance of those last words: it was a play for the crown.

The following day Prince Henry was summoned to a private audience with his father, who had been advised of all that had occurred in the previous day's meeting. The prince bowed to his father who was seated on his throne. To the prince's eyes he seemed to sit straighter, and rumour had it that he had been at practice with a sword, sparring with Lord Grey and other Lancastrian knights. If this were true it would explain his change of pallor, the prince mused, seeing a ruddy glow to his father's cheeks and reminding himself that his father was but forty-seven years old, and kings had still fought at that age.

"My son, we thank you for attending us. We were appraised of the events at yesterday's meeting with the ducal envoys. To this end we wish to inform you of our decision in an effort to seem outwardly unified towards the French.

"Our subjects in Gascony are wedded to the Armagnac cause, and should we side with Burgundy it would be the basis for a civil war of our own in France between our English and Gascon subjects. Think on, we also have interests in Aragon, Navarre and Brittany who would be similarly affected. It would not accord well with our position if we were to be the cause of such discord and division among our subjects.

"We therefore propose a new course of action. We shall lead our forces to Calais and strike fear into the hearts of all the

French that threaten our borders there. Nay my son, do not look at us so, we recover by the day."

"To Calais, majesty? You will lead a force to Calais in person?" The prince asked, shocked to the core by what his father had just said. "You will not favour either side with aid?"

"We shall aid neither Armagnac nor Burgundy. We shall fight for our own territory as God intends," The king rejoined, strength entering his voice as he raised a clenched fist to reinforce his view and his intention.

Chapter Thirty-Four

Rouen, France

Jamie entered the magnificent city of Rouen three days after leaving Le Havre, still cursing the corkscrewed mount he had hired. The palfrey had walked comfortably enough, but she had an annoying and uncomfortable gait at the trot that twisted him as he rose and fell in the saddle. He wished that he had either Richard or Killarney under him instead. His back was sore after three days riding and he vowed to change the errant mare before his return journey.

The great walls that bordered the river Seine turned the town into a veritable fortress, and with a soldier's eye he mentally assessed how difficult it would be to take it by siege, not liking the odds of success for the attackers. He headed for the Place du Vieux-Marché in the centre, and from there made his way to the palace of the archbishop, where he was given to believe the Armagnacs lodged. It looked a great deal more comfortable than their rustic castle to the north that lay outside the city walls.

He walked his horse slowly through the crowded, dirty

cobbled streets of half-timbered houses, hearing accents that were very different from the French spoken in Calais and even Le Havre, some ninety miles to the west. He was careful to speak with a Flemish accent and maintained his disguise as a wool merchant. He raised his cowl against the awful stench of the city, rank in the summer heat and made more obvious after the fragrant fields of the countryside through which he had but recently passed.

As expected, the bishop's palace was gated and guarded, and he saw to his relief the arms of the Armagnacs flew from the spire above: the quartered flag and four lions rampant in red and gold. The ashlar stone glared brightly at Jamie in the harsh sunlight, causing him to shade his eyes from the stark walls as he awaited permission to enter.

A courtier appeared, clearly a man of rank, who bade Jamie dismount and follow him into the splendid building. As Jamie entered, he breathed a sigh of mixed relief and comfort, such was the contrast between the stifling heat of the courtyard and the cool atmosphere inside. The sculpted arched ceiling was beautifully carved with clean lines against the coloured relief of the interspersed panels. The tiled floors and marbled frescoes emanated calm and tranquillity and Jamie felt soiled in comparison to his opulent surroundings. He had travelled for five days in the heat and badly needed a wash and a change of clothing.

"I feel like a pig in such a palace." He muttered to the courtier, who responded immediately.

"Ah monsieur, *mille pardons*, please allow me." He led Jamie to an anteroom and a *garderobe*. There a servant produced a bowl of water and a towel, together with a cool goblet of watered white wine that smelled fresh after the stench of the city without and tasted like nectar after Jamie's long ride.

Once refreshed, and with the stain of travel removed, he followed the courtier into a large inner chamber, where he recognised a group of nobles gathered around a table, discussing plans that were strewn about atop the polished surface. They turned as one at Jamie's entrance.

"My lords, may I present Sir James de Grispere of the English court," the courtier announced.

The young Charles, Duke of Orleans, came forward as the most senior aristocrat in the gathering: "Sir James, I bid you welcome to France. Are you fatigued? Do you wish refreshment?"

"Your grace is most kind, I have been given consideration and am recovered from my travels. As your grace permits, I have news that will be of immense interest to you and the Armagnac faction."

"Pray continue."

"Secret talks have taken place between the proctors of Prince Henry and the ducal envoys of the Burgundians, who reside at this moment in the English court."

The duke was shocked. He had not been aware of such intelligence and bade Jamie tell him all that had occurred. The others present, including the Duke of Berry and the Count of Armagnac, also interrogated him at length until the full story was told.

"Sir James, we thank you for your honesty and that of your king in bringing us this news, and I would beg of you a favour to us." The young Duke of Orleans said eventually. "Whilst you have no vested interest in our cause, we would ask that you abide here for a few days and mayhap return with a message for your king in due course. For you will not be looked for on the road and stand a good chance of securing the delivery of a missive."

"As your grace wishes. If thou dost agree, I needs must depart within three days to attend to my duties in England."

"That will be ample time to secure a reply to your king."

Jamie was invited to join them for an evening meal and a chamber was prepared for his use. Meanwhile a messenger was sent to Paris, the first of a three-man relay. Jamie had noticed an intensification of activity, with more captains and knights coming and going at the palace and a mustering of troops beyond the city walls near the castle, which formed a military headquarters for the Armagnacs away from the bishop's palace. On the third day, as Jamie was becoming more and more anxious that his every move was being watched, he saw a tired horseman make his way up to the gates of the palace. The man slid from the saddle of the third horse he had ridden that day. He made his way stiff-legged into the entrance hall, and from his position of vantage at the duke's table, Jamie saw him being led down to the main chamber where three days before he himself had enjoyed his own audience with the duke.

The duke bade him enter and join him, and the messenger passed Jamie to stand before the duke and hand him a sealed missive. The duke read it and in the silence of the court it appeared as if nobody so much as breathed as he did so.

"Sir James, your arrival has been timely," the duke said finally. "We are most grateful to you for agreeing to our entreaties and waiting for our response. This letter has arrived from Paris and with it a promise to aid us in our fight against the Burgundians. On your honour, I beg you deliver this to your king, for it contains a message asking for his favour in matters of the utmost import. I know that I can trust you as a most loyal servant to his majesty. There is no one else we would trust so, and as an Englishman you bear the honour well."

"Your grace, I am your most obedient servant and will most earnestly fulfil your wishes." Jamie took the sealed scroll and resolved to place it securely in his saddle bags.

"In return I have a gift for you for your journey," the duke offered with a genuine smile. There had grown between them a quality of intimacy which bordered on friendship for two men of different rank who may one day meet on the battlefield as enemies. "But for now you must forgive me, as time is pressing and there is much to accomplish," the duke continued, "Our heartfelt gratitude once again for your efforts in journeying here, and I bid you Godspeed on your return."

Wishing the duke adieu Jamie left, curious to see what gift awaited him. Leaving the cool of the building a few minutes later with his bags packed he crossed to the stables to fetch his hired horse, none the wiser.

The groom came forward with a steel grey dappled mare: "Monsieur, a gift from my master," he offered.

As he came closer Jamie saw that the horse had a kind eye, was short coupled with a good slope to the shoulders and pasterns that promised a smooth and comfortable ride. *Much better than the screwed, cow-hocked animal I rode here on,* he thought. He took the reins and gently mounted, feeling an immediate sense of empathy with the animal.

"What is her name?"

"Tacheter."

Dapple, of course. Aptly named, he thought, nudging her into a walk. Tacheter responded eagerly and Jamie began his homeward journey.

Chapter Thirty-Five

London Wharf

Jamie had been delighted with Tacheter on his return journey, and she had lived up to all his hopes for a smooth ride. He decided to keep her instead of selling her on at Le Havre and paid for her to be transported aboard the next ship to sail, which was a cog that had sufficient room to hold her. She was nervous at first being hoisted aloft in a sling but quickly settled once on board and only fretted a little.

After safely disembarking, the mare now stood shaking herself, eyes wide and nostrils flared as she got used to her new surroundings. Jamie saddled her and made off through the streets towards Westminster Palace. It had been nearly two weeks since he left for Le Havre, and he was keen to return home – but first he had a message to deliver. He had looked at the seal closing the scroll and saw to his amazement that it bore the crest of Queen Isabeau of France. He was intrigued as to why the French queen should be writing directly to the king of England.

Jamie stabled the mare and made his way to Whittington's chambers.

"James," Whittington exclaimed as he was shown into his chamber. "By the rood it is good to see you returned safe and well. Now, tell me all that has occurred. Did you reach Rouen safely and without mishap?"

"I did, Sir Richard. Yet afore I offer a full discourse, I have this directly from the Duke of Orleans to be given into the king's hand." He passed over the scroll that he had carried safely from France.

Whittington took the scroll and looked at it cagily. "You brought this first to me?"

"I did, Sir Richard. I thought that you should be aware of its existence before it reaches the king's hands. Look to the seal," Jamie said.

"The Queen of France?" Whittington was aghast. "How came you by this? Tell me all."

Jamie explained about his stay in Rouen and he calculated that a messenger relay would have been able to visit Paris and return during the time of his stay. Whittington nodded, seemingly understanding all. Jamie looked at Sir Richard and said: "This is a mystery to me. For the queen is loyal to King Charles, despite his vagaries. Why would she correspond with his majesty and on what account?"

Whittington smiled at his naivety. "Because, young Sir James, she is cousin to the Armagnac faction through her Italian ancestry. She is related to the count of Milan, who is a great friend to our king. It was he who made the king's armour for the duel to the death with Thomas de Mowbray, Duke of Norfolk, although as you know the trial by combat was never fought. The queen will not wish the English to aid the Burgundians against her kinsman. That is the favour she asks, I'll warrant," Whittington waved the sealed parchment at Jamie.

"Now take this to the king," he continued. "It shall not be borne thence by my hand, for many will see and rumours will surround me again. I wish this to arrive unsullied by my involvement. Go to, James, and approach his majesty direct."

Jamie left Whittington's chambers and made his way through the corridors to the king's private apartments, where he was invited into an antechamber and asked to await Lord Grey, the king's chamberlain.

"Sir James, good morrow, how may I be of aid?" Lord Grey's manner was blunt and he was clearly pressed on other business.

Jamie was tired from his long journey and was in no mood to be stalled. "My lord I am lately returned from France and have here a missive to be given to his Majesty."

Lord Grey frowned, taking the scroll from his hand: "From France? To where did you journey and from whom is the message?"

"I travelled from Rouen and the Armagnac court, and this was given to me by the Duke of Orleans to be passed in person into the king's hand in order to fully honour the terms of the duke's promise of delivery. My lord, you will see that the seal bears another's crest." Jamie offered, awaiting the reaction that he knew would come. Lord Grey looked at the seal.

"The Queen Isabeau's crest! How long have you been on the road, man?"

"I left Rouen nearly a sennight past."

Lord Grey's attitude changed at once, and when he spoke his voice held a sense of urgency. "Stay, for the king is making plans at this moment, and I am persuaded he will wish to speak with you."

Moments later Jamie was summoned to the presence of the king. He accompanied Lord Grey through to the king's inner sanctum and there on the throne sat his majesty. Jamie bowed thrice and took a closer look at his sovereign, who had gained weight and sat straighter on the throne. His shoulders appeared filled with new muscle, not slack and limp as before. *So the rumours were true*, he thought, *he has been practicing with a sword and arms.*

The king received the scroll, which lay unravelled in his hand. "Sir James, you are a most welcome sight, and it seems that you do us great service yet again," he offered.

"Majesty, it is but my devoir to serve as I may to aid the crown." Jamie answered.

"Your loyalty is noted, and does you credit in these treacherous times. Tell us, were you informed of the contents of this letter? Lord Grey informs us that it was placed in your hand by the young Duke of Orleans. Is this so?"

"As your majesty pleases, I have no knowledge of the contents. Its safe delivery was assigned to me directly by the duke and it remained sealed in my presence. I awaited a messenger that was gone three full days, which time I assumed was necessary to journey to and from the French court in Paris."

"We thank you in all your efforts, and ask that mayhap you will accompany us on our expedition to Calais in September."

"Your majesty is too kind, and I should be honoured."

"Go to then – and not a word of what has occurred here today or your journey to France." The king urged.

"On my honour, majesty. May God be with you, sire."

With that he bowed and left the royal presence, excitement shaking his young frame with every stride. He was to accompany the king to fight in France, that is how he interpreted the king's words.

Hotel des Tournelles, Paris

Jacques de Berry rode hard and made his way to the French court in the heart of Paris. It had been just over five days since

277

he had left London. To his disappointment he found that John the Fearless, Duke of Burgundy, was absent from the court and expected back within the week after inspecting his Flemish lands to the north. He had gained an audience with the king's chief advisor, Lord Pierre Salmon, while messengers were despatched to find the duke and speed his return to court.

He was granted an audience with the dauphin, Lord Salmon, Queen Isabeau and other members of the regency council were also in attendance. The regal figure of Queen Isabeau was seated on the throne in proxy for her husband, King Charles the Sixth, who was indisposed with another fit that had caused him to injure and nearly kill a courtier who had tried to defend himself without attacking the royal personage. The unlucky man had barely escaped with his life after being stabbed twice by the mad king.

De Berry looked around him at the sumptuous court and felt instantly at home. His fatigue left him within the confines of the court that was so familiar. The luxury exceeded that of the English court, with the rooms adorned with vivid colours, deep piled carpets and tapestries from the Far East and Italy hanging from the walls. Velvet pelmets of deep blue embroidered with the gold fleur-de-lys of France hung in swathes from the canopies that shrouded the royal throne. Mysterious scents and perfumes wafted through the air with subtle blends of jasmine and musk. It was a heady mix and he longed for the eternal comfort of the country that he called his home.

Washed and changed from his travels, he made his way to the royal dais, bowing to the queen before him and acknowledging nods of welcome from other members of the council whom he recognised.

The queen sat imperious and inscrutable as Jacques moved to kiss her hand.

"Majesty, you are more radiant than ever." He said, and

meant it. For the queen seemed not to age, retaining the beauty of her youth even into her forties. Her eyes had a dewy sheen, and she seemed to see all with a gentle smile that gave nothing away. She was reputed to have been the dead Duke of Orleans' lover, and fresh rumour insinuated that the same role had been in part filled by the Duke of Burgundy – which would have been a strange irony if correct, as he had arranged for his rival's assassination.

"We see that your time at the English court has not lessened your charm. Pray tell us what brings you to our court."

"Majesty if it please you, I bring news of great import. The offer of terms by your royal embassy from his grace Duke John has been put abroad, and even now I suspect that the Armagnacs are being informed of all matters."

He went to say more, but was stayed by the queen's hand as she silenced him with a gesture. Her mind raced.

"Who was present at the meeting? The king in person?"

"No, majesty. He was not aware until after the talks were finished, as they were held in secret. Only Prince Henry's proctors and the ducal embassy were present."

"Can you confirm to us that no decision has been made as to acceptance or rejection of the terms offered?"

De Berry hesitated. He had been caught out and was in a quandary, desperate that the Duke of Burgundy be present. For he wished neither to deceive a queen nor disclose details that may contradict what the duke had passed on to her majesty.

"Majesty, e'er it please you," he began, hoping to dissemble without alienating the queen. "The terms were for jewels, landed obligations – and," here he hesitated, "the hand of the duke's daughter the Lady Anne in marriage to the English prince." He allowed himself to tail off.

The queen arched an eyebrow at the mention of the Lady Anne, but made no further comment on her inclusion in the terms. "Were any additional terms or codicils added to the bargain?"

"Not as far as I am aware, majesty."

"Very well. It will prove fruitless to discuss this further until my Lord John returns from his travels. We are fatigued and wish to rest. You may leave us, de Berry." She dismissed him, and for one moment he made to speak again, then he realised it would not only be in vain but extremely dangerous to do so. The queen, he perceived, was angry and hurt at his disclosure. He bowed and took his leave of the court, turning to see the queen rise as all those around her bowed in turn.

Chapter Thirty-Six

London

After a freezing winter, the summer weather had proved equally implacable, with a fierce heat lasting into August that roasted the city in humidity. Farmers feared for their crops and the threat of disease reared its ugly head again within the city walls among the closely packed citizens of the capital. The heat brought with it an appetite for lighter meals of fresh fish, a favourite of Thomas de Grispere.

"There is no one quite like Mary to mix a sorrel sauce with this excellent salmon." He exclaimed, attacking the barley bread with gusto. Thomas, who had now fully recovered, presided over his table at supper in the cool air of his dining hall, extolling the virtues of his cook: "So my boy, tell me, are the rumours true that the king intends to lead an expedition to Calais next month?"

"They are indeed, Father, from what I hear at court. Knights are training hard and vying for a position to attend his majesty and his meiny. I have been notified that I will accompany him when he leads his force to France." Jamie explained.

He had been back but two days and after a day's rest had resumed his duties at court today, returning for the evening meal.

"You will accompany the king?" his father exclaimed in astonishment and pride.

"Aye, Father, it was as good as promised to me from his majesty's own lips when I spoke with him upon my return from France. Ships are being sought for the voyage, and my Lord Beaufort has refused to return to the office of Lord Chancellor, vowing to fight with the king in France. He has clearly obtained a taste for battle and wishes to enter the fray."

"I trust not that man." John snorted in disgust from the other side of the table. "His morals and code of chivalry are those of a vagabond. He bears a grudge and would look with envy on Croesus even if he be Solomon!" He rejoined scathingly. "Yet what heartens me is that the king has taken to arms again and rallies right well, I hear. Be this so?"

"Aye John, that he does, according to my Lord Grey and others of the Lancastrian cause. I have seen his recovery for myself, and I know that he spars daily and makes scant allowance for his illness, may God assoil him. He sets the date of the 23rd of September to set sail with a great fleet to drive the French away from Calais and its marches and to regain all lands lost. It would be a great wonder if I could be at his side to fight the French." Jamie said.

"Amen to that," John said. "Would that I were young again and could fight in a shield wall against the crapauds."

Jeanette smiled at the old soldier's spirit, knowing that if pushed he would even now still give a good account of himself in any fight. He often trained with Jamie, and was as hard and fit as ever. He would probably carry a sword to his grave like the Vikings of old. "Afore you sally forth, shall you visit the Lady

Alice?" Jeanette said. "For I hear that she and her family may soon be returning to London."

"Mayhap 'tis you who should spy for Whittington," Jamie teased her. "Your knowledge of all matters abroad surpasses mine with ease. Do you have cognisance of what the French are about perchance?" he asked with a grin.

"Why, that is simple, they plead for aid and beg for war. Is that not so?" she rejoined.

"Ah and there you have it my son, a women's appropriation of the highest affairs of state summed up within a single sentence." Thomas led the laughter as Jeanette fixed an impish smile upon her face.

"Well in truth I hope to see her upon her return," Jamie said. "Providing her father permits such addresses. Naught can come of such an alliance if the old devil is set against me."

"Mayhap saving his life will have softened the earl's stance towards your addresses for Alice." Jeanette offered.

"I doubt it. He is of granite and completely implacable."

"Dost that little grey mare have aught to do with it?" Jeanette continued, teasing her brother.

Jamie had kept Tacheter and decided that he would make a present of her to Alice upon her return to London. "She is a sweet-tempered mare and is the most perfect palfrey. Alice has always yearned for a grey mare, and truth to tell, I am better pleased with Killarney as a riding horse."

Jeanette gave her brother a forbearing grin which seemed to make him all the more uncomfortable. "Well, she and her party are expected on the morrow, so best you groom her in readiness," she remarked tartly. Jamie pretended not to heed her comments and took a mouthful of food instead of replying.

— ✕ ⚜ ✕ —

Two days later the latest embassy from France arrived quietly at the London docks and made its way in secret to the palace. There were no heralds, pennants or announcements this time. The company consisted of just three of the duke's envoys accompanied by Jacques de Berry, who knew well the back passages and corridors of the palace. He secured other men in their chambers with hardly anyone of consequence seeing them.

"We seem to have entered quite unobtrusively," Sir Galliard de Durfort commented, delighted with their progress.

"It would be naïve to assume so. Rumours will spread from ostlers and pages, and by sext I shall be accused of necromancy in spiriting you from France in a basket carried by a swan," de Berry replied scornfully. "Such is the intelligence at court. Now prithee rest here messieurs, and I will facilitate arrangements for a *paroli* with the prince's proctors.

The meeting was arranged, and an hour later the men sat securely in the Bishop Chichele's quarters away from prying eyes. Thomas, the Earl of Arundel, presided over the affairs and along with his fellow members, he was eager to hear what the latest envoy had to offer.

"My lords your visit is timely, for the king plans to voyage to Calais within the month and restore order there as he sees fit."

Sir Gaillard was surprised, and looked to his fellow knights: "The king himself will travel? Is he not unhale?"

"He flourishes yet and continues in ascendancy. He is determined to take the field once more in the van and will not be dissuaded. The royal household is all agog." Sir Thomas finished, letting the words hang in the air.

"We wish to agree terms at the earliest possible moment. Even now Armagnac troops are mustering and preparing for an assault upon the western border of Paris. Duke John makes preparations, yet we fear he is too late and will give ground. If Paris is lost, so is our alliance with Burgundy and the goodwill of his majesty King Charles, may God keep him. For our king will fall under the spell of the Duke of Orleans and his contingent. And do not believe that this will be for the good of England, for with such a bond formed, they will forget all previous tributes and offers, and seek Calais as their next prize." He warned.

"And the duke would not?" Thomas challenged.

"Would we be here in harmony seeking aid and future alliances based upon the marriage of our royal houses if that were not the case?" Sir Gaillard countered.

"Therefore monsieur, let us not tarry. What are you able to offer that may sway the prince and mayhap his majesty?"

"As you please monsieur. In addition to our previous terms, we can also include rights to land in four territories that we will cede to his majesty King Henry. There may also be," here he hesitated, framing the words with care, "other inducements. To wit payment for arms to aid our cause against the Armagnacs."

The English contingent became more excited, yet did not show it, for this was what they had hoped to gain. Bishop Chichele interceded: "My lord, are we able to obtain a written confirmation of such terms signed by his grace? For hearsay is but a stepping stone, and written terms of indenture a bridge." The bishop allowed himself a small smile to rob the words of any sting.

Sir Gaillard was a diplomat as well as a knight, and knew a trap when he saw one. "My lord archbishop, I am sure we can come to acceptable terms that befit such an arrangement."

Chapter Thirty-Seven

As Jacques de Berry had suspected, the landing of the French contingent had not gone unnoticed. The army of spies that policed the docks and other English ports under the auspices of Sir William Stokes were paid to keep him abreast of all matters pertaining to comings and goings by sea. Little time was lost in informing him of the French contingent's disembarkation, and he hurried to Whittington's offices to discuss the implications of the latest much more clandestine visit and how the crown may best be served.

Whittington, as ever, was pleased with the intelligence. "We must essay how best to utilise the knowledge and fortify the crown against ambush to the royal plans. For even now that we are preparing to sally forth to Calais – why even the royal bed is made ready to transport!" He exclaimed, both men knowing that this was a sure sign of intent on the king's part. "What could they offer to entice an English union with the Burgundians, I wonder?" he mused. "I wish his grace the Archbishop of Arundel were here, for he would know on the instant of the king's plans as you know of the prince's, all the better to insure the one against the other."

"Amen to that. Yet my lord archbishop has battles of his own to fight in Oxford – which may yet involve his majesty. I fear there is naught that we can do to aid the king. He will know soon enough and for certes he will foresee the pitfalls of offering support to the treacherous Burgundians. The king is no fool and if his body wanes his mind does not.

"Oxford alone could be the cause of a division. There have been riots there and citizens killed in the name of this heretic Wycliffe," Stokes opined.

"I fear for the prince in that regard. The Beauforts have no regard for Archbishop Arundel and see him as an impediment to their rise in power. They would not hesitate to use Richard Courtney as a hammer to drive a wedge between king and prince. I hear that he resigned as chancellor of Oxford University and yet is to be reinstated in direct opposition to the rules *De Heretico Comburendo*. 'Twill not end well, for he is loved and favoured by the prince, which poses a dilemma upon which he needs to tread with care. The Beauforts will stir mischief to weaken his resolve and cause dissent with Arundel. They plead with the prince daily to petition his father to abdicate, and I know he wrestles with his conscience on the matter. There will come a time I foresee when he must choose a side – and may God himself assoil the prince to side with his father and not the Beauforts and others.

"I feel it would be prudent to ensure that the king is aware of the latest embassy from Burgundy, and I will speak directly with Lord Grey. Yet all will out soon enough. How go the sheriff's gatherings of taxes?"

"Thirty five counties are now included in the muster all is gathering in preparation for war," Stokes answered.

— ✕ ✦ ✕ —

The following day saw the arrival at court of Archbishop Arundel after a hard journey from Oxford. He made straight-away for Lambeth palace, sending pages to see if the king was south of the river. He was in a foul temper, and thin lines of anger scored the skin around his eyes.

"Never have I been so ill treated by anyone, let alone the heretical scullions that inhabit that university!" he ranted at his clerk, "I shall have the king intercede, by God's grace so I shall."

The page returned a few minutes later. "Your grace, his majesty asks that you attend him at the hour of nones in his chamber. Shall I tell him you will agree?"

"Yes, ensure that you do. Wait, what is his disposition? Has aught changed?"

"It appears not, your grace. His majesty still seems hale and intends to lead the muster to Calais," the page replied.

The hours moved on and with the passage of time the arch-bishop's temper improved, as he removed the soil of travel and ate a small repast. It was a more amenable figure that arrived to present himself to the king at the appointed hour. Inwardly he was still furious, yet he mastered his zeal and temper. He bowed before his monarch.

"Majesty, if it pleases you, it does my eyes good to see you in such hale condition."

"You are kind to us, archbishop." The king responded formally as there were others present and only in private did the king allow more intimate conversations to occur.

" We hear that you were not so kindly treated at Oxford if the rumours be true. How are things there?"

"Your majesty is as ever well informed. I was most fortunate that I was protected with a guard and armed with my own sword. For we were attacked by a mob of university students and masters alike led by Richard Courtney, who sought to do me harm. They forced me to leave and forbade me to speak against the intolerable heresy of Wycliffe's teaching. Courtney had the temerity to threaten me with excommunication on the grounds of infringing the university's liberties. Me, the Archbishop of Canterbury!" he fumed.

The king's eyed widen in rage: "We had not been informed of these events. This heresy has continued for too long, and we shall together stamp it out. Fetch our clerk," he demanded of one of the courtiers.

The courtier returned minutes later accompanied by two clerks, who made preparation to begin writing the king's demands. "Let this be taken down and copies sent to our Lord Chief Justice and our son Prince Henry – and most importantly, to the Chancellor of Oxford University my Lord Courtney, whom we demand attend us on the ninth day hence of this September, the year of our Lord 1411.

"There are other matters we wish to communicate to the Royal Council. On the ninth of September, in addition to the arbitration on the Oxford matter, we call for the council to attend us and discuss the pending expedition to Calais. Let it be registered that the sum of one thousand marks will be allocated for the expenditure of the journey."

The King's Keeper of the Rolls, John Wakering, was aghast and barely managed to conceal a sharp intake of breath. It was, he knew, beyond the bounds of the Royal treasury to cover such an amount without breaking the terms of the previous parliament.

The documents were signed and sealed, with copies sent to recipients within the Palace. A messenger was sent for to deliver the summons to Richard Courtney at Oxford. Rumours spread through the corridors of power that the king was once more spreading his authority within his court.

— ⚔ —

Bishop Henry Beaufort sought out his brother privately at his home, avoiding the Palace which was awash with rumours. "Thomas, are you aware of the latest news from the Palace?" He asked.

"No, I have been attending matters pertaining to the prosecution of the pirates Longe and Prendergast. What ails you, brother, to be so excited?

"Writs have been served and an arbitration is to be held upon the matter of the Lollardy and heresy fomented at Oxford. Courtney has been summoned to London to be heard before a court."

"You jest? Yet I see you do not. So, Courtney follows his cousins in his fall from grace. Yet the prince must and will side with him, driving a wedge still further between father and son." Thomas Beaufort thought for a moment. "This serves our cause well. It will be a perfect opportunity to urge the prince to sue for the crown and call for Henry's abdication. When is the date set for the arbitration?"

"There is a council meeting called for two days hence, and the arbitration is set for the ninth of September, twelve days before the king is due to sail for Calais. His majesty our brother cuts it fine and prays no doubt that all will be settled afore he leaves these shores. We have a chance to remove a king from a throne and supplant him with another who will grant us more power."

"There is all to play for at the Council. Come, we must hurry and speak with Warwick and Arundel to ensure we are all in agreement."

The following two days were spent gathering support for the prince against his father, forcing him into the position that they required. Richard Courtney arrived from Oxford on the twenty-seventh of August and was invited to be ready to attend the Council meeting. After a wait of nearly two hours, he was called into the chamber. He bowed to the lords and was presented with questions on the events at Oxford.

Richard Courtney was a tall man, nearly on a level with his great friend the prince. The noble lineage of his breeding showed in his handsome features. With flowing blond hair and blue eyes, he carried himself well, and despite leading the university in an academic post he was by training a knight, which showed in his imposing physique.

"Upon what law do you stand to assert your case for the continuance of service and the permissions to offer prayers in the manner of Wycliffe?" Bishop Henry Chichele of St. David's asked with little preamble. He was very aware of the principles upon which this whole matter was based, and wanted to stick to facts and not be drawn into the web of intrigue that he suspected was being spun by the Beauforts.

"My lords, your royal highness. If it please you, we rely upon the Papal Bull of 1395 that grants the university exemption from visitation allowing them free rein to do as they wish."

"And is this Bull valid?"

"It is, my lord, according to the views held by the scholars of the university. My lord prince, I would humbly ask that you grant us leniency and expedite this matter before the arbitration in September hence." He asked, turning to Prince Henry in appeal.

"My Lord Courtney, you know that we shall give the matter full consideration, yet we shall not be drawn in haste. Now we shall hear more of Archbishop Arundel's actions at Oxford," the prince declared.

Courtney spoke eloquently, naming senior tutors and deans of the university who backed his actions and sought the autonomy they felt they deserved by right of the papal permission. After two more hours the council broke, and members departed to consider all they had heard and discussed. Sir Richard Whittington had been present on the request of the prince. However, he had been prevented from overhearing the final discussion between the prince and his uncles. When the council reconvened the following day, Whittington was to learn more.

"Sir Richard, we call you as our friend, and as such would appeal to you to aid us in our cause. We must attend the king, and he values you for your wisdom and loyalty as much as we do. We must plead with his majesty and would have an independent arbitrator present whom our father would neither suspect nor perceive as a threat to his situation. We would have you say naught, for your presence alone will calm the troubled waters of the realm – of this we are assured."

"My lord prince I am as ever at your disposal. But may I be impertinent and beg your forbearance?"

"As ever my lord. This has not been an impediment to you in matters past," the prince remarked with a rare show of humour. The corners of his mouth twitched in a whimsical smile.

"Highness," nodded Whittington, taking the olive branch that was offered and meeting it with a generous response in kind. "May I suggest that we and we alone attend his majesty, for a show of force or a strong presence will alert him to take a different course of action. For certes the lords of Beaufort, Warwick and Arundel should not attend."

"To lessen the blow, mayhap? You have the right of it, yet t'would be unseemly to attend with no escort, even in humility."

"My prince, I would strongly adjure you to follow this course. Perchance you should take Bishop Chichele and a household knight. Someone who is lowly enough to be of no political consequence yet of sufficient status to protect your dignity and presence?"

"Chichele, yes, I most heartily agree to an ecclesiastical presence. Whom would you advise as my knight in guard?"

"My prince, mayhap Sir James de Grispere. He is of lowly status, has no political aspirations and is well regarded by his majesty, having proved his loyalty to the king on more than one occasion previously."

"Indeed, he may do well. We hear he was recently returned from France bearing correspondence, yet none seem wise to the content. Do you know aught?"

"I must confess, sire, that it was I who sent him on a mission to spy on the Armagnacs, as there were rumours of them mustering for war. Upon his return I sent him to his majesty with a first-hand account and a note from myself."

"Just so. On issues concerning de Grispere, dost thou have further news of matters in the north regarding my Lord Stanhope? It concerns us, for he was known as a strong confederate of our father's, and indeed was once one of his household knights. Now he seemingly embarks upon disloyalty to the crown with no true colours shown. My father will not bring force to bear upon these rebels, I know not why. Maybe 'tis lack of will or illness."

"On that accord I am at one with you, my prince. I have news of more dissent, and Lord Stanhope's power rises as he casts his net wider. My fear is that if he is not brought to book and associates himself openly with others who demand your father's abdication, you could be inextricably linked to their cause and accused of treason in your father's eyes."

Prince Henry looked at Whittington with a mixture of shock and concern. He had considered how it might affect his father but had not thought about the implications of his own involvement. He turned and paced away from Sir Richard, considering carefully what had just been said.

Have I wounded him? Whittington wondered. *Or have I just opened the floodgates to possibilities that had not previously occurred to him?* Prince Henry turned and looked sternly at Whittington, his face now impassive once he had taken the time to school his features as he broke from the discussion.

"Present us with a report giving details of all that has occurred, Sir Richard. Does Lord Roos continue to liaise with you in this regard, for he asked for permission to venture north and investigate?"

"He does, my prince, and even now is in Nottingham. For there is rumoured to be a Loveday Arbitration between Stanhope and the Meryngs, among others. There is fear that violence will be done if authority does not intercede. I hope that Roos is in time to avert an ambush or a violation of rights. For Lord Stanhope grows stronger with each outrage he commits."

The prince said nothing, gently massaging his brow between fingers and thumb. He was torn, Whittington knew, between asserting authority that he had not been directly given and not wishing to seem disloyal to his father, who had clearly lost all focus within his realm, concentrating on everything abroad and the problems in France.

"The worries of the kingdom and its responsibilities weigh heavily upon us, Sir Richard," the prince said at last. "For traitors and malaperts must be brought to book, whether they be royal knights or no. We will not stint from our work of governance, nor cause the authority in us by the council to be wasted by shying away from matters which are unsavoury. We wish to God that our father could see as clearly as we do what needs must be done."

"My prince, he is much occupied with thoughts abroad and

relies upon your governance for internal problems through the good offices of the council."

"Mayhap. Set to, Sir Richard, and arrange for de Grispere and his Grace Henry Bishop of Chichele to attend us on the morrow, for we visit our father in all earnest intent."

"Yes sire, by your leave."

Chapter Thirty-Eight

Spitelecroft, London

The three figures sat their horses well, and having ridden carefully around Smythefeld they released their mounts into a spirited canter across the practice fields before them. Two of the horses and a wolfhound pulled away, leaving the third to a steady canter, the figures in the lead crying with joy at the feel of a good horse and the open fields before them. Ahead of them stood a huge oak tree, and when they neared it they began to pull up gently, easing off their speed as they approached the northern confines of the common.

The pretty grey mare slowed her pace to a steady walk and Lady Alice turned to Jamie, her face flushed with happiness. Her horse blew and snorted, pleased to be allowed to run, hoary breath that flowed back towards Alice as the mare nodded her head up and down, playing with the now slack bit. Alice reached forward and patted her neck firmly, speaking soft words of affection. Forest looked up, panting with exertion, her pink tongue lolling.

"Jamie, how can I ever thank you? She is wonderful. Such a

soft mouth and so responsive. I have decided to call her Tash as a stable name, for Tacheter is too long."

"It becomes her well. I am delighted you approve, for I took to her instantly."

"How could I not, for she will be the envy of all."

"Except perhaps your father." He spoke quickly as her groom approached having been left behind in their onward gallop.

She looked up at his face. Jamie had changed in ways that were almost indefinable, but he had changed nonetheless. He looked more serious, and the lines of his face had matured and hardened. Although it had always reflected the character of a knight forged in battle and all the attendant journeys he had made, there was now a strong and more considered intelligence apparent. His mind and outlook had matured, she reflected. A strength of purpose now prevailed with – if possible – an even greater determination about his jaw, even in repose as it was at this moment. His strength had been brought about by recent experiences, she presumed.

"Jamie, he comes about. He now just grunts when your name is mentioned instead of growling like a wounded bear. My mother works her whiles upon him and soon I foresee a time when he will permit you to visit me." She jested, seeking to lighten his mood. "His leg still pains him and may never quite move again as it once did, for it was a shocking and perilous wound that he received. If your presence had not been so propitious, if you had not arrived when you did, praise God, things would have turned out much the worse on our account. My mother sings your praises for saving my father's life, so that even the cantankerous bear cannot remain so for ever. He softens, truly," she said. "Witness that he now permits me to be escorted by you, where perchance afore he would have run you through with his sword. Surely this is advancement?"

Even Jamie had to laugh at this railment, shaking his head at the absurdity of her words. "My Lady Alice, you never fail to lift my spirits, know you that?"

"Pray tell why do they need raising? Why should you be of a melancholy humour? You sit upon a magnificent horse with a fair maid on a beautiful day. Will that not serve?" she teased him.

"Aye my lady, but I would have it as a fair day and a beautiful maid."

"Now, there is the man I know, for certes his tongue is as effulgent and smooth as quicksilver. But come tell me, what ails you to cause this shadow upon your visage?"

"My Lady Alice, you are as sapient as ever. 'Tis the court, for as ever I straddle a fence and hope I do not fall to either side. In all confidence I am torn, and on the morrow I must attend the prince in an audience with his majesty. Both men I serve with all my heart and loyalty, yet I foresee a time when I shall be forced to choose twixt king and prince."

"On what matters do you attend, or are you forbidden to reveal the cause of your attendance?"

"In truth I know not. Sir Richard's note merely bade me attend upon the middle of the morning and to have on my best livery for I was to attend the prince in his audience with the king."

At that moment their conversation was cut short as two figures rode towards them, dressed in mail with their helmets hanging from the pommels of their saddles. They were hot, and sweat dripped from their brows. As they drew closer Jamie saw that it was Jacques de Berry and Crispin de Lourds. The two men curbed their horses as they drew near, nodding their heads in formal bows at the Lady Alice and Jamie.

"Good morrow my lady, Sir James. It seems you are ever in

good company and travail far," de Berry said, a slight sneer in his voice.

"I seek only company that avails my pleasure in kind. For certes I can vouch that it is of my own choosing, rather than that which may be foisted upon me according to the will of others," Jamie retorted.

De Berry's nostrils flared white in anger: "One day, de Grispere, I shall meet you alone, without a lady to protect you."

Forest sensed the tension and growled; her lips drawn back in a wicked sneer. Jamie motioned with his hand to steady her, while Richard fretted at the bit, sensing the atmosphere through the reins. "I shall look forward to that day," he responded quietly yet with menace. "When you have neither words nor a whelp to hide behind. When there is only your sword and your dark soul between us, I shall be pleased to relieve you of both."

De Lourds went for his sword and de Berry's temper erupted, and whether by accident or design his horse lurched forward towards Richard, who lunged with blinding speed, straightening his neck, muscles taught, ears flattened and teeth bared, snapping at the other stallion's vulnerable neck. De Berry's horse caught a bite in the muscle of his neck and lurched sideways in response, squealing in pain, nearly unseating de Berry as it collided with de Lourds.

"By God's legs, de Grispere, control that cur and that red hellion. My lady." He nodded and spurred his ill-used horse off in a canter, sending turf flying in his wake as the pair left.

"Jamie, you seem to relish the fight wherever you go. Does the devil sit on your back with a whip, urging you on?" chided Alice shaking her head.

— ✕ ✻ ✕ —

299

The following day Jamie attended the prince along with Sir Richard Whittington and Henry Chichele, Bishop of St. David's. The party made its way towards the king's private chambers, the long-limbed prince striding out, causing the bishop and Sir Richard to scuttle in his wake. Prince Henry was in a dour mood, determination strengthening his jawline, his expression focused and impenetrable. He had said but a few words of welcome to Jamie, other than thanking him for attending the meeting with the king. Richard Courtney had been present and seemed for once nervous and less sure of his position than at any other time Jamie had met him. Courtney was said to be the closest confidante to Prince Henry. The tension in the room was stifling as they left him behind, although he nodded with a thin smile to the prince and wished him good luck.

The clerk to the king bade the two guards at the door permit the royal party to enter. The stifling heat of July and early August had abated, yet the room was humid despite a gentle breeze wafting in from casements that had been left ajar.

The group approached the king, their boots crunching on freshly laid rushes that were strewn about the floor. Upon reaching the carpet before the royal dais, the four men looked up to King Henry and the three men who stood either side of him: Prince Thomas, Duke of Clarence, the Archbishop of Canterbury, Thomas Arundel and Richard, Lord Grey of Codnor. The atmosphere was strained, and none present knew how the other side would fare. Although it was as they all knew a meeting of sides, none save the king and the prince had any idea what would be discussed.

The king looked strained, with new lines etched on his face, yet the grey pallor of the past months had left his countenance and he had grown muscle about his shoulders, Prince Henry saw, putting him in mind of the man he had grown up admiring, a man who had been one of the best jousters and knights in Europe. The king's face was grave and implacable, yet there seemed to the prince's tutored eyes to be a latent anger lurking, with no outward sign of affection evident towards his eldest son. His own brother was easier to read, and he saw anger and pain etched into his young and handsome face.

"Majesty, we bid you good morrow and trust that you do well."

"We are as you see, in vigour and hale. The weather suits us and we prepare for France. What say you?"

"Majesty, it pleases us that you are so well intentioned for our kingdom."

"Yet we perceive that you come hither with reasons enough to disturb us, so we prithee proceed. Your visit follows no doubt upon the missive we received late upon the hour yester eve."

Whittington caught his breath, barely stopping himself from looking to the prince. He had no knowledge of a letter written to the king, and felt that he had been duped; led here like a lamb to the slaughter. Jamie stood impassively, his mind in turmoil, realising that the kingdom stood on a precipice yet knowing not which way the day would fall.

The prince was unperturbed, no doubt expecting this reaction from his father. "Verily sire, I would have discourse with you concerning the University of Oxford and other matters that pertain to the order of the realm, both here and abroad."

"You have put us in an unenviable position, you and the so-called Council that govern our kingdom," the king replied. "Did'st think that you could sway us when we have called for an arbitration on the ninth day of September? No doubt that scullion Courtney – whom we have previously held to believe and have sympathy with – has pressed you to such a course. You would take his side against that of your father and sire?"

"We take no sides, sire. We merely wish to enjoy harmony

and justice throughout the kingdom, the better to focus our intent upon our true enemies. We see that the role which you have so well performed tires you, and would therefore seek to aid you. The Council has adjured me thus and wishes you to consider abdication."

There was a sharp intake of breath from all present. Not even Sir Richard had foreseen this attempt to wrestle the crown from the king. The only person present who was not surprised was Bishop Henry Chichele, who was privy to the inner working of the Council and had obviously been forewarned of this presentation of abdication. Thomas clenched his hands by his sides in fury, unable to contain himself any longer and against protocol spoke out in anger and frustration.

"Brother, are you possessed by hell or those devils incarnate who are our uncles? For by the rood I see whence this derives. They would seek to use you as a vessel to usurp the crown to their own ends."

"Enough!" shouted the king. "It is as we have decreed. An arbitration will be held on the ninth of next month."

Prince Henry paled both at his brother's outburst and his father's finding on his plea for abdication. Anger and embarrassment was writ large across his face, his blue eyes smouldering with fire at the rebuke.

"Forsooth sire, we believe you do not look to yourself in this matter. The weight of the crown is wearisome and we adjure you to reconsider."

"We have decided. Let the matter be discussed no more. Is there aught else you would speak with us about?" King Henry asked, his voice dangerously close to full blown anger.

"Your majesty, e'er it please you," the prince uttered, barely containing his own temper. "There are matters abroad within our realm which needs must be brought before you. We know your Lord Chief Justice, Sir William Gascoigne, has furnished you with an affidavit proving the conspiracy of certain lords including Sir Richard Stanhope to foment insurrection in the north. As we speak, Sir William Lord Roos has journeyed there to ensure peace at a Loveday Meet. We beg of your majesty to show these dissenters sterner justice, for Stanhope is one of your knights."

"We trust Lord Roos, who is a good and valued member of our court. Let him bring us proof and we will align with your aims. Now are there yet more matters upon which you would speak with us?

"Yes majesty. The latest Burgundian embassy has offered final terms and Burgundy is prepared to offer full reparation in matters pertaining to Guyenne and others of the four territories, together with all those matters offered previously. To wit land and jewels, and the duke's daughter in marriage." The prince faltered, seeing the mask of insouciance back upon the king's face, a stone cast of granite unreadable. "In return," he continued when the king made no response, "they would have us aid them against the Armagnac cause."

"They are glossiers where their need is most. They crawl like toads before us. I prithee, do they in return for rendering them great service offer us funds to furnish armies that they would have us send on their account?"

"Majesty, it is our understanding that the intent is there with voiced confirmation of coin to fund our insurgence." The prince dissembled as much as he dared, drawing upon the words that had been reported to him by his proctors, which had no doubt been embellished. "They indeed promise funds from the Burgundian *Chambre de Comptes* that we are assured will cover our costs for the campaign."

"We will defer from immediate judgement and respond by the month end. Now we beg that you leave us, for we are fatigued and require respite from matters of court."

The prince was clearly frustrated with the lack of any firm conclusion, shaking his head yet bowing to his father before leaving his presence, his whole body rigid with rage and frustration. "By your leave sire."

Once free of the king's chamber he clenched his fists in anger, shaking them to rail against his father's stubbornness. "By God's grace we know not which way to turn and we are thwarted in every direction." He raged, stalking along the corridor towards his chamber, with Chichele and Whittington puffing behind and only Jamie at his side.

Upon reaching the entrance to his chamber he turned and said: "Sir James, we thank you for the service you did us today and for your support. We prithee on your honour that not a word of this be breathed abroad, for news of this discourse could unsettle matters to a still greater degree, were that possible." The prince offered Jamie a direct stare, fixing him with his ice blue eyes.

Jamie did not flinch, sensing much of the pain and frustration the prince must be feeling. He returned the look with sympathy and a steady eye. "My prince, upon my honour, I shall speak not a word of these matters."

"We will have need of you again I fear, and I will send word."

Jamie sensed he was being dismissed. He bowed once and left the three remaining figures to discuss a course of action, nodding to the other two lords as he departed.

Once inside his private chamber, Prince Henry continued: "Well my lords, what think ye?"

Whittington stayed silent, waiting upon the bishop to say his piece.

"My prince, it is as we expected," Chichele said. "The king grows stronger and will not consider any course but that to which he is already wedded. The Council will be disappointed and so will my Lord Courtney, I fear, yet there is naught we can do to mitigate his fate."

"What say you, Sir Richard?" the prince asked.

"My lord, I had no knowledge of any letter that had been written on Richard Courtney's behalf, and I can only suppose that it will have been reviled by the king. I am not surprised at his objection. Whomsoever advised you on such a course of action should have given more credence to his majesty's present condition." As a rebuke to Bishop Chichele and others not present, it was strong in substance and caused the bishop to blanch. Whittington continued. "As such, my lord, I would advise caution. Allow the king his time to consider and mayhap he will come about to your cause after he has sat upon the arbitration. For as you suggested, there are many matters about the kingdom that require the strong hand of justice."

"Just so, Sir Richard. The words of Solomon as ever. Where would we be without you?"

At which Bishop Chichele smiled benignly but was seethed inwardly. *The lords Beaufort will have cause to gnash their teeth now*, he thought.

Chapter Thirty-Nine

"The news is grave, yet to our advantage, for I hear that our arrow of mischief went near the mark and the division between prince and king is greater still," Thomas Beaufort said.

"Indeed, brother," Bishop Beaufort agreed, "Yet we must press on at the next council meeting and persuade the king to abdicate. Therein lies our strength. He still persists in warring with France, and the arbitration will take place on the ninth of September as planned. I fear that after the prince's intervention things will not go in Courtney's favour." He smiled wryly.

"Amen to that," Thomas Beaufort replied. "It will be of great import to see which way the wind blows with his majesty and the prince at that sitting, and who will emerge the victor."

"There is more we need to achieve before that date, and it still gives me cause for concern that the matter of Stanhope lodges us at the root of the issue – albeit by word of affidavit rather than presence. If Sir Richard and other knights of the shire of Nottingham give us up, it will go hard for us brother, be warned."

Thomas Beaufort snorted, dismissing the idea. "The king

will do naught to secure charges to his own royal knights. He has not the stomach for it and sees only France as the wrong-doer. And should the prince prevail, we shall say we were aiding him to the throne through dissent and anarchy, so we durst not worry."

Bishop Henry was more concerned and tugged at his short beard: "I wish I shared your confidence, for the winds of change are blowing and I know not from which direction." He responded, worry written upon his face. "Lord Roos is even now in Nottingham attending a Loveday parade involving all parties to the dispute, and the outcome of it remains to be seen."

"All will be well, brother, all will be well. In my official capacity I shall hear first of any matter untoward afore most men at court," he assured Bishop Henry.

— ✕ ⚜ ✕ —

Sir Richard Whittington called Jamie for a conference before the proceedings of the arbitration that they were to attend. "We have little time, Jamie, but mark all that occurs in the arbitration today. It may well have a bearing on your future and mine."

"What think ye of the outcome for or against Courtney and the prince, who has nailed his colours to the Courtneys' mast for certes?"

Whittington hesitated, pulling at his ear in that now familiar gesture as he did so.

"I believe that the king will side with Archbishop Arundel and upon that course he has little choice. The law can ever be twisted," he continued cynically. "To side with Oxford would invite anarchy and mischief, and God knows there is enough of that abroad at the present. Now come, we must press on. Once we are at the prince's chambers I will leave you, because the prince presses me for a discussion before the arbitration. I will find you in the hall at Lambeth."

With that the two men left Whittington's chamber and walked to where the prince and his company were holding conference. Jamie moved on to the quay on the terrace to the south of the Palace where waited Cristoforo and Mark, both of whom were keen to see the outcome of the arbitration that was open to public view. They finally managed to obtain passage upon a ferry that had just returned from the south side of the river. The ferry men were busy this day, as was to be expected.

"The king wavers, my prince." Whittington warned. "I hear that he now favours no intervention for either faction. Mayhap he would agree to an embassy to sue for peace between Burgundy and Armagnac. If you were the architect of such a cause, it would show you in a good light, both to your father and to the two French factions, favouring neither side."

"Sir Richard, we thank you for your counsel as ever, and we think it would do well. We shall think on't. Now we needs must attend our father upon the matter of arbitration." Turning to Richard Courtney, who was one of the others present in his retinue, he said: "Shall we venture forth, Richard, and pray that we have more success than previously where my father is concerned? If our head should ache as a penance for success then we have won the day, for by God mine doth pound. We were to wrestle later today, yet I think it a poor idea."

It was a rare show of disloyalty towards his father outside the confines of the council, and showed just how close the friendship was that existed between courtier and prince. The two men were in a dissolute state from carousing the previous evening, causing mayhem about the court and in certain stews close to the palace. The prince for his part, full of nervous energy, was glad to have his drinking companion returned from

Oxford, with whom he could relax and forget his troubles and responsibilities.

Richard Courtney did not look his best either, being of unusually pale complexion, brought on by the evening's festivities and the late hour of his bed.

"Amen to that, Hal, for my head doth feel like a blacksmith's hammer upon an anvil."

The prince's meiny proceeded, including the lawyer Nicholas Ryssheton, whom Jamie had met in Calais and who followed Jamie's path to the prince's private barge that was to transport the party to Lambeth. The arbitration, which was to take place in the hall at Lambeth Palace, was open to all comers and drew a large audience of courtiers and nobles alike. The immensity of the verdict and its implications was apparent to all.

The prince's party, including his proctors the Earls of Arundel and Warwick, had settled on one side of the aisle, and once all was in order the heralds trumpeted and the king arrived, accompanied by his household knights including Lord Grey and Archbishop Arundel. He had taken more care about his person than normal, dressing in full robes and with a padded long doublet in bright red silk trimmed with ermine. His demeanour was erect with no sign of the slumped shoulders that had been apparent on previous occasions, and he looked to all as a new man. There was still about his skin evidence of the disease that ravaged him, but this was offset against the seemingly stronger monarch.

The gathering bowed three times, and with Henry's permission all were seated. Sir William Gascoigne, the Lord Chief Justice, presided over the affairs as each side presented its case, after which there was a final summing up from the lawyers representing both Richard Courtney and Archbishop Arundel. Much hung in the balance with the judgement that was about to be made by the king, who was the final arbiter with no recourse to any other court of appeal.

"Majesty," began Sir William. "You have heard at length the case brought forward by both protagonists in this hearing of arbitration. Do you wish to retire before any judgement you may give binds these parties irreparably?"

There was a pause as all held their collective breath. Finally, the king raised his eyes to seek out his son before answering, as though to give him fair warning of what he was about to declare.

"We do not require any further time to make a determination. The course of action seems to us very clear. Both sides to this appeal have brought forward their case, which rests not upon the intricacies of human nature but upon the law on a matter of heresy and papal permission to transcend the whims of nature.

"We perceive that the case for the Chancellor of Oxford University rests upon the authority of the Papal Bull dated the year of our Lord 1395, upon which the premise is based that Oxford is exempt from the fetters of intervention on any ecclesiastical vein.

"It would appear that this was the intention of the Papal Bull, and falls in line with the actions taken by certain divisions within the university."

Here the audience again held its collective breath and Jamie caught sight of Richard Courtney giving the prince a sly smile. *No doubt he expects full exoneration*, Jamie thought.

The king cleared his throat reached for a bejewelled silver goblet of wine handed to him by a servant. Swallowing, he continued with his judgement.

"Upon such a pretext hangs the question of the validity of the Bull. It was produced within the reign of his majesty Richard the Second, and there is no record of him or his court recognising or ratifying the bull in law. Alas, within our reign we have not brought the Bull into our statute. It is therefore not binding and we do not rely upon it as a defence for practices of heresy and more pertinently Lollardy. We therefore find in the favour of the Archbishop Arundel in full and final settlement of this arbitration."

Murmurs rose from the gathering within the palace, although Jamie was not distracted and watched very carefully the faces of Richard Courtney and the lords of Beaufort. The great friend and confidant of Prince Henry was devastated as his face fell at his complete loss. The Beauforts allowed each other a small smile, clearly delighted with the result.

Now what do you gain by such a verdict, my lords? Jamie asked himself. *A chance to further your ambitions at the expense of others and their honour, I'm bound.* Jamie realised he was beginning to think like Sir Richard. He chastised himself for such cynicism, laughing inwardly at how he was changing.

Chapter Forty

The court cleared after the hearing of arbitration, and all that remained were the close servants and retainers of the king, including his second son, Prince Thomas, Duke of Clarence, who now addressed his father.

"We take instruction from you, father, in how to manage proceedings and to adhere to the intricacies of a Papal Bull that it can be ratified."

The king looked at his son and favoured him with a warm smile. But for all that, the king looked tired. The hours of the arbitration and legal arguments had taken their toll. "By the Lord God I wouldst rather fight my way through a Saracen horde than listen to that twisted web woven about a cause that is so patently against the law of God."

"Yet your finding was just and fair, sire, adhering to all the doctrines of law and ecclesiastical doctrine." Archbishop Arundel commented. "And you, my son, fear not, for we shall thwart the case that opposes your suit of marriage to Lady Margaret."

All knew that it was Bishop Henry Beaufort who opposed

the marriage, yet none would say his name in front of the king, who offered words of comfort to his son.

"Fear not, Thomas, you will prevail and marry whomever you wish, and we will do all in our power to aid you, short of making war on our half-brother directly," he assured him. Prince Thomas gave his father a smile of gratitude, yet privately remained to be convinced for he knew that his uncle and his own brother was against the match. "To wit," continued the king, "we have decided to stay in England and not venture forth to Calais, as there are many matters here that need our attention."

"Father?" Came the young prince's cry of shock.

"We are hale, yet we shall not be bullied into circumstances that go against our will. Your brother and others seek to wrest the crown from our head, and that will not be so easy if we are here to wear it." He laughed roughly at his own joke, whilst those around him were amazed at the sudden turn of events.

He turned to his clerk. "Make it known to all concerned and change the arrangements for our travels. We shall remain at court and fight a different battle, one that is no less serious to the wellbeing of our realm. Have it written so and we shall seal the order."

Sir Richard was glad to be north of the river and back in the palace of Westminster. He walked back to his quarters to seek Jamie's presence, and found the young knight waiting for him upon his return to his offices to discuss all that had occurred.

Once seated and secure in the knowledge that they could not be overheard, Jamie offered his thoughts. "Did you mark the countenance of the Beauforts? They were champing at the bit to clap each other on the back, so delighted were they with the king's decision. I hear rumours now that Courtney is to resign his post as Chancellor of the university. But cynical as I have become, I suspect that it will not last and some subtle means will be found to reinstate him, all the while protesting at his lack of suitability."

Whittington laughed at Jamie's perspicacity. "You become jaundiced with the machinations of the court – and rightly so, for it is the best armour to don in these treacherous times, and it will serve you well. Did you mark the response from the Beauforts?"

"I did. They are a pair of vipers keen to wile their way upwards at the expense of others."

"Verily so, yet they make bad enemies, so beware for their stars are in the ascendent. I believe they are even now in conference at the Council table."

— ✕ 🕯✕ —

The following day rumours spread about the court like wildfire, and Sir Richard Whittington was summoned to the prince's chambers to aid him in his dilemma. When he arrived, Whittington saw that the prince was in a state of agitation. He was reeling from the events of the court the day before and paced the room as he spoke his mind.

"Were you aware of this news, Sir Richard? For we are shocked that our father has pronounced that he will no longer travel to France. Is this what you foresaw?"

"I was not aware, but in faith it surprises me not. His mind has been turned by many events of late, some most pressing, to wit the turmoil within his realm that you yourself have brought to his attention, my lord prince. His hand now firm upon the tiller will be better served at home than abroad, where others may make better embassy in his stead. And should war beckon, why there are many of that disposition who would readily grasp the sword to fight for England's name in France.

"My prince, if I may adjure you, go to your father and appease him in his moment of triumph, for as was apparent yestereve he wished to favour his dear friend Arundel in the arbitration, as you did for master Courtney. If you appear now in humility and suggest an embassy to France to sue for peace and mediate between the factions, it would appear seemly in his eyes."

"Sir Richard, you are our friend indeed and offer good counsel. Whilst we loathe the thought of conciliation and it bears heavily upon our honour, 'tis no doubt the wisest course and verily to strike whilst the iron is hot is a most propitious action to take. We shall meet with the council immediately and repair upon the morrow to gain an audience with my father. You have our thanks as always."

"Highness, is it my pleasure to serve." Whittington bowed and left the prince to his thoughts and actions.

Prince Henry called a special Council meeting for that afternoon. Not all members could attend, yet those relevant to his cause were able to sit as requested, and of those the most important were the earls of Arundel and Warwick together with the Beauforts. There was a tense atmosphere about the chamber as all present had by now heard the news of the king's decision to remain in England. That, following on from the result of the arbitration, had shocked many and caused them to reconsider their own positions.

"My lords, we thank you for attending upon us at such late notice. Matters have arisen that call for us to take action with the utmost expediency. For with his rejection of travelling to Calais, my father opens for us a gate and casts it wide that we may fill the void he has left. We propose to send an embassy of our own to Calais and mayhap aid the Burgundians in their cause against the Armagnacs, who are, we believe, even now fighting towards the borders of Paris. If they are successful, we do not feel they will offer us favourable terms to compare with those of the Duke John.

"I propose that my Lord Arundel, if he accepts the commission, leads an embassy of our own, with my lord of Warwick to accompany him to France."

The Council members were shocked for the second time within twenty-four hours of the arbitration decision. Each member turned to his fellow in excitement at what they had just heard, and the Beauforts smiled at each other in their glee. Yet none was so pleased as the earls of Arundel and Warwick.

"My lord prince, I accept with alacrity, and only ask when we should prepare to leave upon this auspicious journey?" Thomas Earl of Arundel rejoined, quickly seconded by the Earl of Warwick. Both men knew that this would bring fame and standing to them both in the new court Prince Henry was creating.

"I propose that the expedition sets sail on the twenty sixth of this month of September. Let it be so entered into the records." This last was spoken as an aside to one of the chief clerks who were recording the minutes of the meeting.

Thomas Beaufort spoke forth on a matter that had been considered by many around the council table. "My lord prince, in my capacity as Lord Chancellor I must beg you to consider the cost of such an embassy, and I ask how such a venture will be funded?"

All eyes turned to the prince. His face was impassive as he spoke, the steel back in the icy blue eyes, for even for a member of the blood royal it was an audacious question. The prince's voice when he spoke was emotionless and cold: "We shall make provision out of private funds, and this shall not be entered onto the lists. We are persuaded that all costs will ultimately be met by the Burgundian offer of a *chambre des comptes.*"

Again the magnitude of what the prince said surprised even

Thomas Beaufort. The prince continued driving the final nail into the coffin of his father's reign and his governance of the land. "We aim to meet with him tomorrow and expect his blessing on the matter."

The silence around the Council chamber was palpable. The prince was taking over the realm!

Chapter Forty-One

The following day, with the motions recorded and set, the prince attended King Henry at court with a small audience of courtiers, knights and churchmen in attendance. The king looked anything but unwell, in fact he looked healthy and sat ramrod straight upon the throne. There were no visible tremors to his hands as had been the case in times past.

"Sire, we thank you for granting us an audience," the prince began. "We were delighted to hear that you have refrained from making the arduous voyage to France and remain here to govern your kingdom."

The king was no newcomer to flummery and took none of the prince's honeyed words at face value. "Our son, we are as ever delighted to see you here before us in court, and would assure you that we are in hale health and able to continue our governance. With this in mind is there a matter pertaining to the realm that you would discuss? Has some janglery brought you thus?" The king said, with a hint of mockery in his voice.

The prince ignored the barb and proceeded in equanimity: "Majesty, it concerns as ever France. If you are not to lead an expedition there, may we suggest that an embassy be sent from the court to sue for peace mayhap? We would surely wish to prevent bloodshed between the two royal houses of France, and in so doing win favour and the return of our lands as due and promised by the parties concerned."

"The idea holds favour with us. Whom did you have in mind to represent us?"

"Why sire, the earls of Warwick and Arundel and a small company of men in sufficient strength to add credence to their cause."

The king asked more questions of prince Henry, softening as he received the answers he wished to hear and feeling the prince's obvious intent of reconciliation after his previous demand that he should abdicate.

"How should this venture be funded? For God knows there is little resource in the national budget, and we have sheriff's payments made to fund our fleet with little left to spare."

"Majesty, we propose a funding from our own estates to be reimbursed by way of *chambre des compotes* as the Burgundians agreed in their last embassy."

"Very well, let it be so. You have our blessing to send abroad an embassy under the control of the Lords of Arundel and Warwick."

The prince smiled bravely at his father and thanked him for his agreement to the expedition. Bowing, he begged to leave and removed himself from the king's presence to make plans for the voyage.

— ✕ ✦ ✕ —

Sir Richard Whittington met with the prince on the morning after.

"My lord prince, the audience with your father went well, I hear."

"Indeed. Your council to us as ever was well placed and we proceed apace to send an embassy to France."

Something in the prince's tone gave Sir Richard pause for thought. There was a gleeful attitude of a victory gained that would be unseemly for such a request to be granted by his father. He decided to probe a little deeper.

"My prince, I have news most pertinent to your cause. The Armagnacs have taken the war against the Burgundians forward, and my latest intelligence suggests that they now march on Paris. This will pose, as I am sure you are aware, a strong front of resistance and make them far less likely to come to the table of reconciliation."

The prince seemed unperturbed, which gave Whittington greater cause for concern. *What are you planning my prince?* He mused inwardly, his finely tuned brain seeking an answer.

"Fear not, Sir Richard," the prince said. "We will make provision for all eventualities. Now, we prithee, time is of the essence and we must attend to matters of detail for the embassy." At which he gestured to his clerks and servants who were patiently awaiting his instructions.

"Of course, my prince, by your leave." Whittington bowed and left, feeling decidedly unsettled at the turn of events. He made for the private rooms of William Stokes, hoping that he would be there at this time of day. He was given entrance and found William speaking with a servant who was on the point of leaving.

"Just so, Alan, let me know how the provisions progress." With which the young servant sketched a bow, nodded to Whittington and left, clearly in a hurry.

"Good morrow to you, Sir Richard. Abroad as always. What say you to the news of the embassy to France as the king no longer ventures forth?" The sharp intelligent eyes watched Whittington carefully. It was an old game they played, to see if they could catch the other out in being the first to become aware of new intelligence.

"A good morrow to you sir, though you tease me so to catch up on old news. Yet I have new intelligence, as I suspect do you."

"You play a good game, Sir Richard." Stokes smiled gently, pleased with his worthy opponent. "I'faith I do. Alan there works upon the docks in the tax office, and sees much of what occurs. This muster is causing much furore, for it seems greater than a mere embassy, and if the signs be sure it will concern not one, but two sailings. One from the London docks and another from Southampton, where I hear another call to arms is being raised."

"What?" Whittington said, forgetting their game. He had been wrong footed and now he knew the cause. "What numbers are involved?"

"Ah, so you knew not," Stokes grinned, savouring the moment. "You will not like much the tally. For here in London, it numbers above a hundred men including some archers to the muster. As to Southampton, I await the news."

Whittington said nothing. He tugged at his ear, lost in thought. Then he turned suddenly. "He means to send a war party to France, not an embassy! By all the Gods, this will not do. If he joins with Burgundy and fights for their cause it will end badly, and of more import it will cast us for one side and we must live with that choice. The Duke of Burgundy, if victorious with our backing, will not stop at victory for Paris. He will sweep forward to Calais and hold that to ransom as a hostage of fortune for the prince. Hell's teeth, this does not serve."

"I bethought you would not be amused," Stokes offered lightly, "and we are of the same mind."

"Does the king know aught of this?" Whittington asked.

"As yet I have not apprised him of the build up to arms. Others may have, yet all is being done in secret with small pockets of men assembled and ships made ready in isolation. It is a clever stratagem, and one that appears to be working right well."

Chapter Forty-Two

London buzzed with a new sense of excitement as the rumours of war spread. The king's ships, which had stood ready to sail, had quietly and gradually been sequestered by the captains and servants of the earls of Arundel and Warwick. Whittington had been attending a meeting with the Guild, and arriving at Thomas de Grispere's house he asked if Jamie would accompany him down to the London Wharf. The two men rode to the waterside, dismounted and quietly led their mounts along the river frontage. A cool wind blew off the river, heralding the changes of the season as autumn spread its magic among the trees, colouring greens to violent hues of ochre, orange and blood red, a portent of battles to come.

"When is the fleet to sail?" Jamie asked.

"The twenty sixth of this month, just six days' hence," Sir Richard replied. "Mark how there are large companies of archers about, as well as men-at-arms and barrels of fletched arrows stacked by the quayside. Temporary stabling is being made ready, all in preparation for war. This is no peace embassy and it is not what the king agreed to. The prince has exceeded his remit – and at whose encouragement, I wonder?"

"I would look no further than the Lords Beaufort or indeed any on the prince's council, for they all have axes to grind and a profit to gain, in war or in coin, it matters not." Jamie finished disconsolately with a saddened face. His optimism of such a short time ago when he was raised to the status of household knight had wilted in cynicism at the games he had seen being played for power and political gain.

"From your tone I surmise that the prince turned down your request to venture forth with his so called embassy?"

"Aye, that he did, claiming that he would have other matters for me to attend to at home in England. Yet I know not what, for all focus seems to be on France and aught else is forgotten."

"Then beware, Jamie, and I adjure you to caution. You are the leading witness to the treason of some of the most powerful men in England, and you have therefore made some terrible enemies. Lord Roos barely made away with his life when last he was sent to settle the Loveday dispute involving Stanhope, and I hear that he may need to venture forth again.

"Now think on't. If you were at risk of consigning blame to powerful lords who backed your cause, what better time to send abroad to arrest those who might bring them down than when those same lords are abroad gaining glory and wealth for England in the king's name, eh? Recall how much criticism the prince received from the Head of the House, Thomas Chaucer, for arresting Prendergast? And he a traitorous scullion, proved so directly by his actions. All Stanhope, and indeed the lords of Arundel and Warwick, would say is that they were never there and you were mistaken. Whom do you think would win in the Chancery courts?" Jamie looked aghast at Sir Richard as the magnitude of what he faced hit home.

"Yet take heart, for they have now heard of the writ and

have accordingly stayed their hand. They seek more subtle means to gain a crown, to wit..." he waved his hand expansively across the broad panoply of a country preparing for war that lay before them.

"I would wager a considerable sum that when Roos next goes into danger – probably to Stanhope's lands – you shall be asked to accompany him. So, beware and have some good companions about you, I adjure you most strongly."

"So I am merely a pawn in this game for the throne, to be sent to my demise to protect lords of greater standing than myself?"

"Mayhap. 'Twould not be the first time such things have come to pass. Yet they know not with whom they deal, and you will with my help and those of your steadfast companions better them yet. Now let us remount and ride to the palace where I must attend upon his majesty to ensure he is aware of all that is occurring in his name."

When they arrived at the Palace, they found that the king was not in residence, but was sojourning south of the river at Lambeth palace, having left courtiers on notice that he was not be disturbed until the next day. Jamie left Sir Richard and wandered along to the court that so often assembled in the Great Hall, where gossip rather than coin was the currency of choice and courtly secrets were spread wide as a swan's wings. It was a gay scene as minstrels sang gently and music wafted across from the harpists above the hubbub of voices. Fresh rushes had been laid, and the smell of sandalwood pervaded the air along with some new spice which he could not identify. Fires had been lit against the chill of autumn that seeped into the palace walls from the nearby river.

He spotted Cristoforo in discussion with the Contessa, and to his pleasure the Lady Alice. Jamie made his way towards them, smiling in relief at gaining a few minutes respite from the intrigues of the court. The court had already started to change with the seasons, and the silk gowns of the hot days of summer were replaced by luxurious fine woollen garments, caught with inlaid silk within the tippetts and shawls of intricate embroidery in deft pastel colours. The long sweeping collars were lined with ermine fur, and hair was raised with nets of jewels. The contessa wore a gown of an unusual frosted pink, while Alice's robe was the vivid green of rich watercress. The colour lifted her complexion and made her eyes iridescent, he noticed.

"Lady Alice, Contessa," he addressed them, bowing. "Why this is well met and a relief from the drudgery of court to see such celestial beauty in such abundance."

"Fie on you, for clearly the drudgery of courtly intrigue has not affected your silvered tongue, which dispenses compliments like a soothsayer's stories." Alice flicked her delicate fan at him in mock condemnation.

"I am a severely wounded by your rejection of me, Lady Alice. Mayhap the contessa will aid me in my dilemma?"

"Look not to me as a port in your storm, for my harbours are closed and barred to all but one," she replied, flashing her feline eyes at Cristoforo.

"Cristoforo, how do you manage such wilful ladies, for their wiles are beyond me?"

"Ah, *amico mio*, one day I will take you to Italy, where the answers will all be *apparente*." He offered Janie a warm smile.

"Tell me, does Italy hold the answer to all things, even riddles?"

"*Si, è vero*. Why, do you have a riddle that needs solving?"

"Ah, my Jamie," Alice said. "Does the court once again grasp at your soul? Come tell us all, for you are among friends here and we shall be a balm to your fevered senses."

"As ever, my lady, you are more than a balm. You are a veritable panacea to my ills."

"Come then, let us walk easily. Pray tell me all, for it intrigues me and I suspect we may aid you in some small way to find a cure for that which ails you."

At which the four broke into two couples and gently paraded around the hall until they found a quiet corner where Jamie explained what had occurred and Whittington's fears both for himself and for the realm.

"'Tis a fine coil and no mistake," Alice opined. "I fear that Whittington has the right of it, for my father has been approached to see if he would side with the prince should he move to seize the crown from his father." She admitted, looking furtively around as she spoke.

"When did this occur?" Jamie asked, suddenly concerned.

"Someone came to our house yestereve, I saw not who it was and caught but snippets of the conversation from my father's solar. The door was ajar and I wished to know who had called, so I waited perhaps a minute longer than I should, for I was curious and the hour was late. After the mysterious visitor had left, I asked father for more details, but he dismissed me, saying it was just matters of the court. Yet he had a troubled look upon his face, as if he were torn and indecisive. I would not have mentioned it except in passing, for there is ever some plot afoot to swirl about the court. But as you have come hither with fears of the same stamp, I thought it relevant."

"And you have done well, my lady. If you should learn anymore, I beg of you let me know, for my life and that of the king could depend upon it."

The contessa, who had walked nearby and overheard Lady Alice and Jamie's conversation, now spoke up. "My uncle I know raises funds for the prince upon our bank. I would never normally disclose such facts," she said, "yet here I see that the two may be intertwined and one may aid the other." The contessa realised that she breached mannerly terms of convention, yet in her heart as an Italian she knew that she would not be constrained by convention until her dying day, as she had proved on many occasions. She was also aware that this spirited attitude was one of the reasons Cristoforo loved her so.

"Why contessa, you are a wonder," Jamie said. "Do you know for where these funds are bound? For there are rumours of reinforcements for a second sailing being assembled at Southampton. If this be true then a whole army, not a simple embassy, would be travelling to France."

"I will see what I can find out from my uncle. We must have a care of what we divulge, for our business is based upon trust and secrecy and for this alone we are permitted to stay and trade in England whilst other foreigners may not. Yet mayhap even the smallest indication would aid you, no?"

"I have complete faith in you and in your discretion, contessa."

"Ah, master Jamie, you are so charming that you would steal the very food from my lips." She chastised him.

"Not I my lady, yet I know of one who would..." At which Cristoforo, upon whom all eyes turned, merely smiled and shrugged, feigning innocence.

"Now, ladies, by your leave I must depart, for this news brings with it details that I must offer to Sir Richard."

"Will you not allow me to walk with you sir?" Lady Alice asked coquettishly in a very forward move.

Despite his pressing need to impart the news, he could not resist her charms and offered her a place at his side, aware of the heat of her presence and the high colour in her cheeks as she accepted. Her maid, who had kept a discrete distance throughout, now trailed closely in their wake to chaperone her charge and preserve the proprieties as they left the gathering of the Great Hall.

Chapter Forty-Three

Sir Richard Whittington was even more agitated when he received Jamie's news. He noted it down excitedly, but found himself unable to prevail upon anyone willing to allow him an audience with the king. It was not until the following day that the sovereign held any interviews, and even then they were held in the presence of the Lord Chief Justice, Sir William Gascoigne, Archbishop Arundel and Lord Grey. Mercifully, Sir Richard saw that Lord Thomas Beaufort, the king's Chancellor was not present. He needed this moment to be as private as possible and all those present to be unequivocally in favour of the king.

"Majesty, thank you for agreeing to grant me an audience."

"Come, Sir Richard. We are always pleased to see you and obtain the wisdom of your counsel that you so often proffer."

It was a generous offer of encouragement from a hard pressed king, and it was better than most would have received. It showed the value the king placed upon Whittington's advice, as well he knew.

"Sire, you are most generous. I have news which grieves me

to impart, yet it is my duty to so do. Since your decision to withdraw from travelling to Calais I have been checking carefully upon the comings and goings through the ports and reconciling these with Sir William Stokes and the build-up of support for the embassy to France that is due to sail on the twenty sixth of this month." Whittington halted to see what response his words would be met with. He saw the king was interested, his brows knitted in concentration, unsure as to where this discourse was leading.

"Pray continue, Sir Richard. We are most intrigued."

"Sire, with this in mind I have observed well and scoured for intelligence on all movements of troops and coin that may pertain to the embassy. To wit I am certain that the build-up of munitions is tantamount to a war party, for certes not an embassy of peace. In addition, I am also led to believe that a second muster is occurring at Southampton by way of reinforcement to the initial van, taking the number far in excess of what I presume you had intended." Here Whittington stopped, giving the king time to consider. Lord Grey and Archbishop Arundel looked on askance. Clearly neither man had received such news. They had been tied up directly with the king's affairs and little of their concern was directed toward the prince.

At length the king responded: "Do you have evidence of numbers at London?"

"Majesty, from the quantity of arrow barrels at the wharf and the temporary stabling I would for certes estimate hundreds of archers and—"

"Archers in great numbers?" the king cried. "Then this is indeed an army, not an embassy. So, our son has betrayed us again. We pledged our trust in him and it has been broken. And of Southampton?"

"Sire, as yet I know not details, and I pray that these will be available to me soon. I can confirm that monies have been sent to be dispensed in regard to the recruitment of men and the purchase of arms."

"By God's legs he deceives me, and seeks to cuckold me from my own realm. So be it, that is enough. Sir Richard, have a care about yourself, for you have done us great service, yet we fear should news of this exposure be seen to issue from your circle it may go ill for you."

"Majesty, I am as ever grateful of your concern. By your leave, sire." Whittington bowed and backed away until he reached the door of the chamber. Once he had left the room, King Henry instructed his chief clerk. "Have Sir Thomas Beaufort the Lord Chancellor, attend upon us this instant."

"Majesty," the clerk said, and was gone with a swift bow.

— ✕ ✳ ✕ —

By the afternoon the court was in shock once more. The king had issued writs to reconvene parliament on the second of November. Everyone knew that there was no financial reason for such a move. The kingdom's revenues revolved around the wool subsidy and this had already been set by the last parliament. No new statutes were to be passed and no debates ordered by writ, other than this one from the king calling for an unusual parliament. The Palace was rife with rumour.

Thomas and Henry Beaufort met with the prince and his other proctors in a private audience.

"He will be too late, highness. The embassy of Arundel and Warwick sails in five days' time. There is nothing he can do and this embassy has his blessing, it is so written."

"I agree. And how does the party at Southampton progress, Thomas?"

"Well my lord," Thomas Arundel answered. "The reinforcements there will be greater than the van, with more archers and men-at-arms. The tally will be in excess of two thousand men."

"'Tis well done. Then we shall prevail with God's grace and beat the Armagnacs, for I hear that they now gain Saint Cloud and knock upon the very gates of Paris seeking to unseat King Charles and make him a mawmet to their needs.

"We ask therefore what battles must we fight here? Dost my father think to retire from the throne or try some scheme to pull back more power and express his distaste for the actions we have taken? What say you, Sir Thomas? You were there in conference when he signed the writs."

"I know not, my lord prince." Beaufort answered. "He was in a cold rage and was not wont to dispense wisdom or thought, merely to assign the cause as was his right. I seek now to learn more and will pass on all that I can glean."

"Just so. 'Twas well done, and we thank you for advising us so promptly. How go your preparations for the sailing, my lords?" he asked of Arundel and Warwick.

"My prince, all goes well." Arundel answered. "The ships are provisioned and the men nearly all assembled. We await more archers to arrive from the shires and then we shall be a full company upon your orders.

"My captains are to bring forward the day after your sailing with twice as many men from Southampton as you take for the initial foray. Funds are being placed and we shall have ships and arms enough to sway the tide to the Burgundians' favour. You are to join with Burgundy in Paris, yet you must approach from the north east, for the Armagnacs hold the north, west and south and are pressing the duke's forces hard."

"As you command, my prince. By your leave we will go now and oversee the final preparations for the voyage."

"May God be with you, my lords and speed you to a victory in his name."

"Amen to that, sire."

"Now we have other matters to which we must attend, as there is mischief abroad at Wrawby in Lincolnshire by none other than the king's own royal justice."

"Would this be Sir Robert Tirwhit, who has estates in that shire, my prince?" asked Thomas Beaufort, his mind turning to events there, wondering who might be party to any major dispute in that area.

"You have the right of it, Sir Thomas, and he goes against Sir William Lord Roos to settle a Loveday Arbitration that will by all accounts turn into an affray. Our father's hold on these matters weakens, so we must take a stand and rule in his stead."

"Who will you send, my lord prince, with so many of your trusted knights sailing to France?"

The prince favoured him with a smile, wondering if Beaufort himself wished to head the party who would settle the dispute, as there was a chance of some action at arms. He then dismissed the idea, knowing his father would never permit his Chancellor to head such an errand, and answered absentmindedly: "Why, Sir William, Chief Justice Gascoigne, a few household knights and men-at-arms for a show of force and protection. We shall be short enough of men to aid us once the embassy sails for France."

"Ah just so. A goodly force to stay the errant hand of Tirwhit. To go against the king's peace in such a manner is illustrative of how far in contempt your father's court has fallen." Beaufort finished hypocritically. The prince said nothing in response, merely dismissing all bar his clerks, servants, and Courtney.

Upon leaving Prince Henry's chambers the two Beaufort brothers made their way along the corridor, and when they were alone Thomas muttered to his brother. "Have you considered that all those party to events and circumstances here and who have connexions to Stanhope are to venture forth to Lincoln? For I'd wager that Sir James de Grispere will number in the party."

Bishop Henry Beaufort looked at his brother, instantly understanding the intimation. "Do I understand your meaning correctly, brother? If so I shall pray for your soul." The solemn denouncement was delivered with a raised eyebrow and a lengthening of his lips that some could have taken as a wicked smile of complicity.

"Why then brother, I would adjure you hence to the nearest chapel, for I shall have need of prayer if my plan be true."

Chapter Forty-Four

The following day found Sir Richard Whittington pacing his chamber, unhappy with the way in which events were unfolding. A knock at the door disturbed his thoughts, and his clerk advised that Jamie was here to see him.

"James, well met. You disturb me from my reverie, which is opportune, yet I see from your visage that all is not sunny with you."

"I have just returned from Prince Henry, where again I begged to be allowed to accompany the expedition to France, and again he refused to listen to my plea. Instead, he asks that I go with a party to a Loveday arbitration in Lincoln. I am doomed to be a mere hearth-knight, swapping old wives' tales with toothless men of battles past, yet I will have nought to tell save a Loveday!"

Whittington gave a small chuckle at Jamie's frustration. "Ah the impatience of youth. Think you not that you have had adventures enough, and were knighted by the prince himself, no less? Come now, your time of battle shall arrive, as much as I fear it will. Yet in the meantime have a care, for the road to Lincoln may not be a peaceful one."

"Why so? What have you heard?" Jamie's head shot up, eager to hear news of possible conflict.

"There are rumours abroad that Stanhope is causing mischief again, and you will pass close by his lands on your road to Lincoln. Mayhap the prince will ask that Lord Roos intercede there as well."

"Good, for I should like to meet with my Lord Stanhope and that arrogant knave Strelley again, this time without restraint or hidden purpose."

Sir Richard shook his head at Jamie's impetuosity and the eagerness of youth for battle. "When do you leave – and tell me, do you travel alone with the Lord Roos and his meiny?"

"On the morrow, for the Loveday is set for the third of October at Wrawby, and prince Henry bade me take what companions I wished as resources were slim due to the embarkation to France. I have therefore asked Cristo and Mark to accompany me, for there are no others that I would rather have at my back in times of trouble, if it be as perilous as you suppose. I prithee in that regard, durst thou hear of any news regarding the so called embassy to Calais afore I leave? I should like to know all I can."

"I have, and the intelligence is not good," Whittington replied. "The earls and the prince have mustered two hundred men-at-arms and knights, together with eight hundred archers."

"Eight hundred archers? By the cross, that is an invasion force, not an embassy. So the prince means war by any other name. This shall be added to by forces gathering at Southampton, which if by the information provided by the contessa is correct, will more than double that force."

"It will, and it gives me great cause for concern. I do not doubt where it will lead." Whittington said, looking to Jamie the most worried that he had ever seen him since entering his service. "The Armagnacs have taken Saint Cloud and reinforce their position ready to storm Paris and hold King Charles as hostage to their fortune. Mayhap the English force will bolster the Burgundians sufficiently to achieve a status quo with neither side proving victorious, for that would unite France. Now be gone, and make your preparations well, for you have a long ride and much to do," Whittington urged Jamie with a smile, robbing the words of any sting.

Jamie left the palace and rode to the house of the Earl of Macclesfield on La Straunde, reminded of the first time he had called here on the eve of his knighthood and had been barred entry. He knocked loudly upon the solid door, expecting a different response, having saved the earl's life. His steward, who answered, was of a far less frosty disposition than previously and bade him enter, expectant upon Lady Alice's arrival. A groom slid past to take Killarney to the stables at the rear, an accolade in itself.

Jamie was shown through to a private solar, now lit by candles as the weak afternoon sun began to dip low in the autumn sky. A fire was lit in the hearth and trays of scent and fragrant woods above the mantle gave off an air of harmony and sultry spices. He stood with his back to the blaze and warmed his hands, thinking of the journey to come and of Whittington's words of warning. After ten minutes or so, his thoughts were disturbed by a rustle of silk and the sound of soft footsteps approaching on the wooden floorboards – two sets, or his ears deceived him. The Lady Alice and her maid appeared. Alice was a vision in a cornflower blue gown, a delicate weave of gold netting surmounting her hair shot with pearls that caught the light, and an ermine-trimmed stole draped elegantly from her bare shoulders. Her eyes were lined with kohl and seemed to slant upwards in a feline manner, while a pale blue tint shaded her upper eyelids.

She nodded her head in response as he bowed forward, stretching a leg and observing formalities for her maid's sake and that of propriety. His breath was drawn with difficulty as she seemed to steal the very oxygen from his soul. It was not just her beauty, but her vibrance and spirit that bewitched him so.

"My Lady Alice, 'twas good of you to see me. I was not certain that you would be at home."

"Sir James, I am here as you see. Though my father is at court on business and my mother visits friends." The message was clear: she was alone, for her younger brother was now engaged as a squire in training.

"How provident it is that I found you thus disengaged."

"Indeed. Do you have news, or is this merely a fleeting visit on a whim?"

"My lady, I never wish to visit you fleetingly, whatever the cause. Such beauty deserves time to be appreciated. Yet I am afraid that I must depart on the morrow, as I have been tasked by the prince to travel with Lord Roos to intercede in a Loveday dispute in Lincoln."

"Lincoln? Why that is seven or eight days ride."

"Indeed, my lady and I shall miss your company for those days and many more."

"Honey smooth as ever. Nesta, pray fetch some wine for us, for I fear Sir James is in need of refreshment to salve that glib tongue of his that works so hard to enslave me." She smiled coquettishly up at Jamie, savouring his look of discomfort as Nesta left the room, pulling the door behind her until it was only slightly ajar, blocking the view from anyone passing. Alice closed the distance between them to merely a few inches from his face, and he knew not who instigated it, but their lips touched to inflame a passion within them as his arms embraced Alice, crushing the breath from her.

Her perfume and lips inflamed his senses, and all thought was lost to another world. When they finally broke, he looked worriedly at the door: "My lady, Nesta–"

"Will be a long time," she whispered, pressing her lips to his.

Part Four
Lincolnshire and London

Autumn/Winter

Chapter Forty-Five

Lincolnshire

The party of knights, esquires, archers and men-at-arms travelled out on the north road from London in the early hours, seeking to make a good start on their journey to Lincolnshire.

Jamie had only spoken with Sir William Lord Roos on a handful of occasions, but knew him by reputation. Roos was a knight of around forty years old who had left King Richard and sided with the then Henry Bolingbroke when he returned from exile and landed in the north of England to begin a campaign to take the crown from King Richard. He fought for King Henry at Shrewsbury and went on to be not only one of his most trusted advisors, but also a financier who aided the crown when it fell short of coin. The majority of his estates were in and around Lincoln, and he now travelled to defend these lands and their returns.

With him at the van were two other leading knights of King Henry's court: Henry Lord Beaumont and Thomas Lord Warre. They were both solid and chivalrous men, dependable and intractable in their loyalty to King Henry and battle hardened by long campaigns in the early years of his reign. One had served him in Europe and the Holy Land. They were great soldiers and wise in the ways of the world, standing aside for no man. The dangerous times called for such knights to be at the king's side, strong and unyielding, with a capable mesnie following each man to swell the numbers of the party to a good fighting strength. For rumours had reached them that Sir Robert Tirwhit was thought to be bringing a large number of armed men to pursue his cause.

Finally, there was Lord Chief Justice Sir William Gascoigne, another stalwart supporter of King Henry who had been having a difficult time of late, pulled as he was twixt the prince's council and loyalty to the king. He and Whittington were close friends, Jamie knew, and despite his seniority the great lord had spent some time talking with Jamie out of respect for his achievements in aiding the crown.

At this moment the four senior knights were ahead, talking as they rode, out of earshot to Jamie and his two companions, who were happy in each other's company, some distance back from the front of the party. The men-at-arms were at their backs, and behind them was a company of archers followed by the baggage train.

By the end of the day they had made a good twenty miles, as the roads were in good order after a dry summer and little rain.

Mark interrupted Jamie's reverie: "You are deep in thought, Jamie. Is it the journey ahead or the thought of a certain sweet lady that addles your wits?"

"Ah, such badinage with two fools, what more could a man wish for?" Jamie responded in kind, pleased at the lightening of the mood brought on by his two companions.

"But surely there is naught to addle, for where there was once a brain there is now nothing but a beating heart that rules all." Cristoforo opined, joining the banter and taking Mark's side, keen to tease Jamie for his love for the Lady Alice.

"And this from a man who was conquered by a glance and has for evermore been besotted by the sight of a pair of deep brown eyes and the whisper of Italian. You stand as good example of a man encoiled in the arms of love."

Cristoforo rounded in disgust at such an accusation – although he knew it to be true – and the banter continued, with Mark being hoisted by his own petard when the name of mistress Emma was mentioned.

They made for Wicumun, planning to stay the first night there. The size of the town was sufficient to provide for the whole company, and there would be few such towns as they travelled further off the main route so they made good use of such facilities while they could. Lord Roos knew the route and all its foibles well, having made the journey many times.

The following two nights were also spent in towns, but on the fourth night they made camp next to a stream by a forest, with plenty of space to pitch tents and catch trout from the stream.

Finally, they made for Newark on Trent, where they were accommodated in the town. It was a substantial settlement with a royal charter and a strong castle that dominated the central market area. The population was over two thousand strong, and the town bustled with life and thrived on the wool trade as did many northern towns. The senior party of knights was made welcome by the castellan of the castle, while the men-at-arms, archers and servants camped in the bailey, keeping a close eye on their baggage train. The following day they would press on for Lincoln and then to the small town of Wrawby some thirty miles to the north.

Jamie learned that night from Sir William that writs had been served for the arrest of Sir Richard Stanhope and others.

This pleased him, for he wished to see the look upon the knight's face again in his true colours and not as some scullion man-at-arms as he had bethought him before. It made him think deeply about all he had learned from his time in London's court, and instead of passing the evening with the other knights, he excused himself upon the reason of tending to his horse, which he said had shown signs of lameness. He was left alone to wander in solitude around the walls of the castle and think, looking into the darkness beyond. He nodded to the occasional passing guard, but was left alone to consider all he knew.

He considered it strange that he with his companions would be sent on this Loveday, and his thoughts turned to others in the company. Lord Roos was party to accusations – not just of Stanhope, but those against other knights and lords, including Sir Roger Leche, the Controller of the King's Household and a Justice of the Peace, not to mention the implied treason and disloyalty of the king's own half-brothers the Beauforts.

Who else knew of this? Sir William Gascoigne, of course, who was party to the affidavit, and anyone associated with Jamie himself with whom he might have discussed such matters, namely Cristoforo and Mark. Then there were loyal Lancastrian knights such as Lord Beaumont and Lord Warre. If anything happened in battle or skirmish and all perished, every scrap of evidence against the northern meeting would vanish, save for Whittington's word and a writ that could be made to disappear easily enough.

And who would care, he reasoned? Warwick and Arundel were abroad gaining glory and honours. No one would dare besmirch their fair name as heroes in battles to save Calais, as it would be perceived. The king would be severely weakened both physically and financially. Did Prince Henry know this? Was he sending Lord Roos and his company – including Jamie, Mark and Cristoforo – to their deaths to preserve his hold on the crown? The more he thought things through, the more uneasy he felt. For if this Loveday was a ruse, brought about by one of the king's own bench, why could that not be a trap to kill and silence them all?

Thoughts whirled in his head and when he finally lay down to sleep he found himself unable to do so, vowing to speak with Lord Roos in the morning. He turned his mind to thoughts of Lady Alice and how she had lighted a fire within him. She had been very brave and forward to kiss him so, and her maid – bless her – had been complicit in the act. He had swived many a tavern wench in the past, and two widows in Scotland had succumbed to his charms. He remembered them with a smile, yet none had affected him like Alice. Each time he saw her he was smitten anew by her aura and beauty, striking him breathless and wanting for more like a drunkard unable to resist the next cup of wine.

The following morning the party set off for Lincoln and Jamie rode to the head of the line in order to speak with Sir William.

"My lord, I would speak with you, despite my position here as the most junior of the company."

"Pray continue, Sir James, for youth does not preclude valued thoughts, nor should seniority disparage them," Sir William encouraged Jamie. Lord Roos had been impressed by the young knight's maturity and his reputation had begun to proceed him, especially after discussing him with Lord Grey, who spoke well of his efforts to thwart Glyndower at the battle at Stokesey. He also knew Whittington well, as they were joint financiers of the crown, spoke regularly and had much in common via the wool trade.

"I was given to much thought yester eve over our orders

pertaining to both the Loveday and Sir Richard Stanhope."
Here Jamie looked at Sir William Gascoigne, who showed a
wintry smile as though he anticipated what was to come and
echoed the same thoughts in his own mind. The look encouraged Jamie to continue airing his thoughts.

"Verily I say, be not hesitant with your discourse. Pray
continue," Lord Roos said.

"Very well. We are linked by two or three factors, to wit we
are party to the possible arrest of Stanhope and the knowledge
of his misdeeds. We also share a loyalty to the king and his cause
above that of any other, and an intimate knowledge of matters
not known outside our circle and those to whom it would be a
detriment if their plotting were known."

"Of whom do you speak?" Lord Roos asked. At which
Jamie explained his thoughts of treachery, what he had discovered at Nottingham when he had been there in the early part of
the year and the link between that and the current circumstances that led him to believe they were being led into a trap.

As Jamie paused for breath after giving full voice to his
concerns, Lord Roos looked at him anew. "By the rood,
Whittington has taught you well! If what you say is true and
it encompasses the earls of Arundel and Warwick as well as
the Beauforts, dost thou think the prince is party to this
deceit?"

The question hung in the air as the chink of bridles, creak
of leather and echo of horses' hooves were the only sounds
apparent to the knights. At length Jamie spoke. "I know not my
lord, and would hope that despite his differences with the king
the prince's loyalty is not tested in such a manner."

"Which provides no answer at all." Lord Beaumont
commented, his dark eyes flashing with suspicion.

"Therefore, I ask of you," Lord Roos commanded, "what
would you have us do? For we cannot abandon the cause with

which we have been assigned, certainly not for talk and rumour of ambush, yet forewarned is forearmed."

"My lord, you know this area well. Accordingly I would advise that we camp outside Lincoln, with the less evidence of our passing the better. Is there a village or friendly spot where we could camp away from the main road and unseen?"

Lord Roos thought for a moment: "Yes, the bishop's palace at Nettleham. His grace is a friend of mine and I trust him well enough. It is north east of the town and will set us up well for the final leg of the journey."

"That will do well, my lord. From tomorrow I suggest we all ride in at least maille and have a shield at the ready." The knights looked to each other and shrugged. It would be but a day's ride and they had known worse hardships.

"So be it. We will follow your lead, but I pray you are mistaken, for I do not like what it presages at court."

The day continued without event as each man considered his own thoughts based upon what Jamie had disclosed. None was happy at the prospect of an ambush on the open road, and they rode warily, marking potential points of ambush as they went. They rode to the east of Lincoln, circumventing the town and avoiding contact with any of the outlying steadings. A messenger had been sent ahead to warn the bishop of their imminent arrival and to beg for shelter that evening.

As they paused to gain their bearings and rest the horses, Jamie rode alongside Mark and Cristoforo.

"Mark, I have a favour to beg of you. Can you play the bumpkin once more and ride into Lincoln seeking news, gently asking if there is any work? You do this best of all, for no one suspicions you, everyone takes to you and you have the gentle touch for finding favour with others.

Mark grinned back, slipping into the role of country oaf that he knew so well from his childhood. "Why master, it'll be a pleasure to serve 'ee, so it will." At which he tugged his forelock in mock servitude.

"You are a scullion knave. Yet have a care, for they will be wary of strangers if trouble is looked for. Do you have an old jupon in your baggage that would better aid your disguise?"

"I do, and will find it now." With which he departed and went back to the baggage train. Cristoforo raised an eyebrow.

"I know, yet he played the fool right well on board the *Shield* and lulled them all from suspicion. Everyone takes to Mark and he appears harmless, a gentle giant to all but a few that would pick a quarrel. He can turn upon his Cornish accent to good avail when needs be. I will ride with him and tend his horse whilst he is in the town, for dusk will come in two hours or more and he must be out afore curfew."

"No, I shall do that," Cristoforo said." You will be needed here, the better to organise matters on the morrow. Besides, the night is my friend, we are old companions, she and I, and do well together. I shall keep Mark safe, never fear."

Jamie thought of arguing yet knew his friend was right, as he looked to approaching dusk and realised that if anyone could hide two horses safely and guide them back, it would be Cristoforo.

"So be it. Yet have a care and God be with you both."

"We shall return afore the morning, fear not." Mark assured him as the two men rode off towards Lincoln. Jamie watched them until they were lost from sight. No one had gone after them from the camp, nor did they seem to be trailed by any others.

Jamie rejoined the company as they remounted and set forth on the final leg of their journey. Lord Roos was curious: "Where do your companions go?"

"I have sent Mark to scout the town for news and signs of anything untoward."

They arrived at the bishop's manor house and entered the courtyard. It was a fine structure of local stone, built well with a high wall surrounding the house that would keep out all but the most determined foe and prevent any night-time ambush. He would sleep well that night, though they were nearing enemy territory, he knew, and the feeling of impending danger was stronger than ever.

Bishop Phillip Repingdon was a man of middle years, yet he carried himself well, reputed to be as good with a sword as a bishop's crosier. He welcomed Lord Roos as an old friend and bade the company welcome. Listening carefully to all that had occurred, he claimed some knowledge of the events leading to the Loveday dispute. He told the assembled knights that it was rumoured some three to four hundred men-at-arms had been assembled from Sir John Tirwhit's mesnie and were being used to bully and intimidate local communities.

"This surprises me not," Lord Roos replied. "'Tis the same tactics used by other treasonous knights in the district of Nottingham. What concerns us all is why now he should fly against the king, being one of his own justices."

The bishop looked from under a heavy brow, peering hard at his friend: "We are out on a limb here, yet we are not without news or rumour. The consensus is that Tirwhit believes the king to be weak and senses that now is an opportune time to stretch his boundaries and gain more than is his due." Here the bishop hesitated, deciding how much he should proclaim of what he clearly knew. "There is also a feeling that he has been promised more power with a new leader governing the country. How does his majesty? For I hear that he rails and turns for the better, God be praised." The bishop finished, crossing himself.

"He does, your grace. The disease still ravages him, yet he makes better of it than most. He has taken to the sword again and was to lead an army to Calais, yet now he stays at home to

set matters aright here, for they are due and no mistake." Sir
William finished.

"Let us not dwell upon this here. Come, wash yourselves
and food will be served after vespers when you are refreshed."
At which the bishop gestured for the knights to follow him to
their allotted quarters.

The talk over supper continued in the same vein, and it was
after dark that the party was disturbed by a messenger.

"Sir James, there are two of your men without who wish to
talk with you."

Jamie rose and bowed to the bishop. "By your leave, your
grace, I needs must have discourse with my companions."

Once he had left the hall the bishop turned to Lord Roos
and the others, commenting. "An earnest young man and very
dangerous to boot I'd say. What is his history?"

"He is interesting, is young Sir James. 'Twas he that fought
off Glyndower and he who helped capture the pirates Longe
and Prendergast. Rumour persists that it was also he who fired
the French siege machine that was destined to take Calais."

"Then he is to be praised, for no man should build a
weapon of war in the house of God." The bishop stated
vehemently.

Chapter Forty-Six

Lincolnshire

Jamie left the manor for the chill dark of the evening, where he found Mark and Cristoforo waiting for him in the courtyard. They appeared to be in good spirits and not hurt in any way, but Jamie was worried, nonetheless.

"Mark, you are unhurt? Did you find aught amiss?" he asked, concern in his voice.

"I encountered no problems, and the townsfolk were right friendly. I shared a jug or two at a couple of taverns and looked around for a bit," Mark drawled in his Cornish burr. "There was a captain at arms seeking men and there was talk of a fight coming 'to the north', so they said around the town. But most interestin' of all was this captain who was seeking men who could use a bow. Anyone who could were to follow him this eve for there was good pay to be had, he declared. A few went and I was sorely tempted to go to see what he was about, yet I had no way of letting 'ee know nor a bow to my name."

Jamie grinned at his friend's easy going nature. Mark laughed in the face of danger and found it easy to be accepted by everyone. He had the skill of making firm friendships upon first acquaintance.

"So they seek archers? Hell's teeth, that does not bode well. How did you leave? For the gates will have been barred and the watch about."

"That were easy enough. Some stables were set by the wall, and I heaved myself up and skipped over it. 'Twas low at that point and I tumbled down for an easy landing. It was like falling from a throw." He dismissed the action as commonplace. Mark was, Jamie knew very well, athletic and nimble despite his size.

"It is well. Thank you, Mark – and you, Cristoforo, for keeping watch for him. Now get some rest, for the morrow promises to be an interesting day. We may yet thwart this coil in which are caught," Jamie finished. Then he went in search of the Roy, the captain of archers, and Alun of the men-at-arms, to discuss with them plans for the following day.

— ×✤× —

The party set out at dawn, with a grey and overcast sky and a light breeze from the south drifting over the company as they rode off. The weather offered little comfort. Jamie had informed Lord Roos and the other knights of all that Mark had learned, and they were now prepared for any ambush. Unrolling their hauberks from the waxed leather sheets behind their saddles, the knights rode with helmets on and visors ready to slip down. They carried their kite shields by the guige straps over their shoulders, ready to be brought to bear on their arms at the first sign of trouble.

The topography had changed as they ventured eastwards away from the hills of central England. The sweeping vistas gave way as the countryside became flatter, with sluggish, low lying rivers, streams and dykes crossing land that had been drained since Roman times. Much of the country was forested, and gently sweeping grassland came sloping down to meet the main road on which they travelled. With no meaningful rain and only light winds, the forest was still clad with leaves, beautiful in their shades of orange and vermilion, dappled with patches of brown that lifted the yellows like flames from a hearth. The trees had been cut back to prevent ambush as was the custom, yet still the road meandered at times, rising and falling with the contours of the land as they emerged from the final few hills. At each rise and twist the knights became tense.

They watered their horses at Redbourne and followed the straight road through level country towards Hibaldstow, where they felt all eyes upon them as they passed through the small village.

Here the road forked, and they veered eastward towards Wrawby. Jamie had that familiar feeling upon the back of his neck when he was being watched and looked across and down at Forest to see if her ears were pricked, then at Cristoforo.

"*Si, Amico mio*, I feel it too. The trees have eyes, I sense."

"Aye, even I feel it or 'tis my imagination and I've been travelling with you two for far too long," Mark said.

Without saying anything, Jamie nudged Richard into a canter to catch up with the van of the party. He could feel the excitement flowing out of the stallion and kept watching Forest's ears to see if she had picked up on any sound or danger beyond the human ear or senses. Forest seemed on tenterhooks, yet whether this was as a result of picking up tension from her master or some other cause, he could not tell. She loped by his side as he caught up with Lord Roos and the other knights.

"Sir William, a word if I may?"

"Of course. Speak, man."

"Pray stop the cortege for a few minutes and allow the rear

to close up. I know it may seem strange, yet I wish my dog Forest to pick up on any strange sounds. The bend ahead and the greater slope to the hillside next to it bodes ill, I feel, and something presses upon me with a warning."

Jamie nodded to the road ahead that showed a curve, all but invisible as the landscape undulated away from the flatter terrain that characterised this area. Two ridges rose on either side of the road upon which they travelled, and clearly the original builders had cut through a swathe of rocks and land to create a straighter and more level path, until it reached the escarpment edging the lowlands that was now within view in the distance.

"Sir William, how far now to Wrawby for you know this area well?"

"Why 'tis maybe two leagues, for just past the bend ahead lies the village of Brigg and then Wrawby. You suspect an ambush?"

"I do. Forest is unsure, and ever I trust the hound. Richard too frets, and something is clearly amiss. If we are to be attacked, it will be here for certes. I wish to take the archers in two bands to the ridges on either side of the road, along with some of the men-at-arms." Turning then to the lords, he said: "Have your shields ready, sirs, for I suspect we are to be attacked here."

"Will you take the heralds to warn us?" Sir William asked.

"No, my lord. Sir Robert de Umfraville used a different method when attacking in the daylight. You will see a single arrow fly upwards just before we attack, mayhap alight with tow. If you see no arrow then we will appear by the road as you arrive and will give you fair warning so you do not mistake us for the enemy. I fear archers, for they could take you all down in one flight. Then a leaderless band would remain, with no knowledge of what we have, and all matters would then be served right well, both at court and here.

"Give us sufficient time to gain a place of vantage, for we shall walk the last distance, leaving the horses with grooms off the road so as not to be seen by any scouts abroad."

Jamie nodded and cantered back to his friends. In his absence, Lord Beaumont commented: "Sir James has the right of it, for all my senses scream that something is amiss, yet I know not what, and that," he pointed ahead, "is as likely a place for an ambush as any I've seen."

Jamie reached his two companions and the rest of the company, including the men-at-arms and the archers, all of whom had dismounted to rest their horses and take advantage of the break. To any watchers, the halt in their progress appeared natural, a chance to offer the horses and men some rest. Jamie sought the captains of archers and soldiers, calling them into conference with Cristoforo and Mark. Many times he had planned such a raid with Sir Robert, and leadership came naturally to him.

Roy and Alun came forward. Both were seasoned fighters from the wars of France and civil wars in England. Their attitudes were calm, brought on by experience, and they relished a good fight.

"I suspect an ambush at the bend ahead," Jamie said. "But we are going to ambush them, as I explained yester eve. I need two parties of archers and men-at-arms, one to accompany me and one to go with Cristoforo. We will ride off the road and leave our horses out of sight while we proceed on foot. I need good men who know how to move in silence. Nock your bows now and be ready. We approach just below the ridge and away from the skyline, giving cover and making the passage easier. Try to leave one man alive if they are there, for I may be proved a fool this fine day, like a nervous maid at a bridal ceremony."

The men all laughed at his jest, liking him all the more for his lack of arrogance.

He chose two groups, one for each side of the road. They took their horses, riding into the woodland where the mounts could be restrained by servants. The archers strung their bows, each man looking to his equipment to ensure that it did not rattle or creak, then both parties made their way through the woods to the appointed place where the assumed ambush lay. They followed animal tracks worn by time, staying clear of the undergrowth and avoiding all the dry sticks they could from the long hot summer. Most of the men in the party had grown up familiar with country ways, the yeomen leaving a life on the farm for the glories of war, a master's roof over their heads and regular pay. Jamie moved forward, watching Forest as she padded silently by his side. Some two hundred yards short of the place they were aiming for she stopped dead, her ears pricked as she looked back towards him, her coat raised in hackles. Jamie smiled a grim smile, sensing that he had been vindicated.

He turned, motioning those behind to cease movement and huddled down as the leaders of the group gathered around in the limited space on the trail.

"They're ahead, lying in wait. Forest is sure. There will be archers, so beware." Then he called up to Randel who, Roy swore, could move like a ghost. Jamie needed someone like him as Cristoforo was leading the other group of men.

"Randel, move to the far side, for that is where they will have the horses tethered. They'll not want to risk being trapped after an ambush and will flee north to Wrawby and the safety of Tirwhit's men. Do try not to take the horses, for they will whinny and sound an alarm. Silence anyone holding them and slice the girths nearly through, for they'll be saddled like as not.

Should any try to ride free, we shall kill them as they fall. Think ye can do that?"

"Aye my lord, with pleasure." Randel whispered, showing an evil smile that was a mixture of missing teeth and bad breath. He was dressed in faded brown and looked as sun darkened as the trees he crept between, moving noiselessly, seeming to float as did Cristoforo, Jamie mused. Allowing Randel some time to get ahead of them, the party moved forward again, creeping slowly, watching how each foot was placed to avoid stepping on tinder dry twigs or undergrowth. They had to be especially careful as the breeze was behind them and would carry any sound.

There was no birdsong, Jamie noticed. All seemed to have deserted this place of tension. After a hundred yards he looked downhill through the foliage towards the road and saw what he had feared – a line of around thirty or so archers and soldiers.

They had cut back a small clearing in preparation for the ambush, allowing room to draw their bows unimpeded. Small branches and foliage had been clipped back above them to offer them a full firing line to the oncoming travellers upon the road, who were still some fifty yards distant. It was a killing ground. If, as Jamie suspected, they were to attack from one side first, the unsuspecting party would then retreat to the right of the road, straight into the line of fire of the other armed band that Jamie was certain would be on the opposite side, and whose archers and men would slaughter them as they ran towards the apparent safety of the trees.

Through the small gaps in the trees, he saw the party of knights in the distance now making its way forward as if they were innocent of the impending attack. Looking to the north in a small glade he saw the tethered horses, and all was still. As if by magic, Randel appeared at the side of the group from a small trail.

"Roy, strike a flint as soon as we are ready to release the first arrows," Jamie said. They had only ten archers and would be outnumbered, but they had the benefit of surprise. "Now, as soon as you release the first wave, send the fire arrows into the brush at their feet, it will light like a tinder box and the wind is with us," he continued.

"Ready Roy," he whispered. "Now!" Jamie swept his hand down to the twang of bow strings and the whistle of arrows as the shafts sliced through the air. All but two found their mark, knocking back their targets such was the force at less than one hundred yards from a weapon that could pierce armour and kill at three hundred and fifty.

The cries of the ambushed men rose shrilly into the air as an arrow was released upwards as a signal to Lord Roos's party. The flint caught the dry wool, creating a flame that quickly engorged the first tow-covered arrow to be placed in its reach. The arrow spluttered to life and as soon as it was ready, the bowman drew back, bending legs and shoulders into the bow in the time honoured fashion, reaching the full draw weight of one hundred and eighty pounds. He held briefly and then released the cord. The ash shaft struck another victim, who fell back as the small flames leapt to the tinder dry forest floor.

Already the attackers were returning fire, and one man-at-arms fell to the flurry of arrows that was sent back towards them as an arrow pierced his shoulder. It was now each man for himself as the archers fired at will, with fire arrows lighting up the forest floor. There was soon a wall of fire between the two parties, and the wind was driving it inexorably towards the ambushers. Some of the enemy soldiers broke free, fleeing from the blaze and the eye-watering acrid smoke.

They strove to attack Jamie's party, cursing as they hacked through the trees, angry and fierce in their fear. Jamie and the men-at-arms brought their shields to bear, forming a shield wall among the trees, trampling foot space ready to repel the attack and protect the band of archers who continued to light up the forest and pick out targets as they ran.

Then, from the road and the other side, they heard the clash of swords and the cries of battle. The knights were slaughtering any who ventured onto the roadway and harrying any who tried to flee. Then there was no more time, as the soldiers were upon them, outnumbering them two to one. They crashed against the impromptu shield wall, shouting battle cries and cursing through smoke-strained eyes, desperate to get at the men who had thwarted their plans. The wall held and Jamie stabbed through the gap, slicing an exposed leg without mail or armour. As the man fell, he stamped forward over him stabbing down with his sword to kill. A face appeared above his shield and he stabbed upwards, watching it disappear in a spray of scarlet as he pushed his shield forward. Suddenly the soldier at his side had his shield hooked by a poleaxe and screamed as it drove forward into his unprotected face, leaving Jamie's left side exposed to the oncoming soldiers. The poleaxe wielder lunged again, driving over Jamie's shield, causing him to flinch backwards to avoid the wicked spiked end of the axe, as there was no room to swing. Hooking the top of Jamie's shield, his attacker pulled back, seeking to use the same manoeuvre again. His shield down, Jamie stabbed over the top, looking for a target of soft flesh. Driving overhand, he turned sideways to avoid the spike and give himself some extra reach. A flash of silver grey blurred at his side as Forest charged in, attacking the soldier's shin, her jaws agape as she locked onto his lower leg, distracting him.

Looking down at the snarling mass of fur, the man never saw Jamie's strike coming until it was too late to avoid the deadly point that caught his raised shoulder. Jamie twisted the hilt of his sword, bringing a scream of agony from the axeman, and he withdrew, crying out in anger and leaving a gap which another soldier filled. Jamie stepped back bringing his shield up taking the sword slash that cut through slim branches to land upon his raised shield, then he stabbed low, gutting the man through his mail as his blade sawed home.

Forest darted back behind Jamie at his command. Another man attacked and was suddenly ripped from view, thrown backwards as an arrow embedded itself in his eye and forced its point a full two feet from the back of his head. The shield wall closed again and the company stood firm. Smoke and chaos was everywhere, with new cries of battle as men bearing the livery of Lord Roos, a bright red shield bearing three silver water bougets, rushed up hill through the trees to get at the enemy, shouting 'a Roos!' and 'King Harry!' as they came. The ambush turned into a rout as the enemy fled to their horses, some of which had waited despite being alarmed by the smoke and flames while others had fled in horror of the fire. Archers and soldiers bounded along, striving for their last means of escape.

"Follow me men, we'll have our last pickings yet!" With that, Jamie ran forward after them, avoiding the smoke that filled the trees to their right. Some made it to their mounts only to find upon getting to the saddle that the girths broke and they either toppled to the floor to be stabbed and slaughtered where they fell or were plucked out of their saddles by keen-eyed archers who were in a murderous mood and keen to avenge their fallen comrades. Randel had done a good job, Jamie saw, as the riders all fell. A few were taken prisoner as they begged for mercy. They were herded back down to the road at sword point.

Jamie saw to the wounded of his own men and finally arrived at the road, reeking of smoke and with a tear-stained face. He looked to the other side of the road and to his relief saw Cristoforo and Mark appear, driving a few prisoners before them. Cristoforo bore a cut to his head that bled onto his handsome features, and Mark's gambeson was torn in two places from sword cuts.

"How do you both fare?" Jamie called.

"Ha! As you see, we are victors but not unscathed," Cristoforo shrugged.

"Get these malapert whoresons down on their knees," Jamie ordered the men-at-arms, who promptly forced the prisoners to kneel before Lord Roos and the knights.

"This one," Mark nodded at the wielder of the poleaxe, who now cradled his torn left shoulder, "was the captain of arms who was seeking men in the tavern yester eve."

"Good, then he will do well." Jamie decided, walking towards him with murder in his eyes, the battle madness still within him. "You, caitiff whoreson, who ordered you on this murderous account?"

The captain looked at him. He said nothing and spat at his feet. Jamie did not hesitate, there was only cold rage in his head. These ambushers would, he knew, have slaughtered them with no mercy, for these were dangerous times and any show of weakness would be to invite defeat. Chivalry was a grand ideal, yet only a strength of purpose and a willingness to fight and kill for those ideals kept it alive. Jamie kicked the wounded shoulder of the captain, causing the man to cry out as blood oozed from the wound as he fell backwards. Jamie stood over him, stepping on the wound and twisting his foot with the weight of his body behind the move as the captain wailed in agony.

"This is your final opportunity, knave. I shall ask this question once more, then I shall take your right eye, and after that the left. Then I'll geld you and leave you on the road for the animals to gnaw upon. Who sent you?"

The captain mewled like a child. "No, no. I'll tell 'ee. We are here on the orders of Sir Robert Tirwhit. Please, I beg you, let me be."

"I have one more question, then you can live or die. By what intelligence did he learn of our travels and when we should arrive?"

The man gulped for air and nearly passed out with the pain as Jamie pushed with his foot. "No...agh ... He... He had a message from London two days past. Warned us you were all coming."

"All? He knew our names?"

"Aye, Sir Roos and a knight, Sir James de Grispere. You were to be killed at all costs. Now, please sir, I beg the by the Holy Mother, let me be."

Jamie turned to face Lord Roos and the other knights, who had heard the captain's confession and were completely unmoved by his suffering, as was Jamie. They were battle hardened and inured to the horrors of war.

"Christ on the Cross, de Grispere!" Roos exclaimed. "It is as you feared. We were staked out like lambs to the slaughter. Who is behind this? I'll not believe that Prince Henry would be so ruthless. He is too good a man, however hard he may wish for the crown."

"I know not, my lord, yet I could hazard a gaggle of names who would benefit from such an action besides the prince." Jamie looked up at Sir William, his face so angry that Lord Roos blanched at the fury he saw there. "We have been betrayed. By your leave, Sir William, I should like to move from this place and meet with Sir Robert Tirwhit, for there is much I would discuss with him." Jamie growled.

"And I too, de Grispere, and I too. Yet I must offer you our gratitude, for if not for you we should be dying stuck with arrows on the road."

"'Twas nothing, my lord, I remain your most obedient

servant." At which Jamie made a half bow and went to retrieve Richard, who had fretted and pranced wanting to join the fray. Forest padded at his side.

"Well done girl, well done." Jamie praised her, ruffling her ears. She looked up at him with big, soulful eyes. Once he caught up with his two friends, he turned as though he had forgotten something.

"Why Mark, a thought occurred in the fray. I have a gift for you, one to which I believe you will be very well suited. They rode to the pile of weapons that had been collected by the men-at-arms from the dead and captured ambushers, where Jamie dismounted and sought the large poleaxe with which he had been attacked by the captain at arms.

"It came to me that you prefer a quarterstaff over a sword, yet it will not do in battle. So here, take this, for it has the reach and heft that you enjoy and is deadlier than a staff. This is well made, with a good balance."

Mark took the weapon in his hands after he too dismounted. "The balance is indeed excellent. You must show me how to use it properly." He hefted the weapon, liking its feel. It was of excellent quality and Mark knew they were expensive weapons to buy or have made. He wiped it clean and put it into the bow bag he used to carry his quarterstaff when riding, pleased with the spoils of combat.

The captives were rounded up, and those who could walk were roped and taken to the trees. "You have committed a breach of the king's peace, to wit assault and attempt upon the life of his majesty's representatives, a treasonous act against the person of his majesty King Henry Fourth," Sir William Gascoigne declared. "I hereby sentence you to death by hanging by the power vested in me by his majesty as Lord Chief Justice to the crown."

There were pleas for clemency from the few men who had

survived that went unheeded as the death sentence was carried out, and the men were left hanging in the lower branches of the trees so that all who passed would witness their fate and know what would befall any man who took up arms against England. "That will act as deterrent to others who disturb the king's peace and show he still has a firm control upon his realm," Sir William said as the royal party rode off northwards.

Chapter Forty-Seven

The company had lost a few men and only two archers in the battle, leaving the main force intact and able to present a good showing. They passed through the tiny village of Brigg, stopping only to drain the local tavern dry of ale, which was much needed after the battle, before moving on to Wrawby. Here they stopped and pitched their tents at the end of a long day's ride.

"I have posted double guards tonight, for I trust not Tirwhit and he may try once more to cause mischief. We meet on the morrow at the village of Melton Ross, where the dispute arose, which is a mere few minutes ride north of here," Lord Roos declared to the knights around him.

"Do you still fear trouble, Lord Roos, with me as the king's Lord Chief Justice as witness to any assault?" Sir William Gascoigne asked, still incredulous at the earlier attack on the king's men.

"In all honesty, Sir William, I do so worry. I knew Sir Robert when he first joined with Henry and his majesty was merely Lord of Bolingbroke. He lent the king money to fight in the Welsh wars and was both resentful and keen to see that his generosity was rewarded from all sides. Even in the face of this debacle, I am persuaded that the king would go leniently on him for past favours given."

Jamie, on hearing this, snorted and shook his head. Lord Roos took pity upon him. "Aye, you shake your head, Sir James – and rightly so, for the king needs friends and will get them wherever he can. Yet he has always been a loyal master and favours friends well. His majesty always has one eye on the consequences of alienating potential allies and knows those allies may one day side with his enemies against him. The court is a much a battlefield as Crecy or Shrewsbury."

"So I am beginning to learn, my lord. Yet I would rather a clean fight in which I can see my enemy in front of me, look into his eyes and battle him face to face."

The circle of knights offered Jamie broad grins, echoing his thoughts.

"Amen to that, Sir James." Lord Warre opined.

"In that accord, on the morrow we travel in full armour, with bows strung and men ready with their swords. For I fear a large company will receive us, and would not wish to be taken advantage of again," Lord Roos said.

The company retired for the night, with squires preparing armour and men repairing damaged maille and sharpening swords. The following day the company set out early into another cloudy day of overcast skies and a chill breeze coming off the North Sea. A mile from Melton Ross, Lord Roos had the archers move into two flanking positions either side of the company. They marched some two hundred yards apart and forward of the main body, arranged in such a fashion that they could bring their shafts to bear with no fear of hitting their own men.

"I wonder, Sir William, how many archers Tirwhit will possess if he be as aggressive as we suspect?" Jamie asked.

"Not many, I would surmise. He was looking for more in Lincoln and we captured or killed many of those. Please God he is just with men-at-arms and a few knights of his mesnie."

They rounded a slight bend and immediately saw the answer lying before them. Tents had been pitched on a meadow that had been cut for hay. A large canvas structure stood in the middle surrounded by smaller tents, and arrayed before them were squares of men-at-arms, ready and mailed yet with no armour. Mounted men were behind in fewer numbers, and these men were ready and armed. All bore the arms of Tirwhit upon their shields and pageants flew above his tent, fluttering in the breeze. Yet to all the company's relief there were but a handful of archers.

"Unfurl our banners," Lord Roos commanded the heralds who went before them. The archers dismounted and melted away to flank either side of the tented army, their bows at the ready, invisible to Tirwhit at this moment.

"By God he must have upwards of four hundred soldiers ready to do battle." Lord Warre commented quietly.

"It is as I thought, and I trust him not." Lord Roos offered quietly. As they approached the encampment, he hailed Lord Tirwhit.

"Sir Robert, good morrow to you. Are you not surprised to see me here at the appointed hour?" He said, a hint of sarcasm in his tone. "Or not content with an ambush, do you ride for war in some cause of which I have no knowledge? For I was given to believe that we were upon a Loveday arbitration, not meeting on a battlefield with you arrayed for war."

The man before him was in armour, yet no helmet graced his head. His build was typical of a knight, stocky with well-developed musculature around the shoulders from use of arms. His red hair blew in the breeze and his bright beady eyes missed nothing.

"Good morrow, Lord Roos. I believe it is you who are mistaken, for I have no knowledge of what you speak, or of a Loveday here. I merely seek to school my men against any enemy I find on my land, to which I claim all rights to hay and land with no concession given."

"You lie! You have given your word, or like your soul durst it count for nil?" Lord Roos demanded.

Tirwhit's eyes narrowed and his hand went to his sword, ready to command an attack. "You speak bravely now and bait me. Let loose your hounds of war, I pray thee. What have you? Forty or fifty men, to my army here? You are a bigger fool than I thought, Lord Roos, and I shall appease you not. Now begone afore I release my men upon you."

Lord Roos smiled wickedly despite his anger at being duped. He savoured the moment to come as men on either side drew swords in readiness for the anticipated battle. "You are hasty, my lord, and you see and count but poorly. Look again to your left and right."

At which he raised his hand and the two concealed companies of archers emerged, arrows nocked and ready a mere hundred yards away and well within killing distance. Tirwhit looked left and right, aghast, his face puce with anger. "My captains have their best men targeting your person." Lord Roos continued. "We shall arrange for a suitable resting place to bury you in this land of yours that you value so highly. As to the rest, why, half your men will be dead within five breaths. There will be slaughter on both sides, yes, but win or lose you will not live to see the day end. And should you kill the king's Lord Chief Justice, his messenger and lieutenants, you will be hunted like the scurrilous dog you are and put to a traitor's death." Lord Roos finished.

Sir Robert Tirwhit turned and went to his tent, releasing the tension in the air. Everyone breathed a visible sigh of relief.

Swords were replaced in scabbards and bows were dropped into a downward position.

"What will happen now?" Jamie asked, curious as to how this could be resolved. He knew that if this was Sir Robert de Umfraville against the Scots, he would move forward, charge into the tent and drag the screaming traitorous liar out by his hair, killing him where he stood if he uttered a command to rebel.

"We settle and wait, Sir James. I believe this will not be agreed today. What say you, Sir William?"

Sir William Gascoigne looked across at the main tent that now housed Sir Robert. "I find it hard to credit what I have seen and heard these days past. The whoreson cares not for honour and rights, and rides roughshod over any and all. How comes he to feel such immunity from redress? That is the question I would ask. What occurs at court whilst we are away on a wild goose chase, I prithee? Who seeks to gain and what will those gains be? The more we tarry here the more concern this gives me."

Then they saw figures riding away from the party of tents. Once clear they broke into a fast canter and made for the north road, away from the field. At the tail were a group of esquires and the few mounted archers.

"By the Lord Harry, is that not Sir Robert?" Lord Roos cried. Jamie made to give chase, hating the quarry that had evaded him. Lord Roos held out his arm, preventing Jamie from riding off alone. "Stay, Sir James, for if we give chase a battle will be engaged and we shall be the losers, for by the time we disengage my Lord Tirwhit will be safely in his manor, which is but two miles away."

Jamie growled in anger at being so cheated, but listened to the wise words of Lord Roos.

Sir William Gascoigne spoke: "Come, let us away. I fear for

the king and I shall have writs served that will bring the scullion in chains to be arrayed before the Chancery courts where I will preside. Then we shall see how well he fares."

Jamie gave one last look at the receding knight and turned to follow the lead of the other lords, anger and frustration oozing from every pore of his body.

Chapter Forty-Eight

London

The return journey to London by comparison was long and uneventful, with no repeat of ambush, despite anger and frustration at the failure to bring Tirwhit to heel. Sir William Lord Roos had stayed in Lincolnshire to await the writs and serve them upon Tirwhit, demanding that he attend a hearing at the Chancery Court set for the later that month. There were also warrants for the arrest of Sir John Stanhope and all those conspiring with him.

Jamie had been asked to report directly to Prince Henry in the company of the Lord Chief Justice, Sir William Gascoigne. The meeting took place in Sir William's private chambers at the orders of the prince, who was furious at the news. So angry was he that Jamie was convinced that it had not been his intention to secure their silence by ordering the deaths of all present at the ambush. After he was dismissed, Sir William and the prince continued their discussions anew.

"How goes the war in France, my prince?"

"We have news that Arundel and Warwick joined with the

Burgundians on the third of October, and are now proposing to engage with the Armagnacs. They are close, Sir William, so very close. They have taken Saint Cloud on the north bank and target the centre of Paris next. If that happens and we lose, Calais will be their next target. But by your addresses, you fear the raising of arms closer to home. Durst thou think that Stanhope will cause more trouble and fan the flames lit by Tirwhit? For whilst we seek complete government of the realm, we do not wish it to be at a traitor's behest, and Stanhope plots with others, we hear."

"He does, my lord prince. We heard rumours around Nottingham that a riot was caused when he found against a plaintiff of the county, supporting instead one of his favourites. I would adjure you, my prince, to permit me to serve writs upon him and all others causing such affray. That, along with de Grispere's affidavit, will be cause enough for him to be locked in the Tower awaiting his majesty's pleasure."

"The Tower shall soon be full, offering new homes to Longe and Prendergast, Tirwhit and Stanhope amongst others. Yet it must be done, for if we show weakness now, the whole country will flare abroad and there will be rebellion in every province. I will sign the writs personally when they are ready. Mayhap the malaperts will respect my wishes, if not my own justices. If not, I shall raise an army and make war upon them. Let it be known."

The following day, Jamie made his way to Whittington's chambers and gave a full account of all that had occurred. The wily elder statesman showed little surprise.

"So the prince shows his teeth to cure the ills of his father's kingdom. It is high time matters were put to rights in the shires of the north. Well done, for I hear that the prince sings your praises along with Sir William. You saved their lives, I hear, and ensured the survival of the company?"

"Aye, 'twas a close-run thing, and thanks are due to you, for I reasoned it through bearing in mind all that you have told me, and liked not what I found. I was on my guard and well supported by my friends. We should have ridden into a storm of arrows and no mistake. It was a cleverly set trap and they knew we were coming, by God they did."

"Of that there is no doubt. Yet there are many who would benefit from your death and those with whom you travelled. Have a care, Jamie, powerful men are set against you. Yet we must hope that with the arrest of Tirwhit and others the threat will diminish. Now we must seek to protect the king, for I fear for his life now that he has recalled parliament."

"Why so?"

"I believe he seeks to reinstate his hold over the realm, but in doing so he would have to weaken the control of the Council and those attached to it. There are many who stand to lose much should this happen. Not least Thomas Beaufort, who with his deceit would lose the power of Chancellorship, I am bound. Be on your guard, and if you hear aught report to me directly."

"For certes, you fear assassination? By the rood it has been tried afore."

"It has, and on two occasions it was nearly successful." Whittington warned, looking gravely at Jamie. "Come to me directly if you should hear of any plots against the king and I will do my best to keep him safe from harm."

"Amen to that. Now, Sir Richard, I would see the Lady Alice of Macclesfield, for she had word when last we spoke of approaches that had been made to her father, and I wish to see if aught else had been declared in that regard. By your leave sir Richard."

"Have a care, Jamie, there is much at stake, and men become desperate when it is so."

Jamie offered a lazy smile and was gone. He walked to the Great Hall and the court hoping there to see the Lady Alice. He was not disappointed, and found her in a huddle of ladies of the court laughing in the course of a deep discussion that caused much mirth. He faltered, for nearby was the Earl of Macclesfield himself, looking well and walking with only a slight limp as he approached his daughter's party. *Hell's teeth, I shall prevail. This needs must be done and now.* He scolded himself and continued upon his path to Alice. The earl arrived before him, engaging his daughter in conversation. Jamie approached and bowed.

"My Lady Alice, Lord Macclesfield, good morrow. I trust you are both well."

They both turned at his voice, Alice's face alive with joy, her father's expressionless.

"Jamie, this is a pleasure. You are returned I see and unscathed, for we hear there was much done against your party." Alice's father scowled at her impertinence and cut across any further connexion between her and Jamie. The earl growled. "De Grispere, would you do me the honour of some time? There are matters I would discuss. My dear, if you will excuse us for a few moments."

Both men bowed stiffly to Lady Alice and moved towards a trestle supporting wine and sweetmeats.

"You pay addresses to my daughter, Sir James," the earl growled.

"I do, my lord, and would not hide the fact from you. I act with the greatest of honour and the deepest respect, my lord, and I swear to you that I would not treat such a cause lightly."

The earl looked up at him sharply. "Very well. I am sensible of the fact that I owe you my life, and I am not unfeeling in that regard. You may make your addresses, yet have a care, for she is dear to me and I will not see her hurt. Do you understand me?"

Jamie looked him in the eye, unflinching. "Perfectly, my lord."

At which the earl grunted and walked away, joining in conversation with another knight. Jamie breathed out slowly, unaware that he had been holding himself so tightly. When he spoke with Alice, she was amazed.

"He admitted that he owed you his life? Why Jamie, do you know what that would have cost him in pride? By God's grace, he will be smarting even now. That is wonderful, for no longer do we have to skulk around in secret."

Jamie rejoiced at her words, and moved with her maid to enter the cloistered garden as she wrapped her shawl more tightly around her, despite the warm autumn sunshine that pushed through to gild the garden in a gentle yellow haze.

Once free of eavesdroppers in the main hall, Alice became serious, looking over her shoulder before she spoke.

"Jamie now that we are alone, I have more news for you regarding the messenger who visited my father to persuade him to their cause. It was Sir Roger Leche!"

"Leche?" Jamie exclaimed.

"Ssh! Have a care, I adjure you."

"My apologies, my lady. But by the lord Harry he is prince Henry's steward, and was present at the meeting of knights with Stanhope at his manor when first I was led to meet him. Do you have aught else? Prithee tell me all you can."

"There is no more, except that a date was mentioned that I caught. It was the second day of November."

"That is the day upon which Parliament is to meet for its first sitting, called by the king. Today is the sixteenth, which means we are short of time, for certes something is planned as Whittington suspected. What is to do? Pray tell me, durst thou think your father was amenable to Leche's offer?" Jamie paused in his walking, and to all watching it would seem they were engaged in a lover's tiff, for he scowled into the middle distance while Alice gazed up at him.

"I know not, yet I perceive that he is against any actions towards the crown, for he is a loyal subject of King Henry. Jamie, what do you fear? What ails you?"

"I am sorry, my lady. This was to be a happy moment, but it is now marred by matters of court. We – that is Sir Richard and I – greatly fear an uprising against the king, and mayhap an attempt upon his very life. If the prince's steward is involved, then it points a bony finger of accusation towards the prince himself, but please God let it not be so."

"What will you do? Jamie, you must take care for your own sake, for to be caught twixt a prince and a king can avail you nothing but harm." She looked up at him with fear in her eyes.

"I must see Whittington at once. My lady, I beg your leave, for much hangs upon my actions." He bowed and strode away with Alice left adrift on a sea of emotions – not least of which was worry for her father. Upon returning to Whittington's apartments, Jamie found him absent and his clerk informed him he had gone to a Guild meeting with plans to visit wool merchants in Gloucester. Cursing, Jamie knew there was not sufficient time to chase him. He needed to make plans in the absence of his mentor. He strode the corridors and then went to a tavern which was, he knew, a favourite of Kit's, together with other young squires and knights when at their leisure. Jamie and Kit had not passed much time together since the battle upon the *Juliane*, and Jamie enjoyed the company of his friend.

Coming upon the inn, he paused at the doorway, for did not wish to set tongues wagging. Calming himself, he entered, and there found Kit surrounded by other squires and young knights in the middle of ribald story. With his dark curls and boyish good looks, Kit was a firm favourite among the ladies whose company he enjoyed.

Jamie ordered an ale and joined the group. He noticed that Phillip Leche, Sir Roger's son, was amongst them, and he would be around his own age, Jamie supposed. He had met him before and trained with him as an esquire. They had been acquaintances rather than friends, as he had sought other company.

"Ho, Kit, another tall tale. Is any woman safe with you around to swive them all?" he teased his friend in arms.

"Ha now, here he is. Watch out, everyone, for as Sir James appears, so will trouble. Mysterious archers will attack us now – or mayhap even pirates." Kit laughed at Jamie's expense, and the others joined in, for they had all heard of the battle on the Lincoln road and Jamie's involvement, which had become the stuff of legend in a short space of time, exaggerated with the re-telling. Now it was an army of five hundred that Jamie had slain with a mere twenty archers at his back.

"By the rood I shall leave it to you to find trouble, for I hear there is many a father in London who seeks you out with words to say about his new grandson," Jamie responded, maintaining Kit's reputation as a lover of some renown. The banter continued in this vein until Kit made to leave, and with him Jamie, who promised to show him some fine cloth his father had found.

As the two men made their way towards Jamie's home, he made the real reason known to his friend for the time away from the others.

"Not here, though. Ride with me and we can talk privately once we are at my father's house." Kit was intrigued by Jamie's secretive actions and willingly obliged. Entering the rear court-yard, their horses were taken by a groom and they entered through the rear doorway. It was warm inside, in contrast to the day where the sun was fighting a losing battle as the hours moved on.

"Oh Jamie," called a woman's voice from the stairs. "Is that you returned?"

Both men's eyes were drawn to the light steps upon the stairs as Jeanette came into view. She blushed upon seeing Sir Christopher Urquhart. "Oh! A thousand pardons, I did not see that you had company. I bethought you were with Cristoforo."

Kit saw before him a lithe beauty with tawny blonde hair where Jamie's was red gold. She had blue eyes against his green hazel and was tall for a lady, with a graceful step she had shown as she descended the stairs. "Oh, mademoiselle, it is I who should apologise for invading your home unannounced." Kit answered, bowing deeply. Jamie watched the byplay with interest.

"Kit, forgive my lack of manners. May I have the honour to introduce my sister," he stressed the word, "Jeanette de Grispere. This knave, my dear," he continued with a straight face, "is one Sir Christopher Urquhart of his majesty's court, lately of the stews of London."

"Jamie, you are too cruel, and the poor knight so latterly in our home. You are welcome sir. May I offer you some refreshment?"

"My lady, the pleasure is all mine, and I thank you for defending my honour against such scurrilous accusations from the lips of your own brother, which I must stress are all unfounded."

"Thank you, Jeanette. We will be in father's solar, if he is still at the guild meeting, for we have matters of import to discuss. Come Kit, this way." Jamie beckoned as time was marching onwards he knew and there was much to discuss.

He explained to Kit his thoughts on what he knew and suspected he had discovered.

"Sir Roger? The prince's own steward? Do you give full credence to such a rumour?"

"I know not for certes, yet the life of a king may hang in the balance. Would you choose between the difference?"

"No, indeed I would not. What would you have me do, for I am yours to command?"

"I wish you to talk with Phillip Leche. Seek out his thoughts and see if you can find anything amiss. For if I am not mistaken, we have but a few days to find if there is a plot and when it is to be hatched."

"I will do my utmost, rest assured." He cut the conversation short as a housemaid appeared with wine and sweetmeats. Jamie thanked her and continued.

"Learn all you can, and please pass any tiny morsel of gossip or rumour you hear on to me."

The two men agreed to meet daily at the tavern Kit frequented – which was named, ironically, the King's Head. With the plans in place, Kit made to leave. He bowed deeply to Jeanette, making her blush and telling her that he hoped to see her at court soon.

"I look forward to it, sir – if Jamie durst not banish me to a convent, for that is his way," She smiled.

"On that accord I will plead with him and see if aught can be done." At which Kit swept out dramatically and was gone.

"Have a care, little sister," Jamie said. "For he is a holy terror where maids are concerned, and has them dripping off his fingers like honeyed wine."

"Fear not Jamie, I am well able to sift the wheat from the chaff," Jeanette replied. "I have been dealing with men all my life and know well their wiles."

Chapter Forty-Nine

Over the next three days Jamie learned all he could, spending much of his time listening to gossip in taverns and the court with the other young knights and squires. He caught news of a party that was to be assembled one evening later that month. It was described by one of the esquires with whom he drank as a harmless celebration. The man was in his cups, and Jamie himself was unsteady on his feet, so much had they drunk. The squire was a new acquaintance from the north, and when he heard Nottingham mentioned he had persisted.

"And whom do you serve?"

"Why my Lord of Chaworth, did I not say?" The esquire slurred, focussing with great difficulty upon Jamie.

"Who rides with you? May anyone join?" Jamie asked.

"No. My lord likes his friends, and enjoins only those of close companionship to him."

"Mayhap I can gain acceptance? Which night is this rout to take place?"

The man looked owlishly at him through unfocused eyes, as his head rocked gently back and forth. He wagged a finger at

Jamie. "You'll need armour...I was told to have it ready for... for... twenty..." and with that his head banged forward onto the tavern table. He had passed out and Jamie shook him to no avail.

"By God's holy legs, so close, damn you man. So close." He muttered. Trying to stand, Jamie realised how perilously close to collapse he was himself. He staggered up from his seat and made for the door, weaving as he went. Once outside, the cool air hit him after the fug of the tavern. "By the Lord I'm foxed with ale," he muttered, placing his hand against the wall. Shaking himself, he made towards his home through the quiet streets, sobering a little as he went.

A figure detached itself from a doorway by the tavern and followed Jamie on silent feet. It was the same man who had followed Jamie, Mark and Cristoforo when they first gathered to discuss their journeys so many months earlier. He had been paid to follow Jamie and now thought to do more, encouraged by Jamie's drunkenness. *My master hates him, so if I should kill or maim him he will doubtless pay well,* the man mused. He padded closer, drawing his bollock dagger in a reverse grip to stab downwards. Jamie leaned against the nearest wall as his stomach revolted against the beer that still sloshed around inside it. He groaned, ready to throw up, and turning to support his back to the wall he bent low and heaved at his feet. This alone saved him, for as he turned the dagger came down, slicing where his back had been. As he spat the bile from his stomach the figure and the gleam of a dagger caught his eye in the poor light and the attacker cursed at the stench of vomit and the miss of his thrust.

Jamie pulled away backwards, suddenly a great deal more sober knowing his life was threatened. No knight trained at arms for hours and hours needed to give a conscious thought to his next actions. His sword and dagger appeared unbidden in his hands and he stabbed at the approaching figure. His thrust lacked finesse, yet it caught the man by surprise as the sword seemed to appear from nowhere. The attacker gasped as it sliced his ribs, as Jamie's aim was drunkenly off. The man ran off, dripping blood on the cobbles as he went and gripping his side.

Jamie gave no thought to chase him and shook his head, now far less foxed for the encounter.

The following day he woke with the shutters allowing a shaft of sunlight to stab through the window to his bedroom. He was still dressed and booted from the night before and wrapped roughly in sheets and blankets, clearly in an attempt to get warm as the night passed and his body cooled.

He stood, and quickly regretted it. A smith with a large hammer and anvil started work in his head and he fell back to his cot. "Oh, by the Lord Harry I am dying," he moaned, grabbing for a pitcher of water at his side. He drained the contents as best he could into his mouth in swift gulps, with half the water ending up on his shirt.

Two hours later he was beginning to feel human once more, and was displeased to be disturbed by a knock at his door from a servant, who told him that Kit was below and needed to speak with him urgently.

A newly shaved and dressed Jamie appeared a short time later to find Kit deep in conversation with Cristoforo and Jeanette, who with her maid were being entertained by the young knight, telling an implausible story of how he came to fight all the pirates and retake the ship at Smallhythe single-handedly. At Jamie's tread on the stair the party looked up.

"Ah, *amico*, here is the ale knight, back from slumbers, and with a sore head I'm bound," Cristoforo laughed.

"Needs must you shout so and at this early hour? Hell's teeth, man, have you no common courtesy, you damned Italian?" Jamie grumbled.

"Jamie, you look like death, my friend. I hope she was worth it?" Kit laughed, at which Jamie grunted and ordered a thick trencher and bacon from the servant.

"We needs must talk, for I have grave news. There is party of knights who are planning a rout for a night venture soon." Kit began.

"With Sir Thomas Chaworth, I take it?"

"By God Jamie, are you a magician? They will burn you for heresy if you read people's minds thus. Yes, and I suspect more than a rout is intended."

"It is, for they plan to be in armour. Yet I know no more, so we must be aware in the days to come and learn all we can. Is Mark due here today, Jeanette, or does he visit mistress Emma? For I would speak with him."

"I am sure he will be with Emma this eve, but I will send a note to ask that he visit here." Jeanette replied.

— ✕ ⚜ ✕ —

The next two days were hard for Jamie as he sought answers wherever he could. After the attack upon him in the alley, he knew he was being watched. Whittington had journeyed to Gloucester without being able to see him, so he was alone. He pledged Sir Richard's clerk to find loyal pages who would aid him, and with this achieved he arranged to have Sir Roger Leche and Sir Thomas Chaworth watched from the twentieth of October onwards. For two days Leche was followed to meetings, including one with the Lord Chancellor, Thomas Beaufort, which in itself was not a crime Jamie knew, as both were deeply involved in government.

With no one else to turn to and knowing not whom to trust, least of all the prince, Jamie sought an audience with Richard Lord Grey.

"My lord may I speak plainly? For I have difficult matters to discuss and these do not come easily to me."

"As ever Jamie, you have proved yourself a loyal subject to the king and indeed the realm, and I know that your heart is true. Unburden yourself I prithee, for what occurs here stays within these four walls," he gestured about the solar. "Consider this room as you would the confessional, whenever it be necessary to act in the king's best interests."

"As you say my lord, for what I have to impart concerns the king. There are rumours abroad that an attempt will be made upon his life." Jamie halted, unsure whether to continue, wanting to see what reaction he would receive from Lord Grey.

"There are always rumours to this effect, they fly like dandelion seeds upon the wind," Lord Grey replied. "Do you know more, or have you proof of those who would perpetrate the act? For the king is well protected within the palace and has many loyal supporters to call upon."

"There, my lord, may be the fault, for those whom I assume to be traitors are close by and have the royal favour." Lord Grey raised a questioning eyebrow, and it was a measure of the esteem in which Jamie was held that he was allowed to continue. "My lord, I believe Sir Roger Leche and Sir William Chaworth may have cause to be suspected of treason to the king's person."

"No, Sir James. I will not countenance such a thought. We have Tirwhit and Stanhope, and now you accuse Leche? Be there anyone in the king's mesnie who can be trusted? Do you have proof, Jamie? Have you witnesses or written report that confirm this plan of treachery?"

Jamie sighed in vain. "No, my lord. I have corroborative evidence and no more."

"Then there is nothing that can be done to move against someone so highly placed. Seek more proof and I will aid you in any way I can, but without more, there is naught that I can achieve."

"As you wish my lord. Yet I would adjure you to consider this puzzle. You know well the contents of the affidavit I swore on Stanhope and others at Nottingham, who even now are indicted to be arrested. Who else was there at the meeting, or more particularly who was represented? Arundel, Warwick, Stanhope, Chaworth, Strelley and Leche were all present, with representatives of the Beauforts. All those men are close to the prince. All have power within the council – and recently as you say the king's own officer, Sir Robert Tirwhit, plots against his authority. Lord Roos is away and Arundel and Warwick are beyond any blame gaining glory in France. If the power is broken by the king when he sits in parliament again, all those will suffer demotion at best.

"Think on that puzzle, sir, I beseech you, and keep the king in great care. Be on your guard, I beg you. Consider also, sir, that you and Archbishop Arundel are with his majesty constantly and you are his loyal supporters. If you too were lost, then who gains?"

Jamie bowed and dismissed himself, leaving an incredulous Lord Grey standing and watching him walk away.

Chapter Fifty

Westminster Palace, 22nd October

The day started badly, with a colder wind that brought driving rain. Dark clouds scudded low across the sky and it seemed as if the vibrant colours of autumn were being washed out and blown away. With the season's departure, Jamie began to think that his hopes of defeating those who plotted the king's demise were disappearing too.

He wandered listlessly about the palace, feeling disenchanted with his efforts, and eventually went off in search of his friends. Mark had finished practice for the day, having had three bouts with the prince, who he said had been in good spirits. Cristoforo was alone as the Contessa was entertaining friends of her uncle's from Florence.

"They bemoan the English weather, and I defended this grey land, cheered them by saying that this was like summer, and they should come in winter."

"Cristo you are a buffoon, know you that?"

"I do, and am happy in my state. It lulls my enemies into false assumptions," he declared, raising an eyebrow.

It was at this moment that a page appeared and a note for Jamie from Alfred, Whittington's clerk. It was brief, and Jamie looked up at his friends with renewed anticipation. "'Tis from Sir Richard. He says that he has news of movement for tonight afore compline." Mark and Cristoforo looked suddenly eager.

"Mark, see if you can find Kit, have him meet me at Whittington's chamber where we will await him. Compline is at seven of the hour, and it is now nearly five," Jamie said, looking to one of the three huge clocks that graced the palace. They were a marvel that had been installed by the late King Edward III. *We will still be but two knights against unknown odds, and they will be in full armour, yet who to trust?* He wondered. Then a thought occurred. Turning to a page he called out asking him to send a message to Launceston Lane.

Jamie and Cristoforo arrived at Whittington's offices to find Alfred in a state of agitation.

"Ah, Sir James, you're here thank the Lord. A servant arrived a while ago, stating that he knew of plans to have horses ready for my Lord Leche as he planned to leave before compline."

"How many horses?" Jamie asked.

"A full ten, Sir James."

"By God, he brings more than messages to King Henry. Where dost the king stay this hour?" he demanded.

"Why he retires, as Sir Richard knows, and has returned to Lambeth Palace."

Jamie shook his head in disbelief, thumping his hand into his fist. "I should have known. He will be at compline prayers in the king's chapel with maybe a man-at-arms and a page, no more. Mayhap Archbishop Arundel, too! To take both would destroy all witnesses and the prince would be assured of immediate accession to the throne. What a coil we are in. Yet they will ride, for it would draw attention to have ten fully armoured knights take a wherry to the Palace at that hour. They will take London Bridge! It will take them an hour or more. We may have time."

It was nearly an hour later that the message sent to his father's house bore fruit. The page returned with two figures following him: his father's steward Will, bearing a crossbow, and John in full maille that was a little worn and rusty but still fitted him like a glove. He had a shield from his days with Henry Bolingbroke that bore the king's old arms with a background of gules and three lions passant. The red was faded now with time and the lions a honey yellow rather than bright gold, but it was in good order and the steel rim shone dully in the torchlight. He had on his head an old-fashioned segmented helmet and looked as fierce as any man Jamie had met. Another servant of his father's accompanied them bearing a waxed borel sack and a rolled leather sheet.

"So we go to save my old master, God bless his majesty," The old soldier muttered as he belted on the sword that he was not permitted to wear within the city of London. Only knights were accorded that privilege. John then picked up again his spear. Jamie unrolled the leather sheet to reveal an arming doublet, suede hose and a maille undershirt. His father's servant removed the full set of plate armour from the borel sack.

Then Kit arrived with his squire, Phillip, and both men began to put on their plate, aided by the squire and Mark, who helped Jamie into his armour.

Jamie stripped down to his linen shirt and pulled on his arming gambeson of thin, lightly padded leather that fitted him like a second skin, and his suede hose. He pulled over this his maille under-shirt that would protect groin and armpits, together with other exposed areas, ensuring all the waxed laces were free to tie to the armour that would fit on top.

"Why it feels like Stokesey again, Jamie," Mark exclaimed,

remembering the battle at the castle that had thwarted Glyndower, where he had helped Jamie arm for the first time.

"It does, and please God with the same result." Jamie answered.

Within twenty minutes all were ready, with Kit and Jamie finally pulling on their padded coifs followed by visored bascinet helmets. They were now fully armoured, with Cristoforo in a padded gambeson and the others as well protected as they were able.

"Your new hauberk fits you well," Jamie commented, looking at the huge figure of Mark clad in his maille coat that he had made for him upon his return from Lincoln.

"It was a close-run thing in the woods with so many swords and men to fight and arrows flying everywhere. I decided that with you for a companion it would like as not be worth the coin it cost to venture forth again to battle well coated and t'would seem I had the right of it."

Good maille was expensive, as Jamie knew, and with Mark's size he had needed to have it measured and made specially to fit his huge frame. Yet it was a worthwhile investment as his life may one day depend upon it. Mark hefted his newly acquired poleaxe and was ready.

"You carry a shield as well as armour, Jamie?" Kit asked, puzzled.

"Aye, with odds against us and mayhap the need to save the king, who will not be armoured, I shall take it." He slung the shield upon his back using the guige strap.

It was a motley gathering, but all were fiercely loyal to the king and would give their lives for him. The seven men made their way quietly down to the waterway from the palace terrace and hailed a wherry. The ferryman was nervous at the sight of the heavily armed party, and said he could not take all of them as they would be too much for his craft. The party split in two and they waited for a second boat to appear.

Jamie took the first boat and cautiously stepped aboard. One slip and he would drown before time was given to rescue him from the dead weight of armour that encompassed his body. The crossing seemed interminable to the men aboard, desperate to reach the south bank and make headway to save the king. Finally, they neared the southern shore and were hailed by two guards, one a sergeant-at-arms. It was now dusk and they were difficult to identify in the gloom. The two men were naturally suspicious at first, as their job was to prevent unwanted landings near the king's residence at such a late hour. The guard moved his hand to a crossbow by his side, while the sergeant pulled free his sword in anticipation as they saw the band of armed men aboard the wherry.

"Ho! Who goes there?" The sergeant called the challenge.

"'Tis I, Sir James de Grispere, of the royal household and the prince's company. I beg leave to visit the king on a matter of life and death."

"Just you, sir. Come forth and be recognised," the sergeant demanded.

Jamie jumped as best his armour would allow from the boat into the glimmering torchlight cast by a smoky brand lodged in a sconce from the guard post wall. Rain glistened on the steel surface of his plate.

The sergeant was taken aback at the armour, wondering no doubt as to the necessity of it. "Sir James, why 'tis you. What business do you have with his majesty at this hour?"

"I have little time to explain, sergeant, as the king's life is in grave danger. I adjure you let us through or accompany us as you please, for we needs must secure his majesty's person and with it his safety. We are still short of a few minutes before the hour and danger approaches even as we tarry here."

The sergeant hesitated, despite knowing Jamie, having seen him many times visiting the Lambeth Palace on official business. He wavered, then made a decision. "Tom, stay here. I'll escort Sir James to his majesty and the guards within."

At this point the second boat arrived and the rest of the party disembarked including Mark, causing the sergeant even more consternation at his choice of action. But he beckoned them to follow, striding towards a side door of the palace. Only one soldier stood on guard, and he was alarmed to see a heavily armed party arriving and was only assured by the sergeant's presence.

Having settled the guard, the sergeant moved on with Jamie's party following him. The sergeant knew where the king's private chapel was located and confirmed that the king would now be at prayers for compline. The corridors were as great a maze as Westminster Palace on the north side of the river, and they were glad that they had the sergeant to act as a guide. They finally reached the small private chapel, having seen clergy passing in twos or threes hurrying to prayer, casting them sidelong glances of apprehension as they did so. But there was no one else, no guards or courtiers at this late hour, and the sergeant was surprised and puzzled upon reaching the chapel. "Not even any guards without? Mayhap his majesty is not inside."

The sergeant knocked and pushed the door open. The murmured voice became louder, and the scene before him was as expected.

The chapel was small, no more than thirty feet long and twenty wide, with an altar table covered in cloth at the far end on a raised dais. There, on his knees at the altar in front of the lines of pews either side of the aisle, knelt King Henry. Above him was Archbishop Arundel, dressed in full bishop's regalia, a mitre upon his head, chanting the Latin of compline and evening prayers. A page was also knelt in prayer at the king's left-hand side and an esquire on his right. All were unarmed save for a dagger or eating knife. None were mailled. They were clad only in rich courtly clothes and cloaked against the chill air. Weapons and armour would not have been seemly in a house of God. But it meant that the men inside were completely defenceless.

The archbishop looked up upon their sudden entrance, a frown of annoyance upon his face at the unlooked-for disturbance. The king too turned around in consternation.

"What is the meaning of this garboil? We are at prayer, how dare you disturb us!" he growled. The esquire had half risen, his hand going to the dagger at his waist as he put himself between the king and Jamie, ready to defend the king with his life from the presumed threat of armed men entering the chapel. He stood, putting a guarding hand forward his dagger drawn, setting his feet apart in a fighting stance.

"Stay and come no closer, or by God's grace at least one of you will accompany me to our Father above, and this is as goodly a place to die as any," the esquire commanded, standing bravely against the armed party before him.

All of the party dropped to one knee bowing their heads three times to the king in the prescribed manner, after which Jamie spoke, lifting his visor and locking it in place.

"Majesty, 'tis I, Sir James de Grispere of the Royal household. I come to warn you as I believe you to be in grave danger of your life, and my friends with me are here to defend your person from any such attack."

"Sir James," cried the archbishop, "what arrant nonsense you speak! Are you foxed and addled with drink, man? We are safe here in the palace as anywhere. No one would dare to mount an incursion here in such a sacred place!" he stormed back at Jamie.

"Your majesty, your grace, we have little time and I beseech you to listen to my words. And as to the sanctity of this place, have you forgotten Thomas à Becket?"

At this the king's brow furrowed in anger, yet Jamie gave him no time to answer, ploughing on with his discourse.

"Even now, majesty, I believe there is a party of armed knights come to do your majesty great harm and mayhap take your life or your liberty. Witness there are no guards without, dismissed on whose orders? The river is secure, but held only by three men. I believe there is mischief abroad and these mala-perts come by road. For they plan, if my intelligence be true, to arrive within compline. We have little time to prepare for an attack, majesty."

The king had had danger as his constant companion since he seized the throne from the tyranny of Richard the Second, who had exiled him to roam Europe adrift and lordless. Henry's reign had been riven with plots, rebellions and assassination attempts. He came about quicker than Arundel, who still refused to believe such an act could take place upon the hallowed ground of his own palace.

"Sir James, you have ever served us well and we trust you. Pray tell us whom you suspect of perpetrating such heinous acts to our person?"

"I know not all their names, sire, but they are led by Sir Roger Leche–"

"Sir Roger? Why we knighted him ourselves, and he is of our household knights. Do you give your word that this be true?"

"On my life sire, may you strike me down now if you believe it not so." Jamie pulled his own sword with his left hand from its scabbard and passed it hilt forwards to King Henry, kneeling as he did so. The king was humbled at the integrity of the young knight who knelt before him.

"Off your knees, Sir James and take back your sword, for if you are true you may have need of it ere time be much shorter. Now, what would you have us do?"

"I thank you sire. I prithee to allow me to command my company." Jamie bowed to the king and turned to the others of his party. "Will, you are unarmed and have but a cross bow. I'll not have you slaughtered by an armoured knight. Get behind the chapel table and await my signal with your bow locked and ready. Cristo, you too, for this is not for you. They will be heavily armoured and daggers will not serve if visors be down."

Both men moved forward past the surprised face of the archbishop to hide behind the dais.

"John, Mark and Phillip, kneel here behind his majesty, and prepare for prayers if you have them. For this could be our last adventure yet, and to save our king is the worthiest of causes. You sir," he said turning to the brave esquire who had been about to give his life for his king. "Your bravery and loyalty is to be commended. Stay as you were next to your king, and if any reach his majesty, kill them and use a stool as a buckler. T'will serve well." With which he offered a grim smile to the faithful squire and directed the sergeant to go and find reinforcements.

The king looked on, liking what he saw and wishing that he too had a sword to hand. As John passed to kneel, King Henry saw his distinctively scarred face.

"Why, dost our eyes deceive us or 'tis you, John of Northampton, or we're a duck's drake?" The old soldier stood proudly, seeming to grow another two inches before the company.

"As your majesty pleases, 'tis I, sire."

"Well, by God's grace, we fight together again and by the rood there is none we would rather have at our side than you if we are to leave this state of grace this evening tide." The king clapped the old soldier on the shoulder in a rare show of affection from one old comrade in arms to another.

"Majesty, we must not tarry, for they could arrive at any moment, and needs must my trap be well laid, by your leave," Jamie said.

"Forgive an old soldier, Sir James, as you please." As the others all went to their allotted places, Jamie had Kit stand on the opposite side of the chapel to him. Halfway down there were two half rounded stone pillars that rose to receive a large central wooden truss that supported the vaulted roof. They were about two feet in radius and offered sufficient concealment to enable both knights to hide while being able to stand and be ready.

"One last order, your grace. When they enter, move to your left, leaving Cristo and Will sufficient space to bring their crossbows to bear upon the whoresons." The archbishop nodded, allowing the coarseness of Jamie's language to pass even here in the house of God. He stood resolute, calm in the face of the storm to come.

Chapter Fifty-One

The royal party in the chapel did not have to wait very long. The bells of the palace had struck the hour, and some minutes after, the clank of armour was heard from the corridor outside the chapel. No man could move with complete silence in armour, and while the attackers would be wearing strong boots rather than armoured *sabatons,* their passage was heard.

Jamie motioned for the archbishop to begin again the liturgy, and his pulse began to race as it always did before combat. He expected that he was about to face poor odds, yet he was strangely joyful at the thought of battle. Nervous energy seeped into his blood, his hand grasped his sword which was already drawn, and he tightened his hold on his shield in readiness. The noble image of Richard embossed upon the front added drama to the scene.

The footsteps stopped, and there was a brief silence before the door was pushed quickly open to admit a party of knights, their swords drawn and their armour shining in the torch and candlelight. They had arrived with murder in their hearts.

Ten knights entered and fanned outwards behind their

leader, Sir Roger Leche, the pews stopping them from spreading further, causing them to funnel slightly in formation. The archbishop performed his role perfectly, feigning surprise as his lined features creased in anger at their presence.

"What is the meaning of this intrusion into his majesty's chapel?" He demanded.

Sir Roger ignored him, and bowed briefly to the king. "Majesty, we are here to take you hence," he said.

"Upon what authority?" The king answered, hoping to secure names and understand more about who was behind the plot.

"Upon the authority vested in me by the lords of this land and the Council. Now, majesty, I would ask you to agree to come with us."

Jamie had heard enough and stepped from the concealment of the pillar into the light. "I think not, Sir Roger." He said lightly, almost as an aside. As he did so, Kit revealed himself opposite while John and the others stood, raising their weapons in readiness, and Will and Cristoforo rose from behind the altar table, crossbows raised and ready.

Sir Roger Leche was startled. "You again, de Grispere? Are you a wight to be spirited thus whenever there is trouble? Yet here you have overstretched yourself, I fear, for you are outnumbered and I shall be pleased to relieve you of your sword and your troubled soul. You are but two knights and a few peasants." He sneered.

"I ask you to consider the odds," Jamie replied "with a quarrel aimed at your evil heart. You may live, and we are but six to your ten, but we are worthy of any two of your curs. Choose your terms. Surrender or we drop your worthless body in the river for a traitor's death. What say you? Choose or you die," Jamie snarled, wanting the fight, needing it with pent up frustration. He had lived through interminable court intrigue and had watched Sir Robert Tirwhit run from battle, and now he finally had the chance to settle with this traitor once and for all.

Sir Roger made a move to give up and drop his sword. This action was misinterpreted by others of his party as his arm was raised, and two of the unknown knights lunged at Jamie while another went for Kit. Seeing the act, clicks of crossbow triggers whispered from the altar, and a quarrel soughed through the air crashing straight into the gorget of Sir Roger, who flew backwards with the force of the deadly missile and lay on his back on the floor unmoving.

The two knights snapped down their visors and launched themselves at Jamie simultaneously. Jamie experienced the same feeling that he had on the cog when he'd been crossing the Channel, that neither knight could get at him cleanly when they were fighting in unison. Added to which both men were without a shield, relying on their plate armour alone. They were hampered in their lines of attack by the pews to Jamie's right and the wall and pillar to his left. Neither could gain the advantage of a ninety degree angle of attack or greater, which would offer them a huge advantage. The first came ahead slightly, attacking to Jamie's left, sword in the upper guard seeking to drive the point forward, while the other sought to slash from his right. Unlike the men on the boat, they had clearly trained to fight in pairs, two to one.

The slash Jamie knew would avail nothing, no sword edge would penetrate his plate. He made to deal with the probing point that was aiming for a slit in his visor, driving the shield up and deflecting his attacker's sword point, at which he felt the brutal impact of the sword from his right. The plate held, and while Jamie felt the jarring blow it did nothing to disable him. The knight from the right would now seek to smother him, he knew, his mind flying as everything seemed to slow in the heat of combat and his muscles performed the time-worn actions brought on by years of training.

Pushing forward with the shield, he caught its edge against the pig-face of the bascinet helmet visor and pushed upwards, exposing his opponents face. Too close for a sword blade, Jamie drove the cross of the hilt straight into the knight's face, smashing skin and bone and causing him to scream as the blood flowed. The knight staggered, clutching his ripped face. Jamie did not let him go, but pulled him by his helmet towards the second opponent, with whom he collided. As one man raised an arm upwards to support the other, Jamie drove up with his sword, seeking the less armoured armpit and forcing his sword tip up with all his might, piercing the maille and running into the man's body beyond, killing him instantly. The first knight was trapped by his comrade's fallen body, and his visor was still open, gushing blood from where Jamie had hit him with the hilt of his sword. This time Jamie was able to pick his point with precision and drove his sword into the man's open mouth.

Looking around for his next opponent, he saw Kit was engaged with another knight and two were down from crossbow bolts. Mark, John and Phillip had launched an attack, John's spear driving forward behind his shield, with cries of "King Harry" and "Saint George". Anger and rage drove them forward. Cristoforo jumped on the altar table to gain better vantage and a dagger flew from his hand, embedding itself into the face of an unlucky knight whose visor was up.

Jamie began to trade blows with another knight, who came forward wanting to kill all before him, heedless of the cost. Then the sergeant at arms appeared at the doorway with reinforcements and all resistance stopped as the king bellowed: "Halt! You are doomed. Surrender and we shall spare your lives."

At this, the remaining knights threw down their swords,

dropping to their knees in surrender, yielding in unison as the chapel floor echoed to the sound of steel hitting the ornate tiles.

Sir Roger managed to rise, one hand to his throat, which had only been saved from piercing as the quarrel had hit the thick rim of the gorget, badly bruising his throat beneath and causing him to speak with a rough, gravelly whisper. He sat up, his eyes blurred with tears from his damaged throat.

"Majesty," he coughed, "I beg mercy for I was about to surrender, and that purblind fool dead there, did not heed." He finished, pointing to one of the dead knights at Jamie's feet.

The king looked at him without a flicker of emotion on his face. "Take him away," he ordered.

Jamie and the other knights looked on, keeping their weapons raised, guarding their prisoners as the men-at-arms gathered up all surrendered weapons. The knights were then stripped of their armour, roped together and taken away under arrest by the palace guards.

Jamie felt that feeling of anti-climax that he always did after a fight as the lust of battle drained from him. Each man looked to the other knowing how close it had been that the king had been taken or slain, and indeed how their own lives could have been forfeit. The atmosphere was broken by John, who exclaimed: "By the rood, that was the best fun I've had since I campaigned with you, by your leave your majesty."

The tension was broken and smiles came to their faces as the king gave a harsh laugh. "Indeed, John, and even now we should not like to be faced with you in battle."

He then looked at Jamie. "We are very grateful to you and your companions as loyal subjects, Sir James. But for you we should be dead or in the Tower languishing at the Council's behest."

"Thank you sire. It was but our devoir to your majesty.

Long live the king." He shouted, raising his sword at which all echoed the cry, raising their weapons in salute.

They all felt the relief and leaden muscles of a soldier after battle. It was an indescribable weariness that none who had not been at arms could know or fully understand. Each man felt it now and wanted to move restlessly and drink until drunk. The page was sent to raise Lord Grey from Westminster, and clerks were ordered to attend the king upon his move to the private chambers, where arrest warrants were issued for all those knights who had come to assault him.

Turning once more to the company who had saved his life he said: "We are in your debt, and your actions will not be forgotten. We thank you all most heartily and give praise to God that a king was delivered from harm by such loyal and faithful subjects."

With which he turned and left as the company bowed to their departing sovereign.

Chapter Fifty-Two

The story of the assassination attempt on the king had run rife through the palace, exaggerated with each telling. Kit was delighted that he had again been with Jamie when entering the fray. He made great efforts to align himself with Jamie and made the most of the association to flirt with the ladies about the court, who saw him now as the hero who had helped save the king.

There was a more serious side to the events. Prince Henry had been beside himself with fury, openly decrying his former steward who now languished in the Tower under arrest. His position was bolstered slightly by the arrival in London of Lord Stanhope, brought back in chains by Lord Roos under close arrest along with others from the shire of Nottingham. The prince was still greatly troubled and wished that Sir Richard Whittington was returned from Gloucester, but his close advisor was not due back until the end of October, just three days before Parliament was due to reconvene. Two days after the events at Lambeth Palace the prince called upon Jamie to attend him in private.

Jamie wore the prince's livery upon his surcoat as a member of the royal household. He was nervous, not knowing what sort of reception to expect. As he had reasoned with his father the evening before, he had saved a king, but from whom? No one knew if the prince had been secretly complicit in the act of attempting to remove his father from the throne by force, or even of plotting his assassination. Sir Roger had claimed (Jamie remembered his words so well) that he was acting on the orders of the lords and the Council, and the prince was the head of that Council.

Jamie was more worried than he had been when facing the armed knights in the chapel at Lambeth. He wished that Sir Richard was returned from Gloucester to instruct him in how he might proceed. He was introduced by the prince's steward and entered his private chamber, relieved to see that no other courtiers were present. He had worried that the meeting may have been a trap, with either Beaufort or one of the other Council members in attendance.

"Your royal highness," he said as he entered, bowing to the tall figure before him. He was heartened to see a smile of welcome upon the young prince's face, who in age would be but five years older than himself.

"Sir James, 'tis good to see you well and unhurt after your troubles of the eve past."

"As you see, sire, I am well and in good health. I trust that your father the king fares well after his adventures?" Jamie ventured, hoping to gauge what ground he trod upon.

"We understand that he is hale and in good spirits after the events that occurred. To wit we would thank you for your efforts in saving our father from what would very probably have been his death. It is of no little accord to save a king, and a father who is dear to us, despite a differing of opinion on matters of rule."

Jamie's mind raced. Was the prince offering an apology? A reassurance that he would never countenance such an act against his father. He wisely said nothing, schooling his features to give nothing away. The prince continued.

"Yet there are still many matters concerning the government of the country that remain in the balance. The realm is filled with traitors who would rise up against our father and undermine the rule of law. Witness Sir Richard Stanhope and the king's own Justice, Sir Robert Tirwhit, both now in chains at our order, with Prendergast and Longe. All of whom you helped to secure, for which you have our extreme gratitude. We strive to maintain the peace of his majesty's realm and aid him as best we can – both here and in France." Here the prince paused and looked briefly away as though unsure of how to proceed.

Jamie interceded. "Sire, you may depend upon my steadfast and loyal service. At all times for I remain your most faithful servant."

"As God is our witness you are, and have proved so time and again. We greatly value your service, and long may it continue. For certes we would assure you that we will doubtless have need of your services again and those of your friends. For we hear that Mark of Cornwall and the Italian, *signor* Corio, were at the event, as well as old John, a former sergeant of our father's, who we hear is still a doughty fighter. You are formidable, de Grispere, and we would rather have you for than against us, as with the best of men. Remember that and you will go far in my service."

"As your Highness pleases." Jamie answered innocuously.

"Good. Now go, and by God's grace keep well."

"By your leave, sire," Jamie said and left the royal presence.

He was in turmoil. Had he just been praised or threatened to say no more and be careful which side he chose? He knew not and wished to God that Whittington was here. The prince's words had laid his mind to rest on one thing, at least. He was no longer in danger himself. He had spent too long wondering whether the things he knew made him an enemy of the prince. He had not discovered the identity of his attacker that night in the dark streets, but the prince had said that he found him useful that he wanted him close and that he would need him in an uncertain future. It was unlikely, therefore, that the prince considered him a risk.

With a troubled mind he sought the company of Lady Alice, who was in court, and bade her accompany him to the flower gardens of the cloisters where they could be relatively undisturbed, save for the presence of her maid. He had been overjoyed to discover that none of the knights present in the chapel before him that night had been the Earl of Macclesfield. Whether he had been complicit in the action, Jamie knew not – and nor did he wish to, he reflected. For while all remained silent, Alice and her family were safe from accusations of treason.

Now, walking side by side with her, he felt the tension leave his body as he explained all that had occurred. She listened in silence, until at last they stopped at a bench under a rose arbour that now lacked the sweet, scented blooms of summer, with just a few flowers left on display as the last vestiges of the season departed.

"Do you wish my opinion?" She asked gently.

"I do, though in faith it has been a relief to share the discourse with another. That alone has been a balm in itself."

"I believe that the prince is concerned both for his father and the realm which he hopes to inherit. His position makes it unclear which way he is likely to turn, yet he cannot show the least sign of weakness. Witness my father when he thanked you for saving his life. He had gained much and stood to lose more if he thought that you would be untrue to me. The prince, whose burden is greater, would feel the same. He has a kingdom to lose. My father only has a daughter," She finished simply.

"Why my lady, your logic defies belief but I feel you have the right of it. Yet there is still uncertainty in my heart as to which course I should follow and indeed, how I should follow it."

"That will become apparent only as opportunities present themselves," she offered.

"Amen to that. Now let us find Cristo and Alessandria for I am in need of some Italian buffoonery. I would also find Mark. The prince mentioned their names and offered his thanks to them, and I must pass such news on, although this time the royal gratitude does not come with a purse attached! But their company, as yours, lifts my soul."

He received a smile in response. "And a smile as fair as yours, my lady, shall make the clouds above me flee," he said.

— × ⚜× —

Three days later Sir Richard Whittington returned to London and heard of all that had occurred. He was amazed at the attack upon the king, and summoned Jamie immediately.

"I should never have conceived of such a direct attack and rue the day that I was not present to assist you and the prince, for he is in need of help now more than ever I'll warrant," Whittington said. "A more subtle plan I did foresee; some coercion brought about by threats of disorder. To attack him thus in his private chapel, 'tis such a base and cowardly approach.

"The prince must feel it more keenly than most, for he is in the light as a potential orchestrator of such a move. Now the king will be moved to come down harsher upon him and the Council – if indeed he had not planned to do exactly that afore the attack. There will now be little mercy in his majesty. For the choice he now faces is either to abdicate and cede all power so as not to be a threat, or retake the reins in full, which will require tremendous strength of purpose and cunning. There can be no halfway point in such circumstances as I see."

"What will be the prince's position now, do you suppose?" Jamie asked "For if I judge correctly, he was at pains to point out that he was not the perpetrator of the attempt upon the king's life. He said that he still found great promise for his future and mine, if I was on his side. That was how I interpreted the speech."

"Tell me exactly what was said by Prince Henry," Whittington asked, and Jamie reiterated everything word for word, as faithfully as he could remember, for the speech was embedded upon his memory. When he finished, Sir Richard paced the room pulling at his ear deep in thought.

"By his actions he praises and warns you to stay faithful under his protection, and not to go against him on a personal level by siding with his father. Stay true to him, James, and spend as little time in the king's company as you can, for that way lies your ruin. All hangs now upon the impending meeting of Parliament and what is there decided." he finished.

Chapter Fifty-Three

2nd November Westminster Palace.

The Painted Chamber was located on the western axis of the Palace. Sir Richard Whittington had always though it a beautiful room, and he looked upwards at the delicately painted vaulted ceiling in panelled limed oak. Intricate carvings were inset in a linear fashion and painted to reflect the colours of the walls. Large swathes of canvas tapestries adorned the eastern wall, showing fine paintings of battle and chivalric scenes, while the large windows that opened out upon the courtyard south of the library flooded the chamber with light, enhanced by the two huge stained glass windows in the northern wall.

The main entrance was at the south from the chamber of the lords, and there was a smaller and more formal entrance from the east. It was from this side that the king would make his appearance. The Speaker, Thomas Chaucer, sat in the chair of authority over the Stone of Scone, presiding over all. He did not look happy or relaxed in this position, although he had occupied it for many years. He began proceedings by declaring the parliament in session, and called upon Sir Thomas Beaufort to make a pronouncement before the king entered.

"Chaucer does not look at all delighted with his position," Whittington muttered to Sir William Stokes at his side.

"Indeed he does not. Rumour has it that he tried to abdicate the role, yet the king would have none of it," Stokes replied.

"By the rood, that does not bode well for the proceedings," Whittington said. "Here we are, for my Lord Beaufort dost make an appearance and all is to play for, I'll warrant."

Thomas Beaufort, the Lord Chancellor, stood up to address the newly assembled parliament members.

"My lords, gentlemen, I welcome you all to this parliament of the year of our Lord 1411. I have here before me a writ signed by his majesty this day." At which he unrolled the scroll in his hands and read. "His majesty King Henry Fourth begs me to inform you that he will not be attending today for certain reasons. He therefore claims within his authority to prorogue parliament until the date of the 3rd of November. Lords, gentlemen, parliament is no longer to sit."

The noise and hubbub from the members echoed throughout the Painted Chamber as all speculated on the sudden change of plan.

Whittington chuckled, "Why the king will have his turn, and so he does, for now the cat is amongst the pigeons. Look at the expression of the thunder upon their faces. My Lord Beaufort is lost, as is my Lord Chaucer. Why, 'tis more fun than a mystery play."

"Yes, but where shall it lead?" Stokes asked anxiously.

"I know not for certes, yet I would hazard a guess that it will lead to the door of a king who is about to take control. Well, we shall just have to be patient and await the 3rd of November. 'Tis only tomorrow, so our patience will be rewarded soon enough."

"Amen to that." Stokes replied.

3rd November, Westminster Palace.

Parliament was reconvened the next day, and the king appeared before his subjects as head of the house. All seemed to run smoothly at first, with matters discussed including the arrest of Sir Robert Tirwhit, who had been taken into custody and was to be tried before Sir William Gascoigne later that month. Over the next few days the parliament discussed matters resulting to the disharmony in the kingdom throughout the year and the due process of law including the fate of Sir Roger Leche.

After a number of days, Lord Beaufort addressed the house, "It is my view that all matters of the realm should be decided by a loyal council without wilful bias, and that men must show a due obedience and honour to their liege lord."

"By the rood the man is a hypocrite," Jamie muttered to Whittington at his side. Sir Richard showed no sign of hearing, and remained eagerly expectant of what would come next.

"My lord I must protest," Chaucer spoke out, realising what was about to happen. "There should be nothing stated in this house or within the actions of its members that could be held against those members, specifically the Speaker."

There were mutters in the crowd of members then the king spoke up. Chaucer raised his hand and the members were silenced. "Quiet for his majesty King Henry," Chaucer ordered.

"My lords, gentlemen, we would put you on notice that we do not abide by any form of novelty, and would exercise our liberties and franchises in the same way that our predecessors have done." At this there was silence. The king had shown his steel and all could see that he was taking back control. Parliament was adjourned until the thirtieth of November.

The following day Prince Henry received encouraging news from France. "They have succeeded," he cried in joy. "By God's grace we win a victory. Arundel and Warwick have defeated the Armagnacs and Paris is saved. They have regained Saint-Cloud and secured the city."

"My lord prince, that is indeed good news," Thomas Beaufort agreed. "God be praised. What are they to do now? Do they return home?"

"They are to stay with King Charles and will return upon the month of December. It also says that the *Chambre des compotes* has been paid and is lodged with our bankers.

"Why this gives great support to your cause, my prince. We can now press our case and mayhap the king will see how prescient you were in asking for the embassy – albeit a larger force than he anticipated." At which the prince could not refrain from a conspiratorial smile at Thomas Beaufort.

"Uncle, you do us justice, and while we were concerned at the king's last remarks in parliament, we do believe he will now see that we have the right of it."

"Perhaps, highness, if I may suggest another form of embassy – to your father, in the company of my brother, with the bishop present to see if he would now consider abdication? For you have shown great strength of purpose. Stanhope and Tirwhit have been served and are under arrest, the pirates are defeated at your behest and the realm his been restored."

"This may be a propitious moment," the prince said. "Send your brother, his grace to us, so that we may discuss a stratagem."

Thomas Beaufort smiled inwardly thinking, *the prince becomes our mawmet and the game begins anew.* Outwardly he said: "As you command, my prince, by your leave." He bowed, leaving Prince Henry to his thoughts.

Chapter Fifty-Four

The king's anger had subsided since the meeting with his son and Bishop Beaufort. He had been so furious at this last attempt to wrest the crown from his head that he had not been able to speak, such was his apoplectic rage at the temerity of the prince. When he was able, he had firmly informed Prince Henry that he would continue to govern his realm for as long as there was still breath in his body.

Prince Henry rued the day that he made this last plea to his father, and wished that he had listened more carefully to the wise council of Sir Richard Whittington, who had advised him against such an action.

Parliament went again into session on the thirtieth of November. King Henry appeared to all who witnessed his entrance to have a self-satisfied look upon his face. He was not worried or angry, he looked more like a man who had achieved what he set out to do.

Thomas Chaucer began with the king's wishes, asking all the members of the Council to attend him one by one at his throne. The council members looked at each other and proceeded as bidden by the Speaker. As each man went forward King Henry thanked them personally, then addressed the body collectively in full hearing of the assembly.

"We would like to thank all members of the Council for their diligent and loyal work in helping us govern England for the previous eighteen months. We are very grateful to these men, and offer them our heartfelt thanks."

The prince, as the leader of the Council, came forward before his father and addressed him in formal response, though somewhat sourly as much as he dare.

"Sire, we would have been able to serve you better if we had been better funded. The strings of the royal purse were not only tied shut, but expenditure elsewhere prohibited such actions."

The king offered his son a wintry smile and nodded in agreement: "As always we are grateful to our son for his advice and insight."

At this, the collective members of the Council were motioned back to their seats. It began to dawn upon them that they had been relieved of all authority in the cleverest way, without aggression or force. They had simply been removed from office.

"Let it also be recorded that we hereby refute and repeal the restraint imposed upon us these eighteen months past and assume full control of the kingdom once more."

There were sighs and intakes of breath from the house, yet all sat impotent before the king as everyone realised that he had once more taken full control of his government and would rule again by absolute monarchy.

The speaker called for the House to be upstanding for the king, who left the Painted Chamber. Once the monarch had left, Sir Richard Whittington, who was seated in the public gallery with Jamie, shook his head: "I witnessed it, yet still do not believe it. That was the most immaculate regaining of power I have ever seen or heard of."

Jamie too watched in disbelief realising that he had just seen history made before his eyes.

Leaving the Painted Chamber and the palace, Jamie ventured towards the King's Head where he had arranged to meet with Cristoforo and Mark. They were to his mind as much an antidote to the secrets and intrigue of the court as anyone else. They understood all the characters taking part in the panoply but were not intrinsically linked to them as he was. Jamie also knew that he could be completely honest in their company without needing to be constantly on his guard as to what he said and to whom.

Upon entering he saw that his two companions had already arrived and were sitting at a table in a quiet corner. Buying a tankard of ale, he moved to join them, and taking a seat he allowed himself to relax for the first time in many days. He interlaced his fingers behind his head and stretched his elbows backwards, releasing the tension from his shoulders and exhaling deeply as he did so.

"Well? What ails thee?" Mark asked, sufficiently well versed in his friend's moods to know all was not well.

"It is the damnedest thing I have ever witnessed. Truth to tell I am not certain how it was achieved, even though I was present." He paused, still considering the drama he had just seen enacted as he supped more of his ale.

"Pray thee, Jamie, tell us more, for there is a tension of rumour and counter rumour about the court and we all are agog." Mark demanded while Cristoforo looked on in puzzlement, unsure of what was happening.

"Why the king marched into parliament and sacked all before him. Everybody! The whole Council was disbanded, yet the strangest point was that the Council members were not sure that it was happening, nor quite how the king achieved his aim. Even the great lords of Beaufort and Le Scrope were amazed and disbelieving. Yet there was naught they could do. His majesty thanked them for their service and bade them adieu. By the rood, it was cleverly done. My Lord Chaucer was himself open-mouthed, and as like as not to lose his position as speaker of the house."

"Tell me how is this possible," Cristoforo asked, clearly confused by the difference in language and culture. "He has the right to dismiss them all? Just like that?" he snapped his fingers in a dramatic gesture.

"He does. To wit, he repudiated all restraints and conditions that had been placed upon his power by the same council some eighteen months past."

"By the good Lord, that is amazing," Cristoforo exclaimed. "Will he kill them all in their beds now and mount their heads on poles?" Jamie shook his head and laughed, and Cristoforo asked for a blow-by-blow account of each phase of the proceedings so that he might better understand his new country.

"Well if that be the case, shall I be in need of finding a new master to wrestle with?" Mark asked, half in jest. The other two laughed at this comment and Jamie nearly choked on a mouthful of ale at his friend's response, spoken with such a straight face.

"I think not Mark, the prince's purse is deep and with no Council to occupy him, why I suspect he will want to wrestle all the more!"

19th December

The final session of Parliament for 1411 had just been concluded, and all had been adjourned until the following year. More events and judgements were made, which may have been less surprising than the dismissal of the Council, but were still as shocking, with their reverberations felt throughout the court.

Jamie had joined Sir Richard Whittington in his quarters to discuss a new climate of politics that they knew would affect them both.

"So the king's brothers did not find favour with the king's council, for I hear that Thomas Beaufort is sacked as Chancellor and will be replaced by Archbishop Arundel. By the Lord Harry I would have paid much to see the look on his face and hear the words he spoke upon such a demotion – and to be replaced by his enemy Arundel! The earls of Arundel and Warwick supplanted in power and Henry le Scrope sacked as treasurer – and my Lord Roos made up. Why 'tis a revolution in all but name," Whittington said.

"On Beaufort's fate I rejoice," Jamie replied. "For he is a traitor and a hypocrite. Yet I hear that Tirwhit is released upon a public apology and payment of fine of oxen, wine and twelve sheep! Why he nearly killed four household knights and this is the punishment he receives? Stanhope and others released from the Tower but with no pardon. Pray explain how the court's games work. My enemies and those of the crown plot and scheme to bring down a king by using a prince, and I am caught twixt service to one and loyalty to the other.

"I am set upon by enemies on all sides, who are pardoned or released by the very men whom they threatened at the behest of a prince who demands the level of loyalty exclusive of that to a king. A king whose very loyalty seems fickle indeed. I find myself upon a knife edge, where one ill-judged move will result in my death. I know not which way to turn." Jamie finished, lamenting his position as Whittington allowed him to vent his spleen.

"James, you turn to me. For I have ventured upon these waters before and I understand well how they swirl with whirlpools of unrest that would drag many a good man down. I have served two kings so far and wouldst seek to add to my tally.

"The vagaries of the court rise and fall as a tempest, James, and you must learn to neither topple from the peaks nor get drowned at the troughs. Steer a steady course instead, and maintain a buoyancy to thwart those who wouldst sink you in their wake.

"You should not underestimate your position, for you have the favour of both prince and king. These final words I durst not dare whisper outside these walls, but the king will not live forever. Go to now James, go to. Husband your power and use it well, for you have more than you know." Whittington encouraged.

Jamie left Sir Richard, still uncertain, but possibly better prepared to serve in what may prove to be the second and final stage of King Henry Fourth's reign.

HISTORICAL NOTES:

NOTE: there are spoilers in here if you are reading ahead of the story.

As I explore this period in greater depth I continue to unearth fascinating facts and events that have me more surprised than ever that they could all be contained within a single year. I am again indebted to a number of excellent books, without which I would not have been able to carry out my extensive research. On that note I have received feedback through reviews and directly regarding Jamie's age. The reviews ask whether he would have been able to do all I say he did – and perhaps as importantly, would he have been allowed to do so? With this in mind I wanted to offer some general information on the era, as well as health and age, to put things into perspective.

Age and longevity

It should be noted that only 50% of the population at the time managed to live to see 20. Of those lucky fifty percent, a further half died before they reach 40, and only 5% of people born in this age lived to 65!

A man was therefore considered to be in his prime at 20 years old and mature at 30. Children had a very short childhood, and seven- and eight-year-olds were expected to do a full day's work. Even the well off, such as a merchant family like the de Grisperes, would expect Jamie to accompany his father Thomas from the age of seven to learn the trade, travelling around with him all over England and abroad at his side, listening and gaining experience. It was a hard world with no tolerance for slacking.

Twelve-year-olds were allowed and expected to attend jury service and could judge their peers and adults alike. Teenagers were encouraged to wed and have children as early as possible due to the high mortality rate and the level of infant mortality. Childbirth in itself was a perilous affair.

Young boys of twelve to fourteen years old were sent away to train to become squires and ultimately knights, after three to four years. This training would always take place away from home in the service of another knight or nobleman. It was a brutal but effective way of producing warriors ready to do full battle and serve from an early age. To put this into perspective, Prince Henry was given leadership of his father's forces in the Welsh campaigns at just fourteen years of age, where he learned a great deal about castle sieges and guerrilla tactics through first-hand experience. Then at sixteen he was given command of a full wing of his father's army at the battle of Shrewsbury. Half way through the battle, he received an arrow to his face and carried on fighting with it lodged a quarter of an inch from his spine. His injury was not treated until four hours later. The initial prognoses was poor until John Bradbury, a noted surgeon of the day, came along and said he could heal the dying prince.

The catch? The prince had to be transported on a rough cart for another four hours to Kenilworth, where Bradbury was having made a specially designed new implement to remove the arrow head. Two journeys and some ten hours later, with no aesthetic, he was operated on with success. The head was removed and the prince, of course, survived. He was up and around and fighting again ten days later. There is to this day no picture or painting showing a full face of Henry V due to the scar on his cheek.

Leaders who commanded in their twenties were well respected often by men much older than themselves. Edward III (1312-1377) led an army into battle against the Scots despite being heavily outnumbered. He led nobles and knights much older than himself who followed him to victory.

Finally, a note on squires or esquires. The modern view is that they were young men not of age, yet squires often stayed as such all their lives, never wanting nor aiming for knighthood. Being knighted brought with it demands and responsibilities, both physical and fiscal in the form of military support and payments of dues above that of a squire, who could hold land and fight without all the onerous terms demanded from a knight.

Therefore, for Jamie to be called to aid the crown at the age of nineteen was nothing out of the ordinary, and many would have been doing so at an earlier age

A note on time

Clocks were few and far between in the early fifteenth century, and approximate times were:

Terze: 9a.m.

Nones: halfway between noon and sunset,

Lauds: 3 a.m. or at dawn.

Prime: around 6 a.m.

Tierce: around 9 a.m.

Sext: midday.

Vespers: was the twelfth hour, or sunset.

Church bells were rung at these times. However, there was no such thing as Greenwich Mean Time, and indeed there was no such thing as standard time until the nineteenth century when railway timetables meant that clocks across the country had to be regulated. The timing of the bells therefore varied between one location and the next. However, the bells regulated the daily lives of everyone who could hear them.

Stanhope and the North

Sir Richard Stanhope did rise up as I describe with all his loyal knights (including Sir Roger Leche, who was there with his coterie and the prince's steward). Stanhope caused chaos in the shires and weakened the king, threatening the court and destabilising the king's rule with a view to putting Prince Henry on the throne. There was virtually a war between the Meryngs and others, so I thought why not put Jamie into the fray? Ultimately, Stanhope was arrested as I describe and taken to the tower under arrest with evidence against him. All around Nottingham were afraid of him and his cohort of villainous knights, who rode roughshod over law and order in that area. They were startling times where loyalty see-sawed as the rivalries demanded, and no one could be trusted.

Piracy and the Treaty

Everything I describe happened, from Prendergast and Longe to the Courtneys failing to apprehend the pirates and the Treaty being put in jeopardy The pirates threatened the whole economy of England and its future, for everything hinged upon the Wool Trade together with the knock-on effects for Calais and the rest of France. The Courtneys were as I describe, and Hugh (who became the 12th Earl) really was a renowned pirate, and therefore maybe not the best person to go pirate hunting! They did sail from Plymouth, close to Mark's home, which gave me that perfect opportunity to insert him as a spy with the crew. William Stokes was also real. He was a Financial Spy as described, who knew Richard Whittington well.

The prince's ship *Juliane* was captured on the Channel and taken by Prendergast. It was this final act which so annoyed Prince Henry that he sent Lord Beaufort to get it back for him. However, what surprised me the most were the events that led up to Longe's and Prendergast's capture, for they did sail the *Juliane* up the river Rother as I describe and were captured at Smallhythe where they surrendered, with Prendergast escaping and claiming sanctuary in Westminster Abbey. No one knows quite how he managed this, so I have inserted what may have happened.

All the numbers, sums of money and dates are accurate, together with amounts paid in taxes, subsidies and to Thomas Beaufort to apprehend the pirates. It was a vast sum at the time, yet it did the trick. With all these resources at his back, Beaufort's strategies succeeded. The Treaty was consequently signed, opening the floodgates for the Armagnacs and the Burgundians to approach the English court for help, with embassies and offers flying hither and thither across the Channel.

The battle for the favours of both king and prince was as I describe, and ultimately both men wanted the same thing – political stability and the re-gaining of English lands in France! What changed was the side whom they backed. The 'embassy' to France did escalate into war party, which really annoyed King Henry, who saw it as a threat to his power. This, along with the Beauforts demanding his abdication, pushed him over the edge.

Lincoln and the Loveday Arbitration

The events leading to the Loveday ambush did occur. The party was ambushed and Lord Roos was apparently lucky to escape with his life. I have of course inserted Jamie into the scene for the sake of my story. Tirwhit (there are many versions of the spelling of his name and I have adopted this one) did deny his previous agreement to a Loveday – effectively a peaceful arbitration – leading to the violence shown in the ambush. He was later brought to heel, but with only a minimal penalty, it would seem. I would have liked to have killed him off, but history was sadly more lenient.

King Henry

The king was in Gloucester when I show him to be, and was warned about the council meeting that was to be called, so why not use Cristoforo? These were treacherous times, and it showed in the real plight that Prince Thomas had when trying to marry John Beaufort's widow, which will come into play later.

The king's health was as mercurial as I have described it. No one knows for certain what exactly was wrong with him. Some say it was leprosy (not quite the kind that we equate with the disease now, but similar) others a wasting disease. He did have boils and sores about his face and his health was constantly changing. Sometimes he regained all vigour and was back to almost full strength again for short periods. This must have been terribly sad, considering what a great knight and fighter he had been in his youth, to be so stricken in later life when only in his forties – although as I mentioned earlier, forty was pretty good going for those times.

He did arbitrate upon the matter of Lollardy at Oxford, finding for Archbishop Arundel in a decision that had a huge influence upon events to come between prince and king.

King Henry's reclaiming of full control at the November

parliament was nothing short of miraculous, and happened as I describe, with no one really understanding how he managed it. The attempted attack upon him by Sir Roger Leche was also real, although I have no exact knowledge of the blow by blow events, only that Leche was arrested together with other knights on the 22nd of October. It seems almost too much of a coincidence that Sir Roger was the prince's steward, attached to Stanhope, and that the assassination attempt occurred just before Parliament was due to re-convene at the king's behest. I wonder who was behind it?

I hope that you enjoyed this second story of Jamie de Grispere. He will return in 1412 as history unfolds. Do please write to me with any questions or comments as I love to hear from my readers: simonfairfaxauthor@gmail.com

A message from Simon:

I know that you have over a million choices of books to read. I can't tell you how much it means to me that you choose time to read one of my books.

I really hope that you enjoyed it and that you found it entertaining. If you did, I would appreciate a few more minutes of your time, if I may humbly ask for you to leave a review for other readers who may be trying to select their next reading material.

If for any reason you weren't satisfied with this book please do let me know by emailing me at simonfairfaxauthor@gmail.com The satisfaction of my readers and feedback are important to me.

Best wishes,
Simon.

Acknowledgments

First of all my great thanks to my editor Perry Iles who helped so much in making my book come alive and my trusty BETA readers David, Deb, Patricia and Sarah.

As always research has been the key to my work and it always surprises me how much went on in a single year in 1411.

To this end and in an effort to fully understand the events and people of the period I again read extensively, including Chris Given-Wilson's excellent book *HENRY IV* and Ian Mortimer's *THE FEARS OF HENRY IV*. Both give a brilliant insight to the events of the period. I would also recommend Ian Mortimer's *The time traveller's guide to medieval England* and I apologise if I have made any factual errors as a result. I would also mention Christopher Allmand's *HENRY V* which gave me such a fascinating view into this extraordinary King's life, events and personality.

Also, I would add to my bibliography this excellent book, that enabled me to understand fully the ships of the day, how they were constructed and used in warfare: *Medieval Maritime Warfare* by Charles D Stanton.

I have studied martial arts for most of my life from teenage years onwards, including, Wing Chun, fencing and judo, all of which came into play for this novel as many of the throws and holds from judo are very similar to Cornish wrestling. Yet to add veracity, I attended the Armoured Combat Gloucester 'knight school' to wield a broad sword for real and see if everything I had written worked!

On sword fighting I also delved deeply into *The knightly art of battle by* Ken Mondeschien who explains the art as propounded by the brilliant Fiore dei Liberi. Also, Hans Talhoffer's *Medieval combat in colour* and *Armourers* by Matthias Pfaffenbichler.

Finally, my thanks to all the horses and particularly polo ponies- including Richard- who taught me so much.

Made in United States
North Haven, CT
19 November 2023

44267039R00264